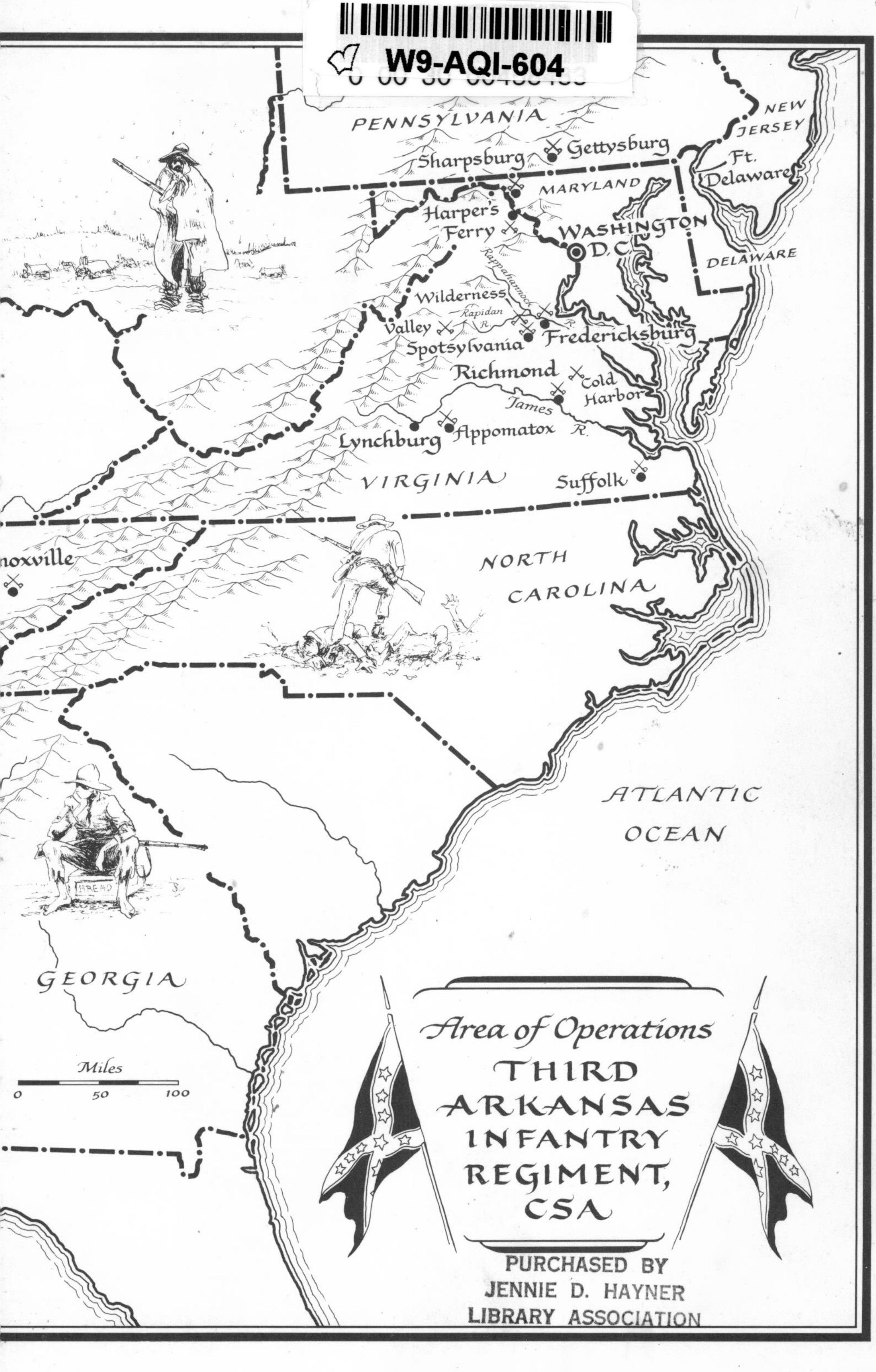
PENNSYLVANIA
NEW JERSEY
Gettysburg
Sharpsburg
Ft. Delaware
MARYLAND
Harper's Ferry
WASHINGTON D.C.
DELAWARE
Rappahannock R.
Wilderness
Rapidan R.
Valley
Spotsylvania
Fredericksburg
Richmond
Cold Harbor
James R.
Lynchburg
Appomatox
VIRGINIA
Suffolk
noxville
NORTH CAROLINA
BREAD
ATLANTIC OCEAN
GEORGIA
Miles
0 50 100
Area of Operations
THIRD ARKANSAS INFANTRY REGIMENT, CSA

# THE BAREFOOT BRIGADE

OTHER BOOKS BY DOUGLAS C. JONES

*The Treaty of Medicine Lodge*
*The Court-Martial of George Armstrong Custer*
*Arrest Sitting Bull*
*A Creek Called Wounded Knee*
*Winding Stair*
*Elkhorn Tavern*
*Weedy Rough*

# THE BAREFOOT BRIGADE

## DOUGLAS C. JONES

*Certainly they were a breed of soldier*
*the like of which the world had never seen*
*and will never see again.*

—JACK COGGINS,
ARMS AND EQUIPMENT OF THE CIVIL WAR

**HOLT, RINEHART and WINSTON**
**New York**

PUBLISHED BY HOLT, RINEHART AND WINSTON, 383 MADISON AVENUE,
NEW YORK, NEW YORK 10017.
PUBLISHED SIMULTANEOUSLY IN CANADA BY HOLT, RINEHART AND WINSTON
OF CANADA, LIMITED.

LIBRARY OF CONGRESS CATALOGING IN PUBLICATION DATA
JONES, DOUGLAS C.
THE BAREFOOT BRIGADE.
1. UNITED STATES—HISTORY—CIVIL WAR, 1861–1865—
FICTION. I. TITLE.
PS3560.0478B3 813′.54 82-892 AACR2
ISBN: 0-03-060041-3
FIRST EDITION

DESIGNER: JOY CHU
ILLUSTRATIONS BY THE AUTHOR
ENDPAPER MAP BY ANITA KARL AND JAMES KEMP

PRINTED IN THE UNITED STATES OF AMERICA
10 9 8 7 6 5 4 3 2 1

# Author's Note

This is a story of common soldiers. It is not a story of causes or politics or social systems, nor of generals and grand strategy, but of simple soldiers and how they were in some ways amazingly different from modern soldiers, and in others amazingly the same. There were a great many like these who, despite all odds, at least attempted to do whatever was asked of them.

# ONE

FURY was a constant state of being for His Honor Judge Guthrie Scaggs. He went about everything angrily, to include eating and sleeping, breathing and copulating. Those who knew him claimed that he had issued from the womb with a scowl on his face and, as the years advanced, never once observed anything that had the capacity to change it. On this May morning, as he guided the mule down the mountain to the small tributary of the Buffalo River, he was more furious than usual.

The larger part of it came from an upset stomach. Being a circuit-riding judge of Arkansas in this year of 1861 threw him on the mercy of tables set for him at the various farmsteads where he stopped the night during his rounds. On this particular morning he had breakfasted on hog jowl and gravy, a greasy mess he had wolfed down without regard for the consequences, and had been forced since on at least four occasions to take soothing draughts from the bottle of corn whisky in his saddlebags.

And he had not slept well, having shared a bed with two gangling and bony sons of his host, neither of whom had yet consigned his winter underwear to the boiling pot, nor taken his annual spring bath. His Honor Judge Scaggs did not consider himself a fastidious man, but he had been cursed from birth with an extremely sensitive nose, designed by its breadth of nostril to pick up scents and odors lost on other men with less classic proboscises.

And still another part of it was this business of the convention in Little Rock that had procrastinated for so long before seceding from the damned Union. The governor himself had implored the convention to sign the articles of secession. But they had refused, voting down such a resolution again and again, bone-headed and stubborn as the mule that Judge Scaggs was now astride. Only when Sumter fell and Abe Lincoln called for volunteers had the convention voted the necessary document, taking it as insult and even threat to freedom that the Federal power would ask them to send soldiers for an invasion of sister states in the South.

Had His Honor Judge Scaggs been running things, the Union would have been dissolved back in Andy Jackson's time, when there was all that nullification business, four years before Arkansas became a state, when it was in fact still a territory peopled mostly by bottomland men along the rivers and by wild Indians. And Judge Scaggs himself a boy of only thirteen, learning the rudiments of cotton and hatred of strong central government while he worked alongside his grandfather's Negroes in the delta country west of Memphis.

There were other irritations, too. Here he was riding a circuit he had never ridden before because some idiot judge in these northern districts had run off to join Federal armies in Missouri or Illinois or some such place, leaving this area without the proper dispensation of justice. His Honor Judge Scaggs thus found himself in this mountain wilderness, attending to matters he had no desire to attend to, in a strange country and among people who had never seen his name on a ballot—a great many of whom, heaven forbid it, supported the Union. Dumb bastards, His Honor Judge Scaggs thought viciously, and pulled the amber-colored bottle from his saddlebag.

The woods that bordered the winding road were thick-leaved and gleaming green, and from among them came the calls of jays, the hammer strokes of woodpeckers on hardwood, the chattering of squirrels. As the road pitched down into the valley of the stream, the trees changed character, oaks and hickories thinning, their place taken by the redbud and sycamore and willow of lower elevations. The stream glistened in the sun, running fast and clear and cold. Looking ahead at the ford, His Honor Judge Scaggs pulled up and studied the proposition, glaring between the mule's ears.

It was impossible to gauge the depth of the water, for even though he could see the shine of gravel at the bottom of the stream, the dazzling sunlight on the surface could be deceptive as to what lay beneath. Judge Scaggs made a quick and unalterable decision, and dismounted.

He slipped off his frock coat, then the collarless gray shirt, and draped them over the saddle. He pulled down his doeskin pants—which were so short in the leg that they failed to reach the tops of his shoes—then the shoes, and there were no socks beneath. He stood now, glaring around, clad only in his stovepipe hat and flannel underwear that had once been red but had long ago washed out to a ghastly pink.

With only a moment's hesitation, he peeled off the underwear and, standing naked, took a copy of the Statutes of Arkansas from the saddlebag and wrapped that and the clothes in a large bundle resembling an army bedroll. Placing bare toe to stirrup, he swung up, his naked butt slapping against the saddle leather. He kicked the mule forward, holding the bundle high above his head in one hand.

The mule marched daintily into the water and toward the far shore. Soon, the water had risen to the mule's hocks. Judge Scaggs glanced down as they approached the center of the stream. The water was still at the mule's hocks. Farther into the stream the mule trod, but the water rose no higher up his legs. Judge Scaggs began to suspect a miscalculation.

With his nakedness shining in the bright sunlight, he glanced along the far shore. There, in a thicket of willows, were three young women wearing poke bonnets and calico dresses done up high-waisted with ribbon, like the ones their grandmothers might have worn during the Revolution. They stood with eyes popping and mouths agape, motionless as statues, watching the tall, naked figure now passing midstream on his mule.

When he saw the young women, Judge Scaggs did not flinch. He did not try to twist his body to hide his manliness behind the pommel. He did not lower the bundle from above his head. He looked at the young women for only an instant, and then observed the far bank directly ahead as the mule approached the gravel bar there.

He had always been a deliberate man, and he was now. As

the mule came to a halt on dry ground, Judge Scaggs dismounted slowly and began to unravel his bundle of clothing, his naked back toward the women. After slipping the Statutes of Arkansas back into the saddlebags, he began to dress. As he pulled on the doeskin pants, he glanced over his shoulder, and where the women had stood was now only the salad-green foliage of the willows. There was no movement there, not even the rustling of leaves marking their departure, and His Honor Judge Scaggs snorted and buttoned his pants.

He paused a moment, making another decision, or judgment as he would have called it, and finally pulled the bottle from the saddlebags and took a long swig.

"By the living God," he said aloud, "these hill people move quiet as wolves, even their bitches!"

And then he mounted the mule and with great dignity rode along the valley road toward the town.

THEY called it Town. Just that. There was never any mistaking the place to which they referred because it was the only town they had. There was a proper name, which could be seen on any map, but most of them had little use for maps, and many couldn't read any of the names on such a device anyway.

It was the only settlement of note within miles, boasting a population of well over five hundred. It was impressive, too, because it was a county seat and the home of the sheriff. Town lay in the valley of the Buffalo, its single street twisting alongside the bank of the river, with buildings on either side, most of them slab-side or shingle. But there was one sandstone edifice. The courthouse. It was not an imposing building to someone like Judge Guthrie Scaggs, who had seen such places as Little Rock, but to the hill people it was the symbol of government and power. And for most of them, such symbols were entirely negative.

The sheriff had his office there. The courtroom was there as well, a small room with a few chairs facing a table that had Queen Anne legs and served as bench. Across the hall from the courtroom was the single jail cell. It stood empty most of the time.

Except for the sheriff himself, there was no jailer. The only people locked up were murderers and highwaymen, and there were not many of these because most were never apprehended, and those who were seldom survived arrest. Sometimes there were casual shootings between members of families who disagreed on property boundaries or the ownership of milk cows, but not many of these affairs, even the lethal ones, came to trial, witnesses somehow becoming as scarce as hard money.

The hill people came down into Town to pay their taxes and discuss the news. They came from as far away as a day's ride on horseback because the county, like all others in the state, was laid out geographically so that no matter where a man might settle he could get to his seat of government on a single stretch of daylight.

Their school system was nonexistent as a state-supported institution. But Town had what they considered a good one, sustained by donations of hogs and chickens and free labor to repair roof and windows and siding.

Even so, most education was left to the scattered families, and that meant that a good many men, and even more of the women, could not read or write. Learning in the hills was usually taken at the knee of some ambitious mother who taught her children the verities of subject and verb from the Bible.

There were a sawmill, a blacksmith shop, a mercantile, and all the other things a town needed.

Everything worked pretty well. Boys and girls sparked and were coupled by mutual agreement between the heads of families. They wed and had their children, usually one each year for a time. There was plenty of wild land to be cleared; there were homesteads to be made, fields to be plowed, hogs and chickens to be raised. They were not close enough to any hostile Indian tribes to be worried about such things as sometimes troubled the western counties.

In all the hillside fields around the county seat, there was not a single black man working, and in Town there were only two, and they the property of the sawmill operator. The people of the county stayed well clear of the two blacks, for Negroes were as foreign to them as were solid black mastiffs among all their own mottled and varicolored hounds.

And there were no whores or beggars and only a couple of men who were habitually drunk. The townspeople recognized few diseases—although some could recall a smallpox outbreak a few years earlier—and they died of the usual maladies of the time: consumption or the vapors or measles. Or simply of old age when their time ran out.

Up to now they had felt themselves far removed from the hot whirlwinds of the nation. But now they could no more avoid those storms than control them, and for Noah and Zackery Fawley the whirlwind came in the form of His Honor Judge Guthrie Scaggs.

"STAND to the bar, Noah Fawley," Judge Scaggs rasped. He glared across the small room—empty now except for a cluster of Fawleys sitting along one wall and looking defiant, the prosecutor, and the complainant in the case, a small, weather-reddened man in homespun who from time to time cast an apprehensive glance in the direction of the Fawleys.

The youngest of the Fawleys, a tall, slender, hard-muscled man of seventeen years, rose as the prosecutor motioned to him. Stepping out to stand before the table with the Queen Anne legs, he glanced back once toward his family.

There were his mother and father, both tough looking and hard-faced with thin lips, and his four brothers, Tyne, Britt, Cadmus, and Zackery, all of the same stamp with thin blond hair and pale eyes that were more green than blue and, in certain light, almost yellow. The woman wore her hair pulled back to a bun; it was gray, matching a face etched like her husband's from exposure to sun and wind, although she was no older than forty-five.

"Charged with stealing a pig, on complaint of this gentleman," the prosecutor was saying, waving a hand in the direction of the small sun-bleached man without looking at him. To the younger man stepping forward he barked, "Take off your hat!"

Noah Fawley pulled the floppy, wide-brimmed hat from his head and stood with a spray of silky hair falling across his high forehead. He stared squarely into Judge Scaggs's eyes.

"Are you represented?" Judge Scaggs asked.

The young man stood uncertainly, but his gaze never wavered. One bony hand rubbed the seam of his homemade trousers, the other held the hat at his side.

"This here's my people," he said, looking back toward his family once more.

"I mean, have you an attorney? A lawyer?"

"What for?"

"I'll not dawdle with you, young man," Judge Scaggs snapped impatiently. "How do you plead?"

Once more Noah Fawley stared, uncomprehending.

"Did you steal the pig as alleged?"

"He was drinkin' that blackberry wine," the woman shouted from her side of the room, and the small man in homespun gave a violent start as though ready to bolt through the open door at the rear of the building. "It was Lucinda's weddin' day."

Judge Scaggs looked at Mrs. Fawley for a moment, but his curiosity soon overcame his sense of courtroom propriety.

"Who, may I ask, is Lucinda?"

"His older sister," the woman said. "She was married that day an' all the neighbors was in for dancin' an' my son sipped too much of that blackberry wine an' never knowed what he was about when he taken that pig."

"Your Honor," the prosecutor said, "it seems to me . . ."

"That'll be enough, sir," Judge Scaggs cut in sharply. He turned back to the woman. "Drinking blackberry wine has nothing whatsoever to do with the crime charged to this young man." And back to Noah Fawley. "Tell this court how you plead."

"I never plead with nobody," Noah said. Some color had begun to rise along his bony cheeks.

"All right, just tell me if you stole the pig."

"Well, me an' another boy taken it an' roasted it down on a gravel bar at the river an' et it."

"You ate the whole pig?" Judge Scaggs asked, his eyes bulging.

"We never et the hide ner the head," Noah Fawley said.

His Honor glanced from the boy's face to those of his family. The Fawley men were tight-lipped and hard-eyed, standing around the mother like a guard of wolves.

"And who was this other boy?"

"Ben Shackleford," Noah said. "He's gone off to Missouri to join some army he heerd about there."

"Noy," the boy's father said, pronouncing his son's name as all the family did, without any hint of the "ah" at the end, "you needn't tell about Ben."

"You keep quiet, sir," Judge Scaggs said, but once more his curiosity got the better of him. "Which army was it this Ben Shackleford joined with?"

"He never said which one. Just an army, he said."

Judge Scaggs reared back in his chair and tapped the fingers of both hands on the tabletop.

"Son, how do you stand on the separation of powers?"

Noah looked at him blankly. Judge Scaggs seemed to shake himself angrily.

"How old are you, sir?"

"Seventeen."

"Sound of limb and mind, it appears," Judge Scaggs said. He allowed his nervous hands to lie quietly on the tabletop and drew a deep breath.

"Sir, under the authority vested in me by the sovereign state of Arkansas, Confederate States of America, I sentence you to enlist in militia of said state, in one of the companies recruiting south of this place, and to remain loyal and true to your oath to said unit until the present war of aggression against the South has been brought to its glorious and successful conclusion, which it is the Lord's obvious will that such be done, and failing this on pain of arrest and sentence to a proper jail in aforesaid sovereign state for the duration of five years. Sir, do you have any statement to make before this court?"

Having little grasp of what had just been said, Noah Fawley shook his head. "I reckon not," he said. "Except the pig was no account. When me an' Ben Shackleford et it, we got sick as Old Nick."

"FORTHWITH," the judge had said. And forthwith it was, with only one more night spent at the hillside farm that sat among the small cleared fields and the hardwood timber.

These were a forthright and simple folk, of English origin. The old man's people had come from east of London, hers from Cornwall. Each counted among their ancestors men who had scouted for the British Army during the Revolution, men who were then and through all their following generations distrustful of the United States government for no apparent reason other than willful ignorance of any institution found in cities.

In fact, Old Man Fawley had immigrated to these hills to place as much distance as possible between himself and that government and such cities as might house any extension of it. The Fawleys had not come alone. Others of their kind had settled in the valley of the Buffalo, many also of old English stock, and their language was still colored with the strange sounds of other places. They called a sack a poke, and sassafras was termed grub hysin.

Twenty-six years ago they had come, Zack being born on the march and all the others born here in a house built with Fawley's own hands, surrounded by fields cleared by his own labor, among the woods that he hunted, for many years alone.

None of the five boys had ever been away from the farm except for a day or two from time to time when they helped some neighbor with his butchering or stump pulling or barn raising. None of them had ever been far outside the county. Thoughts of what lay beyond the distant blue mountains had seldom entered their thinking. Now, two of them would go, because of justice and because Pap had said it was to be.

"Zack, you taken this," he said, handing his eldest the family Dragoon revolver, the powder flash, the caps in their tin box, and the heavy lead balls. "You go an' look after your baby brother in this war you're a-goin' to be at."

And Noah, almost six feet tall, stood proudly by, knowing there was no stigma attached to his conviction for crime. In this family, as in most of the others in these hills, transgressions against outsiders were not considered transgressions at all. Pap had said nothing to that effect, but he didn't need to. He had just put substance to it by giving Noah his prized possession, a gold watch that Noah could feel now in his trouser pocket like a hot, heavy mule shoe.

They were on the front porch overlooking the lush valley of the Buffalo. The old man and Noah and Zack were on one side, making their arrangements; the mother and the other three brothers, Cadmus, Tyne, and Britt, stood near and watched, saying nothing. Now and again the boys looked out across the long valley to the far hills, making a great to-do about keeping all expression from their faces. The woman watched her youngest son with each move he made, and when he finally turned to her and they embraced, there was an added dampness in her eyes, which the other boys tried elaborately to ignore.

Noah turned to his brothers who would be staying, each in turn, and took their hands, still with no one saying a word. Then he and Zack lifted their blanket rolls and stepped down off the porch. Zack embraced none of them, nor shook their hands. He kept his eyes away, but along his beardless jaw the clamped muscles stood out like young hickory nuts.

"You, Noy, be a good boy," his mother called. "An' do what you're told by your elders. Mind your brother."

"Yes'm," he said, turning away down the yard.

"And you, Zack, watch out for your little brother and keep him clear of the Yankees," she said.

"Yes'm," Zack said, not looking back.

The father said nothing but watched his sons walk down to the rocky road and turn south along it. They walked with backs straight, their feet clad in the new shoes bought on credit the day before, after the trial in Town. There was about their walk a certain awkwardness, yet also a distance-consuming grace. Their slouch hats cast a dark shadow across their heads and shoulders.

The family remained on the porch to watch the two boys come to the first bend in the road, beyond which their home would be lost from sight.

"Who are them Yankees, anyway?" Cadmus asked.

"Outlanders an' city scum," his father said. "They're a-comin'. They mean us harm. The preacher tole me so."

"It ain't Yankees I'm afeared of," the mother said. "It's all them no-accounts they got in armies that carry bad habits. God keep my boys," and she turned quickly and disappeared into the house.

NOAH Fawley wished that he had never seen that damned pig. A young man of many regrets, he was always contrite for actions brought on by his impetuous nature. His brother, by contrast, never appeared to regret anything.

Noah was leaving more than family, too. There was the lovely Luanne Lacy, her family's farm only a mile up the hill from the Fawleys, with whom Noah had already tasted the sweet flavor of loving in an old, abandoned smokehouse. It had been in the afternoon, broad daylight, and neither of them brave enough to actually look at what was happening but bringing it to culmination just the same. There had been a gathering of the clans that day, for religious services and late supper on the ground. Those frantic moments in the smokehouse had been a delicious experience—away from all the others, secret. Now, as he walked down the road toward the Buffalo, Noah could see Luanne Lacy's face, the lips pouting, full, and inviting.

In a month or so, when this Yankee thing was finished,

he'd be back. And sweet Luanne Lacy ripe for marriage. Fourteen years old!

He was in this wise unlike any of his brothers, who kept emotion in check as a matter of pride. Many of the hill folk said the Fawley boys would all end bachelors unless their Pap made business arrangements for wives, which he had never shown any inclination to do. It had seemed important to him only that daughter Lucinda be married off to someone capable of impregnating her, which had happened now. As for the boys, if any of them ever longed for soft company on a permanent basis, they made a good job of concealing it.

Except Noah. He was growing from hot-blooded boy to hot-blooded man, given to quick temper, fistfights, and violent spasms of passion.

Beautiful Luanne Lacy! He would tell her grand stories as they lay together after more of the loving that had come but once so far, but that he knew was ready to be had at his taking. Tales to be spun of far places and of people he would see—even the Yankees, maybe. He was unclear in his mind what a Yankee was, with no definite idea of where they came from or what they intended. He wondered how they might look, and if they wore hats like other men and spoke in words he might understand.

"Where's this war at?" Noah asked.

"We're bound to find it, wherever it's at," Zack said in his flat voice with its sound of oak barrel staves clapping together.

"What's it about?"

"Pap says the Yankees aim to come make us live like them."

"How's that?"

"Hell's fire, I don't know," Zack snapped impatiently.

Anxious to end this conversation about things he did not understand, Zack moved off the road and sat on a fallen hickory log. He took out the Dragoon pistol and slowly began loading it. Noah stood still in the road, watching.

"You aim to use that right off?"

"It ain't worth a Gawd damn unloaded."

Zack charged all six cylinders but capped only five, letting the big hammer down on the empty nipple. He shoved the pistol back under his coat, rose, and moved back into the road.

By Gawd, thought Noah, he thinks there really is a war, don't he?

But to Zackery there was no thought of war. Rather, he saw little logic in hauling about an empty weapon, now or ever. All of this was a matter of the moment to him. He was taking this journey because Pap had said to go, but he did not concern himself with anything except tomorrow's dawn. Time enough then to consider the new day and what it might bring.

Although of the same blood, looking brothers every inch, they were as different as two men could be in all other aspects, as each was aware. Now they were going together up the valley of the Buffalo to its head, thence across the intervening ridges into the watershed of the Arkansas, and then along that river to someplace—they had no idea where—to offer their service. Going together in a cause neither of them understood, in total ignorance of why, except for the judgment of His Honor, Guthrie Scaggs.

# TWO

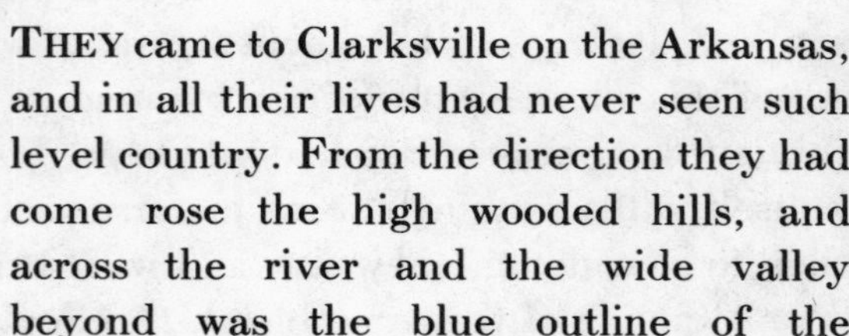

THEY came to Clarksville on the Arkansas, and in all their lives had never seen such level country. From the direction they had come rose the high wooded hills, and across the river and the wide valley beyond was the blue outline of the Ouachitas. But where they stood it was flat, the floodplain carved by the river through all the centuries since the Ozarks were thrust up to form a northern barrier and direct the course of flowing water.

More astonishing still were the masses of people, the hurried activity along the riverfront, the carriages and wagons, the horses, mules, and oxen, and the steamboats.

"She's a bitch, ain't she?" Zack asked.

Noah was staring openmouthed.

"We best fin' some place to earn a little money. I'm hongry as all get-out."

"Pap gave you two dollars. I seen him do it," Noah said.

"Yeah, an' his new razor an' a chunk a' soap. But the money I aim to take back to him unspent. So we'll work for our keep, here as we elsewhere would."

"He give it to us so we could spend it."

Zack looked at his younger brother with calm eyes.

"Two dollars in your pocket," he explained patiently, "don't call for stoppin' daily work."

"I thought we come down here to join up with an army, not to work."

"I don't aim to starve while I'm lookin' fer it!"

Work there was aplenty. They hired on for the afternoon and into the night loading rough-cut lumber onto a small riverboat. The wage was four bits and found, the found being a hunk of ham and coarse-fibered bread, paid in full after the loading was complete.

"How'd you like to have this here boat on the Buffalo?" Noah asked.

"I doubt it'd fit."

There were four others on the loading crew, trooping up and down the gangway with the lumber bouncing on their shoulders. Three of them were regular river men, from downstream, perhaps even as far away as the Mississippi. They were a loud-talking, burly bunch with stocking caps, and trousers cut just below the knees. Laughing, showing tobacco-stained teeth, they made jokes about the hill farmers come down to get seasick on the river.

"Why them men keep lookin' at us?" Noah wanted to know.

"Leave it be," Zack said. "Them's lowlanders. You've heard Uncle Questor talk about lowlanders after that time he went to Fort Smith."

Noah laughed, thinking of Uncle Questor, Pap's brother and holy as a Baptist preacher, Pap always claimed, unless there was a jug of good moonshine available or a young woman ready to accept some heavy-handed flirting. Bachelor he was, Uncle Questor, tending his small farm as little as possible, wandering the wooded hills, always searching for solace or solitude, nobody was sure which, but appearing at Pap's door periodically with a brown paper sack filled with sourballs. For as far back as he could remember, Noah had looked forward to those sourballs.

The fourth stranger on the crew was a farmer, too, showing the marks of toil on his callused hands. He was large and well muscled, and his skin was sun-darkened under light brown hair.

"Hasford's my name," he said, extending his hand to them. "Martin Hasford from Benton County."

"We're Fawleys. From Buffalo River in Newton County," Zack said, shaking the man's hand.

"Where at's Benton County?" Noah asked.

"On the border. Next to the Indian Territory," Hasford said. "You boys live a tad east of where I do."

"I reckon that's so," Zack said, noting a book in Hasford's coat pocket. He took it for a Bible.

"Sure hot, ain't it?" Noah said.

"That's the river. Makes the air muggy," Hasford said, bending to a stack of lumber. "Where you boys bound?"

"We been recruited," Zack said, and laughed shortly.

"That's what I'm here for," Hasford said, balancing lengths of lumber on one shoulder. "Come to join the forces. The past few days I've been drilling with a Clarksville militia company, but I didn't sign up. It's not much army."

"Where you reckon the army's at?"

"Gawd damn, Noah, you ast a lot of questions," Zack said.

"Little Rock. There's recruiting at the arsenal that we took away from the Yankees. I'm going there tomorrow, down the river." Hasford started up the gangway, stepping easily with the heavy load.

As the river men worked they sang a strange trilling song, and neither of the Fawleys could understand a word of it. Nor could Martin Hasford, though he was aware of the language.

"I suppose the daddies of these men were working this river when my people came along it going west," he said to Noah. "Maybe they were here, too. Just sprouts."

"What's them words they're singin'?"

"I don't know. But it's French."

And with that Noah added another deficit to stand beside the bad manners of these men. He had to his knowledge never seen a single soul of French descent, but passing down the lineage of his family from father to son over the years had been the story that the French fought against the English during the Revolution. Also that they ate snails and used perfume by the waterglassful, even the men.

Noah could smell no hint of perfume on this crew, but the idea of those snails stuck in his craw, more even than the fact that their grandpaps might have tried to inflict bodily harm on his own grandpaps back in 1776.

"Them's Frenchmen," he whispered to Zack.

"They ain't botherin' you," Zack said. "Stop tryin' to make somethin' out of it."

The sun was gone by the time they had completed their task. They were paid in coin and meat and found a place to eat in an empty riverfront mule pen. There were stacks of baled hay there and a bed of discarded harness.

Both Fawleys watched Martin Hasford take the Bible from his pocket before he ate. He removed his hat, read a few passages, lips moving, then said a silent prayer, eyes closed, the book clutched in both hands. The three river men were watching, too, from across the pen. And laughing among themselves.

The ham was stringy and tough, but they made no complaint, wolfing it down with the bread.

"How you aim to get to this here Little Rock?" Zack asked Martin Hasford.

"On this same boat. I talked with the master. He'll take me down and pay me again for unloading his cargo. It's going to the arsenal, bought for the army."

"Maybe he'd take us along, too," Noah said.

Hasford made no answer. He was deliberate in his eating, as Zack suspected he was in all things. Slow and sure and confident, doing each job thoroughly, whether it was mending harness or sowing a field or making decisions.

His family had come from Germany, he had said, two generations ago. There were a few scattered families of Germans along the Buffalo, and they were all cut from the same bolt of cloth. Methodical, stolid, efficient.

Not bad companionship, Zack figured. Dependable. And of course Noah was always ready to go with anybody so long as he heard the flute. Zack almost laughed, thinking of the story their Uncle Questor told of that piper fellow in a foreign land leading all the rats out of town with his playing.

"It don't make a damn to me," Zack said.

"I suppose it could be managed," Hasford said. He stared at Zack's face for a long moment while both of them chewed slowly. "As a general rule, I don't believe in oath-making. But I count as friends many who have the habit."

"Yeah," Zack said, neither offended nor feeling any apology necessary. "I seen your Bible. Mama does all the verse-readin' in our family, her an' this uncle we got who's a preacher of sorts."

"Can you read?"

"Enough to know our names. Me an' Noy both."

"That's good. Many can't," Hasford said. "Now, on this swearing, some take it as a deadly sin. But I look on it as only a small disfavor to the Lord, if it is properly repented in the soul."

"Yeah, that's about the way I got it sized up," Zack said, and thought: This here man would please Mama. All it needs now is for him to start quotin' Scripture like Uncle Questor always does. Which could become a pain in the backside!

"You know anything about the Yankees?" Noah asked.

"I know they'll come into our land and lay it waste," Hasford said, as calmly as if he were speaking of plagues of locusts, which were inevitable and beyond the control of mortal man. Zack expected a quotation with it, but none came.

Maybe he ain't as bad as Uncle Questor after all, Zack thought.

Noah started to ask another question, but stopped and looked across the mule pen. The three river men had finished their meal and now sauntered across the open space, finally squatting in a line along the fence near Noah, whispering and laughing. After a while, the largest of them rose and moved directly before Martin Hasford. Noah could see the black hair curling up through the man's collarless shirt, joining beneath his chin with a thick beard that apparently had never felt brush or scissors.

"*Mon Dieu!*" the river man said, grinning broadly. "You 'ave a parson man who reads 'is little book, yes?"

Zack glanced up briefly, then lowered his head, his hat brim shading his face.

"Perhaps 'e 'as a little sermon for us all?" The river man stood with hands on hips, fists clenched.

Martin Hasford looked into his eyes but made no move to rise. "I'm no preacher," he said. "But I allow the Book is not to be made fun of."

"Ah, is this true?" The river man glanced toward his companions, and they laughed and slapped their thighs. "We forget that book, then. But I mus' tell you. We are river men. We 'ave this river for a long time, see? An' now you gentlemens who slop hogs come an' take the money we 'ave been thinkin' of. My friends say I should rassle you for this four bit you make."

"Leave him alone. He ain't botherin' you," Noah said softly, but Zack could hear the temper in his voice.

The Frenchman laughed, head back, and turned abruptly to stand before Noah, his feet planted well apart.

"*Sacré Dieu!* Look at this young one! 'E is another country 'eard from, yes? With the new shoes. You think we 'ave a rassle for those shoes, young one?"

Noah measured the man's chest and the sloping shoulders and the hard line of jaw under the beard. He dropped his head and looked sideways at his brother. Zack was idly plucking lint from his trousers, face still in deep shadow under the hat brim. He's gonna let me run this full course, Noah thought.

"Aw, no. Not the shoes," the Frenchman said. "But you 'ave the 'at. I like him bes'. I try the 'at, see?"

With a sudden movement the river man swept Noah's hat off and had it almost to his forehead before Noah came up fast and drove a fist into the center of the black beard. It was like hitting a jack-oak fencepost. Noah felt the shock of it all down his arm and into the socket of his shoulder. In that instant before the river man reached out, Noah knew he had bit off a tough chew.

The blow had snapped the Frenchman's head back, but he was still laughing, with the blood running through his beard from a split lip. Noah started to swing again when the Frenchman's hands caught Noah's shoulders, gripping like sprung traps, yanking forward.

They struggled into the center of the pen, Noah flailing with both hands now, and the river man laughing. Then the bigger man was in close, clamping his arms around Noah in a bear hug, and they went to ground, grunting and panting, a cloud of fine dust roiling up around them.

From beneath his hat brim, Zack watched. Martin was coming to his feet, jaw clamped tight and fists balled, when Zack spoke to him.

"Leave 'em be!"

The two figures rolled in the pen, scattering the mule droppings, raising a thicker cloud of dust, clubbing each other, and the river man's elbows going into kidney and neck. Legs thrashed out of the dust cloud, and Noah gasped as the river man got a hold on his ear with those long, tobacco-stained teeth. They rolled into a pile of harness, and Zack saw his brother's arm, hand grasping through the dust, then fingers closing on a singletree, and then the singletree coming down in short, vicious arcs. There were the thick, muffled sounds of wood on solid bone, again and then again.

The two river men who had been watching with wide grins started up from their squat, serious now and with hands clenched. Zack pulled back his coat and slipped the Colt pistol free, his eyes cutting sharply toward them. They stopped, half standing, half squatting, and their eyes widened. There was the hard metallic click of the hammer rolling back. The two men sank back on their hams, still staring into the black muzzle of the revolver. Zack held it almost casually across one thigh.

Noah was up now, his hair flying and blood running from his ear down the side of his face and blackening his shirt. He had the singletree in his hand, and his eyes were glassy. Behind him in the pile of harness the Frenchman was moaning, holding his head with both hands. Noah charged across the mule pen toward the other two, who were still squatted rigidly under Zack's gun.

"You gonna get it, too, you tadpole-eatin' heathens," Noah roared, swinging the singletree before their faces. They drew back against the fence as Noah ground his teeth.

"Well," Zack said easily. Their faces turned to him, and they saw his unevenly spaced teeth as he smiled. "Which one a' you boys is next to tie in?"

The pistol had disappeared back under the flap of his coat, but the river men knew it was still there.

"We mean no harm. Only a little of the fun, you see?"

"You gonna fun yourselfs right into an early grave, you son of a bitch," Zack said. He rose slowly and looked at his brother. "Come on, Noy. Let's fin' us a place to sleep the night."

"I'm havin' these two with this here tree," Noah said, his anger still making his voice harsh.

"No, you ain't," Zack said. "You've had all the jamboree you need fer a spell. Mr. Hasford, you like to come along? These here boys might not be too sociable onct Noy puts down that stick. We can take another boat downriver to this here Little Rock."

Hasford, who had watched all of this with a mixture of excitement and repugnance, rose as well.

"I think that would be wise," he said. "But just a minute."

He went across the pen to the fallen man and bent to him, feeling the man's head. After a careful examination, he wiped his fingers on his trousers, leaving a smear of red. They heard him speak softly. " 'If thou doest not well, sin lieth at the door.' That's from Genesis, brother, but I can't recall chapter and verse at the moment."

As Martin Hasford came back across the mule pen, they could see his smile, and when he passed the two river men still squatting motionless against the fence, he touched his hat to them.

Backing away, Noah tossed the singletree aside, but with some disgust. He had wanted badly to whale into the other two as well, wanted in his scalding wrath to feel the smash of the wood against their skulls. But by the time he had retrieved his hat and blanket roll and hurried after Zack and Hasford, his rage had gone cool, as it usually did, and he laughed softly to himself and felt with his fingertips the sticky course of blood along his cheek.

"Was that a pistol I saw under your coat?" Noah heard Martin Hasford ask from the darkness ahead.

"It's Pap's old Dragoon."

"I brought along a musket myself, but I sold it yesterday. I heard there's regiments recruiting that supply new weapons—rifles, I hope."

"We'll tag along," Zack said. "I like the idea of rifles give to us."

"I'll say this, it's good to be among hill folk. I feel more at home with you two boys than I have since I left my family in Benton County. There's been times when I thought of turning around and going back."

"No army's gotcha yet," Zack said. "You can turn aroun' if you feel a mind."

"No," Martin Hasford said, shaking his head as though to convince himself. "I'll see this thing through to the finish."

"Well, it ain't likely to take very long," said Zack.

THEY shipped downriver on a boat loaded with hogs. The vessel had originated at Fort Smith and had been held up at one of the ports of call before Clarksville. Due to hot sun and lack of enterprise by the crew, the smell grew bad enough to drive them all ashore even though it meant forfeiture of pay.

Such things were of minor concern to the Fawleys and Martin Hasford. They shipped on board and, as the boat paddled downstream, spent the better part of the morning flushing out pens with buckets of water pulled up from the river.

After that there was nothing to do but sit in the sun by the railings. For a time Martin Hasford spoke of his farm in Benton County, of the crops they grew, of the virtues of family life and himself lucky in it with a strong son, a pretty daughter, and a faithful wife. But soon he was finished with this outpouring of loneliness, and he fell silent.

Zack slept, a cud of tobacco still in his cheek, his arms folded across his lank stomach as he lay back against the cabin wall.

Noah found it insufferable, this sitting and doing nothing. On a walk through the mountains, at least one could think of placing one foot before the other. But now there was nothing to take his mind off the nagging disquiet of being away from familiar ground and people.

To relieve himself of such tension, he began taking Pap's watch from his pocket at short intervals and announcing the time, even though no one was listening.

"It's four of the clock."

But then the watch seemed to make things worse. Casting back in memory was a thing he had never particularly enjoyed. Sometimes it was downright painful. Even when Uncle Questor or Mama tried to draw a moral from the Scriptures having to do with certain family events, his mind wandered to more immediate things before the lesson had time to take root. Luanne Lacy in the smokehouse, he liked to ponder on, but even that had now taken on the color of melancholy.

Yet, try as he would to concentrate on watching this new land slip past the boat, each time he touched Pap's watch his thoughts went back, hurtfully, against his will.

The mists rising in the springtime from the valley of the Buffalo in early morning when he and Pap and the other boys went down to the rocky fields with hoes over their shoulders like muskets . . . and how Mama would look up from the stove when they came in, a fine dew of sweat across her upper lip and the kitchen rich with the smell of cooking meat . . .

He thought of the rain falling on the shake shingles of the house, himself snug under the goosefeather tick made by his own sister's hand. And he thought of the cool woods, he and Zack alone in the thick timber waiting for the sight of deer, and when it came, Zack dropping the buck with a clean shot to the shoulder.

Among all his brothers he was somehow closest to Zack. Sitting beside him now, Noah felt assurance and confidence. There was even comfort in the soft liquid sound of his brother's snoring.

Noah was glad his father had sent Zack instead of one of the other boys. Not because Zack was the eldest or because he was better than the others with weapons, or yet calmest when weasels got into the chicken coop or a wild hog raided the sows' sty. But because of the special closeness of the two, Zack and Noah, oldest and youngest of the brothers. Noah began to understand the wisdom of his father in seeing this, and with that came a realization of the heartache that must have been the old man's as he watched the first and last of his boys march down the mountain and away from home.

He sometimes gets cantankerous as an old boar squirrel, does Zack, Noah thought. But it's good to have him here.

It was always Zack out into the timber on winter mornings, in the darkness, after deer or turkey, and back sometimes with meat before breakfast. Though other times not until noon, cursing some hound that had followed him and disrupted his stalk. For Zack was a still hunter, a man who could abide dogs only for running fox and coon, and neither of these for killing but only for the sounds of the dogs' baying.

The day finally came when Zack had wakened Noah, the boy still not old enough to hold and shoot the ancient muzzle-loader with a flintlock. Noah had seen plenty of dead game in his boyhood, but it was on that day with Zack in the deep woods that he had seen his first deer brought down, and it had created such excitement that he had almost thrown up. And then for days afterward he bored Mama and Pap and his brothers with the telling of it.

In all his years he had never shot a deer, only rabbit and squirrel. Yet he had been eager from that first morning awakening to tag along with Zack, to watch the woodsmanship. Even now, a grown boy of seventeen, he could thrill to the flow of his brother's movements in the woods, with the game and the timber and the streams, becoming a part of it as soon as he stepped across the split-rail fence into the shadowed wilderness.

"We'll be at the arsenal by tomorrow," Martin Hasford was saying, breaking into Noah's thoughts.

Zack grunted and sat up, stretched, and spat a long stream of accumulated amber juice toward the river. Most of it splattered across the deck, short of the mark.

"I never thought I'd be this far from home," Noah said, and was immediately sorry he had put words to it.

Zack stared at him a moment, then snorted, his way of laughing sometimes. He began to chew slowly, shaking his head.

"Why, hell, you got a wounded ear already. An' you gonna like all this so much, you likely have to be tied an' carried to get you back up in the hills."

# THREE

IN NORMAL times the Little Rock arsenal had been a group of four-story stone buildings set in groves of oak and sycamore and elm, the well-kept lawns and the cannon and stacks of cannonballs providing idyllic picnic settings for gentlemen and ladies on Sunday afternoon outings. There were cool breezes from the river, and the odor of cut grass, and from time to time the staid, measured march of the few soldiers stationed there, having their afternoon parades before storing arms and going into the city for more enjoyable activities.

But now the Union blue uniforms were gone, and the once quiet grounds were a pandemonium of sound and color, of whirling, patriotic zeal spiced generously with mercantile efforts and the frenzied, joyous socializing attendant to recruiting a new army, an atmosphere as yet unclouded by posted casualty lists.

*"TO ARMS! TO ARMS!"* exhorted the placards tacked to every tree and storage-house wall, and all other available surfaces.

"DEFEND YOUR *HOMES* AND *LOVED ONES!* 300 ABLE-BODIED MEN WANTED FOR SERVICE IN THE *ARMIES OF THE CONFEDERACY* AND FOR *ARKANSAS!* YOUR STATE IN *DANGER!* RALLY TO HER *STANDARD!*"

Or sometimes it was five hundred needed, or even enough for a full regiment of one thousand. And beside these, smaller, less elaborate posters indicated that the universal hysteria was not so overwhelming as to obscure the obvious opportunity for profit:

"All the necessaries and most of the luxuries at lowest cost to the soldier if paid in cash. Goodall's Mercantile, Main Street, Little Rock."

Many of the merchants had not been satisfied to await business in their emporia, but had come with wagonloads of assorted salables. The streets around the arsenal were lined with them, and the grounds sprouted stands for lemonade, ice cream, and meat pastries, and some, discreetly out of view, sold thimble-sized drinks of whisky. And at a greater distance were buggies where women in silk dresses looked out above their fans and invited newly recruited soldiers to even more delicate fare. All business done in cash.

Men in frock coats and women under lacy bonnets and with dainty parasols moved confidently about the grounds, and among them the recently uniformed troops, raised in companies by monied planters or politicians.

The soldiers showed more variety in their dress than did the civilians: jackets, coats, or capes; trousers or pantaloons; kepis, slouch hats, turbans, or skullcaps. There was cadet gray and ocean blue, red britches with yellow piping, white plumes in officers' hats, chamois gauntlets and feet housed in new yellow leather, sleeves decorated with the golden whorls of company-grade officers—braid that would have been pretentious for a marshal in Napoleon's army. Gleaming sabers everywhere, and newly issued rifles and muskets—some so old they would have given pause to a soldier serving in the War of 1812. Or zouaves with saber bayonets—vicious looking, but so long and unwieldy they could hardly oppose an unprotesting hog. And knives and pistols, large and small, none authorized by regulations, most purchased from Goodall and other such enterprising men.

Food, too: mince pie and roast pork for sale, and the older ladies of the town laying down potato salad and scalded greens for the men who had just signed on with the Wilson's Whippets or the Mena Rifles or the Garland County Abe Killers.

In an unanticipated part of the scene, a few of the new soldiers were slipping behind the buildings, opening their trousers for a brief moment, embarrassed at leaving the tracks of their requirement splattered along the wall and down the new pants, cursing and wondering why there had been no latrines provided, properly screened from prying eyes with canvas. Latrine—the first of all the military terms they had learned.

And along the roadsides, a little distance from the arsenal, a few of the troops, as yet still looking well-pressed and tooth-clean, bent over ditches and vomited, their stomachs twisting, their minds wondering: Jesus God, why is patriotic whisky so damned ornery raw?

A whirlwind of brave talk swirled over the grounds, impelled by an urgency to have the men in uniform before the Yankees were whipped and sent home, the war over; and if no opportunity then for native sons to have known the sting of gunpowder in their noses, at least to wear the gray.

The sweet-faced young women seemed to say it with their eyes, the older ones with their potato salad, the merchants with their necessaries, the recruiters with their promise of thirteen dollars a month in pay, and the whores with their delicious fantasies promised for cash. Oh, young men, hurry to the colors! Before it is too late!

And all the while a frightful number of kisses being stolen. Not from the professionals in their buggies, silk-clad and eyes above their quivering fans, but from the sweet innocents who paraded in rows like ranks of flowered infantry, close under the watchful eye of parents and guardians. The brazen conduct of the young soldiers was overlooked. This was Southern manhood, off to slay the dragon of Union, and why not a little kiss here and there beneath the sycamores to send them on their way? Unspoken but understood, it had become an immediate and prideful duty for the young ladies of good family to pucker when a soldier boy presented his grinning face.

And everywhere the flags: the original emblem of secession with three horizontal bars—two red, one white—and a blue field with a single star; and the newer one, with the field showing a circle of seven stars; and even a few of Old Bory's flag, the stars and bars, banner red as blood and manufactured by the ladies to Confederate specifications, forty-eight inches on a side—a flag only a few of them would fight under, but that would become the emblem of their pride, and for some their shame.

A DARK, heavily built young man sat astride one of the old Mexican War cannons, watching the carnival of mobilization with a sardonic grin, white teeth showing in a thick black beard. He had taken his share of kisses already and might take more, although there was nothing about his clothing to suggest the soldier except for the long bowie knife thrust into the belt of his trousers.

He fanned himself with a floppy short-billed cap, much like those seen on riverboats of the Arkansas, yet somehow with a distinctly European look about it.

"You there," he called to a man passing with a pushcart steaming from a charcoal fire beneath a row of double boilers. "What's for sale this time, is it?"

"Meat pies," the man said. He paused, glanced at the long knife and the stout hands of the young man, the cords of muscle showing on his arms where the sleeves were rolled up to the elbow.

"Meat from the cats of Little Rock streets, I'd wager it."

The man flushed and drew himself up indignantly. "Sir, these pies are made from the finest pork available."

"Of course they are. But nothing wrong with cat, so long as the seasoning has it right. Dish one out, man, before I starve with all this war talk."

The pie was dished out, a turnover brown and glossy with butter. The man served it on a folded section of newspaper, took his six cents, and trundled off to the rattle of his pots, looking abused.

Liverpool Morgan ate his pie, the grease running into his black beard. He continued to watch the throngs, listening to martial music from a brass band that had just marched out from the city. Nearby, a small black boy was dancing on the hard-packed yard beside an arsenal building, a crowd around him, some tossing pennies.

"Wars bring out the music in us all," Morgan said, and laughed. He winked elaborately at two passing girls, who giggled and hurried on as though half afraid he would leap from the cannon and assault them, half afraid he would not.

And then, his pie mostly finished, he saw the three men

standing near, two of them tall and built like hickory saplings, the other older, heavier. His smile grew as he watched the gawking expressions on their faces, and he knew they were seeing a pageant of patriotism for the first time.

"And what is it you're selling now?" he asked, taking the last mouthful of meat pie and wiping his fingers on the front of his short-sleeved jacket.

"We're not selling anything," the oldest of them said, a little startled at the question.

"Oh, but everyone here sells something," Morgan said with a laugh. "A pie for six pennies, a kiss for the flavor of it, or perhaps ourselves for the glory. You're here to enlist, I'd wager."

"We were inclined in that direction."

Liverpool Morgan leaped down from the cannon, landing awkwardly on both feet, like a buzzard, and extended his right hand.

"You've come to the wrong place," he said. "I'm Liverpool Morgan. Some call me the Black Welshman."

The older man took his hand, looking at the black beard and the black hair splayed out beneath the cap and the heavy black brows over gray eyes.

"I'd never have guessed such a thing," he said. "Hasford. Martin Hasford. These here are Fawleys. Down from the hills to be recruited."

"Zackery," Zack said. "This here's my little brother Noy."

"And a fine little brother he is," the Black Welshman said, taking their hands in turn, extended to him with hesitation, even reluctance. "Now tell me, are you here to join the dancing and kissing, or looking for a fight?"

"We aim to tie into the Yankees," Noah said. "As soon as we can fin' some."

"Aye, and well said, little brother. But I tell it again. The wrong place this is. Most of what you see is state militia. They'll likely never leave the county, it's the truth. You need to go downriver. With me."

"Downriver?" Hasford asked.

"Downriver and recruiting for Virginia and the war. And likely some good English rifles in the bargain, though I hate to give the bloody English anything."

"Rifles?" Zack said, his eyes showing sudden interest.

"They tell me. Rifles. Bought with good cotton money. And money, as you go to war. You can hire on a boat and make a nice wage. A soldier always needs a nice wage wherever he can get it, because it won't come from the army."

"We've just come off the river," Hasford said. "We shipped a boat down from Clarksville."

"Ship a little farther, then. I even know the boat. Leaving the docks this night, headed downstream."

They studied on that a moment and Noah fidgeted, looking across the grounds toward some of the concession stands.

"I'm hongry," he said. "That river grub don't do much towards fillin' a man up."

"Wait here, little brother," Morgan said. "And think on going downriver to a real army. I'll call back a man I know here who sells excellent pies. I'll set you a table on this old cannon."

Morgan stepped off a few paces and began to call to the meat vendor in a hard Welsh bass. Zack and Noah looked at one another, but Hasford seemed lost in thought, gazing off over the buildings of the arsenal toward the northeast, where Benton County lay more than two hundred miles away. Zack shrugged. "This don't look like no army to me," he said.

"It looks like a circus," Martin Hasford said, seeming to shake himself. "Without the tiger cats!"

They studied Morgan's proposition silently, each with his own thoughts—Noah's mostly about something to eat, and Zack's about those rifles the Welshman had mentioned.

"What's a Welshman?" Noah asked, watching Morgan some distance away bartering with the meat vendor.

"A man from Wales," Hasford said. "Across the seas, in Britain. I've seen a few in Benton County. A brawling, hymn-singing crew if there ever was such a thing."

"Ain't there none of our own folks down here?" Noah asked.

"Not so you can tell it," Zack said.

They studied it again, then Zack looked at Noah and the light in his eyes told Noah that his brother was thinking hard on those rifles.

"We might as well make a few dollars on the way to the war," Zack said. "Virginia is where the war is at."

"Well," said Hasford, "some is likely to be here, too. There's a Yankee army in Missouri."

"We been goin' in the wrong direction for Missouri ever since we started."

"Missouri's clear up north of Harrison," Noah said.

"Yes, an' ever' step we've took taken us a piece farther away from it. Besides," Zack said, "I ain't ever seen Virginia."

"You ain't ever seen Missouri, either," Noah said.

"What the jumped-up hell's wrong with you?" Zack said, suddenly spitting his words. "You heerd all the talk along the river about a big battle in Virginia. You come to get in a big battle, didn't you?"

"I come 'cause that judge tole me I had to," Noah said, and Martin Hasford's eyes widened.

"What judge?"

"Never mind. It's a long story about two drunk boys an' a hog. Maybe he'll tell it to you one of these days."

"Well, all right. Our people have taken this place, and last month they took over Fort Smith, and from the talk, those Missouri Yankees are all in a muddle. Maybe they won't get this far before it's all over and done."

"Then let's tie into Virginia," Zack said.

"So be it," Hasford said, and Noah saw his eyes go toward the northeast again.

Morgan returned with a double handful of pies, and they stood around the cannon, eating.

Noah thought about Virginia, a foreign land. On the other hand, he had heard of Missouri all his life. And although he knew that Martin Hasford would be an ally if he insisted on staying at home to take a chance on fighting in Arkansas, he said no more. Zack had already made his decision for him. I could say I'd as lief tie into Missouri Yankees, he thought, an' Zack would say you'll tie into whatever Yankees I tell you to. Besides, Mama said mind Zack, an' besides that again, if I never done it, Zack'd likely knock the ole piss outa me.

"Now then," Morgan said, "Virginia or no for you, tonight I'm bound in that direction."

"For us, too," said Zack, chewing and watching the Welshman with that glint in his eye.

"Best we do it quick, before they whup them Yankees an' this war is over," Noah said.

Morgan looked at him sharply and started to say something, but then clamped his jaw shut.

"So be it," Hasford said softly. "This don't taste like any meat pie I ever had before!"

THERE was still plenty of time to enjoy an occasional passing covey of parasols, so Liverpool Morgan contended. Sitting against the old cannon's wheels and astride the barrel, they sucked the lemons Morgan had bought from a vendor and sliced with his bowie knife.

"Pap bought a sack of lemons onct," Noah said.

The Black Welshman took a pair of double eagles from his purse and passed them along for the others to feel. Noah had never seen two twenty-dollar gold pieces in the same place before, and precious few of them singly. The coins felt oily and soft to the touch, warm and powerful.

"My da earns many of these each year with the sawmill," the Black Welshman said.

"You a lumberman, then?" Hasford asked.

"I tell it so, but I've spent little time at it. When I was yet a boy, the wanderlust struck me. I've stoked steamboats to New Orleans, I've been a blacksmith's apprentice at Fort Smith. The shame of my da I am, going off from those sweet-smelling pines of the Ouachitas where he set up the mill when I was a babe."

"Where'd you get that name, Liverpool?" Noah asked,

chewing on a lemon rind. "I never heerd a name like that before."

"Born on the docks of that city, when my da was on his way to this land with his family. And a good land. But I never grew to love those pines as my da did, because I suppose I never spent half my days in the black pits above the Dee, as my da did."

"The Welsh I know are all fair-headed," Hasford said.

"Then you haven't seen the true Welsh," Morgan laughed. "We were the first, and then the fair ones came. They brought the Celtic language to us, so now they claim to be the original Welsh. Of which is horseshit."

"It sounds of ancient times to me."

"Yes. Before the Romans came."

"Ah! The Romans. There's a people I've read about," said Hasford.

More than read about, in fact. Studied in Mr. Gibbon's book and in other places. He had even named his children Calpurnia and Roman, for which he was sometimes a little amazed at himself because it was a Latin who had sent Christ to the cross. He always explained that away by telling himself the blame did not lie with Pontius Pilate but with the Jews—those Jews who had wandered the desert in the old days, wearing heavy robes and sacrificing goats on holy days. At least he supposed from his readings they did such strange things.

Fireworks were going up from somewhere on the far side of the arsenal grounds, and although it was not yet completely dark, the red and blue and white bursts made Noah gasp.

"That must be like cannons look."

"No, little brother," Morgan said. "Cannon looks most black and smells like brimstone."

"How'd you know that?" Zack asked.

"Why, man, I went to join the great Giuseppe Garibaldi in the fight for Sicily. I'm just returned. Heard there was a little fuss here to be cleared up."

"You go from one war to another?" Hasford asked.

"If there's a war to go to, I'm for it," the Black Welshman

said. "Why, hell's jumped up, brothers. If you can get used to the stink and the gore and the screaming of horses, and the bad food and the wet nights sleeping on the ground and the bloody flux, war's more fun than anything you might imagine."

"Fun?" Hasford said incredulously.

"A game it is, but not for all. But for me there is a certain excitement."

Morgan rose and stretched, the muscles of his arms swelling tight against his rolled shirtsleeves. He slapped his belly like a drum and smiled, his teeth showing bright.

"Visiting enough, brothers," he said. "Let's off to the boat and Virginia."

"That's more like it," Noah said, feeling some strange exhilaration, some urgency to be on the way.

The fireworks continued to pop in the darkening sky behind them as they moved onto the streets, Morgan leading.

"Causes are fine," he was saying. "My da says he, the English have sucked the blood of the Welsh these generations, and now the Yankee factory owners would do the same to the South, says he. True or not, I don't know."

"I don't know if it's true either," Hasford said.

"Then why would you be off to this war? You seem a man who would fight only for causes or to save his slaves from the abolitionists."

"I've never owned a slave, and none of my people ever have," Hasford said a little abruptly.

"Well then?"

"A state or a man has got the right to do what he thinks best for himself."

"That's cause enough for me," Morgan said, and suddenly he lifted his voice in song, the words and tones sounding even stranger to them than those they had heard from the French river men.

"An old Welsh mining song," he explained. "Good to be sung for all sorts of causes."

Walking behind the other two, Noah bent toward Zack and whispered, "I don't understan' half of what he says."

"Just fill in what you want," Zack said. "I don't think he knows half a' what he's sayin' his own self."

The boat was a large sternwheeler with scow keel and two open decks, the lower one crowded with mules on their way to the cotton country, the second stacked with empty hogsheads bound for the same destination.

"I see you made it back," the master called down from the pilothouse. "Figured you'd get to that arsenal and never find your way here again."

"The militia recruiter hasn't been born who could stay me."

"It wasn't the recruiters worried me," the master shouted. "It was all them women. Any you boys interested in a hand or two of five-card bluff?"

While Zack Fawley and Martin Hasford bedded down with the mules, Noah watched in the cabin as Morgan played cards with the master and his two deckhands. Toward dawn, the Welshman lost one of the double eagles, holding two pairs to the master's three jacks.

It was graying in the east when they went down to the main deck to sleep, leaving the boat crew behind them to make preparations to pull out into the stream. There were black clouds moving close across the riverbottom flats south of Little Rock, and then it started to rain, the water coming down hard, striking the surface of the river like buckshot. It had cooled, and Noah unrolled his blanket.

"Damned gold pieces. They burn holes in a man's pockets," Morgan grumbled. "But no matter. I've still another."

"Why'd you stay in that hand?" Noah asked. "He had a pair showin' an' you had both yours up, an' with him raisin' your bet, you shoulda knowed he had another knave in the hole."

"The salty old bastard called the game himself. Bluff, he said, and by his name I played it."

"It's what we call it, too. What name do you call it?" Noah asked.

"Poker, little brother, poker. The soldier's solace and downfall all in one, like whisky and lovesickness."

"You shoulda stayed with the mules."

"I can't pass a challenge to games of chance," Morgan said. "I suspect your Bible-toting friend would not appreciate such things."

"He ain't a parson, but I expect he's again gamin'."

"Every man needs a few of the gentle vices," Morgan sighed.

Noah lay awake, listening to the stoker throwing chunks of oak into the boiler, the call of the other deckhand as he threw off the ropes. Soon he felt the tremble of the decks beneath him as they moved out into the river and turned downstream, toward the south.

He turned to ask Morgan a question, then heard the heavy breathing and instead lay back and listened to the rain and the sound of the boat's flat bottom rippling through the water.

I wonder what it's gonna be like, he thought. This Welshman knows because he's seen a war already. Before we get there, I'll ast him what it's like. I never seen a man die. Seen plenty in their coffins, though. Old Granpaw Fawley that time he died because he was almost eighty-five an' worked hisself to death, an' they had him in his coffin an' all us young'uns had to go up an' look at him before they put him in the ground. But I never seen him when he died. Just after. I reckon in a war you see some men when they die. I'll have to ast this Welshman.

I wonder how Luanne would look in one a' them fancy Sunday dresses all the ladies at that arsenal was wearin'. Maybe she'd like one a' them little umbrellas, with the lacy stuff all aroun'. Not much account for rain. Reckon I ought to buy one a' them an' take it home with me as soon as we've whupped the Yankees.

The rain beat down on the river and on the upper deck, sounding with hollow little vibrations as it struck the empty barrels. Noah liked rain, especially during sleeping time, but now the throbbing of the steam engine and the thrashing of the paddlewheel kept him awake for a long time. Before he finally slept, he wondered if it was raining along the Buffalo River.

# FOUR

IT WAS still raining when they pulled into March Landing to unload the mules. The four of them were awakened to pitch in and found themselves thoroughly soaked before the job was finished. Two of the critters had to be bodily shoved onto the planking that led from deck to dock. Zack and Noah pulled from the front, the two heavier men pushed from behind and tried to avoid the vicious little kicks from first one hoof and then the other.

"I'd like to be able to figure out which foot a mule's going to use next," Martin Hasford grunted, his hands on the mule's rump.

"Any being that's son of a jackass has some privilege to act unpredictable on occasion," Morgan said, dodging a slashing hoof and grabbing the mule's tail like a towline and yanking forward. "Now watch him, he'll likely shit all over you."

And then the soldiers came, through the rain, shouting and laughing and showing on the lapels of their jackets the wilted boutonnieres of violets and moss rose that had been pinned there by admiring feminine fingers that very morning. Martin Hasford tallied them—as he would cattle in a field—at about eighty strong while they moved down the single March Landing dock to the boat and mounted the ramp the mules had just departed.

First aboard was a small man with a Beauregard look about his face, mustache trimmed close above a firm mouth, the triangular slip of hair beneath resembling an escaped stream of tobacco juice. He carried a saber and wore a thigh-length coat with a double row of shining buttons. On his head was a French forage cap with a white havelock that fell to his narrow shoulders.

Immediately behind the officer came a black boy leading a bay stud that looked as though he were offended at being brought out of his stable in such weather.

Liverpool Morgan, standing at the gang rail, tipped his hat. "Cap'n, it's good to see you again."

The small man turned his black eyes slowly, taking in the lower deck. "Where's the master?"

"In the pilothouse, Cap'n Gordy," Morgan said. "Hanging on to the wheel from lack of sleep. And his pockets heavy with my coin."

"I told you to stay clear of cards," Captain Gordy said, his voice as flat as his eyes, no inflection, no emotion. He looked back once at the approaching troops. "I'll deal with you later, Morgan."

"At your pleasure, Cap'n," Morgan said, smiling, watching the little man move quickly forward to the ladder.

Then came the rest, all in short jackets of generally the same color, wearing forage caps, a few in hats. They made a great din as they boarded the boat and spilled across the decks, the butts of their long rifles thumping the wooden planking. Some surged up the ladders to the second level, ignoring the rain, whooping and shouting to one another, canteens slapping their buttocks, cartridge pouches flopping, new shoes sending vibrations through the boat.

Two baggage wagons followed, and one kitchen, all drawn by horses, their contents only partially protected by canvas tied across the bows. There were two steers as well, pulled aboard by soldiers tugging at lead ropes, the sand-colored brutes bellowing and raising protest as though they suspected the reason for their being here.

And then the last of the company, a few staggering and all of them smelling of corn whisky, herded along by the second officer, a tall man with the bars of a lieutenant on his collar and wearing a black stovepipe hat. Zack was the first to recognize him.

"By Gawd," he swore, "it's the judge!"

His Honor Judge Scaggs swept the decks with his eyes,

gripping a huge cavalry saber of Mexican War vintage, still furious, his mouth a grim slash in a newly cultivated beard that had only just begun to look like real whiskers. When he saw Noah Fawley standing at the far rail, his breath exploded like the air from a paper sack bursting.

"What's this?" he bellowed, and seemed to paw the deck of the boat with his feet before charging across to Noah and Zack and Martin. He stopped short before Noah. "Sir, don't I know you?"

"I reckon you set in judgment on me onct," Noah said, and remembering the courtroom he quickly pulled off his hat and stood rigid.

"By the Lord God, I do know you. Why in hell aren't you in the army?"

"We been lookin' fer the right one," Zack said, and the judge's eyes snapped around in his red face, focusing on Zack hotly. One corner of his mouth twisted.

"You, too, then," His Honor Lieutenant Scaggs said. "I remember you as well. Never forget a face in court. By God, you've found the right army now. And we get two for the sentence of one, is that it?"

"I reckon that's about it," Zack said.

"Good," Scaggs shouted, and suddenly slapped both Noah and Zack on their shoulders. As the twist came to his mouth again, Noah realized that it was supposed to be a smile.

His Honor Lieutenant Scaggs wheeled, the saber clanging, and marched toward one of the ladders, shouting troops out of his way as he went. In the wheelhouse, he found Captain Gordy and Liverpool Morgan.

"Three good men it is, at two dollars a head," Morgan was saying.

"Three, hell," Scaggs burst in. "Two of them boys came here because I sentenced one of 'em to it for stealing a pig."

"Mind the agreement," Morgan said. "I recruit good men for two dollars a head. These three would be drilling right now with some Little Rock militia outfit if I hadn't brought them along here."

"Good men?" Gordy asked, his eyes dark. "A pig stealer?"

"That young one?" Morgan said. "Why, hell's on fire, Cap'n Gordy, he's just in his growing pains. You and me have both done worse than that in our youth."

"Speak for yourself, Morgan."

"Now that older one, strong as a horse."

"And likely eats like one," Scaggs put in.

"And that other one. That Zack. You take one look into his eyes and you know he'd bark your hide as soon as look at you."

"I won't quibble over it," Gordy said, producing a purse and counting out six silver dollars.

"And a couple more for the Black Welshman?" Morgan said, still grinning.

The captain stared at him for a moment, coldly, then took two more dollars from the purse. "I'd likely be better off paying you ten dollars to enlist in some other regiment," he said. "But if we can take that hill bunch, I don't suppose you'll do us any additional harm. And keep those cards in your pocket."

"It's the least I can do for my country," the Black Welshman said.

SO IT was done. They were a part of the army now—not the state militia, but the Army of the Confederate States of America.

"We're the Third Arkansas Infantry," Captain Gordy explained, all of them standing in the wheelhouse, the captain's eyes searching each in turn, a gaze so penetrating and cold that Noah felt naked.

"Two companies already in Virginia, five more on the way, and three yet behind us, to join soon. You aren't from our counties, but we can use good men. It rounds out to eighty-five in the ranks," the captain said, confirming Martin Hasford's tally.

They signed their names to a list produced from Captain Gordy's coat, unfolded and placed before them on the chart table, and among all the eighty-one names above their own, more than half were *X*'s.

Each bent to the paper, Noah first, his tongue between his lips as he laboriously printed out the letters.

Lieutenant Scaggs stood near, nodding vehemently. "You're enlisted for the war's duration," he said. "None of this six months and home foolishness. But, by the Lord God, don't fret about it, son. We'll have the Yankees routed before six months is up anyway."

Then Morgan with a flourish, and Hasford with concern and some scarce-hidden foreboding in the squint of his eyes and the thin line of his lips. Finally, Zack, who after the struggle with the "Zackery," had to glance up to see Noah's signature before he could remember the symbols to make the "Fawley."

"There are no more uniforms, but we have rifles for you," the captain said, and Zack's eyes widened. "But first, you'll have to see the surgeon."

One of the drunken men who had come on board turned out to be a civilian contract physician, although with no contract yet and little prospect of one until they reached Virginia. He questioned each in turn, within hearing of the others, blowing his foul breath in their faces and wheezing as he felt their elbows and knee joints with dirty fingers.

"You ever get blood in your stool?" he asked.

"My what?" Noah said, and Morgan began to laugh and continued until his own turn came.

They were issued Enfield rifles, and Zack's nostrils flared as he tested the cool metal and rich walnut stock with his fingertips. They received no ammunition, Scaggs explaining that Captain Gordy didn't want the troops taking potshots at mud turtles and gars as they went downriver.

"When do we hold elections for officers?" Morgan asked.

"Already had elections," Scaggs said sharply. "You take what you got and proud to get it."

The company sergeant was a man named Small, only he

wasn't that, being well above six feet and with carrot-red hair that hung below his ears.

"You got a mess group. You'll fall in with 'em and you'll eat with 'em and fix your grub with 'em and fight with 'em. Whoever does the cookin' is your own lookout. But while we're on this hyar boat, they won't be no fires lit. You'll eat cold and do what you're tole. And keep them rifles out of the wet."

"When do we get bayonets?" Morgan asked.

"What the hell you want with bayonets out hyar in the middle of this river?"

"They make good spits for roasting meat," Morgan said, grinning. "An old soldier like you ought to know that."

"I ain't no old soldier," Small said, his face reddening. "I'm a cotton farmer. And I jus' tole you, they ain't gonna be no fires on this hyar boat. When time comes, you'll get your bayonets."

They found their mess unit at the stern near the paddlewheel, squatting along the rail in a tight group, one of them obviously drunk.

"This hyar is Hysel," Sergeant Small said, and the youngest of them, no older than fourteen, stood and grinned and stuck out his hand. There was a parade drum hanging from his front like a chunk of tree stump, red-sided and with cowhide heads dotted with rain. "They tole us to brang along a regimental drummer boy, and this hyar is him."

"Folks call me Billy Dick," Hysel said. "I'm from Pine Bluff, right over yonder beyond the landin'."

Next came Sidney Dinsmore, the drunk man who had already lost his forage cap and would pay for it from his first month's money. He stared owlishly at the newcomers, slack-jawed, isolated patches of gray whiskers across his face showing beads of moisture. Beneath his watery eyes were fleshy bags, blue-veined and sagging. Sprawled on the deck, he looked like a discarded rag doll.

And Beverly Cass, who alone of them all was dark-skinned, black-eyed, and raven-haired. They learned he was first cousin to Captain Gordy—"and he owns eight niggers."

His face was as coldly set as Gordy's, but it showed almost fragile bone beneath the olive skin, and his hands and fingers had the texture and grace of a woman's.

And Dad Johnson, dour and scrawny and parched-looking, with the texture of old leather about his face, unstretchable, unbreakable. His eyes were birdlike, small and constantly moving. Across his lap was a homemade banjo.

At first, Hasford and the Fawleys stood back a little, so that the mess unit was like a cell that had just divided, the two parts still in proximity but somehow repelled. Each group sized up the other, eyes covert. Only Billy Dick offered his hand until the Black Welshman forced his way among them, almost seeming to dare a refusal to take his handshake, laughing and calling them by name as though he'd always been a part of them, working the same cotton rows, baling the same fiber, driving the same mules to the river landing.

"I ain't a farmer like these other men," Billy Dick said. "My daddy runs a mercantile in Pine Bluff."

"And preaches hell's fire ever' Sunday at the Baptist church," Johnson said sourly.

"You could use some preachin', Ole Dad," Dinsmore giggled, then gagged and leaned toward the boat's side. They watched expectantly, but he didn't throw up.

"Who's head man of this little band?" Morgan asked, and they all stared at him blankly. "Well, see here, we need some organization if you expect this to be in fighting trim for the Yankees. We need a head man."

"As soon as I sober up, I'll rassle you fer it," Dinsmore said.

"Why don't we just call this a squad, boys. A squad with the principal purposes of killing Yankees, eating high on the hog, and making the ladies happy."

Billy Dick laughed. "That's the kinda talk I enjoys."

"You oughta be ashamed, actin' like a sojur already," Johnson said to him.

"And not even old enough to be away from your mammy's tit," said Dinsmore, and giggled and gagged again.

So it became Morgan's squad, and he began to call it his just as a general might claim his army. Everyone knew that no one would rassle the Black Welshman for anything, least of all Dinsmore, who although a man nearly as old as Dad Johnson, was not a stone heavier than Billy Dick Hysel, even now in his uniform soaked with rain.

The boat was still tied up at the landing when the call came along the decks for mess parties. Johnson and Billy Dick went forward to the baggage wagons and returned with a small trunk packed with cooking gear. Among the pots and skillets were six canteens split in half, making a dozen plates, more than enough by two. There were metal forks and spoons, and holding one of these up, Morgan gave his first command.

"Now, messmates, we take these utensils and these mess plates, and we add them to our blanket rolls and carry them wherever we go."

"Why?" Beverly Cass asked, his voice as flat as his cousin's.

"Because sometimes you'll need to eat and the wagons won't be nowhere nearabouts," Johnson said.

Morgan slapped his belly. "Ole Dad, you speak from the experience of war."

"I was in Mexico with Taylor in forty-six."

"I knew there was the smell of gunpowder about you."

"More the smell of Mexican donkeyshit than gunpowder."

"And the vocabulary of an old soldier, too."

A carrying party brought two pots, one filled with slabs of cornbread and the other with the edible part of the cowpea, a gray, lumpy mush.

"What's this stuff?" Noah said, speaking for the first time since they had joined the group.

"Them's black-eyed peas," Billy Dick said. "Cooked with pork fat, and some of it done in my mama's kitchen."

"And likely prayed over, too," Johnson mumbled.

Martin Hasford pulled out his pocket Bible and allowed that this was the proper time for a short reading and blessing, what with breaking their first bread together. He read a verse from Judges, then asked the Lord to make the food useful to their bodies.

"A man can't get away from preachers, even in the Gawd damned army," Johnson grumbled, already eating.

After they had eaten, Sidney Dinsmore produced a small jug and it was passed around, everyone except Billy Dick taking a sip.

"Well, it's good whisky," Hasford said, smacking his lips. "I make a little for sipping each year in Benton County."

"At least that proves you ain't no Baptist," Johnson said.

"Methodist."

"The secret is the agin'," Dinsmore said, his speech still a little blurred. "You char a hickory kaig, then you fill it with your drippin' an' bury it in manure, horse or cow, it don't matter. You let 'er set six months, then dig 'er out. When you knock out the bung, you get a swish of air that looks like blue fire. Then you know you've got good whisky."

"I never heard of that," Martin Hasford said.

"Try another sip."

"I guess I will."

BEVERLY Cass leaned against the rail, his gaze on the river beyond, a part of this group yet somehow detached, silent and brooding as the conversation swelled over the lip of Dinsmore's jug. He had taken a drink himself, but it was not his kind of libation. He inclined toward the brandies of France. Lack of such things was another of the hardships of war that he expected, that he accepted with a feeling of grand self-pity.

He could hear Maurice Gordy speaking to various of the troops as he moved among them on the main deck. Without turning, Cass knew his cousin was drawing near. When Gordy spoke to his own mess squad, Cass remained facing the river, forcing his mind to the hatred accumulated over the years. After a moment, he heard Gordy move away, and his lips turned down in a sour smirk.

He thought about the name: Gordy! Maurice Gordy, son of

his mother's brother. How he despised the sound of it, and now at the boat railing, watching the rain, he recalled its lineage as he knew it, remembered its harsh outlines as he had done each day of his life since he had been old enough to realize that the social station of his own mother was held beneath that of his Uncle Gordy, father of this company's captain.

Grandfather Gordy had come upriver from New Orleans with his young wife after a term of service with Andy Jackson. The record of that service had been dim from the beginning, and Grandfather Gordy had refused to shed light on it. But he had money, a fortune many of his neighbors assumed he had made from privateers, maybe even pirates.

He came boasting only of forebears who had attended the courts of the Bourbons, and it irked Beverly Cass that in his own growing years he should have developed a similar admiration for things Gallic. He refused to believe that he had inherited anything from the old man. Cass often thought, If there were an ounce of my flesh that reflected him, I would cut it out with my razor like a malignant wart!

The eldest Gordy had become one of the big cotton planters of the Delta country, raising a red brick mansion in a grove of red oak trees in the midst of flat, red land, and had seen his son married in the style of his caste with roast pigs and New Orleans pastries and rust-colored whisky, a wedding party that lasted ten days. But for the daughter, when her time came, no wedding celebration at all. The old man even refused to attend the ritual of taking vows.

The bridegroom in that affair, the first Cass in the various cotton counties of the area, had come up from New Orleans, too. Darkly handsome but a hell-raiser and gadabout, he had made as little comment on his origins as ever the old man had on his money. It was hinted that perhaps there was Indian blood in him, or maybe even a strain from Africa.

The Casses took up housekeeping in a small local hamlet, and there Beverly was born, his father away at the time on one of his many travels along the river. Likely gaming on the boats, everyone said, for no one could pinpoint any other means of livelihood for the man, even though he always seemed to have cash.

From those times, Beverly Cass could recall his first inkling of division within the house. On Christmas Day, he and his mother would be invited to Gordy Mansion for dinner, but not his father, even if he was around. And never an invitation for Christmas Eve and the fireworks and the coming of Saint Nick and spending the night in one of the large upstairs bedrooms where the bonfires from the yard sent red lights through the windows to flicker across the high ceilings.

As a child, Beverly Cass heard of how it was at those Christmas Eve parties from the children of neighbors who were invited. But he and his mother were never there to see it for themselves.

When the old man died, he left the better part of his land to his son, father of Maurice. The daughter got what was left, mostly swamp.

No, the Cass land was not meant for cotton, nor the man meant for farming. There were times when starvation was close by and perhaps would have come, had it not been for the charity of the big Gordy household. And each handful of corn and pail of molasses given with a smirk. Perhaps because of that, or because of the unknown lineage, the man drank too much and womanized too much and fought too much, and was finally shot to death in an affair of honor on a Mississippi sandbar near Helena.

Beverly started cultivating rice, still in his teens but now master of the Cass plantation. Times were not easy. He borrowed heavily from Little Rock banks and struggled slowly to self-sufficiency, meanwhile watching his neighbor cousin—silently, viciously.

The young Maurice was coming into his own, taking over more and more of the plantation management from his father. He was buying blooded horses and building better quarters for the field hands and striking the best bargains for his cotton in markets all along the river. Before his majority, Maurice Gordy was already a force to be reckoned with in the county, a man everyone supposed would never run for office but would elect or defeat those who did.

Now both of them were in their late twenties, Beverly a business success—he never cared for politics—but still silently furious when he heard the whisperings that the reason his farm was a good one in a new crop was because of his Gordy gumption and drive and get-up-and-go.

He was a Cass, he told himself, and proud of it, no matter the lack of specified ancestry. Perhaps that was even a reason for his pride. What he was leaving behind he had made himself, while Maurice Gordy's success had been passed along by birthright—intact, viable, profitable.

With the war, Maurice had stated his aim: to raise a company of men and fight in Virginia. Beverly could have done the same, but in some perverse fashion he refused to follow the lead of his cousin. Watching the rain, he was aware of the contradiction in his hatred of Gordy while now having enlisted in his company as a private soldier—perhaps to flaunt his own superiority, even though forced to do so at a more demeaning level. It had always been that way.

Start from scratch, he thought, and best him anyway—and in his sight, where he'll know. When he was a boy and I was a boy, we never played together. On those Christmas days at the huge table, he would watch me, and there was in his face an invitation to romp in the barns afterward. But even then, a child, I would not give anyone in the old man's house that satisfaction. And, most amazing, the son of a bitch has never understood my feeling for everything that Gordy Mansion represents. Never had the imagination to understand my mother's humiliation, having as she did to live like white trash until the rice came. And still, even now, looking with longing in her sad eyes across the flat country toward her father's house.

With the elder Gordy in his grave only this past year, there was no one left on either plantation except the women. There were the two mothers, one of them living on Gordy ground and not a Gordy at all, the other on the Cass farm and a true Gordy—which only fueled the malice—and the wives, the one at Gordy Mansion with three young sons, and the other childless.

Not that Beverly Cass had failed to sire his share of offspring. He was silently proud that like his father he had cast his seed from the Gulf to Saint Louis. Most remarkable to Beverly Cass was the fact that the black boy, Tug, who tended the captain's red stud, was his own son out of a young household slave of Gordy Mansion, a circumstance of which the captain himself seemed completely unaware—and a circumstance, too, which to Beverly Cass was alternately a delightful irony or the cause of deep depression.

Dinsmore was offering up the jug once more.

"Have another little sip, Mr. Cass?"

"I think not," Beverly Cass said, taking a clay pipe from his pocket and stoking it with home-cured tobacco. Before lighting the pipe he brushed his beard with the palm of one hand. It was cut in a style that exactly duplicated the face hair of his cousin.

"Better have another sip," Dinsmore grinned. "Ain't gonna las' much longer with this here crew."

"No, thank you just the same. It seems to upset my stomach."

THEY moved only a few miles downstream before dark, when the master pulled the boat into a sandbar to lay out the night. It was still raining, and he wanted better visibility as they neared the big river.

Soon they were to sleep, lying like cordwood laid bark to bark along the lower deck, protected from the rain. Some were snoring, Dinsmore among them, mouth open and whisky-fumed. Dad Johnson grumbled in his sleep, cradling his banjo. Billy Dick Hysel stayed awake, crying for a while, thinking of his bed at home, but soon his fatigue overcame even that.

Martin Hasford thought of his warm farmhouse and the large room that was both kitchen and bedroom, of his wife's full body beside him on the feather mattress, the chatter of guinea hens stilled now, the soft tinkle of a cowbell on the slope behind the barn, the last soft movement of his children's bare feet in the loft above as they moved to their beds. Perhaps during the night there would be the sound of the Butterfield stage moving along the road below the house, and his wife would sigh in sleep and roll against him, and he would feel her warmth even as he slept on. Impatient with himself for his weakness, Martin Hasford tried to swallow the hard lump in his throat, but with little success.

With the paddlewheel motionless, Noah was asleep quickly. Beside him, Zack listened to the rain, thinking of deer in the mountains. Wet ground made easy stalking. After rain was a good time to take venison, Noah alongside him, watching because that was all he wanted to do.

Zack listened to Noah's breathing, so heavy and childlike. Before he slept, he reached over to pull the shelter half up across his brother's shoulders.

And in the pilothouse, the Black Welshman, with Captain Gordy and Scaggs now safely sleeping below, played euchre with the master.

BY MORNING the rain had stopped, but it was still cloudy. They drove through the gray water quickly now, the troops standing along the rail and waving to people they could see in the fields, most of them black. The cotton workers stood and watched them pass, a few waving back, and twice small boys raced along the bank trying to keep pace with the boat, packs of dogs yammering beside them.

Twisting and turning along the course of the river, they passed old Arkansas Post. The master blew the whistle, short, urgent blasts, and a few townspeople ran down to the river's edge with flags, as they had done for other boats, other troops moving to the east and the war. The soldiers cheered and waved their hats furiously.

Although generally an unschooled lot, most of them knew that this was the site of the first white settlement in Arkansas, and one of the first west of the Mississippi. Here the old Frenchman Henri de Tonti had set up a trading post and way station in 1686, a century before the Revolution and generations before the forebears of most of these men had arrived in the Western Hemisphere. And although they could hardly put it to words, most of them felt a broader sense of history in the gray waters running under the flat keel, for this flowing river had been the highway of traders and settlers into the virgin land, when the area had been a part of Louisiana and then of Missouri and, finally, in 1819, the Territory of Arkansas, its borders stretching from these flat bottoms to the very edge of the Staked Plains. The route of commerce, this river, with the Quapaws and Osage. And then the road of dispersal for the Choctaws and the Chickasaws and the Creeks and the few Seminoles the Federal government could root out of the Everglades.

After Arkansas Post their faces grew quiet, except in the eyes where excitement would not be denied. Away now from recruiting exuberance, they were becoming more unto themselves, waiting, wondering. Thinking themselves soldiers, but not soldiers yet. Each of them knowing that and a little afraid of the fact.

But beneath this new solitariness lay a yearning to be more than themselves alone—to be a part of something none of them could easily identify, not the hill men nor Billy Dick Hysel nor even Cass or his cousin, the captain.

The Black Welshman, beside Noah as they looked across the river, mused aloud, speaking so softly that Noah had to lean near to hear.

"Now it's soldiers we are," Morgan said. "No longer a matter of politics and issues, lad, but of this undertaking. Only now what you'll learn is best about it all: the camaraderie! The birth of the regiment. That's the grand feeling."

Noah understood little of it, but the Welshman's words made the hackles along the back of his neck rise.

When they came to the big river, to that vast expanse of water where the Arkansas merged with the Mississippi, some who had never been there said, "That must be like the ocean is."

But they could see the dim shoreline to the east, a blue pencil mark against the gray sky. Noah couldn't believe that he was looking on a foreign land for the first time, seeing a state not his own, seeing Mississippi.

"This hyar river smells like rotten fish an' mud," Noah said.

And Zack, thinking the same thing without speaking but recalling how Pap had always told him, "You an' that Noy ack like you wasn't even kin one time, an' the next you ack like you was goin' at thangs from the same set a' brains!"

As the boat turned upriver they learned from Sergeant Small that Memphis was about a hundred miles away, and they relaxed to the monotony of the slowly passing shoreline. Zack squatted on deck, cleaning his rifle, and Ole Dad complained that there were rumors they would be color company, and hence from experience were assured they would draw Yankee fire like gnats to tainted meat.

"Well," Noah said, "we'll be shootin' at them pissants, too."

Zack looked up slowly, blinking, shifting his cud deliberately. "You best get outa the habit of that kinda talk before you get back in earshot a' Pap," he said.

Night caught them short of Chickasaw Bluffs and Memphis. Under a lantern on the main deck, the Black Welshman learned that Captain Gordy's black boy, Tug, was adept at rolling dice.

"I lost the other double eagle to that little bandit," he muttered, getting under his shelter half beside Noah.

Around them were the dark cocoons of the men, each rolled in his own length of canvas that was supposed to provide half of a two-man tent but would never be used that way.

"My purse is empty as an Englishman's heart!"

Noah reared up on one elbow and bent toward Morgan's form.

"Listen," he said, "I'm gettin' a little tared a' you always doin' that bad talk about English. Pap says we're English, an' I'm gettin' tared a' your talk about 'em."

"Oh, dear God," Morgan sighed, then abruptly laughed. "All right, little brother. My word on it. No more about the bloody English."

Noah lay back and watched the stars now that it had cleared. A rim of them was visible under the eaves of the upper deck. "I'm sorry about the double eagle," he said.

# FIVE

THEY SAW little of Memphis except the rail yards, passing quickly out of the city aboard an eastbound freight train with a boxcar, a dilapidated coach, and a flat attached for their use. Sergeant Small exhibited his qualifications by shouting them aboard and getting everything nailed down with a minimum of chaos, treating them like field hands. His red hair earned for him the nickname Woodpecker, but soon this was shortened to just Pecker—so long as the sergeant was not close enough to hear.

By then, too, His Honor Lieutenant Guthrie Scaggs had become Ole Jury Duty, and Captain Gordy was Li'l Chicken Guts, from the whorls of gold braid on his sleeve.

They even invented a name for Beverly Cass, a thing seldom done for a private soldier in the ranks. But regardless of the honor and recognition, the rage in Beverly's gut smoldered hotly each time he heard it: Li'l Cousin.

With all the starts and stops and pulling off on sidings for other trains, it was midafternoon before they reached Corinth. Just beyond that they lost their train. No one was quite sure why. Certainly the conductor's explanation that there was a higher priority in Memphis did not satisfy Captain Gordy. Whatever, they were dumped without ceremony in the countryside and told to march to Decatur, Alabama, on the Tennessee River, and there other cars would be available for them. With that, the train backed out of sight in the direction of Memphis.

Captain Gordy excepted, it suited them all fine. Soldiers were supposed to march, they figured, and with the sun bright but not too hot, what better time to start?

Scaggs and Sergeant Small got them into some semblance of a formation, and they started along the dusty road, paralleling the tracks for a short time before veering off into cultivated fields and woodland patches. At some unknown point they crossed into Alabama.

Birds were calling along the way, and sometimes meadowlarks flashed up from beside the road. There was the smell of recent rain on turned earth, and in the woods the heavy sweet scent of honeysuckle. With no weight of ammunition or anything else except rifles and bedrolls on their backs, they were having a hell of a good time.

"If we aim to march clear acrost this country, may as well have a little song on the way," Dad Johnson said.

He loosened his rifle sling, swung the Enfield across one shoulder, and with the same movement brought the banjo onto his belly and began to strum.

"Sing the one about the gold rush, Dad," Sidney Dinsmore said, eyes red-rimmed, his jug long since empty and cast aside. "Make me forget my misery."

"Mr. Johnson been clear out to Californy in the old days," Billy Dick Hysel shouted, and Ole Dad threw back his head and started "The Days of '49."

The hard twang of the banjo strings sent vibrations along the column, and the men began to swing their legs out, biting off three feet of road with each step. They straightened and pulled their caps and hats down close over their eyes. They shouted encouragement, grinning.

About Lame Jess, Old Dad sang: " 'And in his bloom went up the flume, in the days of 'forty-nine!' "

When it was finished there was a ragged cheer, some of them still slapping their rifle butts in time.

"Nobody goin' up no flume till we've scalded the Yankees," someone shouted. Another cheer, high-pitched.

From the tail end of the marching company, Ole Jury Duty roared, "All right Dinsmore, 'Black-Eyed Suzie'!"

In a hard, straightforward lead, Sidney Dinsmore started the old tune. Others began to join in, especially on the chorus, shouting the words, heads back.

" 'All I want in this creation, pretty li'l wife and a big plantation!' "

Zack picked up the lilt of it, adding his tenor to Morgan's fine bass, and beside them Noah, grinning, joined Dinsmore in the lead. The feet were beginning to pound the road, two-four time, the marching rhythm now affecting the entire company. It seemed to take no breath at all, marching and singing, the scissoring legs like a bellows pushing up each new word on a gust of wind. The shoulders were coming up square, the chests going out, the arms swinging in unison, the gleaming rifles racked above their heads toward the blue Southern sky.

"Left foot on my strongest stroke, in the army and goin' broke," Dad Johnson shouted between verses, whanging at the strings, while Billy Dick Hysel tapped the cowhide with his drumsticks.

"Get out from amongst those men with that damned drum," Scaggs bellowed from the rear, "before you knock somebody down."

Billy Dick skipped out of the formation, taking his position alongside the column, his sticks continuing to make little rolls across the drumhead.

Dinsmore: " 'Up red oak, down salt water, some ole man gonna lose his daughter!' "

Noah could feel the surge of it through his body, like dancing. He remembered the spring evenings at home above the Buffalo, when his Pap would take out the Jew's harp, and Cadmus the jug, and they would dance up and down the front gallery, which looked out across the disappearing vistas of blue-timbered hills. His sister, Lucinda, would dance with each brother in turn, Pap stamping his feet on the rough boards, and then Mama would join in, dancing with two of them at once, the bun slipping down from the back of her head until the hair swung out silver behind, she scattering hairpins and chicken feathers and limestone dust, outdancing them all!

" '. . . some ole man gonna lose his daughter!' " The voices snapped out the words in cadence to the feet slapping the dusty road.

Zack, his high harmony clear, admired this Black Welshman marching beside him, a better bass even than Uncle Questor when the family would gather at Christmastime and sing the ancient Anglican chants, running through the Psalms and canticles handed down from England. It was as close to religious fervor as Zack ever came, those chants, and now he felt almost the same subtle thrill, though it was only "The Black-Eyed Suzie."

But Martin Hasford marched in a deep depression. He knew from the newspapers he had read that already in Missouri Yankee armies were driving the Confederates of Sterling Price toward the northern border of Arkansas, toward his own farm in Benton County. And here we are marching in the other direction, he thought bitterly.

Well, at least we're going toward the scene of coming action—the Yankees pushing into western Virginia, threatening the Shenandoah Valley and collecting an army along the Potomac, and everyone saying they would make a strike toward Richmond before the summer was out.

Little chance of seeing that, Hasford thought, what with all this talk amongst the officers about going into training. I don't know how long it takes to train a bunch of men like this, but it's bound to be a considerable spell.

And in Richmond, that man acting as the chief advisor of President Davis and trying to pull all the Southern forces together where they're needed. We'll likely hear little of him in this business, being like he is attached to the throne and never in the field. Yet the name rings familiar. Likely from Ole Scaggs's Mexican War or maybe with the frontier army someplace before the war. Lee. That's it, Robert Lee. Called Bobby Lee.

They've already got Joe Johnson commanding in Virginia, and Ole Beauregard's coming up from South Carolina after taking Sumter, and there's Albert Sidney Johnstone in Tennessee. Not much room in the field for this Bobby Lee. Likely never hear much about him.

I wish to God I'd stayed in Arkansas. That much I'm sure of.

And riding the red stud at the head of the column, Captain Maurice Gordy did not look back. His Beauregard face was set in its usual dark French expression—brooding, lids hooded over black eyes. He could feel the stud beneath him prancing to the rhythm. He could feel the pounding of feet from his company, of them all only Dad and Morgan and Scaggs with any past military experience. Yet all of them marching now, the fire in them. And in the eyes beneath the drooping lids, his own slow, brittle flame began to glow.

THEY had passed the house a few miles short of bivouacking for the night, a fine little farmstead of red brick and white trim, with beech and holly trees along the fencelines. And with impressive chicken coops.

Now they were back, two of them, in the moonlit darkness, the Black Welshman and Noah, crouched in the woods that skirted the barn lot. Across the road they could hear a chuck-will's-widow, and farther along the countryside a yard dog was barking listlessly.

"Wind's right," Morgan whispered. "Be there dogs, we are in and out before they know we're about."

"Unless they sleep in the henhouse," Noah said. He could feel the cold sweat on his hands and running down the tight muscles of his back. This was nothing like stealing the pig that day of Lucinda's wedding. This was cold sober, and there was a growing knot in his belly.

"Pleasant is the prospect of a plump hen toasted over the coals, spitted on a bayonet."

"We ain't got bayonets."

"Ramrods, then, little brother. Now, close to me it is," Morgan whispered. "Once in the coop, wait a spell for the eyes to become accustomed to the dark. Then you for the eggs. The chickens, me."

"I think we'd be better off back with the company."

"Worms in the gut, is it? Just remember, if the captain had slaughtered one of those steers this night, we wouldn't be here. You want to eat that cold mush slop all your army days?"

"I'd as soon be back."

"Very easy, all of this, and never a light in sight. So come on with us. Never pea soup for me, with chickens waiting."

The distance between woods and coop seemed to stretch

out forever, and each step of it Noah expected a snarling dog with big teeth. The whole place was dreamlike, doll's blocks set in a landscape like snow, the moonlight turning everything blue-white.

They were at the gate, and the hinges made a frightful squeal as Morgan pulled it open. They ran across the lot and to the open door of the coop, then inside, smelling the acid odor of chicken litter and the warm, suffocating smell of feathers.

Noah remembered the time, him still a boy, when the foxes had raided the Fawley flock, and Zack had sat three nights in the coop, smeared with chicken litter to kill his human smell. On the third night—with a moon like this one tonight—the family wakened with the sound of the gun, both barrels. Zack then skinned the fox and hung it outside the coop as a warning to other predators, and to shame the dogs who had allowed the intruder in in the first place, sleeping sound and warm under the front gallery.

And now, Noah thought, he knew how the fox had felt just before Zack pulled the trigger.

They stood against the wall, either side of the door, panting softly. It was black as coal tar.

"Now," Morgan whispered, and Noah felt rather than saw him move.

Groping along in the dark, Noah found a row of sitting hen boxes, all in a line nailed to the wall. He slipped his fingers into one. There was the startled cluck, and he felt the warmth of the hen as he slid his hand beneath. Then his feet caught something, and even as he fell he knew it was the coop ladder reaching to the boxes.

"Oh, Gawd damn!"

He whispered it frantically, falling back and pulling the row of hens' boxes with him. There was a sudden wild screeching, and he felt the fat bodies whipping against his face and tasted loose feathers. The blackness of the coop was now a fury of flapping wings and great plump forms buffeting his face as he scrambled about trying to rise, kicking over another ladder in the attempt and sending more birds squawking into the whirlwind of their sisters already on the wing.

Morgan may have said something, Noah wasn't sure in all the noise about his ears. He regained his feet, sliding in the deposits of litter on the dirt floor. Something sticky and hot ran through his fingers, and he knew he had found at least one egg. He made a staggering dash for the bright rectangle of the door, cursing and kicking chickens aside. Then he heard the dog.

Noah turned back into the coop, driving madly for the far wall, looking for another way out. Instead of a door he found a second rack of chickens, and sent them scrambling in the dark. Again he lost his footing. He made it back to the door on hands and knees, then out into the lot, a puff of chickens coming with him like smoke from a fired cannon.

Morgan was standing in the moonlight, still as an oak stump, a chicken hanging from each massive hand. Before him was the dog, barking furiously, lips peeled back from vicious-looking teeth. And in the open gate, a bent figure, hat shading his face and a shotgun in his hands.

"Good evening to you, sir," Morgan said.

"What is that, Jude?" It came from the dark house, a woman's voice.

"We gots us two chicken stealers, Miz Earline," the man with the shotgun said. Noah was behind Morgan's back, trembling, the broken egg running from his fingertips, silver in the moonlight.

"Starving soldiers we are, ma'am," Morgan called. "Soldiers enlisted to keep the Yankees out of your dooryard, and a long way from our mother."

"I gonna shoot you fulla buckshot holes," Jude said. "An' den get dat sheriff from over Decatur."

"Away from your mother?" the voice came from the house again, soft and mellow, a quavering in it. "Jude, bring those boys over here."

"I fin' me a chicken stealer, I gonna shoot 'em fulla buckshot holes," Jude muttered, waving the shotgun.

"Ma'am, your man here is about to shoot us," Morgan shouted. "Only two starving soldier boys a long way from home and hungry and here only to protect your hearth and home."

Noah was more conscious of the shotgun muzzle than of

the exchange. He wiped his palms on his trousers and felt his heart thumping against his ribs. The dog was still yammering wildly, still showing teeth.

"Jude, I said bring those boys over here," the woman called. "And get that dog to hush his racket."

Jude escorted them across the yard and to the open kitchen doorway. They paused a moment until a coal-oil lamp was lit inside, and then were propelled into the house with the snout of the gun in Jude's hands. He was muttering, threatening buckshot for chicken stealers.

The kitchen was still warm from supper cooking and smelled of fried meat and white flour. There was a table, and across from it stood the woman, warm and round and staring with large liquid blue eyes, holding a dressing gown close against her chest but not enough to conceal a dark-shadowed cleavage.

"Where did you come from?" she asked, her eyes on the Black Welshman's face.

"Ma'am, walked all the way from Texas, we have, me and my baby brother hardly out of the cradle, trying to catch up to our company. Two weeks on the road it is, and only scraps to eat, and thirsty, too." Morgan swept off his hat, having switched both chickens to the same hand. He stepped back sharply with the left leg, the right extended before him. "Make a leg for this gracious lady, little brother."

Noah snatched off his hat and tried to duplicate the bow and, doing it, saw the fringes of chicken litter oozing from beneath his shoe like speckled divinity.

"Hard it's been, ma'am," Morgan said tearfully. "But we haven't been able to catch up. Our dear mother left weeping, yet her it was who said we should come to fight for Alabama."

"Well . . ." she said uncertainly, "there was a body of men passed along the road only this afternoon. Maybe those are your friends. All from Texas? So far?"

"Yes, ma'am, and not a soul along the route to give us food or drink."

"I can't believe it," she gasped.

"Oh, yes, and no way we had of knowing if you were a Union sympathizer . . ."

"Good heavens!"

". . . and we starving. We'd pay you for these fine chickens, ma'am." Morgan held them head-high, and their marble eyes shone in the lamplight. "But the last of our money was taken by a scoundrel in Little Rock, a cheat and a thief. And our poor mother left alone in Texas amongst the Comanches, after giving us her last penny to see us on the way, and warning us not to trust strangers."

"Oh, it's awful what war does to some people," she gasped. Indeed, everything she said seemed to be gasped, making her breasts above the dressing gown heave like liquid melons.

Jude had moved to the far side of the stove and was squatting there, the muzzle of the shotgun still showing. He glared at them, his little eyes bloodshot in his black face.

"I gonna take dese hyar chicken stealers to Decatur."

"Hush, Jude, and let me hear this boy's story."

Noah had never heard such a story as the Black Welshman spun. Names he had never known, places and events, sweethearts lost to mountebanks, money to profiteers, and always the poor mother in the background, weeping, playing her harpsichord, until the Widow Earline—as she professed herself to be—was almost in tears, gasping her exclamations and finally inviting them to sit down and eat.

"There's buttermilk biscuits and some ham and huckleberry pie. Jude, run out to the well house and fetch a crock of sweet milk."

"I'm gonna take dese chicken stealers to the sheriff," he muttered, but grudgingly rose, still with the shotgun, still glaring, and disappeared through the back door.

Morgan placed the chickens back down in the woodbox, stroked their necks for a moment, and left them lying mesmerized.

"My land, look what you've done," the Widow Earline gasped. "I never saw the like."

Morgan laughed and said, "My dear father taught me before taken off from us, he was, and killed by the Mexicans." And suddenly he was sorrowful again.

Noah was aware that the widow hardly looked at him at all. Her eyes were on the Welshman, the gaze darting back and forth from flashing teeth to brawny arms, as hypnotized as the chickens with the words that came like the music from one of his Welsh songs, in a minor key.

By the time Jude was back with the sweet milk, they were at the table like invited guests, plates of a blue China design set before them and real linen napkins and silver heavy to the hand. And always the widow bending over the table toward the Welshman, gasping about an unappreciative population treating soldier boys so wickedly. With each gasp, the opening in the dressing gown grew larger, revealing more of the fleshy pink canyon underneath.

Before Noah was finished eating, Jude glaring again from the fortress of the kitchen stove, Morgan was up and walking about as though he owned the place, exclaiming at the fine furnishings and the delicate beauty of the Widow Earline's taste. And always that rich Welsh lilt of language. By the time Noah was into the huckleberry pie, Morgan and the widow were in the next room, speaking of chair legs and sofa pillows and hunting tables.

Noah looked at Jude, and the eyes in the black face were fierce.

"You ain't no brothers," Jude said. "You ain't lef' no mama cryin' in no Texas. You ain't nuthin' but chicken stealers an' white trash, stealin' Miz Earline's hens an' comin' in hyar talkin' an' makin' Miz Earline all star-eyed with them tales 'cause that's the way she gets all the time sinct Mister Bruce died las' year, an' they ain't nuthin' I kin do wid her an' she won't listen to nobody when she gets to wheezin' lak she is."

Noah finished the pie and ate another hunk of ham and poured another cup of sweet milk. In the next room the voices droned on, too low for him to hear the words. The Widow Earline had begun to giggle.

"You ain't no brothers," Jude grumbled.

It seemed a long time for Noah, sitting there under Jude's baleful eye. He thought, I reckon the Welshman wasn't too hongry.

Finally, Morgan appeared in the doorway. He had taken off his jacket. He looked at Noah and winked. "Little brother, along the road with you it is now, and see if you can find that company of men," he said. Noah started to speak, but Morgan raised his hand. "Aye, separation for a while it is, but the widow's afraid of the dark, and it's only right I console her and comfort her awhile for all this fine grub."

Jude made a choking noise from behind the stove.

Glad to be out of this with no puncture in his hide, Noah grabbed his hat and stepped to the door, leaving his tracks of chicken litter across the clean kitchen floor. The dog met him at the door, and he kicked at the brute viciously.

"Stop kickin' that dog, white trash," Jude yelled.

Noah turned the corner of the house and found the road in the moonlight. He turned along it, the dog back now under the front stoop, still sounding. It was only after the dog had stopped and Noah was far along the road toward the company that he laughed.

That Welshman was hongry all right, he thought, but not fer no grub. "That's the craziest man I ever seen," he said aloud, and thought, I'll never steal no livestock again, of any sort or fashion. All it gets a body is trouble. Only maybe it got the Welshman more'n that.

IT WAS two days before the Black Welshman caught up to the company again. Luckily for him, they had been detained in Decatur, camping beside the tracks to await their cars. He arrived as they were loading, this time one boxcar and two flats, and in his hands he carried four chickens and a gunnysack filled with gingerbread.

Sergeant Small hauled him before the captain, though staying his distance, even with the Welshman laughing. Morgan stood before Maurice Gordy, the booty hanging from his hands.

"Absent without leave," Gordy said, his eyes cold.

"Without leave, is it? No, sir, only taking provender for the troops." He lifted the four chickens, all held by the feet in one large hand.

"Morgan, you can't supply an army by stealing. In some places you can get hanged for trying."

"Stealing? No, sir. Given. All of it given freely from the hand of a gracious and patriotic lady of Alabama."

"You can't feed eighty-five men on four chickens."

"A good stew it is, Cap'n, and the pieces cut nice and tender. That for the company, and the gingerbread a gift for my own mess squad."

"Gingerbread? Let me see that."

Gordy took the sack from the Welshman and pulled forth a square of fluffy brown pastry and ate it, his eyes never leaving Morgan's face.

"And for the stew, there's even this to buy a vegetable or two." Morgan pulled from his trouser pockets a fistful of small coins. "Another charity for the cause of the Confederacy from the lovely Widow Earline."

"Earline who?"

"We never got that far," Morgan said, grinning.

They sent Billy Dick Hysel on the run to a greengrocer in town to buy Irish potatoes, thinking that if the train pulled out before he returned, it would be small loss. Then they shoveled a mound of sand into the boxcar and set a fire there, taking one of the larger pots from the kitchen wagon.

The red stud, stalled at the other end of the car, made a great fuss when the smoke began to roil around him. But by the time Billy Dick returned with the potatoes, the chickens were cleaned and cut, the train was whistling to warn of motion toward the east, and the red stud had quieted—the black boy, Tug, was standing at his head, stroking him between the eyes and speaking horse language to him.

As to Morgan, he was turned over to His Honor Ole Jury Duty, now the company disciplinarian on account of his long tenure on the bench of law. He sentenced the Welshman to be bucked for twelve hours. A shouted, eye-bulging sermon on the evils of absence without leave went along with it, including the empty threat that next time Morgan would be stood up and shot.

That first night out of Decatur, Noah moved back to the flatcar where they had Morgan bound. He found the Welshman under one of the wagons, a stick gag in his mouth, his knees pulled up to his chest, and a second, larger stick thrust beneath them, his arms below the stick and hands tied with rope across his shins.

Nearby stood a soldier with his Enfield ready. He warned Noah that he'd best stay clear of the prisoner.

"I jus' aim to talk with him a mite," Noah said.

"You best leave him be."

"He got you a bellyful a' hot chicken soup," Noah said, handing the soldier a crumbling piece of gingerbread. "An' this hyar is my own offerin'."

"Hit don't make no difference to me," the soldier said, taking the gingerbread.

Noah loosened the gag and placed the stick carefully by so he could find it in the dark.

"Well, little brother," Morgan said, and Noah could see his teeth shining in the blackness of the beard.

"I tole you we never shoulda done nothin' like that."

"Aw, but the price made a bargain of it," Morgan said, and laughed softly. "I can see her still, the Widow Earline. Beautiful she was, with love in one hand and a chicken in the other."

# SIX

IT WAS midsummer before the entire regiment was assembled at Lynchburg, Virginia, and the Richmond Light Infantry Cadets came down to teach them about being an army. The cadets were mere boys who came from good families or good military schools, or both, and they understood infantry drill. They brought the news that Federal armies were massing in many places along Virginia's border and that the leading newspaper editors in Richmond—who had their own spy networks in the North—predicted a move toward Richmond soon.

The young men in their neat blue cadet uniforms taught the Arkansans how to dress into line from a column formation, how to send out their skirmishers two hundred yards ahead of the regiment, how to use cover in defense, how to aim low. Noah and the others sweated, grumbled, fixing bayonets and standing at attention, learning to shift arms to the marching salute, to stack rifles like the exposed poles of a Plains Indian tepee. And how to dig straddle trenches, and the necessity for using them.

Noah was embarrassed about dropping his trousers over one of these narrow ditches, with all creation able to watch if so inclined. He therefore began to hold his natural calls to those hours beyond sunset, which sometimes caused discomfort and once humiliation when he stumbled in the dark and fell into the trench. The squad refused to have him near them again until he had submerged himself, clothes and all, in one of the local streams.

"You sure didn't help none, did ya?" he said to Zack afterward.

"Some thangs a man caint help none," Zack said.

"Well, you don't need to get such a big kick out of it, either."

"When a man falls in the toilet, it calls fer a little laughin'."

"Well, you sure didn't help none."

"Noy, when you get shit all over yourself, don't expect me to run clean it off," Zack said impatiently. "I don't reckon Pap intended I should have to do that."

Noah laughed suddenly, and Zack showed his teeth in a grin and reached over and shoved Noah gently.

"Lucky it wasn't daylight," Zack said. "You musta been a sight!"

"Yeah, I reckon I was."

The cadets taught them the prescribed drill of men under arms, although there was not enough ammunition for much range firing. The men in the company pretended to load and fire, giggling like boys, grown men being tutored by real schoolboys who were the only ones taking it seriously.

They were issued six rounds each on the day before colors presentation and election of regimental officers, to celebrate the occasion. They tried their hand at hitting what looked suspiciously like empty whisky kegs at a hundred paces. Most of them had been shooting all their lives, and the marksmanship they displayed surprised the Richmond Light Infantry cadets. Zackery Fawley cut a new bunghole in his keg, placing all six shots within a three-inch radius.

With that there was some talk of having a few matches with sharpshooters from other companies—with wagers on the side—but it was abandoned. The officers figured that it might be good for morale but bad on the ammunition supply.

Beverly Cass was almost as good with an Enfield as Zack was, with Dad Johnson not far behind, although he explained that any target beyond ten rods was a little fuzzy to his vision.

Only Billy Dick Hysel had trouble with the big rifle, spilling much of his powder after he had chewed off the end of the paper cartridge and before he could get the charge rammed home.

"Sprout, you're eatin' more of that powder than you're a-gettin' down the bore," Dinsmore said. As for himself, he had little trouble whacking the keg with each shot, however drunk at the time.

There was no mystery about where Sidney got his drinking whisky. The contract surgeon who had boarded the boat at Marsh Landing and come to Virginia with them was a Dinsmore, too—Sidney's nephew, who Dad Johnson claimed was sorry for doctoring but hell for good whisky-making. If any regimental surgeon in the army could maintain his supply of medical alcohol, it would be Sidney's nephew, and damned fine whisky, too, what there was left of it after he had done his own sampling.

They marched into a big cow pasture for the colors presentation, the entire regiment on line. They were met by a delegation from Lynchburg who had come out in buggies and traps and hacks. Everyone was allowed out of ranks before the ceremony to socialize, and there was lemonade and ginger snaps, and some of the elderly men of the town offered more high-spirited libation from small pocket flasks.

Then they aligned once more. The new commander—a man named Rusk, formerly a United States senator with a constituency consisting in part of the entire regiment, but whom Noah and Zack had never heard of—stood in front of the troops with his staff.

There was a speech by the mayor and a splendid matron spoke, too, of valor and fortitude and the cause for which they would soon be fighting. From her hand the flagstaff was passed to Colonel Rusk—the banner with crossed bars dividing it into four blood-red triangles—and from there to the color guard, who marched back and took their place along the line of troops at one flank of the company, where Dad Johnson was muttering again about the damned thing drawing fire.

Colonel Rusk made his speech. It was growing hot in the ranks. Sidney Dinsmore had turned pasty white, was soon showing spots of green, and would have collapsed in place had not the Black Welshman hooked a hand under his arm, holding him upright until the colonel was finally done. None of them could remember a word that was said within five minutes of the saying, and with a general sigh of relief they marched back to their encampment, Martin Hasford and Morgan on either side of Dinsmore, dragging him along like an empty meal sack.

But they sang "The Black-Eyed Suzie" as they marched, in Sidney's honor, and managed somehow by mutual but unspoken agreement to cut all the most ribald verses.

Dinsmore spent the better part of that night throwing up and crying, feeling sorry for himself alone in Virginia and away from his old lady of twenty-five years and mother of his two grown daughters. The other men in the squad could hear him gagging and sputtering and talking to himself well past midnight.

"Old Sid's been at the kaig all his natural life," Dad Johnson explained from his blanket, "but his belly ain't never 'come accustomed to it yet."

The company pulled its share of garrison detail, which meant standing guard around the camp during hours of darkness. They posted sentries, two at each station, four hours' duty at a stretch.

Noah and Zack always drew the same schedule, but neither was sure whether it was an accident or whether maybe Ole Jury Duty did it by design because they were brothers.

It was pleasant, standing on one of the little hills where most of the trees had been cut and the ground laid to crops or pasture. If their tour was early in the night, they could see the lights from scattered farmhouses across the landscape. And the cookfires of the regiment spread before them like the glowing tiny glass beads in the veil Mama had made Lucinda for her wedding day. After the dust of drill and the close human confines of marching formations, these night watches with just the two of them alone had a clean freedom Noah liked.

One night while standing picket they saw four meteors. Zack was lying on his back in the thick clover that blanketed their little hill, and Noah was standing beside him, leaning on his rifle.

"Seems like we seen more shootin' stars hyar than we ever done at home," Noah said. He was looking up, measuring the

Big Dipper and the position of the North Star. "But the rest of it looks the same."

Zack grunted. From the camp of the Richmond Light Infantry Cadets they heard the faint notes of a bugle.

"That there's taps," Noah said.

"Yeah, you're gettin' the hang a' this business pretty fast," Zack said sarcastically.

"Well, they's sure'n hell lots to learn in one a' these armies, ain't they?"

"It appears so."

"An' them Light Infantry boys knows all about it, don't they?"

"They been at it awhile. Most of it's right easy, onct you get the knack fer jumpin' when the sergeants shout," Zack said. "You wanta chew? Help you stay awake."

"I ain't goin' to sleep on guard," Noah said, but he took the plug that Zack handed up and bit off a mouthful. He found it diffcult to speak around the cud. "Some a' these men take badly to them sergeants. You ever get peeved at the way they hurrah us sometimes?"

"No."

"Well, sometimes they sure get under my skin."

"Army ain't no place fer hair-trigger temper," Zack said. "One a' the thangs you're suppose to learn is to take horseshit from the sergeants while you're learnin' all the other stuff."

"Yeah, well, except fer the ones in the Light Infantry, them sergeants don't know no more'n anybody else." Noah gave up on the tobacco and spat it out into the darkness. "I don't see how you chaw on that stuff all the time."

"Now them sergeants, they may not know more'n we do, but they got the authority who says what to do. Like at home. You don't argue with Pap when he says somethin'. Sergeants is like Pap."

"I ain't seen one I'd like to be kin to yet," Noah said, and laughed. He cocked his head, listening to some sound from one of the treelines at the base of their little hill. "What's that?"

"One a' them night warblers they got aroun' here, I guess. Hell, I don't know."

It was growing late now; only a few fires were still alight in the camp below them. Still, there was the scent of wood smoke in the air along with the smell of clover.

"The officers seem all right."

"It's like mule colts," Zack said. "Sometimes you get a good one, sometimes a son of a bitch. I reckon we hit it fairly lucky. Ole Jury Duty, he's rough talkin', but he's all right. Cap'n Gordy, he don't talk hardly at all."

"I heerd the boys in some a' these outfits gripin' 'bout their officers. Mean gripin', like they'd not mind takin' a shot at one of 'em."

"Dad Johnson says all officers is bred from jackasses, good or bad," Zack said, and they both laughed. "But takin' a shot at one could get a man hanged."

They heard a string of wagons pulling out of the camp, headed for Lynchburg, where there were still a number of lighted windows, drops of orange light in the blue-black night. Ration wagons, Noah thought.

"Well, it sure ain't like I thought it'd be," he said softly.

"A man jus' puts up with whatever comes. That's the biggest thang you learn in an army, it looks like."

Noah laughed again. "They sure made a big fuss outa givin' us that flag, didn't they?"

"Civilians has to get some fun outa this war, too."

And, Noah thought, here we be, thinkin' ever'body else is civilians an' us separate an' apart. I reckon that's somethin' you learn in an army, too.

THEY HAD their first payday outside Lynchburg, and within hours of pay call most of the money was in a few pockets. Liverpool Morgan won thirty-eight dollars and lost it all that same night throwing dice with Tug, the captain's batman.

"Who looks after that red stud when you're off takin' money from us white folks?" Dinsmore asked.

"Don' take no lookin' after all the time." Tug grinned, rattling the dice in his dusty brown hand. "Ole Red enjoy a little lef' alone time, now and again. Mister Liverpool, I sees three dollars uncovered."

"Impudent you are, you African road agent. There's the money. Roll!"

Before the evening was out, Tug began to deal three-card monte and soon had cleaned out the entire squad, except for Beverly Cass, who played a few hands silently, eyes hooded, picking the red queen on three straight attempts and then drawing back from the game. The eyes of these two players never met, nor did any word pass between them, squatting near the fire, the boy's long, brown, supple fingers swiftly placing the cards, and each time the long, brown, supple fingers of Beverly Cass flipping the queen and taking the money.

Martin Hasford watched, thinking, If a body were to see only the hands, it would be hard to say which is the player, which the dealer. Or which the white man, which the darky!

"You got this boy's size, Mr. Cass," Dinsmore said with a giggle. No one in this squad called him Li'l Cousin, as did other men in the company. Billy Dick Hysel had tried it once, in a spirit of comradeship, and Cass had lifted his head and stared with a look that was knife-sharp, almost capable of drawing blood.

They heard about Manassas—Bull Run, the Yankees were calling it—and their irritation and frustration grew because this war was about over with them still drilling and not an enemy yet seen or heard. But when they spoke of such things, the Black Welshman smiled silently and shook his head.

Sometimes the good people of Lynchburg invited them into town for a meal, in twos and threes. On one such occasion, Sidney Dinsmore got so drunk he lost his way back and ended in the next county. At a small settlement called Appomattox. None of them had ever heard of it before. Some of the cadets hauled Sidney home, and Ole Jury Duty sentenced him to stand for three evenings on a keg with a placard around his neck proclaiming that here was a sot and a malingerer.

Sidney spent his time on the keg singing "The Black-Eyed Suzie," and making up a few new stanzas that would have shocked the ladies of Lynchburg or any other town short of Sodom or Gomorrah, Martin Hasford said.

Everyone noticed that Martin did a lot of letter writing. He was cheerful enough in his messages home, although he complained about all the army vices—swearing, drinking, gambling. Maybe it didn't matter what he wrote. The Confederate postal system was as unpredictable as a rutting boar hog, and thus far Martin had not received a single letter in return.

Often in the evening, just before sunset, he would sit and stare at the mountain ridges to the west—pensively, saying nothing, fingering the new growth of mustache he was cultivating. Zack called it his Benton County look, fingering his own new sprout of hair along the upper lip, a straw-colored wisp that seemed to grow fastest at the corners of his mouth, dropping down like frazzled cornsilks in a summer drought.

For Noah, it was Pap's razor every day. Of all the company, only he and Billy Dick Hysel were still clean-shaven, he because he wanted it that way, Billy Dick because he couldn't grow hair on his face if he wanted to.

Finally their orders came, and they marched north toward Staunton and the mountain passes where a Yankee column was imperiling the western end of Virginia. They went with singing and laughter and a spring to their step, glad to be away from those Richmond Light Infantry cadets and the boredom and the salt pork and turnips.

For all their high spirits, they were as yet unacquainted with the methods of their first commanding general in Virginia, one T. J. Jackson. Ole Blue Light, the troopers called him, and he was a hard-driving disciplinarian and the fastest marching commander in the army. Others called him Stonewall, from his famous stand at Manassas.

Nor was their enthusiasm for this war yet dampened by the high slopes of the Appalachians drenched with rain.

"I WROTE a lie today," Martin Hasford said. He and Zack were sharing the dubious shelter of an oak in the darkness. They were wet to the skin, even wrapped in their blankets and shelter halves. They leaned against the tree trunk, half sitting and half lying, the heavy drip of water through the leaves all around them.

"You done what?" Zack asked, his voice muffled in the damp wool of his bedding.

"I wrote a lie to my wife. I told her I've been in the army since Clarksville, that my company came here from there, and Captain Reedy was my officer."

"That Company K officer? Why the hell'd you do that?"

"Captain Reedy's a well-known man, I suppose. Maybe that part was pride, wanting her to think I was serving with a well-known man." He drew a deep breath and expelled it, blowing the drops of water from his new mustache.

"You could have told her you was servin' with Ole Jackson. He's a well-knowed man, of which I hope we ain't servin' with too much longer."

Zack realized that Hasford was keeping his face turned away, as though ashamed to have Zack see it, even what little could be seen in the darkness.

"But I told her I'd joined at Clarksville, and my company came over here to be a part of this regiment."

"We all ended up at the same place. What's the difference?"

"I wanted her to think I joined quick, close to home. That I made my commitment close to Benton County, not way off downriver."

"Has Dinsmore been sharin' some of his whisky with you tonight?"

"I wanted her to think I'd done it quick, close to home so at the very start it was too late to turn back and go home where I belong."

"Oh, I see," Zack said. "Well, get to sleep. That damned fool Jackson'll have our arses up before light again to run up an' down these mountains."

"My wife likely don't know where Clarksville is. She likely don't know it's any closer to Benton County than March Landing. But my daughter, Calpurnia, might. I wanted them to think my commitment was made close to home, and they'd understand I couldn't turn back."

"I wist you'd tell this all to somebody who could do somethin' about it," Zack said. Oh, hell, yes, I'm enjoyin' this, he thought. His legs ached and he felt his nose running and his bowels had been like soap water for a week.

He had been living in mountains all his life, and he knew that any fool had enough sense not to get out along these vicious slopes and run up and down day after day in driving rain. And for what? To catch a few fleeting views of Yankee patrols, to get shot at by sharpshooters, with small chance to shoot back. Even out in the valley they were generally behind some artillery outfit that cut the muddy roads to ribbons.

Worst of all was Ole Jackson. He had them march frantically in one direction, and then just as frantically back to where they had started, and never a word why. Colonel Rusk didn't know, Captain Gordy didn't know, nobody knew. And always his damned staff officers riding the column, forcing them on. A few times the sour old Presbyterian himself had appeared on that scrawny sorrel horse he rode, glaring at them from those pale eyes and muttering, "Close up, close up!"

I would like jest one chanct at standin' up to a bunch a' Yanks an' havin' it out, Zack thought, an' get shed a' this damned runnin' up an' down through the brush. An' get shed a' that damned Jackson, too.

Zack coughed and raised his head far enough from the blanket to spit. It was ailment time, all right. Billy Dick back in some hospital with measles or some such thing, and every man in the company spending half his time nose-blowing. Some said it was the food—raw pork and soggy cornbread—and sometimes just the meal itself, without any cooking to it. Rumor had it that already twenty men in the regiment had died of first one sickness and then the other, and only three in the ground so far from enemy fire, killed in the few skirmishes they had had—the "little catfights," as Dad Johnson called them—when the Yankees tentatively probed their positions. Only three casualties from enemy action for the regiment, out of the more than eight hundred who had come up from Lynchburg.

Worst of all, Ole Jackson was rumored to have said that this Arkansas outfit was just a rabble, no good for anything, couldn't march, couldn't shoot, couldn't maintain any sort of camp discipline. A rabble! And Colonel Rusk knowing that he was being sent west to some obscure command, and the leadership of the regiment already in the hands of somebody named Manning, a south Arkansas lawyer not yet twenty-five years old!

This is gonna be one helluva hard winter, Zack thought. An' I'd as soon the war was over right now an' get home without ever drawin' bead on a Yankee. Maybe Hasford's right. Maybe we don't none of us belong hyar. An' that Noy, takin' to it like honey.

It was true. At the moment, Noah was on picket far up the slope in heavy timber, his rifle held muzzle down under the blanket draped across his shoulders. He was wet and miserable like all the rest, but somehow it made him feel a part of the army.

You gotta be miserable in an army sometimes, he thought. That's what the Welshman says. Jus' like a family, the army.

Through his entire life he had known only brothers and uncles and Pap and a few scattered neighbors, and not many of these had he known well or seen often. Now he was with men who had been strangers a few months ago, yet he felt he knew them better than he knew Cadmus or Tyne or Britt or Uncle Questor. Maybe even better than Pap. Together now with these men who were no longer strangers, eating and sleeping and marching with them. And suffering.

Well, he thought, not much sufferin'. Not so far. Except that blister on my right foot when we come up hyar from Lynchburg. That was sufferin'. Till Zack opened it an' then packed it with mud an' made me walk barefoot till it healed.

He wondered what Zack thought about all this. That Zack! Tight-lipped as Pap an' all the other Fawleys, except for Uncle Questor, who takes a pride in lettin' words come out his mouth.

Well, this is jim-dandy woods. Best timber I ever seen. And he thought of clearing a patch of it and using the fallen logs to raise a one-room cabin for a new bride.

ZACK was right about the winter as well. It was hard for all of them, and even Noah had enough suffering to suit him. They were issued overcoats before Christmas, and the commissary department did a fair-to-middling job of keeping them in pork and cornmeal, but the endless marching prevented their settling into any sort of comfortable winter quarters, so to them it was all for nothing.

The inaction was almost intolerable. At one time or another all of them were under the care of surgeons, which Dad Johnson said was worse than being in a Federal prison pen.

"One of them bastards wanted to bleed me," he snorted. "An' all I had was the vapors!"

One night Captain Gordy rose from the fire, the cape over his shoulders showing the wet. Near him, well back in the shadows, squatted Tug, eyes bright, and near him lay the blanket-bundled form of Scaggs, the stovepipe hat and Mexican War saber on the ground beside him.

Beverly Cass came up to them abruptly, not touching his hat as was the custom when addressing an officer. He stood on one side of the fire, Gordy on the other, their faces set in hard lines.

"We need to talk," Cass said.

For a moment Gordy looked into the face before him, then said, "Very well. What's your pleasure?"

"It's nothing to do with my pleasure," Cass said. "It's the men in this company. They want to know why we're here in these mountains and what's happening in this war."

"Each of them is accountable to duty in this regiment, no matter where we may be stationed."

"That's evasion," Cass said, and a flush spread across Gordy's face. "You owe these men some explanation of their situation. If you know it."

Ole Jury Duty's head appeared as he pushed back his blanket and blinked in the firelight.

"What's the ruckus?" he asked.

"A soldier has come to speak with me," Gordy snapped, and when Scaggs saw it was Cass, he quickly pulled the blanket back over his face. But Tug continued to watch, the hint of a smile on his face.

"Then am I to assume you are the spokesman for the men in this company?" Gordy asked.

"I am not their spokesman. I am one of them!"

For the first time, Gordy's gaze went from Cass's face to the fire.

"Very well. We're here because we're needed here. The Federals are attempting to move into the Shenandoah Valley, and if you are aware of geography, you know these mountain passes lead there."

"My knowledge of geography is as good as yours, although not learned from some plantation school."

Gordy's face came up again, and his lips tightened. "There's this, too. The Federals have pushed up the Tennessee River, taken our forts there. Likely a big fight soon, to keep them from taking the whole of that territory. But it's not our concern. We'll stay in Virginia, more than likely. They say the Federals will try to take the peninsula and attack Richmond from the east. We may have something to do with that."

"Why aren't we there? We came to fight this war, not rot in these damned mountains."

"Tell them to have patience."

"Patience be damned," Cass said, and turned away and stalked into the darkness. But Gordy's calling voice stopped him, and he turned as his cousin came up to him, holding the cape tight around his shoulders. There seemed a softness in the face now, but Cass thought it might only be the effect of shadows away from the fire.

"I thought you might like to know," Gordy said, moving close to Cass, "I had a letter from home today."

"Your home? Of what interest is that to me?"

Now Cass could see the jaw muscles go rigid, and even the shadows did not hide the cold slant of the lips.

"All right. Let me advise you that you are a soldier in this regiment like any other, and henceforth if you do not show proper respect for your superiors, I will not hesitate to have you court-martialed."

Cass laughed. "No favors, cousin! I've never had any from your tribe, and I expect none now. Good night, *sir*!"

As he thrashed his way through the trees toward the mess group, Cass thought, Maybe that son of a bitch *does* know how I feel about him. It's about time!

THEY lost the red stud in January. With Captain Gordy up, the big horse slipped on a ledge of moutain ice and came down like a clap of thunder in the frozen underbrush, a foreleg snapping. Gordy came off expertly and wasn't harmed.

He stood looking down at the animal for a long time before handing his pistol to Tug. The black boy—almost lost in an oversized coat—shot Big Red behind the left ear, and while Gordy walked away through the woods, they skinned out the horse, butchered him, and roasted him over a smoldering fire.

Beverly Cass ate with some strange kind of ravenous appetite, and Dad Johnson said it was better than Mexican donkey, even half raw.

Later, after the horse's bones were picked clean, Morgan said, "There seems a satisfaction in our Beverly Cass at each misfortune that comes to his cousin, the cap'n."

"He don't ack sociable to nobody."

"Sociable, is it? I'd wager there's a spite between those two."

"You come up with them crazy ideas enough to make a body tired," Noah said. "Hell, them two's family! A man don't work up a spite with family. They're jus' a little strange is all."

"Well," Ole Dad said, grinning and licking the grease from his fingers, "us folks in the county know about the spite between 'em all right. But we don't mention it in polite company."

With the coming of green to the countryside, the last of them was back from hospital. Not a single man had been lost in the squad, and they said, "There's that big Welshman's luck." Billy Dick Hysel was back, more rail-fence skinny than ever, now with faint pockmarks across his cheeks but still with a brightness in his eye, especially when tapping out the rhythm to "The Black-Eyed Suzie" as they marched, singing, always singing wherever they went.

And now the overcoats were returned to the commissary officers because someone, in his wisdom, realized that as the weather warmed, the coats would end in some ditch on the first long march. Their wagons had been used for firewood long since, so now they carried everything on their backs. Their elbows were showing through rents in jacket sleeves, and their shoes were coming apart. A few were already barefooted. Only the rifles looked as they always did, bright and shining and deadly. But still mostly unused.

The food was getting more monotonous: sowbelly roasted over the coals and cornbread for breakfast, for supper, too; poke greens and sometimes dry beans when they had time to stop the infernal marching and cook them. The men of each mess group squatted around their fire and made cornmeal paste, which they layered along a ramrod, held over the heat until it crusted, then applied a second layer, and then a third. Salt was scarce and coffee nonexistent. They drank a brew made from dried ground okra seeds and called it coffee. But they had ample chewing tobacco.

Sometimes Zack managed to trap a rabbit, even in countryside where armies had been quartered for a year now. They would roast the little morsel late at night over a low fire, the scent of it making men of other mess units grumble, and each having his taste of the crusty meat before rolling into sleep.

They began to hear about battles. There was the affair at Wilson's Creek in Missouri, and Martin Hasford brooded about it for a long time.

"It's not two hundred miles from my front door in Benton County!"

Then there was Shiloh and a ruckus along the Mississippi, and the name of Grant was popping up here and there, a name Dad Johnson had heard in the Mexican War.

Not many were talking any longer about this war being over soon, but by then at least they had been moved out of Jackson's command, a blessing all counted large. They spent some time in tidewater Virginia, and then a short stint in North

Carolina, near Goldsboro. They complained about the boredom, about the drilling, about being shuffled aside, as they heard the news of battles breaking out everywhere, and them far from the action. Like their hearing of Jackson back in the valley, driving the Federals before him.

"Ole Blue Light waits till we're off here before he really ties into the Yankees," Dad Johnson grumbled.

Martin Hasford's thoughts were much on home. The ache seemed incurable. In his mind he saw the long valley in Benton County, the ribbon of road running down from Missouri, his wife and children making ready for spring plowing now—patching the harness, graining the mule. When planting time came, his son, Roman, going down through the stand of locusts before the house, the sun not up yet, the white blossoms of the trees above him smelling like fresh honey.

And sometimes in the spring, his wife hitching the mule to wagon and driving to Elkhorn Tavern for a cup of spiced tea, gossiping with the family who kept the inn for the Butterfield line that ran through the valley from Saint Louis, and on south into Texas.

No, he thought, not likely the Butterfield still runs, what with the war. And the telegraph, too, that was strung along the road in front of his house, silent now with the war. Everything changed in his peaceful countryside.

He had had two letters from home. His wife never mentioned the changes, so he had to guess. She did complain about the cavalry patrols along the road at all hours, but she didn't bother to say which army, even if she knew.

He wished for something that would take his mind off home. Anything.

Then they were back in Virginia and the greatest frustration of all, watching the last of the Seven Days' Battle from south of the James River, out of gunshot range of anything. They could see the heavy smoke rising from the woods around Malvern Hill, the last of this week-long fight that saw the Yankee army trying to take Richmond from the peninsula and failing.

They knew that a new man was in the field over there,

commanding the Southern armies. Robert E. Lee. By then they had heard a great deal about Lee: West Point, of course; distinguished service in Mexico and on the frontier; a good engineer who had designed some of the harbor defenses at New York; superintendent of the United States Military Academy. And rumor had it he had even been offered command of all the Yankee armies before he opted for the older allegiance, to the Old Dominion.

Well, thought Martin Hasford, I guess we'll be hearing about him some more after all.

And they knew that an Arkansas battalion had been at Gaines Mill, one of those fights of the Seven Days. It infuriated them!

"Where'd them bastards come from?" Dinsmore cried. "This here is supposed to be the only Arkansas bunch in Virginny."

"Well, it seems we're not the only fools around, coming all this way when there's plenty of war at home," Martin Hasford said bitterly.

"You can go back anytime you feel inclined, Parson," Dad Johnson said. "Long as you feel lucky about stayin' clear of provost guards."

It was something a few had begun to speak of seriously—going home, to put in crops at least, and then return. Maybe. But His Honor Ole Jury Duty was keen to the mood of this outfit. He warned often that any man who deserted and was caught—and he would surely be caught somewhere along the eight-hundred-mile walk back to Arkansas—would be tied to a tree and shot!

"We come over hyar to fight, not sit on our Gawd damned arses," Dinsmore snorted, whisky-scented.

"Serious Ole Jury Duty is this time, boys," the Black Welshman said. "Patience! We'll see the elephant yet, and soon, I'll wager."

And soon it was. After Second Manassas—which they also missed—the rumors began to circulate through the regiment that they were off to join Bobby Lee near Groveton, and then north to retake Harper's Ferry.

By then they were a tough, camp-wise body of men, profane and dirty and garrulous as a cage of monkeys, disdainful of authority, contemptuous of cavalry. More than a little cynicism had crept into their thinking about why they were into this thing.

Noah had filed a notch in his rifle butt for each new state he had seen, and now there were five—for Mississippi, Alabama, Tennessee, Virginia, and North Carolina. It was in itself a thing unbelievable to him, for there had been a generation of Fawleys now who had never seen beyond the hills along the Buffalo.

"Best get ready to hack another slot in that rifle butt," Liverpool Morgan said. "Another notch you'll be needing soon. For Maryland."

# SEVEN

THE DAY they came down to the Potomac fords, the sun was shining and there was a glitter across the surface of the wide river as the long, widening columns crossed into Maryland. The cavalry and artillery horses looked sleeker than they were with the water shimmering across their rumps, and the metal of the guns sparkled while a band on the far shore played "Maryland, My Maryland."

Looking grim, Martin Hasford said, "I came into this army to stop the Yankees. Now they've got us going into their country!"

Noah thought little about the remark because his mind was completely taken with the grand parade of troops across the stream, like a living snake glistening with steel in the sun. But later, when they were camped near Frederick and Martin Hasford disappeared, he thought about it and all the others did as well, believing they had lost one of their number to desertion because of this invasion of Northern ground.

"Maybe we ought to try an' go find him an' bring him back," Noah said.

"You'd have a helluva time doin' it, findin' him amongst all the others who have done the same on this trip," Zack said.

The Black Welshman shook his head. "Each man is his own boss in this army, little brother, and plague take the provost guard."

But about midnight Hasford slipped back through the picket lines and into their camp, a ripe watermelon under each arm. The squad began to rouse itself and, as they came awake, to jeer at him. Martin Hasford looked sheepish, scratching his mustache and grinning.

"They looked like the ones I grow in Benton County," he said.

"You ole melon thief," said Dinsmore.

"You ole horsefeathers parson, liberatin' Maryland ground fruit," Dad Johnson said as Morgan sliced the melons with his bowie knife and they ate, the meat red and dripping sweet and sticky against the backs of their tongues.

They stayed in that camp for two days, along with the rest of the army. One time they heard that the cavalry officers had held a big dance, and another time that there had been a light skirmish somewhere in the neighborhood. A few of the Frederick townspeople came out with food, but most stayed in their wagons, the young women well hidden behind the bulk of their elders, as though a little afraid of this ragged bunch. It was just as well they didn't step down for a round of kisses; the regiment was crawling with body lice, a condition now so common that the men ignored it except now and then to joke about the graybacks that marched through their jackets and trousers in columns of regiments.

Then movement orders came. Back across the river and along the south bank toward Harper's Ferry.

"It's better not to have any shoes," Dad Johnson said. "At least that ways a man don't have to tote the extra weight of leather."

"Better till the snow flies anyways," Dinsmore said.

He had had some Maryland whisky from his nephew, the surgeon, and a little too much green corn uncorked, and occasionally he had to abandon the column to lower his trousers, to the hoots of passing troops. But each time he caught up afterward, his loose shoe soles flapping as he ran to take his place.

None of them was completely shod. Each showed a line of dirty toes where the soles had parted from rotten uppers, and Zack and Dad Johnson had no shoes at all.

But they marched hard, and along the roadside they passed many men who had fallen out, lying sprawled in the grass and weeds, pale from exhaustion. Some they passed unawares, those who had refused to march toward what they felt sure would be a real invasion of Yankee country and had simply slipped away from the column, into the woods.

Noah cast sidelong glances at Martin Hasford, wondering

if he might bolt again, this time for good. But Hasford stayed with the column, his face set in a hard scowl, his jaw clamped tight shut even when the others sang.

There was less and less singing as the day passed. Even the talk was stilled, the banter gone. Jackets were marked with sweat, and their eyes stung with it. All along the route, mounted officers urged them on. Worse than Ole Jack himself, by Gawd!

Maybe it happened because they were exhausted, or maybe because they had waited too long to see action and nerves were on edge. Or again maybe only because they were caught off guard.

Captain Gordy was somewhere ahead, or perhaps even to the rear, conferring with the other company commanders and the regimental staff—they were never sure which. They were moving along a straight stretch of road that would lead them to Loudon Heights, high ground overlooking the confluence of the Potomac and Shenandoah rivers, below which Harper's Ferry lay like a pearl in the canyon of some buxom matron's breasts.

It started at twilight with the mutter of small-arms fire somewhere to their front, distant and lasting only a few minutes. They marched with faces drawn, expectantly, their hands beginning to grow slippery on the rifles. They were approaching a wooded area, from whence had come the firing.

There was a sudden flurry of movement at the head of the column, and they saw men running from the road, shouting, scrambling across the fences. And then they made out the words:

"Yankees! Yankee cavalry!"

Later, there were those who swore they heard the beat of shod hooves. But shod hooves or no, the regiment was diving for the fences, getting clear of the road, their minds flashing with the image of blue coats on grain-fed mounts, gleaming sabers swinging.

The panic swept down the line like wind roiling placid water, the infantryman's natural scorn for mounted troops abruptly gone.

Jesus Gawd, Noah thought wildly, leaping over the fence

and into the bordering orchard, belly down behind the railings, panting, glassy-eyed, like all the others around him. Even Zack. Jesus Gawd, Ole Jack says we're a rag-tailed rabble, an' we are. Even the Welsh!

Only Ole Jury Duty, of all the regiment, stood firm in the center of the road, deserted by his troops now, waving his gigantic Mexican War saber and screaming foul oaths, standing alone before the onslaught!

And then from the woods they came! About twenty lumbering dairy cows, a few with bells gently clanging about their necks, a few walleyed from some fright they had taken up ahead, some lowing and frothing at the mouth. The regiment lay silently behind the fences and watched in astonishment as the brutes lumbered past, heavy udders swinging.

"You God damned spineless pissants," Ole Jury Duty screamed, rushing alternately at the fence where his troops cowered and then again back to the animals going past, slapping fencerails and cow butts with the flat of his saber. "Get up! Get up from behind there, you God damned worthless mongrel sons a' bitches. Get up!"

Liverpool Morgan, himself a part of the mad flight, shook his head and grinned, but none of the others were laughing, the cows by now having completed their successful charge and disappeared along the road. The men began to climb the fences, back to the road, hangdog, not looking at one another. Noah, for one, could feel the heat in his face and was ashamed of the wild hammering in his heart, the shaking hands, the mindless fear.

His Honor Ole Jury Duty was apple red, running up and down the column of re-forming troops, swinging the saber as though about to use its cutting edge, bellowing obscenities.

"You God damned scum! Cormorants! Debilitates! Supposed to be defenders of Arkansas honor and the virtue of her daughters, and you miserable whore-begotten bastards routed by a herd of cows! And not even Yankee cows at that, you God damned tit-sucking weaselbacks!"

It was a long way down that darkening road before Noah felt he could afford a glance at his brother. But by then Zack was chewing placidly on his cud, no expression on his face. And on his other side, Morgan saw the look and reached out with one huge hand to squeeze Noah's shoulder.

"Out of mind the cows, little brother," Morgan said softly. "Count it off to war's experience. Spread of fear by rumor. A disease of war, panic. And of cavalry. Remember what the boys are calling when the mounted lads pass by: 'Who ever saw a dead cavalryman?' Far on the flanks they are. You'll see. The infantry for serious slaughter. You'll see."

But Noah was glad it was dark now, so he didn't have to look into anyone's eyes. If we think so damned little of the cavalry, he thought, why'd we run like chickens before a dog when we thought they was comin'? Ole Jack was right. And it made a cold knot in his belly beside the green apples.

Zack had known that mindless fear once before, and as he marched in the darkness now he tried to dismiss it as unimportant. He had been ten years old and out in the wild timber with a group of grown men looking for a strayed sow. As they came to a limestone outcrop partly shrouded with a stand of gum trees, there had been a terrible scream, and above them on a ledge they saw the tawny form of a cougar.

The men had scattered wildly, weapons forgotten, running in blind fright. After a long, painful time of thrashing through the brush and timber, Zack found them again, almost unaware that he had run, too—furiously, without thought.

The men laughed in relief when they saw him, and then made fun of him for being so fast on his feet, and of themselves for their own fear and no good reason for it.

"I heerd Great-granpaw Fawley tell 'bout that happenin' onct in the Seminole War," Uncle Questor had said. "But never knowed it to happen with growed men spooked on an ole painter. Zack, boy, you scooted like you was scalded."

There had been no shame in it then, there was none now. But he could feel the shame in Noah.

"You gettin' tared?" Zack asked quietly. "You want I should pack your piece awhile?"

"No," Noah snapped in the darkness.

Zack knew the shame had turned to fury and said no more, aware that Noah's anger could mean a fistfight at the slightest provocation. Zack never tempted Noah to that, never pushed him beyond the edge—hadn't even when Noah was only a sprout. Noah had fought every other brother in the family, most of them more than once. But never Zack.

So Noah was allowed to march in his furious solitude because Zack had no inclination to provoke him.

Hell, Zack thought, he might jus' whup me to hell an' gone. Besides, there was pride in the fact that Noah had never balled a fist at him. Against all the others, but not against him. It had always given Zack a small taste of what it was like to be Pap.

THEY watched the next morning from the Heights as Harper's Ferry was bombarded—out of it still, detached, yet feeling the crushing weight of metal and sound.

"Them boys is catchin' hell," Dad Johnson said in admiration.

"Them poor sons a' bitches," Dinsmore said.

It came from three sides: along the ridges of their own position; from Maryland Heights, across the Potomac, where they could pick out individual gun positions until the smoke blanketed them; and from behind the town itself, across the Shenandoah, where Jackson had his troops.

"There's a battery of Napoleons," the Welshman said, pointing toward Maryland Heights. "And there beside them, bigger guns. A fine show from the long arm, lads."

The noise rolled along the narrow valley, seeming to ripple the waters of the rivers. The smell of it stung their noses, the rumble shook the ground beneath their feet. They could follow the black trajectory of the solid shot going in, where flames and dust and smoke were rising in a massive column from the valley.

When the white flag went up, they expelled a long sigh, sorry it was finished but glad, too. At first they started down the slopes toward the Shenandoah to cross into the town quietly, almost panting from the exertion of simply watching. But then they began to visualize the booty that surely lay below, and began to chatter and laugh. Dad Johnson even did a quick rendition of "Hell's Broke Loose in Georgia," accompanying himself on the banjo, Billy Dick beating the time.

But they were too late for real loot. Ahead of them had arrived the three divisions of Jackson and the troops of McLaws from Maryland Heights, and even most of those who had been with them along Loudon—in short, all the units involved in the siege. Already, too, there was a rush and scramble in the town to get captured weapons counted, food-stuffs cataloged and sent in Yankee wagons deep into Virginia. And they were disgusted to find that the word had already passed along: Get ready for the road north. Lee's in trouble at a place called Sharpsburg!

The streets were milling with troops—Florida and Virginia and Mississippi and all the others. Frantic commissary officers were trying to take control of Yankee spoils, mules and horses walleyed in the rush of things, wagons grating out of town toward the Shenandoah Valley. Captured Yankee soldiers stood along the walls of buildings, sullen but well shod. Noah looked at them, and Zack, each feeling the strange thrill of seeing the enemy close at hand, although subdued. When Zack found one with feet large enough, he offered a plug of tobacco for his shoes, a trade quickly consummated.

"We're on short supply with chewin' tobaccy," the Yankee said in a hard staccato voice. Zack said nothing but pulled on the shoes, laced them, and moved on.

They saw the engine house of the old arsenal, and Beverly Cass said, "There's the place Bobby Lee rooted out John Brown."

"And for the gallows," Morgan added.

Along the edges of the town, troops were lighting fires to cook as the afternoon wore on into evening, trying frantically to get warm food into their bellies before the order came to march. And toward the north along the Sharpsburg road, the artillery of Jackson was already lined out, groaning into the night, gunners on the limbers looking back and chewing their Yankee bread and herring.

"Gawd dammit," Dad Johnson said. "I'd like jus' onct to get a finger into a Yankee sutler's wagon before somebody else has stripped 'er naked!"

But at least some of the worst shod got Federal army shoes without having to make a trade like Zack, and there were pairs of blue Yankee trousers distributed—to keep your arses from fanning in the breeze, as Ole Jury Duty put it.

Extra ammunition was issued—forty rounds per man, a heavy burden on top of their standard basic load of forty, none of it yet fired.

"I don't like the looks of this," Johnson grumbled. "I don't like the looks of this at all."

"No longer a spectator to war, us," the Black Welshman laughed. "Now we're for it, up the road yonder."

"Use this Yankee stuff first, boys," the ordnance officer said. "It's for their Springfields and a mite bigger than those Enfields you got. But until your bore gets choked with powder carbon, these'll fit neat as a spinster's pin."

Of delicacies there was a Federal ration of bacon and coffee, which they were warned not to start cooking yet, but nothing at all from the sutlers' stores.

"Some of these boys who got here early even found Yankee horses to carry their plunder on," Dinsmore complained, dried out now and sour.

"Sutlers are the cakes and cookies," Billy Dick said. "An' our own with nothin' but sorghum molasses. When you can fin' one at all."

"Sutlers, is it?" Morgan said. "We'll see about that."

And with that he disappeared from the company for more than two hours, until long after dark, returning then with a gunnysack over his shoulder and in his black beard the old broad white smile.

The Welshman had brought edibles Noah and Zack had never seen. Canned milk! Taffy candy! Dried apricots! Brown sugar!

"What's this stuff?" Noah asked, fingering white meat from a long tin.

"Lobster it is, little brother. Lobster from the grand coasts of New England."

"A man might live offen this fare," Zack said, chewing slowly, as though the shellfish were a cud of quality plug. "But I hate to hafta cut wood on it all day."

Of all of them other than the Welshman, only Beverly Cass had tasted such things, but he consumed the food as hungrily as the others. Squatted in an alley of Harper's Ferry with the rest of his hairy, ragged company, he ate and almost smiled. He was thinking of the French cafés he had seen on his trips to New Orleans to sell the rice. The rich sauces, the finely delicate ocean catch. Candles in golden holders and a beautiful woman across the eggshell-white linen tablecloth. Napkin rings gleaming, violins playing. The waiters in satin jackets, black faces shining and laughing as they bent with silver tureens, lifting the lids to release the pungent scent of gumbo.

And now here, stuffing morsels of captured Yankee grub into his mouth with his fingers, squatting like a nigger in the rubble of bombardment and the horseshit that marked the passage of cavalry. Across from him no fair-skinned lady, but the scruffy visage of Sidney Dinsmore, hunks of white flesh in his grubby hands before disappearing into the brush-encircled mouth. No white linen between them, but rather the shattered stock and wheels of a Union cannon. Again he almost smiled.

While they waited to march, devouring everything Morgan had brought in his loot bag, Tug appeared with an entire cured ham and gave it to Cass without a word, then turned and disappeared back to his post as horse tender for Captain Gordy, even though there was no longer any horse to tend.

"You want me to carry that awhile, Mr. Cass?" Billy Dick snickered.

"You'll get your slice along with all the rest," Cass said, tying the ham into his bedroll. "When we get back across the Potomac."

"Back across the Potomac?" Dad Johnson sputtered with dismay. Then, looking at his new Yankee shoes, "By shit, I reckon these shoes could use a soakin'. They feel like pine lumber with the splinters still in. How's yours feel, Zackery?"

"About the same."

"What's lobster?" Noah asked.

"A big ocean crawdad," Martin Hasford said shortly, with no humor.

"And this, lads," Morgan said, grinning and taking the last item from his bag—a new, unopened deck of playing cards.

Then the drums started, the sound carrying down the streets where the civilians of Harper's Ferry had come out to gawk at them and shake their hands and wish them well. Units were forming into columns. Billy Dick Hysel was suddenly serious, his face shining in the light of fires that had been lit all along the streets and byways. He clamped his jaw as he beat the long roll, His Honor Ole Jury Duty Scaggs standing beside him with a sardonic half smile on his bristling, scrubby face.

What followed was the hardest march of all thus far. They plowed through the road's dust, pacing out in those long strides that ate away the distance, fatigue forgotten in their excitement, unaware of the landscape passing in the darkness.

"Time for 'Ole Suzie'!" Scaggs shouted from the rear.

Sidney Dinsmore, sober for once, was gritting his teeth, sweating and keeping pace, not falling out to leave his signature alongside the road as he had done so often before. He started the song, and they all swung into it wildly, just for the pure hell of it, egging themselves on toward Boteler's Ford. It was sixteen miles distant, and they took only two ten-minute rests along the way. At about midpoint, Zack and Dad Johnson had their new Yankee shoes off, strung around their necks by the laces.

It was 2:00 A.M. when they forded the river, back into Maryland once more, and were dispersed for sleep. Ahead they heard the sounds of the army going into position. Artillery and cavalry and infantry units like themselves, going through the darkness with an almost silent pulse of vast and overwhelming movement. When Noah fell to the ground to sleep on his rifle, aware of Zack beside him, he felt secure among the multitude.

"BY GOD!"

They all looked startled. It was the first time they had heard Martin Hasford swear.

"It's real coffee!"

They were still along the slopes leading down to the Potomac, and it was midmorning. They had been told to cook what they had of rations and the Yankee bacon, and coffee was put on the fire eagerly, and they were hopeful that they could finish it all before their call came.

There was time. They ate the greasy meat and gulped the coffee, a fistful of brown sugar in each steaming cup. They smacked their lips and marveled at the line of troops coming up from Harper's Ferry, crossing the river near them. The troops streamed past, wet from the ford, going on over the brow of the hill and then toward the east.

That morning they had heard roosters crowing. And now there was a cowbell somewhere, a gentle sound among the rattle and tramp and rumble of the army in motion.

It was an Alabama regiment. They were fresh from the ford, going past, when one of their number raised his yell.

"Hey, Arkansas. Where's your cows?"

The Alabamans laughed all along the line, their grinning faces turned toward the men standing now stock-still and with unchewed bacon between their teeth, furious at first and more furious still as other passing soldiers took up the call.

"I got your cows, Arkansas!"

"Better get behind the river, boys. They got goats ready to charge you, too."

"Fix bayonets, Arkansas! Here comes the udders!"

Noah almost choked on his mouthful of meat. He felt the tears of anger come quickly, hot to his eyes and cheeks.

There was a mutter of rage, and perhaps of shame, among them. Then Bev Cass moved up and pulled the Harper's Ferry ham from his roll and held it high.

"You boys tie into pigs, too, I see," one of the Alabama soldiers shouted, and there was a note of envy in the tone. But their taunting was finished, and like the other units before them, they passed over the brow of the hill and out of sight.

Captain Gordy was among them then, unnoticed before, his face showing no emotion.

"Take no notice of bad manners, boys," he said, and with that the tension broke, and it was back to the Yankee grub, with a mouthful of dried apricots to finish it.

Before he turned back, Gordy's dark eyes went to Bev Cass's face, and the cousins stared at each other, the lengths of three breaths passing. Gordy opened his mouth to speak, but under Beverly's cold stare he clamped his jaw and turned away, eyes hooded. Cass watched him go, then bent to replace the ham in his bedroll.

"We'll save this for a later time still," Cass said matter-of-factly. "We may need to show it off again."

"Maybe Li'l Cousin's human after all," Zack muttered.

"Why, hell, man," Dad Johnson whispered, "he's the humanest man in our whole Gawd damned county!"

But neither Johnson nor any of the others suspected Bev Cass's thoughts: I wish he was now in those ranks coming against us, my mother's brother's son, where some possibility might exist of shooting him.

When the order came to move, they were ready. Trooping up the slope and across the rise, they saw Sharpsburg for the first time. It was a small, quiet-looking town, above it the spires of two churches and around in all directions slowly rolling fields and woodlots and roads marked by fences. Everywhere the frantic, disciplined movement of troops and artillery and wagons.

They marched along a road to the south of town, enclosed with snake rails, then through a break in the fence and across a cultivated field and down the slope toward a small meandering stream. There was a scatter of trees along the edges of the fields, and houses with barns nearby. Somewhere they could hear a woman calling her hens into the coop. To the north, even with the town along the creek, they heard the splat of an occasional skirmisher's quarrel, the rifle fire sounding hollow, without meaning or danger.

They went to ground along the edge of a potato patch, scraping out depressions in the loose ground with their half-canteen plates. They loosened bedrolls, cradled rifles to check the nipples for caps. A few drew the loads from their Enfields and tamped in fresh rounds.

Then, lying there in the late sun, looking between the fencerails and on across the Antietam, they saw them.

"Jesus Gawd!" Dinsmore swore.

On the far slopes, in every direction and back to the crowns of the low hills, was the Federal army. The columns and lines and artillery positions stood out like the arrangements of lead soldiers across a green carpet—thousands, tens of thousands—as far as they could see.

They could hear the faint shouts of command, see the froth coming from the hard-worked artillery horses as battery after battery was wheeled up, unlimbered, and run out, muzzles toward the Confederate lines. They could see the Federal standards, red as their own in this setting sun. Mounted staff officers in clusters, hospital tents far behind the cannon, beyond the range of Southern guns, yellow flags brilliant. And beyond all that, the dust from many marching feet, rising in dense clouds to mark unseen columns coming closer.

The blue infantry came down to the far bank and fanned out, undulating like billows, moving into line with their bayonets already fixed, catching the red sun's rays. They could hear drums and the tiny piping of fifes.

"Yankees you wanted, lads," the Black Welshman said grimly, "so there we have it. And not rat-arsed bluecoats wet in the mountain rain and shivering like pups, but these proud and bold. It's the Army of the Potomac, sure as we're all born."

"Jesus Gawd!" Dinsmore said again, and Martin Hasford echoed him and then slipped lower behind the fence and turned to the Book of Judges.

Among them on that late afternoon, watching the blue soldiers coming into battle position, there was a tightening of the guts—though an inordinate number of them slipped back from the fence for a moment to open their trousers for a quick and nervous spurt—and sweaty faces no longer still.

As the day closed there seemed no end to the clouds of approaching dust. When one faded, another took its place. After dark the far slopes of the Antietam were dotted with their fires, lined out like lightning bugs for miles.

From the darkness now, still the rumble of artillery moving, their own as well as the blue, and a braying of mules somewhere in the town, and swearing. The night had an oppressive weight; the breathing of the thousands exhaled into the darkness.

Noah wondered what all those on the far side were thinking. For himself, a calm had descended, almost from the time they had first seen the opposing army. It left him somehow breathless and cold, but with his senses tuned sharply to every sight and smell and sound.

I ain't ever even shot a deer before, he thought. But tomorrow . . .

They had hardtack, taken from the Yankees at Harper's Ferry, and a few morsels of bacon, which they ate raw. And some of the taffy candy from Morgan's loot bag. Appetite seemed unaffected by any of this. Only the bladder.

"Zack," Noah whispered, "you a-sleepin'?"

"Not yet," Zack said from the darkness, his words rhythmic with his chewing, moist and natural and secure.

"This is the most we ever seen. Up close."

"Most we ever seen close or far off either."

"You reckon that whole bunch is gonna try an' come acrost the creek?"

"I reckon so."

"Well," Noah said, and paused a long time, listening to Zack chew, "the Welshman said we'd be seein' the elephant soon."

"Yeah, I reckon. Tomorrow."

Noah lay his face against the cold steel of his rifle barrel. He was alone now, even with Zack just beside him, alone and suddenly tired and afraid and wanting it to come on quick, to be over and done.

He touched the tip of his tongue to the rifle barrel, cool and hard. He remembered the time that winter morning, when he was only old enough to talk a little, that Tyne had dared him to lay his tongue on the axe blade, the double-edged metal silvery with frost. It felt as though his mouth were turning inside out when he tried to pull away, and Tyne and the others had laughed, rolling on the back porch.

A long time ago, Noah thought. A long way off. An' I reckon when them boys acrost the river come, we'll see the elephant.

He slept calmly, without dreaming. Once, he sat up, fully awake immediately, hearing the sounds still around him, then the breathing of those nearby—Zack and Morgan and Cass and Ole Dad and the rest—and he lay down and slept once more, feeling safe again, unknowing that he was one of less than forty thousand. And across the Antietam, twice that number.

Tomorrow.

# EIGHT

HE COULD hear a mockingbird in the rain, somewhere along the woodline below the house. One of Mama's red roosters was crowing, always the second sign after the mockingbird that the day was coming from behind the far mountains.

He wondered what they would be hunting this day; wondered if the mists would be up along the Buffalo and the fallen leaves damp and soundless for stalking; wondered if Mama was up with biscuits and pan gravy for them before they took to the woods. More likely, she was still sleeping in this predawn darkness, and he listened for the sound of Pap's breathing.

He sat up soundlessly to avoid rousing their brothers—as always when he and Zack went into the deep timber—then saw Zack's long, angular face, dim in the half-light, and all around, the stirring figures; not even visible yet, though he knew they were there now, were the far slopes across the Antietam, and the Federal army.

"Time to get up."

Zack thrust a chunk of salt pork into his hand, and Noah took it and tried to eat. But he made little headway at it and finally stopped trying.

"You want it?" he asked.

"No," Zack said, chewing his own raw breakfast, slowly, deliberately. "Put it away somewheres. You'll want it after a while."

Noah shivered, his back damp. He could see crystal beads of gray moisture along the rim of his brother's hat brim.

"Gawd, it's misty an' damp, ain't it?"

"Rained a mite. But clearin' now."

"I slept right through it."

It was still too dark to see a hundred paces, but then they

heard the first firing, faint little puffs of sound, skirmishers in heated dispute north of Sharpsburg. Soon the sound swelled and became the intense, persistent crackle of infantry engaged.

"How far off?" Billy Dick Hysel asked, his eyes shining in the predawn.

"Maybe four miles," Zack said, looking toward the north and past the town, where the mists were thinning. "But gettin' closer."

Each of them who felt the need moved back a few paces, dropped their trousers, and made their deposit, having been soldiers long enough to know that such things needed doing when there was time for doing it. Even Noah had by now overcome his embarrassment with such things.

"Cover that up," Ole Jury Duty kept saying. "I don't want to step in any of it."

They heard the first artillery fire as soon as it was light enough to sight the guns, growing quickly from a disgruntled growl to a trembling roar. Noah slipped the watch from his pocket.

"It's six of the clock."

"And the ball has opened, lads," Morgan said.

Rolling clouds of powder smoke rose slowly from beyond the town, snow white where the new sun shone. Now, with the cannons thundering, there was the furious, ripping sound of small arms in volley, ascending, slackening, then rising to greater intensity.

"Hell's broke loose, sure enough," Billy Dick kept saying, his eyes so large they seemed to swallow his face.

Martin Hasford took the Bible from his pocket and read from Joshua, loud enough for all to hear.

" 'And there was no day like that before or after it, that the Lord harkened unto the voice of man: for the Lord fought for Israel.' So be it."

There was a quiet agitation among them, feeling the earth tremble from the battle north of Sharpsburg. Captain Gordy and Ole Jury Duty paced behind their line, Scaggs chewing furiously on an unlit cigar liberated from Harper's Ferry. All faces were turned north, where the smoke billowed and drifted.

There was a lull in the sound of fighting, but only for a few moments, then it burst forth again more violent than before. They looked at one another, silently. For an hour it went on, and then for another, and they were so intent in their listening they failed to see the mounted courier dash up to the regimental staff.

"Marching order, column of fours," Ole Jury Duty yelled.

"By shit, I knowed it," Dad Johnson said.

They formed quickly, Scaggs running alongside the column with his Mexican War saber, Sergeant Small shouting, carrot-colored hair hanging down his neck. They started north, headed to skirt Sharpsburg on its eastern edge.

They began to see the balloons of smoke and points of muzzle blast from Federal gun positions on their right, across the Antietam. There was small-arms fire, too, along the lines drawn near the creek where blue formations had already crossed. But this was only minor disputing; they all knew the battle was to the north, on Lee's left flank. Across the fields and along the fenced lanes they moved, always toward the sound of firing.

Across a rise, then, and past the town, with the rising clouds of combat closer. They saw a sunken road to their right flank, and there a line of butternut soldiers, bayoneted rifles thrust toward the fords. They passed well behind these positions and on along the slopes of a low ridge where a large body of mounted officers stood. Detached from them was a single soldier, field glasses to his eyes, a man with thigh-length coat and narrow-brimmed hat on a lionlike head, and the gray of his beard shining in the sunlight like a banner.

"It's Bobby Lee!" The word passed along the column. "It's Bobby Lee!"

They did not cheer, only lifted hats and rifles as they passed. The field glasses were lowered and the burning gaze swept along their ranks, and Lee lifted one hand to his hat in answer to their salute.

"By Gawd, look at him!"

"There's a general fer ya!"

"Ole Bobby Lee, by Gawd. He's bigger'n I thought he was."

" 'Black-Eyed Suzie'!" Ole Jury Duty bellowed, but only time then for one refrain and they were into it.

"Drop them rolls," Sergeant Small yelled above the noise that was engulfing them from a gap between woodlands to the front. They slipped off bedding and left it piled along the fenced road—Hagerstown Pike it was called, though none of them were aware of the name at the time—and began the movement taught so long ago by the Richmond Light Infantry cadets—from column into line, two ranks—the rifles now lowering toward the belching wall of smoke.

They were gasping for breath, most of the three miles from south of the town having been taken at double-quick time. The dense air scalded their lungs, the swirling smoke tasted harsh in their throats.

The sound was overwhelming. From somewhere beyond the woods to their right, Federal artillery was in action. They saw the bursts of spherical case and heard—felt—the passing solid shot. Now, too, the whipping, whining slash of Minié balls, and they all knew the regiment was closing with Yankee infantry.

First, there was a ragged line of figures in gray and butternut, materializing from the smoke, falling back, faces white and staring. Ghastly faces, stunned and powder-blackened. Some of them were still firing, but others had no arms at all and were simply running.

There was a square, whitewashed church off to the left, scarred and pocked, dense timber behind it. Across the yard, broken bits of guns and men were scattered. And nearby, a Confederate artillery battery, and yet another, an entire battalion, firing toward the north. And closer still, they saw more of the dead, fallen in lines and ranks as they had stood when struck.

Pressing forward, Zack at his right shoulder, Noah stumbled on something soft, and looking down he saw the bloody wreckage, hands outstretched. He didn't look down again, but with his feet felt more and more of the yielding forms that carpeted the field.

He heard a high-pitched wailing, sustained and carried through the other noise like the sound of hunting horns. And realized then that he, too, was yelling, along with all the rest, passing the retreating Confederates, shrieking the vibrant, unlearned shout. And lunged forward with the heat and passion of it.

A blue presence through the smoke—undulating, weaving, laced with fire—and from it a deep shouting. Noah felt the shock of the rifle butt against his shoulder without even being aware that he had raised it, let alone fired it. Biting off the end of the next cartridge, ramming it home, hammer back, cap pressed onto nipple, he fired again. The blue haze ahead took shape, showing faces and arms and bright brass belt buckles, his bead drawn each time on that gleaming smudge in the smoke. The kick of the rifle, again and again, and the screaming.

Zack beside him—stumbling, too, on bodies underfoot—never reseating the ramrod after each loading, holding it loose in the left hand under the Enfield stock, firing and loading, four shots to the minute, faster than anyone else in the regiment.

Then the blue images before them were fading, and the heavy shouting stopped, leaving only their own keening. Just a pause, and back the Federals came, blazing, only a few feet away. Morgan was swinging his rifle like a club, the butt and stock shattering like kindling wood in his hand against the head of a Union soldier, the barrel pinwheeling across the front of the regiment.

Dad Johnson, hat gone and a scarf of red running down each side of his head from the gashing bullet wound in his scalp . . . Billy Dick pop-eyed, stumbling over the bloodied bodies, stumbling over his drum, stumbling over his rifle . . . Bev Cass, his face black from biting cartridges, the hard light brilliant in his eyes, shooting low . . . Ole Jury Duty, saber cased now and a rifle in his hands, giving orders nobody could hear . . . Tug, moving beside Captain Gordy, a rifle in his hands, too, firing with his lips peeled back from the bitter taste of cordite and sulphur . . . Martin Hasford marching ahead, mouth open, swearing vile oaths his own ears refused to believe, ramming home the loads, tearing the flesh from the back of his hand on the bayonet . . . And Sidney Dinsmore screaming the vilest stanzas of "The Black-Eyed Suzie."

"They've broke," Ole Jury Duty shouted above the din. "They've broke! The Satan fornicators broke!"

Noah could see no movement now in the smoke ahead, only the faint outline of plowed ground as the wind began to dissipate the shroud.

"Get behind them rocks!" came the order, and they staggered for the scant cover, looking across the desolate and horrible ground, the smoke slowly blowing away.

They could hear it still raging to their left, in the woods behind the church. But for the moment, their own field was not swept by fire.

Noah lifted his canteen and found it empty. He couldn't remember having a single drink since starting the run from south of Sharpsburg. And then he saw the jagged tear a bullet had made across the bottom of the canteen.

Zack shoved his own water into Noah's hand, and Noah drank, never having been so thirsty—gulping it, the water running from his mouth and along his neck. Zack watched him, and suddenly Noah laughed. Zack's mustache was caked with black powder, the lean flesh of his face darkened with it.

"You're blacker'n that boy of Cap'n Gordy's."

"You ain't much fer purty your own self. Get loaded. Them boys is likely to be back."

Noah shoved aside a bloody Union body, positioning his rifle across it. He saw the red on his fingers. But no time to think about it. His heart pounding again, and the senses all leaping to the surface, tingling, as he saw the next blue formation coming across the field before them.

"Hold it," Gordy shouted. "Hold it. Volley fire, boys. Now!"

They rose and their fire swept across the front of the advancing Federals like a sheet of flame and smoke and metal. The line recoiled and tried to re-form and come on again. Then the second volley. Then individual fire, until once more the plain was lost in smoke, impossible to see. But ahead, the return fire suddenly ceased, and once more the smoke drifted lazily aside. To reveal yet another line of blue advancing toward them.

"By shit," Dad Johnson yelled. "They're comin' in column a' regiments!"

"Tough and persistent they are, the old Army of the Potomac," called the Black Welshman, a captured Yankee rifle to his shoulder now.

They had to give ground, slowly and stubbornly. Each felt the pinch of panic as the blue infantry came closer, shouting. They had no idea help was at hand, so intent were they on the desperate work to the front.

But quickly now, unexpectedly, through their ranks came a charging rank of fresh butternut troops, and yet another rank and another, shouting the high call. McLaws's division!

They were left in its wake, panting on the ground, trembling with shock. The struggle surged away from them, thundering, unreal. They had no concept of how long it had lasted, no feeling for time and its passage. But finally the angry, ghastly clamor subsided to a distant grumbling, and then only to a murmur. On the left, the firing was dying out as well, and for the first time they were aware of the wounded calling for help, crying for water.

"Re-form here," Gordy was shouting, and they rose like sleepwalkers and staggered back to align themselves along the picket-and-rail fence that bordered the Hagerstown Pike.

I never even taken notice a' this road before, Noah thought, an' walkin' right along it, an' fought over it, an' seen the elephant astraddle of it.

They lay gasping behind the fence, most of them out of water now, some scrambling about over the field, collecting canteens from the dead. And ammunition. Rapid fire consumed powder and ball with ravenous appetite, and even with a double issue going in, they were running low.

Every member of the regiment was trying to find his own mess group in that line. Many looked in vain. After their head-on clash with the Yankees, some companies numbered less than twenty-five.

But luck still seemed to hold for most of Morgan's squad, although each of them was bleeding from at least one minor wound. Except for Zack, who had gone unscathed.

Noah was amazed to find his trousers soaked with blood, and only when he saw it did he realize a stinging sensation along one side.

"Lemme see that," Zack said, and ripped away the cloth to find only a grazing wound, signature of a passing Minié ball. Zack emptied what remained of his water into the ditch, and with that and a little spit made enough mud to pack the wound.

"I don't reckon I could spit now at all," Noah said.

"Where's Cap'n Gordy?" someone called.

"Gone to the rear," Ole Jury Duty replied.

"Hit in the arm. I seen the bones stickin' out."

"That nigger boy taken him back."

"What?"

"That nigger boy," Bev Cass grated, his eyes fierce and the powder marks across his face like a smudge of thick grease against his olive skin, with a tear in his jacket at the shoulder where the blood showed.

Then Noah saw the Black Welshman and felt an intense, almost painful relief. Morgan came along the line, the Yankee rifle in one hand, a cluster of canteens in the other, grinning, his beard caked with the blood of a vicious little gash across the jaw.

"Water for the thirsty soldier, is it?" he said.

Back among his own, Noah's heart still pounded against his ribs—even now, when his eyes could see clearly that those around him were the men he knew and not the vague shapes of motion and violence, the screaming, lunatic demons they had been only a little while before. His lungs ached from the acrid fumes, and he was thirsty, and his side was beginning to throb painfully.

But there was yet some kind of wild exhilaration. Because he was still alive.

Jesus Gawd, he thought, I'm shakin' clean down to the bone.

"My gun's stuffed full," Billy Dick Hysel was wailing.

The laughter started along the line and spread, hysterically, so hard that tears ran down their blackened faces. Billy Dick had rammed one load after another into the Enfield, failing to cap each time, pressing each round down against the one before. When Zack took a worm to it, he withdrew twelve cartridges from the bore.

"Boy," Zack said, "iffen this ole girl don't slam hell outa your shoulder each time you pull the trigger, then you ain't put a cap to nip."

"I thought it did," Billy Dick said. "I felt it kick, I did. I felt it kick each time."

But the barrel was cold, while all the others were hot, smoking hot, and they laughed out of control, knowing Billy Dick had not fired a single shot.

"Saving ammunition he was," Morgan said, and they laughed again. "Never mind, lad. Bringing the laughter after battle is worth ten dead Yankees."

Now, once more, after the pandemonium and the insanity, they began to realize the battle was shifting. Along the fenceline they found themselves more squarely facing toward Antietam Creek, more toward the center of the Confederate position. And action there was developing rapidly. Artillery from across the stream was sending shell into the sunken road that wound down the slope directly before them, and Union infantry was across the creek in massive formations, deployed and advancing.

Along the ridge to their rear was frantic movement, artillery coming into position to dispute this new advance, the guns run out along the ridge where General Lee had stood when the regiment marched by him.

There was Longstreet and his staff, helping position the guns, the fire of Federal batteries dropping around them, Ole Pete himself dismounted and holding horses for those who served the guns, wearing house slippers because he suffered from sore feet.

And along the left flank, where the morning's fight had begun, Jackson in his seedy little forage hat, sitting the sorrel, looking out across the west woods and past the Dunkard church where the bodies of blue and gray and butternut were strewn like fallen leaves. Dead horses, shattered limbers, gouged earth.

And John Bell Hood, his pale eyes blazing, his gaze across the cornfield where the stalks had been cut to within a few inches of the ground by rifle and artillery fire, not a single one left standing, and there his own division shot to pieces with McLaws's men and the troops of two Union corps.

And Sidney Dinsmore, lying where he had fallen, like a piece of folded flannel, red-soaked and discarded where the regiment's counterattack had first gone in.

Back along their own piece of fenceline the men of the Third Arkansas were grouped, still shaken but taking control of their shock, looking to weapons.

"We seen it, Welshman," Noah said. "We seen the elephant."

"Yeah, an' we're fixin' to see some more," Zack said, looking through the railings toward the slope below.

Up from the Antietam, the Union formations were raising their deep, measured shout. And suddenly the gray and butternut line that held the sunken road broke to the rear, leaving a gaping hole in the Confederate center.

IN ALL the years afterward, they would recall it as their finest moment, the day they saved Bobby Lee's center. They and another single regiment, the 27th North Carolina, who stood beside them, would be mentioned in dispatches, and when they stenciled "Sharpsburg" on their battle flag, they would remember that fight on the slopes above the Antietam.

There were efforts to restore the position along the sunken road. Remnants and pieces of any unit found were rushed into the gap, and artillery along the ridge behind stayed to fire, even though under murderous shelling themselves.

As the Union wave swept forward against the makeshift line, its right flank was left hanging, exposed to the rifles along the Hagerstown Pike.

"Gawd!" Zack said, eyes squinted against the high sun's glare as he watched the long Federal lines, flags before them.

Weapons came up along the fence now, and in the fusillade that followed, they saw for the first time the disastrous effect of fire enfilading a line of standing troops. They butchered the right flank of the advancing Union divisions with volley fire, and as that fell back in bloody confusion, their bullets found targets farther along the blue formation, collapsing it from end to end like flame eating along the length of a fuse.

A pause then, as the blues reorganized far down the slope toward the creek.

There were a number of farm buildings to their left front, a few on fire from artillery, and Liverpool Morgan pointed to one of them.

"There's good luck for you, little brother. The sign on the road says it's the Roulette place. A name proper for the occasion."

Noah stared at him blankly, and the Welshman laughed.

"Roulette. A game of chance, lad."

Chewing off the end of a paper cartridge, Noah thought, I hope his luck is better hyar than it ever was with that nigger boy of Cap'n Gordy's.

The Federals realized their hazard from the fencerow now, and began directing fire against it. As if in answer, the colonel of the North Carolina regiment leaped across the fence and took his stand behind a small hickory tree to their front, directing their own fire, exhorting them to shoot fast and low.

"Where the hell's *our* colonel?" someone shouted above the din.

"Ain't got none left. Cap'n Reedy's commandin' now."

"Besides," Dad Johnson shouted, ramming in another load and having to beat it home with a rock because of caked powder in the bore, "they ain't no more Gawd damned hickory trees out yonder."

The blue assault wavered, started back up the slope once more, and once more was met with sweeping volleys. And now, too, more troops were being pushed into line directly across their path. They wavered a second time, came on, and wavered yet again.

"Them boys can take punishment," Zack said, searching for the last of the ammunition in his belt pouch.

And at last—again, they had no idea how long they had been firing—the Union attack collapsed and the ragged lines moved back toward the creek, soldiers leaping over the rows of dead and wounded.

Nobody was ever sure who started their own charge. Perhaps the colonel from behind his hickory tree, hot for pursuit. Or perhaps the North Carolina boy carrying their colors, who leaped across the fence. The Arkansas standard bearer, not to be outdone, followed. No matter. Suddenly they were all rushing down the hill, screaming their quavering call, those who had not already done so working bayonets onto hot rifle barrels.

They began to overtake some of the Union laggards, who turned wild-eyed, ashen-faced, and threw down their arms. They collected a number of prisoners, pushing them down behind haystacks that had somehow escaped combustion.

The Union artillery across the creek had not yet adjusted to their range, and there was almost no small-arms fire coming at them, so they ran shouting, like boys in a footrace, fear forgotten. But they went too far.

Before them appeared a fence, solid of wood and stone, and behind it rank on rank of fresh blue infantry, waiting, bayonets gleaming in the sun. Even the most exuberant paused, stopped, and squatted, panting, knowing their ammunition was almost gone, and they had only clubbed rifles and steel against this powerful position.

The North Carolina colonel surveyed the situation, but

only for a moment. He ordered them back up the slope. They moved calmly at first, stopping now and again to turn and fire what little ammunition they had left.

Then the Yankee artillery began to find them. And long-range rifle fire. They moved faster, all their shouting stilled. They began to run. The prisoners left behind the haystacks were forgotten in the headlong dash for safety, and some of these took up their discarded rifles and shot butternuts in the back as they passed.

Noah was running beside Martin Hasford, within a hundred yards of the Hagerstown Pike. Ahead he saw Billy Dick Hysel fall after a burst of flame and smoke nearby, then painfully pull himself toward the fence. He saw Sergeant Pecker Small pitch forward, limp as a rag, bouncing when he struck the ground, and not moving. Then there was a sharp report, close behind them, and Martin Hasford grunted and was on his knees.

Pulling him up, Noah felt the wet across Hasford's back and saw the red mark on his chest and thought, Hit went plumb through him!

Behind them, at one of the haystacks, crouched two Union soldiers, one desperately ramming a new charge into his rifle. Then Zack was running over, dragging his rifle in one hand, the old Dragoon pistol in the other. His teeth were grinding in rage, his blackened face contorted.

Frantically, pop-eyed, the Union soldier lifted the rifle and fumbled with a cap. Zack shot him in the head, so close the muzzle blast seared flesh, and then deliberately turned to the other, who was cowering on his knees, hands out and empty, and shot him also.

When Noah reached the fence, dragging Hasford's deadweight, Zack was there to help him. Also Dad Johnson, whose head had started bleeding again and who now displayed across his rump a large smear of crimson.

"They shot me in the arse," he cried. "Them Gawd damn Yankees shot me right in the arse!"

The regimental bandsmen were there by then, doing their

double duty as litter bearers. And there was help from the walking wounded, bleeding badly enough to require medical attention but still on their feet. They dragged away Hasford and Billy Dick Hysel, now wailing for his mama, and Ole Jury Duty sent Johnson to the rear as well, despite vehement protest.

Once more, those remaining sank down behind the fence, quivering, soaked with sweat and wanting water. The canteens were as empty as the cartridge pouches.

"Here they come again!"

Noah groaned and rolled over and looked through the fence. The blue lines were coming directly at them this time, no veering to one side and offering a flank shot. But that wouldn't have mattered anyway. No shot went out to greet them. Both Confederate regiments were out of ammunition.

"Wave them flags!"

As the shout went up, both color bearers leaped to the top fencerail and swung the standards back and forth, defiantly.

"Shake them pieces!"

They lifted their empty rifles and shook them above the fenceline. Zack crouched in the ditch to reload the revolver, his face taut, the jaw muscles working into knots.

"We stay here, boys. We'll hold 'em with the bayonet!" an officer shouted.

A bullet caught the Arkansas color boy, and he toppled back onto the Hagerstown Pike. Bev Cass pulled the staff from the boy's clasping hands and scrambled to the fence, straddling the top rail, waving the banner.

"Now a little music, boys," the North Carolina colonel bellowed. They let loose a cheer and then the wild, high, screaming keen, until their throats were raw.

The Federal lines advanced, rows aligned, striped flags in front. The Confederate artillery along the ridge began to hammer them. On they came. Then slowed. Then calmly turned and walked back down the slope!

The men stood breathless, unbelieving, behind their fenceline, staring at the backs of thousands marching away from them.

"My Gawd! They ain't comin'! Boys, they ain't comin'!"

The gray and butternut line was up cheering, jubilant, reprieved. Until a last random shot from somewhere along the creek echoed across the lines, and Beverly Cass tottered a moment and fell forward into the field, the colors draped around him.

A dozen men leaped out to pull him back across the fence. He was hit low on the left side, the dark light in his hooded eyes fading. Noah was swearing, tears running down his cheeks into his gaping mouth, salty and bitter like all the pent-up rage he'd had this day.

"Don't take on," Zack said, pushing Noah back against the fence.

"He's gut-shot! Gawd dammit, he's gut-shot."

"Maybe not. Maybe it ain't so bad. Don't take on now. They'll get him to the horspittle."

"Gawd dammit!"

Noah sagged against the fence and blew his nose on his fingers, wiping his hand on his blood-stiffened trousers. He looked around slowly, seeing the faces. Only a few he knew. Zack and Morgan and no more from the original mess squad. Three left out of eight.

"Gawd dammit," he said helplessly. "Why'n we stay hyar behin' this fence where we belonged?"

He saw the Bible then, dropped from Martin Hasford's pocket in the ditch along with that clutter of broken and discarded equipment found on all fighting lines. He scrambled over and took it and, back at his place, opened it. On the flyleaf were the carefully printed words:

Maximillian Hassfurt, born 1800, Bavaria.
Died 1837, Benton County, Ark.
Calie Stockburger Hassfurt, born 1801, Bavaria.
Died 1845, Benton County.
Martin Hasford, born 1820, Georgia. Married 1845,
Benton County.
Ora Hasford, born 1826, Georgia. Cousin and
beloved wife.

Calpurnia Hasford, born 1846, Benton County. Daughter.
Roman Hasford, born 1847, Benton County. Son.
The War for Southern Independence, 1861.
God's will be done. Amen.

The battle had shifted once more, farther to the south. They heard it swelling while waiting anxiously behind their fence for ammunition to be brought up. Nothing came during the rest of daylight, but it didn't matter because the blue formations along the Antietam showed no inclination to assail their position again.

Smoke appeared beyond Sharpsburg, from the positions where they had started that morning, and as the intensity of the fight on the far right flank increased, a few thought with horror that they might be asked to go back there.

For most of them, thinking anything at all was a struggle. They were exhausted, footsore, scarred, and bleeding. Limp and thirsty, they listened with only a vague, disoriented interest to the crash of the fight as the sun lowered slowly and at last was gone.

And with it the fighting. As twilight settled over the gently rolling fields and the shattered woodlands and burning barns, it was quiet except for the cries of wounded men and dying horses—a hideous, chilling symphony. Slowly, behind them, the army supply system was once again in motion; they could hear the groan of wagons and the shouts of teamsters.

Before full dark, a general officer none of them had ever seen before rode up and conveyed compliments for their action that day. Sitting his horse stiffly, the general saw Ole Jury Duty still standing resolutely at the fence, the big saber once more in his hand.

"And you, sir," the general said, "are to be complimented on your colorful language." He paused a moment, then added before reining away, "Although General Lee does not approve such usage, I am sure he would agree with its effect."

Ammunition arrived and was distributed. Of rations there were plenty now, once more captured Yankee grub from Harper's Ferry. Now it was pickled beef, tough and salty, with the consistency of hard-packed gunpowder, and desiccated vegetable cakes, cooked in hog fat and as scratchy on the throat as chestnut burrs. But they ate it and drank the water carried forward from the Potomac fords or drawn from local wells around Sharpsburg.

Dad Johnson came back with one of the carrying parties, wearing a new pair of trousers, his head in a turban of white bandage. It made their spirits rise, even though Dad could tell them nothing of the fate of the others who had been evacuated.

"Horspittles and mortuary tents, they make my skin crawl," he complained. "You oughta see all that's back yonder. By shit, boys, it's a wonder an army can move at all, havin' to drag all that around behind of it."

The night was black and clear, and toward the Potomac they could hear a whippoorwill. Down the slope before them, Federal litter parties were collecting their wounded. The burning buildings had gone to embers, and across the Antietam sparkled the many fires of the Union army. They heard little movement of artillery from there.

Liverpool Morgan was sucking a clay pipe violently, his face still agitated from the fight, his eyes gleaming in the hot light from the bowl each time he drew in a lungful of smoke.

"What brand of men be we, Noah Fawley?" he asked suddenly, urgently. "What brand, indeed? Oh, scoundrels and cowards there are amongst us and those left hiding in the woods in Virginia to keep from being here. But not us! You and me and brother Zack. Not us. Nor Jury Duty nor Bev Cass nor even that little African with his dice, nor good Cap'n Gordy, bless him and his arm shot to hell.

"I've seen this madness before. Men willing to do this work of slaughter. How could mere Yanks hope to beat such as us?"

Noah sat listening to the harsh and brutal tones, unspeaking. But from the darkness near them came Zack's voice.

"Because they's more of 'em."

"What?" Morgan's head snapped around toward the words.

"I said because they's more of 'em. I never knowed they

was so many till today. An' it appears to me they're just as ready to tie in as we are."

"You bastard!" Morgan hissed, and it was the first time Noah had heard anger in the voice. "Always the practical one, you."

"Don't wool me around too much this night, Welshman," Zack said, and his words had a cutting edge, though calm and faceless in the dark. "I'm spent now, an' I won't take much woolin' around from any man this night. An' not from you, either."

"No." Morgan sighed and knocked his pipe out on the remnant of his shoes. "I meant no push, just an observation. Damn, Zack, you take all the fun out of it!"

Noah lay against the fence, the rifle across his legs, cool at last. Like the night. September cold in the darkness. He shivered, and the images in his thinking began to rearrange themselves into some semblance of order.

I thought this day would never end. The thang Martin read from his Book, it's the place where that ole warrior made the sun stand still. I 'member Mama readin' that onct.

He saw in his mind more clearly than he had with his eyes the shattered forms on the field where they had first known action: the gaping wounds, the scattered arms and feet and legs severed, the blood-soaked ground, the staring, wide-eyed faces turning black and bloated before the last light of sun left the earth.

He knew he should despise this with a deep intensity he'd never known before, and that made it all the worse because even knowing the hatred should be there, and maybe was to some degree, he knew he liked it, and that frightened him more than Yankee bullets had power to do.

Zack, against the fence, too, was chewing slowly and listening to the movement of ambulances along the ridges—and remembering the man he had shot at the haystack, a man unarmed. But not with concern or shame or even contrition. Only with a kind of detached amazement.

A man never knows what he'll do when the spit hits the stove, Uncle Questor always said. An' he was right.

And Noah again, trying to structure the sequence of events, but unable to. Put your mind on somethin' else, he thought. Home. But now the visions of the Buffalo and his family would not come. Nor even visions of the beautiful Luanne Lacy. The dismembered bodies continued to intervene.

Soon, exhaustion overtook them all, and mercifully they slept. In the night, well toward dawn, Noah wakened and rose stiffly, finally moving across the Hagerstown Pike to relieve himself. As he returned to his place in the line, he saw a figure huddled in the road, head down. As he drew near, he heard the sobbing.

Noah bent closer and saw the tall stovepipe hat and the oversized saber lying in the road beside the crying man. He stood for a moment uncertainly, listening, then quietly went to his position. But he did not sleep again.

# NINE

THEY MIGHT have wondered why Lee stayed another day at Sharpsburg, but they were too stunned and drugged with action to think of anything but sleep, until the morning found them still along the Hagerstown Pike and no order to move for the Potomac fords.

They lay waiting all day, counting each degree of the sun's march across the September sky. Rations were brought up from the rear, and they ate more than they could remember ever eating in this army. Through all of it they expected to see the Federals moving again, but the only activity along the Antietam was defensive—the Yankees digging their own positions, as though expecting attack.

"By Gawd, I hope they don't ast us to go over yonder," Dad Johnson said through a mouthful of half-cooked rice. "After yestiddy, they ain't half this regiment left."

"Bobby Lee seems not in an attacking mood," Morgan said.

Noah was amazed at the Welshman's freshness. For himself, he felt worse than he had the day of Lucinda's wedding, when he had gotten drunk and stolen that pig and was sick from it all.

Slowly the hours wore on, the two armies staring at one another and neither willing nor able to move. Then darkness, and they began the march back to Virginia. It was midnight when Noah felt the cooling waters of the Potomac around his ankles, and with it a vast relief. And yet the loss of some strange excitement, too.

"One thing about it," Zack said, his shoes tied around his neck, "Virginny roads is softer'n them we walked in Maryland."

Now there were no bands playing. There was a sullen silence, a feeling of disappointment, of unfulfilled hopes. No rifles gleamed in the sunlight. Instead, they stumbled along in the darkness, hearing the moans of the wounded from the wagons and ambulances. Horses were breaking down, and many were passed that had been cut from the harness and left to die in the ditches alongside.

There were rumors of Yankee cavalry about to swoop down on their column, but now they were contemptuous of such rumors, thinking, Let the bastards come!

The next day found the army moving toward the Shenandoah Valley, where it would lie in camp and refurbish with material being sent up from Richmond. Men began to appear from the surrounding woods, rejoining their units now that the army was back in Virginia. Within a few days, the Sharpsburg casualties were replaced by these soldiers who would fight only on home ground.

Except in the Third Arkansas, it made little difference.

"We're too far from home," Zack said. "What good does it do a man to desert the army from this regiment? He ain't got nowhere to go, 'less he wants to walk halfway acrost the country."

Within a week, Billy Dick Hysel was back, with ghastly stories about the hospitals. Piles of amputated limbs, men lying unattended because of lack of doctors, wounds flyblown and festering, everywhere the smell of a slaughterhouse.

His own wounds had been of little consequence, like those from long-range buckshot where the spherical pellets break hide. He showed them the scars, still red and scabbed.

"Lucky you wasn't a few steps closer to that shell when it busted," Noah said. "I seen it and thought you was up the flue."

"Hit was close enough. My right ear still rings."

"You see that nephew of Sidney Dinsmore's?" Dad Johnson asked.

"I seen him. He was drunk most of the time, but he give me a drank of whisky."

"Whisky?" Dad Johnson's eyebrows lifted elaborately. "You takin' whisky? A sprout like you, and a Baptist besides? By shit, boy, you're likely to make a sojur yet, iffen we can find you a whore somewheres."

Billy Dick flushed and became intensely interested in tightening the head on his drum.

"I see you managed to brang that damn thang back with you," Dad Johnson said in disgust. "I'd as soon you'd brang a jug instead."

THE company outdistanced the rest of the regiment on one of the quick marches they made that fall. The resulting gap in the column required that guides be posted at a crossroads so the following units would take the right route. Zack and Noah drew the duty.

It was a pleasant day, not too warm, and there were clouds in the deep blue sky and birds along the row trees beside the fields. Vegetables were being grown there now, instead of tobacco or cotton, and the rows were well tended and marked off by snake-rail fences. To the west, far distant, stood the pale outlines of mountains.

They waited in the grass along one of the fencelines, watching for dust that would signal the regiment. Noah lay back, grunting, touching the sore side where the Yankee bullet wound remained as an angry welt. A rifle shot away along one of the roads was a whitewashed frame farmhouse, and behind it a cluster of outbuildings.

"You got any water left?" Zack asked, squinting toward the farmstead. In a small patch of plowed ground near the house, he could see half a dozen men working.

"Not much," Noah said, handing Zack his canteen. "Take some iffen you're thirsty."

"No, you drank it. I'm goin' down to that farmhouse an' see about some fresh water."

Taking both canteens and leaving Noah lying in the grass, Zack walked to the house. As he passed them, the field hands stopped working and stood immobile, watching him. He could see now that they were picking tobacco from the small plot. For home use, he supposed.

There were large oaks in the front yard, standing behind a white paling fence like heavy sentinels before the house, dappling it with shade. Zack stopped at the gate and took off his hat.

"Hullo the house," he called. The field hands were still motionless, watching him.

A small woman appeared like a white-draped bell, her skirts flowing out from the waist to fill the doorway. When Zack asked for water, she seemed reluctant to speak and stood well back in the shadows.

Caint say I blame 'er, Zack thought, rough as I look an' carryin' this hyar gun.

"Me an' my brother is sojurs, ma'am," he reassured her. "Down at the crossroads hyar to guide the regiment on when it comes up. We're a-runnin' low on drinkin' water."

She continued to stay well back inside the doorway, but she directed him around the side of the house in a soft, almost inaudible voice. Zack found a well in the backyard, with latticework built over it and vines that he did not recognize climbing up to shade the curbing. He drew up the water with the blacks still watching, nothing having moved except their heads turning to follow him along the road, through the gate, and into the yard.

He dipped into the bucket with a hollow gourd hanging on the curb, and drank. The water was cold and good, and as he drank he looked at the barns. Well tended, although unpainted. Beyond them and a horse paddock was a line of cabins, and there he saw more dark figures, some children but most of them women in flowered dresses and turbans, and all of them as still and watchful as the men in the tobacco plot.

It startled him when the woman called from an open window.

"Luther!"

The largest of the field hands detached himself and walked

from the tobacco patch into the yard and to the back porch, his eyes still on Zack.

The canteens were filled, and Zack was corking them when he saw from the tail of his eye the massive form of the black moving toward him, a small sack in one hand, a crock pitcher in the other. The man stopped a few paces from Zack and watched as Zack slung the canteens over his shoulder and lifted the rifle from the curbing.

"Miz Marsy says you an' dat utter sojur man to hab some muffins an' sweet milk," Luther said. "I takin' 'em along to da crossroads an' brang back da pitcha."

"All right. Much obliged to your Miz Marsy."

"She say she ain' much fer no visitin', feelin' poorly lak she do wif Marse Benjamin off to fit da Yankee states."

He's one big son of a bitch, Zack thought.

Back through the gate and into the road, Luther followed behind, but not too closely. As they passed along the road the field hands were still watching. Zack waved a hand to them, but they made no response. He could see their eyes shining in the shadows of their hat brims.

This ain't much bigger a place than some in Newton County, Zack thought. Only hyar they got all them people workin' it, all them colored people. What the hell does the men do, with them colored people doin' all the work?

When Zack and Luther came to the crossroads, Noah sat up suddenly, eyes bleary from napping. He stared at the big black, his mouth hanging open.

"Lady up yonder sent some victuals," Zack explained, leaning his rifle against the fence beside Noah's and dropping the canteens onto the grass.

Luther moved up slowly, placed pitcher and sack on the ground, then backed off to the center of the road and squatted there. Noah was still staring.

"This here's Luther," Zack said, opening the sack, lifting the pitcher. He sat beside Noah and began to eat. "Good sweet milk. Ain't had none a' that fer a long spell."

"What's he want?" Noah whispered.

"Somebody's gotta take the lady's pitcher back."

Noah reached into the sack and pulled forth a muffin and inspected it as though it might be poisoned. Then he ate, and they passed the milk back and forth, drinking from the pitcher. Luther had turned his face away from them. He looked along the road and toward the far mountains, elaborately avoiding watching them eat.

Polite son of a bitch, Zack thought. Maybe they teach 'em they ain't suppose to see a white man takin' on grub.

"How long you been on this place?" Zack asked, his cheeks bulging with muffin and the crumbs of it in his mustache.

"All mah born days," Luther said, not looking at them.

"You raise a lot a' tebacky, do you?"

"Naw sah. Not now. Mostly taters an' corn, an' da army buy mosta dat."

Noah watched the slave with quiet intensity, as a cat might watch a vicious dog. He ate quickly and drank, but his eyes never left the black man's face.

"Menfolks off with the army, you say?"

"Yas suh. Marse Benjamin, him an' Marse Bennie an' Miz Marsy mite put out wit dat, Marse Bennie goin' off an' not growed yet. Dey's up yonder somewheres wif a fine Virginny gen'man name a' Pickett."

Luther stared down at his hands hanging between his knees. He rubbed the big fingers together gently. Noah could see the pale palms and the pale fingernails.

"You gen'mans ain' from Virginny, is you?"

"No. Arkansas," Zack said. "West of the Missip."

"Lawd," Luther laughed, looking again now at the road as it wound away to the mountains. "I hear stories 'bout dem red Innians."

"We ain't got no red Indians, 'cept a few that farms like us."

"I knowed you gen'mans wasn't from Virginny, da way you talks. You gen'mans farmers?"

"Yeah. Hill farmers. No flat lan' like this."

For the first time since they'd started to eat, Luther looked at them, but only briefly, as though making a quick assessment.

"You gen'mans got lotsa niggers in dis place you come from?"

"No. We work the lan' our own selves."

"Yah, folks here ain' got so many now. Gone to cotton country."

When they finished the muffins and milk, Zack carried the empty sack and pitcher back to the middle of the road, and Luther rose to take them.

"She ain' say nuthin' 'bout brangin' back no sack," Luther said.

"Go ahead an' take it back, too. Tell your Miz Marsy we're much beholden."

Luther held the sack and pitcher in one hand and with the other lifted his hat. For a moment his eyes met Noah's, and there was the trace of a smile across his wide mouth. He turned back along the road, in no hurry, and Noah watched him go, still intently. Only after the big slave was far along toward the farmhouse did Noah lie back once more, pulling his hat over his eyes.

"Whatsa matter with you?" Zack asked. "You acted like a nervous cat with that big colored man."

"Them people set my teeth on edge."

"I never noticed you act like that aroun' Tug."

"Hell, he's jus' a sprout. That 'un there was bigger'n Uncle Questor's bay mule!"

Zack lowered his head and laughed, shaking his head.

"Besides," Noah said defensively, "he was jus' thinkin' we're some kinda white trash you hear 'bout aroun' hyar, don't own no niggers."

"Maybe you oughta buy you one."

"What's one cost?"

"Christ, I don't know."

"Well, hit don't matter. I don't like 'em aroun'. They're spooky. That one looked like he could cut a cord a' firewood without raisin' any sweat, didn't he?"

"Yeah, he's hell fer stout." Zack looked up the road where

Luther was just turning into the gate, the pitcher dangling from one hand. I wonder why they don't all run off to Yankee country, he thought.

They saw then the dust of an approaching column and realized the rest of the regiment was coming on. Zack was still grinning and shaking his head when Noah caught his eye.

"Better buy you one," Zack said. "So the others won't think you're white trash."

Noah snorted and looked toward the dust plume, and Zack knew his brother was anxious to be back in his own element, where things were a lot simpler.

IT WAS time for drill again, a lot of it, and of reshuffiing. Lee was organizing his army along corps lines, and the company found itself assigned to the Texas Brigade. They hated to end their association with the North Carolina boys who had stood with them at Sharpsburg. The Texans received them with sometimes hostile stares, but that soon passed. Before long they were at home with the new outfit, what with the geographical proximity of the two states. They exchanged lies about the size of fish and the weight of wild hogs and deer in their respective homelands. And the beauty and purity of the women.

There was a barber and Indian fighter in the Fourth Texas who called himself Burton. They never learned any of his other names. He was old, white-bearded but clear-eyed, durable as buffalo hide even at sixty. He was a fiddle player as well, and soon he and Dad Johnson with his banjo were joining at night to render "Leather Britches" and "Coon on a Log" while the others danced.

Because they were the youngest, Noah and Billy Dick always played the part of women. Long before Sharpsburg they had danced, but only to Dad's music. Then Martin Hasford had been with them, and Beverly Cass. The swarthy little rice planter had danced, too, surprising them all. He did it rather elegantly, with some disdain, but working up a sweat nonetheless, and sometimes even smiling. He taught them a fancy two-step, the lady whirled on the extended arm of the gentleman.

But now Hasford and Cass were gone, with only the Welshman and Zack to play the menfolk. Zack went at dancing as he did with singing, whole hog, his usual reserve slipping away for the moment. Noah could recall his clog step those summer evenings when the family took their recreation on the front porch at the farm, but there was even more exuberance now in Zack's stomping, though afterward he would usually retire into the darkness to chew and think alone.

At those times Noah pondered what was in his brother's mind, what images and shapes were built behind those pale, calm eyes. But he never had the courage to ask. Among Fawleys, the thoughts of the elder menfolk were private domain, never visited without invitation.

With the second winter of the war coming on, Noah had begun to look more and more on Zack as though he were of an age with Pap or Uncle Questor. Beyond the understanding of the young! And, as an elder in the tribe, inviolate in his privacy of thought.

They had their last pleasant bath of the year near the valley of the Shenandoah, the whole company marching down to a small, clear stream. They shouted obscenities back and forth, peeling off their clothes and leaving them in ranks of rumpled tatters along the bank beside the stacks of rifles. Two men were stationed as pickets, upstream and down, to warn of any approaching females.

Afterward, dripping wet and naked in the sun, they trooped back to their clothes, where Noah discovered that Pap's watch was missing.

"Gawd dammit," he whispered. Zack glanced at him, pulling on his own trousers.

"Whatsa matter?"

"Somebody stole Pap's watch!"

"You likely jus' dropped it."

"The hell I did."

They searched through the grass and weeds but found nothing. Marching back to camp, Noah glared at the troops around him, furious and tight-lipped and whispering to his messmates that the watch was stolen.

"Armies is all the same," Dad Johnson said, staring ahead along the column and little interested.

"Casualty of garrison life," the Welshman said. "We'll keep an eye out, lads. A good watch seeks the light of day sooner or later."

"I'm gonna tell Ole Jury Duty. By Gawd, we'll search the company," Noah said savagely.

"No, we won't neither," Zack said quietly. "If it's found, we'll find it, an' whoever took it won't get no thief placard hung aroun' his neck. We'll handle it our own selves."

"Garrison punishment, too," Morgan said. "The best kind. What was it you had in mind, brother Zack?"

Zack glanced at the Welshman, but there was little heat in his eyes.

"Breakin' a thumb er two might work. That's easy done."

Morgan laughed.

With fall turning toward winter, there were rumors of the Army of the Potomac moving again, and they began to line out on the roads from the valley of the Shenandoah to the fords of the Rappahannock.

They chose to sing new songs. Never "The Black-Eyed Suzie." They remembered Dinsmore and what a worthless son of a bitch he had been, and they remembered his tune by pretending they had forgotten it. Mostly now it was "Buffalo Gals" with as many ribald verses as the old "Suzie" boasted. But now their singing was not the joyful thing it had been before, rather a required exercise of toughness, with the harsh memories of the Antietam showing through. After Sharpsburg, they would never do anything quite the same again, even to looking at one another.

At Fredericksburg they sat on their weapons and listened to the battle, in reserve and grousing that they were not in this one. Especially this one, where the Federals were coming across open fields against strong defensive positions and being massacred in rows.

Afterward, in the night, they watched in awe as the blazing aurora borealis lit the northern sky. Some said it was a good omen, others said it was bad. Billy Dick Hysel, after his first look at the flaming blue lights wavering along the horizon, turned his head away and would not look again for fear of being cursed.

Later, in daylight, when they saw the slaughter pen along Marye's Heights, they marveled at the strength of the Confederate position. For they looked at ground now not as planters and harvesters but as infantrymen whose eyes picked out cover and defilade and fields of fire without even being aware they were doing it.

Soon, while the army squatted along the Rappahannock around Fredericksburg and Spotsylvania and Chancellor, the cold December rains began.

Noah Fawley, standing his turn as camp guard in the freezing drizzle, recalled those wet nights in the mountains when they had been with Ole Jackson. A long time past, it seemed. And him a raw recruit, eager to do all the unpleasant things.

But not so raw now, and grousing at each call of his name from the duty roster, as was expected of a veteran. And it was a veteran he felt himself to be, for he could strut with the best of them now and show his Sharpsburg wound—even though it hadn't been bad enough to get him evacuated.

He was aware of Zack watching him sometimes—quietly, calmly, chewing his cud with a thinking that was impossible for Noah to fathom.

He's sure doin' a pride a' studyin' on me, Noah thought. More'n jus' watchin' out fer me like Pap an' Mama said to do.

When his eyes caught Zack's at such times, Zack would blink and slowly look away like a mournful old hound caught stealing eggs from the chicken coop.

"Somethin' the matter?" Noah would ask.

"Nothin' I know of." And Zack would blink slowly, keeping his eyes turned away.

It appeared to Noah that his brother was somehow smaller now. Even frail, with an Adam's apple so prominent it looked painful when he swallowed. And a sadness in the eyes sometimes, just like Pap's had been when they laid Granma Fawley in the ground.

It came to Noah finally and with a bit of shock that Zack was likely pretty much the same as he had been when they left the Ozarks. Only his own perception had changed. And so he passed it off as his coming to manhood, almost nineteen years old.

He thought less of Luanne Lacy now. Before, the face appeared in his thinking unexpectedly, unbidden. But now he could think of her if it pleased him and shut her out if it didn't. Only sometimes dreams of her came so vividly they were actually physical, and he would waken in the morning all atremble, hollow-eyed.

And it would be Zack's time to ask, "Somethin' the matter?"

"Nothin' I know of," Noah would say, avoiding Zack's eyes, for now homesickness seemed a weakness to him, to be controlled or kept hidden.

They built huts with scraps of tenting and scab lumber and trees cut from the surrounding countryside, even though they were not supposed to take timber from private property on threat of court-martial. They used mud bricks and sticks and old empty barrels for chimney flues, and then wondered where they would get the wood to burn when real winter came.

The lucky few who had taken Yankee shoes at Harper's Ferry were still well shod, but for most of them there were blanket wrappings to reinforce rotten leather, or raw cowhide distributed by the commissary department, which they stitched together as best they could. Billy Dick Hysel had a pair of these homemades, and they stretched out in front of him like barrel staves, almost as long as he was tall.

But now at least they were no longer harried by the thought of serving under Jackson again. They were a part of Longstreet's First Corps.

"Ole Pete," the Texans told them. "He ain't such a wild man as that damned Presbyterian!"

The food started running low before Christmas. Once, when they were on detail at the end of the rattletrap railroad line that ran up to their positions from Richmond, they saw the meager stacks of supplies. They looked at one another silently, questions in their eyes, knowing then without being told that Lee was scrambling to keep his army from starving.

Sometimes there were breaks in the growing winter weather when the rain stopped, and at night the stars came out clear and it was warm. It was on a night like this that they heard the music from across the river. They moved down along the banks, sat in rows far back up the slopes, and listened to the Union band playing on the far shore.

At first there were only the Yankee tunes, and after each a lusty cheer from the east bank while the grayjackets hissed. But then a single shout came from the west bank: "Play some of ours!" The band struck "Dixie Land." Now the cheering and hissing reversed, and still again when the band played other Southern favorites.

Zack and Noah sat enraptured by it—the best they had ever heard. The Confederates had bands, too, but they were usually ragtag, famous for loudness but not too much on quality.

"A queer breed over yonder," Zack mused. "We shoot hell outa one another fer a while, an' then they play us tunes fer a while."

Moving among his men was the tall figure of Ole Jury Duty, the company commander now, complete with stovepipe hat and Mexican War saber. He was puffing a short stogie, its gleam before his face like a red-hot nailhead, reflecting in his furious eyes.

Other officers had come, too, some from the general staff of the First Corps, but if Ole Pete Longstreet was there, nobody saw him. Rumor had it that some of the officers—likely cavalrymen, they said—had brought ladies out in buggies to hear the concert.

"Damned horse soldiers! They don't take many volleys," Noah grumbled, "but they get all the jularkies."

Liverpool Morgan appeared, breathing hard, and with

some urgency asked them to come with him. They rose and moved out of the crowd of troops, stumbling in the darkness. They followed the Welshman along the slope until the music was only faintly heard behind them, and then cut down across the fields and into a woodline near the bank of the river.

"Who's there?" someone challenged from the riverbank, and they saw the dim outline of Dad Johnson's face and the rifle in his hands. "Oh, that you, Welsh?"

"Any more from the Yanks?" Morgan whispered.

"Nary a sound since you left a while ago."

"Come on, then."

They moved to the river, where Johnson was supposed to be on picket duty along with Billy Dick Hysel, who was farther upstream, somewhere in the timber.

"All right, let's have all your tobacco," Morgan said.

"What the hell's goin' on here?" Zack asked.

"A bit of common enterprise is it," Morgan said. "Give me your tobacco."

Zack handed him a plug. If there was a single commodity this army had in plenty, it was tobacco.

"Now then, who's for the swim with me?"

"The what?"

"The swim. Need two, to carry this stuff and keep it dry."

Noah could see now that the Welshman had two large bundles of tobacco wrapped in handkerchiefs—collected, he supposed, from various members of the company.

"I gotta stay on this picket," Johnson said. "Ole Jury Duty's got a habit a' comin' 'round, an' I ain't lookin' fer one a' them punishments he likes to pass out."

"Either of you two swim?"

"Wait a minute hyar," Noah said, beginning to realize what was happening. "You aim to swim that river?"

"Across and back," Morgan said. "The current's like a baby's breath."

"Fer Gawd's sake! What's the matter with you?" Noah said, exasperated. "They's Yanks over yonder. You fixin' to get your head shot off?"

"Nothing of the sort. It's a mutual enterprise."

"But . . ."

"I reckon I can swim 'er," Zack said.

"Fer Gawd's sake. You tradin' with the Yankees?"

"Not so loud, little brother. You'll have one of our own provost guards down on us."

"Well, by damn, I ain't tradin' with no Yankees. I never come to Virginny to trade with no Gawd damn—"

"All right," Zack cut in. "Quit makin' so much fuss."

He was on the ground, taking off his shoes. Morgan had begun to undress, down to long-handled underwear, ragged at the knees and elbows, and with no seat at all.

"We're gettin' away from hyar," Noah whispered. "Come on, Zack, we're gettin' away from hyar."

"No, we ain't," Zack said, rising now and peeling off his jacket and trousers. "That water cold?"

"Warm as Molly's milk," the Welshman said, grinning.

Noah watched speechless and astonished as the two figures moved down the bank and slipped into the black water, each a pale outline in his underwear and carrying a bundle stuffed with tobacco. From downstream, they could hear the Union band, still playing.

"Damnation," Noah heard Zack whisper as the water came up to his crotch, and then there was only the soft sound of ripples, like two dogs paddling through the stream.

Dad Johnson leaned against a tree, Noah beside him. They stared into the night, toward the far shore, each of them breathing heavily. Zack and Morgan had disappeared within a few feet of the bank.

"Gawd, Zack ain't never swum anythin' as wide as this hyar."

From somewhere out in the river, Noah heard a low whistle, then a muffled shout.

"Yank, we got your tobacco." Morgan's voice. And from the far shore, an answering whistle.

"Gawd!" Noah whispered. "That damned Welshman's addled. An' my brother ain't much better."

The music downstream had stopped now, and they could hear the soldiers moving back to their camps, shouting and laughing. Some of it came very close to them, moving along the edge of the woods. Noah felt his heart thumping. Then Dad Johnson grabbed his arm.

"Somebody comin'," he hissed.

Noah stood rooted, staring into the trees along the river. Then he saw the tall figure, coming directly toward them. He jumped when Johnson made his challenge.

"Halt! Who's yonder?"

"Friend." Noah recognized Ole Jury Duty's voice.

"Oh, that you, Lieutenant?" Johnson said, lowering his rifle.

"God dammit, you're supposed to ask for the password and then give me the countersign," Scaggs said furiously, moving in quickly.

"I seen it was you, Lieutenant."

"God dammit, can't you people ever learn how you're supposed to—"

He stopped short and stood a few feet away, bending forward, his eyes bulging and white.

"Who's that?"

"Noy Fawley, Lieutenant," Noah said.

"What're you doing down here? You're not on duty here."

"I was jus' visitin' a spell."

"Well, get the hell on back to camp where you belong. You're not supposed to be visitin' with men on picket duty!"

Noah moved back into the woods, well out of their sight, and squatted, thinking about what would happen if Ole Jury Duty caught Zack out in that river. Firing squad, likely. Jesus Gawd!

He heard them talking in low tones, and finally the sound of Ole Jury Duty's feet scuffing through the leaves, moving upstream toward Billy Dick's post. Noah tried to keep his own breathing from making enough noise to attract the whole First Corps. He waited a long time, and then slipped back down to the riverbank.

"I figured that son of a bitch would be along," Dad Johnson whispered.

"What'd he say?"

"Said it was a nice evenin'."

"You see anything yet?" Noah asked. "Out there?"

"Hell no, boy. This is gonna take a spell."

Noah shivered. The night was suddenly cold, but he could feel sweat along his back. The water lapped gently along the bank, and now and again he started when there was a loud ripple or splash. He wasn't accustomed to the sounds of this river, so unlike the Buffalo, where he had fished and gigged frogs and set trotlines. This was a very quiet river compared to the fast-flowing streams Noah knew, and its silence magnified the sounds that came from around it.

A crescent moon had appeared by the time Noah heard the ripples, like critters swimming silently. He strained his eyes into the darkness, and then he saw their heads, like black logs, and each of them with one hand holding a bundle above the water. Zack was on the bank first, gasping and dripping and holding out a large tin box. Morgan came out, still grinning, shivering.

"Back to the hut is it," he said. "Cold! For a fire, us."

"What'd you get?" Dad Johnson asked.

"I don't know. But we'll save a share for you and Billy Dick."

They pulled on clothes over the wet underwear and started through the woods, bending to take up what firewood they could find on the way. At the hut they opened the prizes in the light of a small blaze in the fireplace, the Welshman laughing all the while.

They had a tin of figs, another of Yankee army bread, a third of coffee—"Gawd damn, coffee!"—and a slab of cured bacon.

For the next three nights, Zack and the Welshman went back to the river, but each time Noah remained in the hut, pacing, cursing. Then on the fourth night it snowed.

But Morgan continued to disappear each night, alone now, going absent without leave from afternoon drill until morning muster. He would arrive just in time to stand in line—eyes puffy in the gray dawn, suffering from want of sleep, keeping his own counsel.

They knew he was not swimming the river now—too cold, and suddenly become dangerous, Yankee pickets potshooting swimmers on the way over, butternuts equally prone to shooting on the way back. Besides, he brought no delicacies to bolster the fatback and rice diet, so they knew he was not trading with the blues.

Only the bleary eyes and the silence, and sleeping during the day when the opportunity permitted, even when there was a good card game going. Then gone again in the night.

It lasted for two weeks, and then was finished on the night after the provost guards found two women in one of the Mississippi regiments—or maybe it was an Alabama regiment; nobody was sure which. They were wearing soldiers' clothes and carrying rifles and, more astonishing still, were veterans of the battle of Sharpsburg. Taking visitors now in their mess group hut at a dollar a whack.

Noah made no connection between apprehension of the whores and Morgan's sudden attendance to normal nightly slumber in the squad's canvas-and-mud winter home, but Dad Johnson and Zack did. They said nothing to Noah or to the Welshman, but Dad Johnson had his own remark for Zack's ears.

"Now don't you know them was two sweet and gentle ladies? By Gawd, a sojur in rut will mount anything. An' a sojur's always in rut, ain't he?"

"I reckon," Zack said.

THE RIVERS all flowed toward the east and the oyster waters of Chesapeake Bay, moving swiftly above the fall line, but slowing after tidewater, hesitant like a recoiling groom before the wedding of fresh water and salt. They had been there a long time.

Potomac, Rappahannock, York, and James—English names, Indian names, each making its place in the history of the continent and in the markings of maps, each fished and navigated and used for commerce and war by red and white and black.

On opposite banks of the Rappahannock River now, the blue and the butternut watched one another and the water where the Powhatan had fished, equidistant between Washington City on the one hand and Richmond on the other. The hills were white, with bare-branched trees like naked gray sentinels standing rigidly along the slopes.

In the Southern army they were writing letters that winter. They received few in return, so few that sometimes when one came it was passed around among comrades so all would have something to read from home. And when there were hints of tenderness written there, ribald jokes were shouted about sweeties—jularkies—and sometimes minor fistfights broke out.

And they were playing cards until the pasteboards were limp and fragile like wet leaves, the faded index almost impossible to read in the meager light of hutment fires—poker, and when there was no money, euchre, and then back to bluff again, playing for percussion caps.

Finally, the butternut army seemed to get religion *en masse*, and the smallpox came!

THERE were long, dismal afternoons in the gray snow, well back from the army encampments, burying the dead. Not gunshot dead, but taken by the pox because there was not enough vaccine to immunize them all.

After the burials each day they tramped back to the clearings where logs were used as benches for the open-air religious services. Chaplains and pastors from civilian churches appeared before them and thumped the Bible for two hours as the troops sat shivering, led in hymns of praise for the Lord and in prayers of contrition for their sins. Then it was back to drill, always hungry, and next day again the burial details, planting hundreds of their comrades in that soil, knowing there were thousands waiting in the camps for a break in their fever or else the end.

They carried Dad Johnson to the hospital just before New Year's Day, hot to the touch and with skin splotched, and swearing mightily every step of the way. Within the week, Burton, the Fourth Texas barber and Indian fighter, came to their hutment and said he had been on the detail that buried Dad Johnson somewhere in the windswept snowfields near Spotsylvania.

"He never left much," Burton said, "jus' that ole banjo in the corner there, I reckon, an' this stuff."

He poured out the contents of a small leather pouch onto the hutment floor. There was a single coin, a banjo pick, a finely whittled oak toothpick, a crumpled letter with brown ink long ago faded with wetting until it was illegible. And Pap's gold watch!

They squatted around the pitiful pile of loot, staring at the watch, until finally Zack lifted it and snapped it open.

"I expect he forgot to wind it," he said. "It's stopped."

Noah was thinking, That son of a bitch played banjo so good, too. He could work up no outrage, even though he tried.

"Here, take it," Zack said.

The watch might have been a hot coal, Noah took it so gingerly, then with a sudden jerk he closed the cover and shoved it into his pocket, out of sight.

"Why, that ole man," Billy Dick said, "he done—"

"All right, lad," Morgan cut him off.

Burton looked around at the silent faces, perplexed at this last reaction, then deciding it was because of their loss. He sighed in sympathy.

"Well, by Gawd," he said, "I'll cut you boys' hair. Allus helps a man's disposition to get his hair cut and the lice combed out for a change. I brang my scissors."

And later, when they were alone, Noah said to Zack, "Damnation! Tryin' to get rid a' lice jus' stirs 'em up."

He scratched violently at his flanks like an old dog in the sun.

"This is the scratchin'est army I ever seen."

Zack laughed suddenly, a real laugh, and Noah took it to mean that his brother was in a grand mood, which came on less and less since Sharpsburg.

"How many armies you got to compare?" Zack asked.

"By Gawd, they can't be no more scratchin' than we do," Noah said, smiling because he no longer flared his hot temper at Zack's banter. "Mama'd have a conniption fit if she knowed how many varmints we got crawlin' on us."

As his fingers moved along his sides, Noah felt the shape of the watch in his pocket.

"Why you reckon Ole Dad took Pap's watch?"

Zack's expression went blank, his face turning away, the laughter abruptly gone. He made no reply.

"I guess it's better we never found it out before," said Noah, thinking of what Zack had said about breaking thumbs.

But still Zack was coldly silent, and Noah took up his scratching again, embarrassed and sorry he had broken Zack's good mood. And embarrassed for that old man who had stood beside him along the Hagerstown Pike and then turned thief. In armies, he thought, there's always somethin' new to be learned!

# TEN

ON THE third day of the New Year, Beverly Cass and Martin Hasford came back. The others saw them coming, two gray figures moving slowly along the lines of huts, hospital blankets held around their shoulders. Billy Dick was the first.

"Damnation, boys," he cried. "Lookee there. That's Mr. Cass, sure as hell. An' the ole parson!"

"Sure as hell it is, lad," the Welshman said, waving his cap. "You've got the eyes of an eagle!"

There was shouting and back-slapping and laughter, Cass taking it with his usual lack of emotion. But it had its effect on Martin Hasford. He wiped at his eyes with his hard, blunt farmer's fingers, shook his head, and smiled. They had arrived in time for evening muster, and Ole Jury Duty came around to make a point of welcome.

"We'll issue you some weapons," he said. "And henceforth don't clutter up my formation with them blankets. You look like scarecrows flapping in the wind."

As the ranks broke and the men started for their hutments, Noah drew Hasford aside and spoke to him softly.

"I got your Book in my bedroll," he said. "I picked 'er up when they taken you off that day. I been savin' 'er fer when you come back."

"How'd you know I was coming back, son?" Hasford asked, his voice husky.

"I never knowed, but I hoped."

Hasford touched Noah on the shoulder briefly, then withdrew his hand as though flustered with such a show of affection. He turned aside and blew his nose with his fingers.

"I even read a few Scriptures out of 'er," Noah said. "I foun' some a' them verses Mama used to read."

"You can read it anytime you want."

"I ain't too good at it. I reckon I've done enough to last me fer a spell."

"Where's the latrine?" Hasford asked.

"Over yonder, beyond that line a' huts."

Later, when he came into the hut, Martin's eyes were dry, and he sat with Bev Cass and they recounted their stories of hospital life and showed their scars. Billy Dick Hysel agreed with everything they said, nodding emphatically with each statement, his eyes glassy with importance.

"See?" he said, as though none of them had ever believed his own tales of horror. "I tole you how them horspittles was."

"We heard the pox has carried off a lot of men," Bev Cass said.

"Like flies, in some regiments," Morgan said. "Only a few from our company so far. Most of them the new recruits they sent up from Richmond and from home."

"Recruits from home?"

"A few in last week," Zack said. "The pox taken off some a' the old ones, too. Dad Johnson."

Cass looked around the hut at each face in turn, and nodded.

"I knew it wasn't the same. I couldn't put my finger on it. I'll have to write his old lady."

"They told us there isn't enough medicine to vaccinate the whole army," Hasford said. "But they did it to us at the hospital."

Cass slipped off his jacket and rolled up his left sleeve. They all bent forward to look at the ugly scab on his biceps, black and with harsh red edges. Cass fingered it gently.

"In a few days now, when this thing's ready to come off, I'll vaccinate all of you."

While the others brought Cass and Hasford up to date on what had been happening in their absence, Zack slipped out through the canvas hanging door. He was back in less than an hour with a quart bottle.

"Ole Sidney's nephew," he explained. "It taken a few bloody threats."

They passed the bottle around, each taking his sip—Billy Dick gagging on his—and then once again around the circle.

"You boys built a nice little place here," Hasford said.

"It keeps out most a' the wind," Noah said. They passed the bottle again.

"Clear whisky is more to my taste," Zack said.

"But whisky of any kind, a bright light in a dismal world, next only to a warm woman," said Morgan. He and Zack glanced at one another, both remembering the two whores who had been discovered in the Mississippi regiment—or Alabama or whatever.

"You're the judge on that," Zack said, and Morgan laughed.

The bottle was empty before midnight, by which time they were all a little drunk. Except Billy Dick, who was unconscious despite a recent trip to the company street to be sick in the snow.

The days went down and Beverly Cass finally pulled the smallpox scab off his arm.

Noah and Zack were not overjoyed at the prospect of a homemade vaccination, but with Morgan's assurance they submitted to it. Cass used the point of Morgan's bowie knife to scratch a small wound in their arms, implanting it with residue from the scab. Billy Dick bit his lip and tears came, but the sight of it was worse than the hurt. They went to their blankets that night already feeling the soreness, and Billy Dick expected to die before morning.

All of them developed fevers, but not enough to keep them out of ranks. But at each morning muster, Noah's legs seemed to grow weaker, and finally Ole Jury Duty came over to peer closely into his face.

"Boy, you look peaked."

"I feel peaked."

"Well, it'll be all right soon. Go take a day at bed rest," Ole Jury Duty said harshly. "I don't want you falling down and making a God damned spectacle of my formation."

That night in the hut, with Zack mending clothing and

Billy Dick already sleeping, and Martin Hasford off with the Welshman attending one of the revival meetings, Noah settled himself beside his brother.

"I think we oughta write a letter to the folks," he said.

Zack frowned over his needlework, putting rough stitches in his jacket sleeves at the shoulder, in hopes the repairs would hold the thing together.

"That's fine," he said.

"I feel like we ought. A man never knows iffen he'll get another chance."

Zack looked at him then, some question, some amusement in his eyes.

"What's all the hellfire need now?" Zack asked. "The parson wrote one fer us las' summer. An' another one before that."

"They wasn't much. Maybe Pap an' Mama'd like one from our own han'. An' a man never knows when he'll get another chance."

Gawd, this boy's growed, Zack thought. Almost as big as Uncle Questor an' mind to match, settin' things straight an' in order. An' Pap sent me to look out fer him.

Somehow it gave him a little pinch of pride and sudden fear that some stray Yankee metal or some unheard-of ailment could take this brother off, and nothing left to show he had ever been except for a few trinkets like they had seen from Dad Johnson's pockets.

An' how the hell would I be able to go home and face Pap then?

Well, Pap's two dollars is long ago spent, no matter good intentions. An' the bar a' soap gone, too. This hyar has turned into more than a two-dollar, one-bar-a'-soap war.

"That little scratch Cass put on your arm got the fright in you, didn't it?"

"I lay hyar all day thinkin' 'bout it, an' I got to figurin' a man never knows."

"Little scratch on the arm bothers you more'n Yankee shot, does it?"

"I reckon. I got to thinkin' 'bout Ole Dad Johnson."

"All right. You write 'er then."

Zack looked across the firelight to Cass. Cass was watching them, his face immobile. Without saying anything he rummaged through his duffle and came up with a few sheets of what had once been wallpaper, and passed it across to Noah, along with a quill pen and a small bottle of pokeberry ink.

"They carry letters to Richmond on them supply trains, don't they?" Noah asked.

"Yes," Cass said. "No telling if it'll get any farther. But it's a start."

Noah arranged a sheet of the paper on the head of Billy Dick's drum. He frowned, holding the pen awkwardly and licking his lips, blinking. "I ain't very good with one a' these things," he said. "What you want me to write?"

"She's your letter. You write 'er."

With the drum held between his crossed legs, Noah's face worked in deep concentration as he wrote:

> Deer Pap and Mama and all hear we be still in ole virginy we hav bin in sum fites and a big battle and me and zack is all rite a big battle is not like somethin you ever saw befor but we tie into it with delite to give the yankees a good whuppin they dont fede this armie enuff to keep a smal dog from starvin the meat is mostly hog and old enuff to lived in the bible befor it was kilt the sojurs have the flux lots of times and now we got the pox but me and zack has bin vasinated by a real smart man named cass he is from south arkansaw and owns some niggers but seems real nice tell all the boys not to bother comin into the armie the fites and battles are alrite but all the drill and pigit duty and bad grub is not worth it in fites and big battles men get tore up real bad but each one figurs it aint gone to happen to him if you see luanne lacy say me and zack is all right your son noah fawley

Noah studied his work, reading it over with his lips moving. When he looked up, Zack was watching him.

"You wanta write somethin'?" Noah asked.

"No."

"You wanta read what I wrote down?"

"No."

"You wanta put your name on it?"

"No."

"Well, I tell you, writin' letters is more work than diggin' straddle trenches," Noah said with a sigh.

Cass had sealing wax, and they folded the letter with the bright flowered pattern of the wallpaper on the outside, and Noah boldly wrote across the pink and yellow roses an address that he hoped would take it finally to the valley of the Buffalo.

IT CAME to be called the Great Snowball Campaign. It was the best thing that happened to them all winter on those slopes above the Rappahannock.

From the first snowfall, white missiles could be seen flying about the camps. At first it was haphazard, no real plan or design to it. A great deal was done from ambush. Ole Jury Duty had his stovepipe hat knocked off by some hidden marksman, and after a respectable display of his best battlefield vocabulary to all in hearing—a considerable distance—the company commander composed himself and regained his dignity long enough to order a ban on snowballing. The order was promptly ignored. Soon the small fights spread into larger, more ambitious affairs.

"As is the nature of all wars," said Cass.

Regiments became engaged against one another, and sometimes even brigades. The more forceful privates organized these battles, but it took only a short while for the noncommissioned officers to appreciate what fun they were missing and take over themselves.

"As is the nature of all noncommissioned officers," the Welshman said.

Commissioned officers watched from a distance, though not too far to avoid being splattered from time to time.

The challenge to the Third Arkansas came in the form of a note carried by Martin Hasford on his return one evening from a religious meeting. The thrown gauntlet was passed up the line to the regimental sergeant major, who conspired with his counterparts in the brigade's other regiments for the coming fray.

The enemy in this case was a brigade of Jackson's Second Corps, an enemy they hoped would be led by Old Blue Light himself. They knew that was wishful thinking, but getting a whack at some of Jackson's men was the next best thing—almost as good as getting a whack at the Yankees.

"They say them boys from Louisiana are real scissorbills," Noah said.

"I hear they're almost as foreign as the Yankees," Billy Dick put in.

"And a few Irish amongst them," the Black Welshman laughed. "A good lick at the Irish is better than kisses."

There was a small stream that ran across the countryside between the two corps encampments, and here some trees were left standing with cleared ground between for maneuvering. The challenge had identified this as the battleground, devil take the hindmost, throwing to start immediately after the religious services on the following Sunday.

"Working on the Lord's day is not to my liking," Martin Hasford said, but then his face brightened. "But fighting is all right. Even Ole Jack himself does it."

The sun was out that day, after almost a week of drab skies. They thought it a good omen and sat through sermon and hymn-singing impatiently. When the last Amen was intoned, they formed ranks with the Fourth and Fifth Texas and a few men from the 18th Georgia—also of the Texas Brigade—and marched to the field of encounter.

There across the small creek and along a woodline stood the enemy, in ranks like the Army of the Potomac, yelling insults, taunting. Aware of the reputation of his brigade, the sergeant major of the Fourth Texas—acting as brigade commander—ordered a charge. The yell went up and their own lines advanced. The high, keening notes were bloodcurdling. Soon they were in range of the enemy and began to take a few peltings from well-packed snowballs.

Noah, in the forefront, took a solid smash in the forehead from a missile the size of a horse apple and as hard as solid shot. It knocked him down and raised a welt on his eyebrow.

"Them sons a' bitches is throwin' ice," he exclaimed, leaping up to rejoin the advancing line.

One of the Louisiana regiments was suddenly in peril, its colors threatened. The Texas Brigade charged in, screaming, some going to ground with the enemy, shoving snow in their faces.

And then with victory in their grasp, they were hit on the open flank by a fresh, unused regiment, lying hidden to this moment. The Louisiana troops were well prepared, dragging blankets behind them piled with snowballs, ready-made and ice-hard.

It was too much, and the Texas Brigade fell back, followed now by the well-armed enemy, belted repeatedly across backs and butts, and only a few able to scoop snow for return fire.

Back among the huts they could hear the victor's shout, insulting, controlling the field. Their fingers were blue. Zack's nose was bleeding. Hasford was amazed, panting and a little ashamed that once more in the heat of the fight he had uttered vile phrases better suited to Ole Jury Duty's mouth than his own.

They went to their huts, speaking little, beaten and knowing it. They squatted down around the fireplace in the dim light, no fire, their breath making heavy vapor in the cold air.

"They was throwin' ice," Noah said bitterly.

"Outmaneuvered we were," said Morgan. "A green lot, us, at this snowballing."

"Well, we can fix the ammunition part of it," Hasford said.

He led them outside, and they began making snowballs, allowing them to melt a little in the sun, then dragging them into the shade to freeze—and overnight as well, a heap of missiles like white cannon balls growing beside each hut, turning to ice.

The Texas Brigade hungered for revenge. They expected the Louisianans to be back the next day, after Monday-afternoon drill, and they were right. Now it had clouded over again, and the field was in gray shadow under the trees where the lines of Jackson's people waited.

They charged, but this time held their fire, dragging their sleds of snowballs behind. The fury of it when they came in range was almost lethal. The ice balls brought blood on bare skin.

The same flanking movement came against them, but this time the First Texas had joined their fight, too, and struck hard against the flank of the flankers. It was a screaming, milling melee, a madhouse.

Noah was stooping for another ball when he was struck, his hat flying once again. He whirled, and there before him was a large man, larger than that riverboat brawler he had met at Clarksville. The man was grinning, his teeth showing through a tangle of orange beard, and in one hand he held Noah's hat.

Why the hell is somebody always after my hat, he thought.

"Gotcha hat, Arkansas."

"Gimme that," Noah bellowed, lunging forward. Orange Beard laughed and pushed Noah back. "Gimme that damned hat!"

"Hold on," the man roared, and those around him stopped, watching, grinning, snowballs in their hands. "Here's an Arkansas who wants a tussle."

"I want my hat," Noah said. He swung and missed, the big man moving away easily.

All along both lines, men were watching. Above them on a nearby ridge were a number of mounted officers.

"No tussle in the sight of the mighty," the big man said. "But you come here tonight, Arkansas, and you can have your hat if it's a tussle you want and can win it."

Another of the Louisiana soldiers was moving over now, also grinning.

"A tussle you'll get, lad, with hisself Chauncy Ryan, Pugilist, on this spot in the dark of evenin'."

Noah started forward again, his temper flaring hot, but Zack had him then, and pulled him back.

"Leave this one be," Zack said. "You always pick the biggest one you can find, don't you?"

"I never done nothin'," Noah raged.

"You're gonna hafta sew that damned hat on your head. What's the matter with you?"

"I want it back, Gawd dammit."

"He'll break your jaw for you," Zack said, pushing Noah back toward the stream. "You come on now. Remember what Pap told you. Mind your elders!"

Most of the brigade was backing off then, all the fun gone out of it. They moved across the stream where their advance had broken the ice, and the water was cold through their rotten shoes.

"Son of a bitch," Noah said, almost in tears.

But Zack had him in hand now, and they moved back into the hutment area and waited for the others. Noah fumed as they came up, kicking at the snow.

"Damn!" Martin Hasford said. "Beat again."

"Well, I'm goin' back fer that hat tonight," Noah said. "An' I'm takin' a gun."

"No, you ain't takin' no gun," Zack said. "You caint go shootin' none of our own people."

"Well, by Gawd, I'm goin' back!"

"You're too bullheaded to talk out of it," Zack said. "But you ain't gonna tie into that big Irish fella. You heard what the man said. Pugilist. He'll break your face for you."

"Right Zack is, little brother," Morgan said. "Diplomacy, that's what gets the hat back."

"Well, by Gawd, I'll have it one way or the other."

Like all butternuts, Noah might go without shoes or overcoat, but never without his hat. Every one of them understood that. Taking a man's hat was as much an insult as telling bad tales about his sister.

The clouds broke up that evening, and there was a new moon. It was bright as day in the clearing beside the stream, the cold blue light shimmering across the snow. Only the woods were shadowed.

They were supposed to be in their beds. But they were there, the regiment hunkered in a long line on their own side of the creek and the men from Louisiana facing them across the clearing.

They waited a long time, and then a dark figure emerged from the far trees. He moved square into the clearing between the lines of troops, and the moonlight showed Noah's hat in his hand. Near the stream, he bent and gently placed the hat on the snow, patted it, and stepped back. Immediately a cheer came from the Louisianans.

"And now, ladies and gentlemen," he yelled, and there was another roar from the bayou soldiers, "we congregate here for a contest of skill and stamina, not to mention quickness of eye and hand, between the man in that Arkansas outfit without any hat"—a great cheering now—"and our own champion, the right honorable Chauncy Ryan, Pugilist. May the best man win."

The Arkansas line was deadly quiet. They had seen this Ryan, and there was little to cheer about. Now they saw him again, coming from the dark woods and peeling off his jacket. He walked to the hat lying in the snow and stopped, his head back and laughing.

"All right, then," Noah said and started to rise. But there was suddenly a massive hand on his shoulders, and Morgan was whispering in his ear.

"Not for you this time, little brother. It's me, for the diplomacy."

Noah tried to pull clear, but Zack had him, too, from the other side.

"Do what he says. Stay still."

"Gawd dammit . . ."

"Do what he says!"

The Black Welshman moved out into the clearing, dropping his jacket and the little river cap. As he approached the Irishman, he seemed dwarfed by the size of the pugilist. Morgan gave a slight bow, making a leg.

"So, Irish is it?" he said loud enough for all to hear, now

that the Louisianans had stopped cheering. "Irish! Who sleep with pigs because they can't tell the swine from their own women."

Noah saw Ryan stiffen, his eyes bulging, the grin fading from his face. But then the Irishman laughed, and suddenly swung a hard right. Morgan moved back only a few inches, but the blow missed. They circled, Ryan's fists up, Morgan's still at his sides.

Ryan stepped close and swung again. Morgan ducked, his own hands coming up now, circling in the snow, shuffling. The pugilist stepped forward and missed with his right hand once more, and Noah could not believe what he was seeing, even as the blows fell.

The Black Welshman struck first with a quick, straight left hand, then an overhand right, and finally a hooking left. Three moist sounds, one, two, three, like a meat cleaver driven into a raw ham, *chunk*, *chunk*, *chunk*! And Ryan, Pugilist, collapsed like an empty sack, slowly, agonizingly unfolding to lie spreadeagled, face up, eyes glassy bright in the moonlight, and moved no more.

In the complete silence they could hear Morgan's shoes in the snow as he moved to Noah's hat, bent to take it with one quick movement, then crossed the stream for his own cap and jacket. He came to their lines without apparent haste.

"Out of here now, and fast," he said softly.

The regiment moved, backing away from the silent host in the trees beyond the stream, and still the dark sprawl of the pugilist like a great crow shotgunned in the snow.

"By Gawd," said Zack, "that Irishman mighta been better off iffen you had brought a gun, Noy!"

It was the last challenge to a snow fight they ever had from any of the units in the Second Corps.

LYING in the darkness of the hut that night after both the fire and the talk of the fight had died out, Beverly Cass considered the contradiction of soldiers.

Here we are, a group of men, planters and farmers and merchants and buggy-whip salesmen, trained to fighting. Trained to the most earnest contest of all against a deadly enemy. And when there is no enemy to fight, what do we do? We arrange to fight one another!

All of us children again, he thought. Making games. An exact copy of the thing that was no game at all, except that snowballs flew instead of metal.

Maybe that's why the young are so good at war, the old ones not. Because the young, in addition to being strong, can play that game with an exuberance lost on those of greater years.

I'm a young man by most standards. Not yet thirty. But perhaps too old for this. Too old to capture the excitement of the contest, of games long past.

Even so, there was an excitement in it if only to a degree, this snowballing. Maybe only because the deadliness was missing.

But that thought disturbed him, and he wondered, Maybe that's only for me, because in some of these others sleeping in this very hutment it seems that stimulation increases as the deadliness does.

Is that a weakness in heritage, or simply a sign of advancing years? Less than thirty, yet I have done man's work from the time I was a boy, who should have been enjoying the games. Maybe that has put the gray hairs in my spirit.

He could hear the wind coming up, battering against the walls, sweeping under the canvas door. He pulled his shelter half tightly around him, but still it was cold. From the darkness he could hear the heavy breathing of the others, each of them so much a part of him now, yet he himself still strangely apart.

Well, there was a kind of brutal beauty in that Welshman's diplomacy!

THEY were growing lank on scant rations these early months of 1863—becoming almost accustomed to being hungry when they went to bed, hungry each morning, hungry in midday. And blaming it all on the government at Richmond, never on Bobby Lee.

" 'Member that Harper's Ferry ham?" Noah asked. "I wonder whatever happened to it?"

There was talk throughout the encampment of the document President Lincoln had issued on New Year's Day, proclaiming slaves freed in states in rebellion.

"What about the slave states not in rebellion?" Cass asked bitterly. "What about Maryland and Delaware and the others?"

After carping briefly that the proclamation was only a thing to keep England and France out of the war, they went back to more serious concerns—staying warm and fed.

They wintered without overcoats and with only tattered blankets. Toward the end of February a few new shoes were issued, and Billy Dick Hysel discarded his homemades. Yankee trousers captured at Harper's Ferry and Manassas Junction the year before were issued, too, along with a few coats, which were promptly sheared off at the waist because by now they had become proud of the name "grayjacket" and wanted to keep it that way, even though by spring much of the army would be clothed in Union blue.

More appalling to them than their own misfortunes was the condition of the army's animals. All of them had worked with horses, and when the gaunt artillery animals paraded past them, they watched silently, with anger and dismay, seeing old comrades gone to skin and bone but still required to do heavy pulling.

But through it all they still felt themselves lucky. Of the original eight, six still remained. It was better than any other mess group in the company, perhaps even in the regiment. And before the snow had begun to melt from the hills around Fredericksburg, their number was increased by yet another.

It was evening, and they were sitting in their hutment around the small fire. Billy Dick was exclaiming about the flocks of cardinals he had seen that day, swirling among the huts where once there had been low foliage for their nesting. Kingfishers had been flying along the river, too, and each day there were jays in the trees around the headquarters camps where some timber was left standing.

Burton, the Fourth Texas Indian fighter and barber, had been in after drill to cut Noah's hair and shave him. They gave him Dad Johnson's banjo, taking it from the corner where it had been standing since that day they had taken him off to the doctors and to his grave.

Of them all, only Noah was still clean-shaven. Zack's mustache was now a puff of cornsilk plumage above his lip. Martin Hasford was developing a beard almost as magnificent as Morgan's, with a red glint in it. Cass wore a well-clipped Vandyke, looking much as his Cousin Gordy had. Even Billy Dick was letting the fuzz accumulate across his cheeks wherever it would grow.

Their faces turned toward the canvas-flap door as it was pushed aside, and for a moment they stared openmouthed. Tug stood there grinning, his brown face shining in the firelight, across his shoulders a coat cut for shoulders larger than his own, and on his head a forage cap with havelock, suspiciously like the one Captain Gordy had always worn.

"Well, damn me," the Welshman broke the silence. "The African road agent is it."

They were around him then, laughing and jostling, slapping his frail back, snatching off the forage cap and tossing it aside, asking their questions.

"Cap'n? They cut off his arm, them surgeons," Tug said. "But now he's fine. I taken him home."

Only Cass remained still squatting at the fire, pushing small sticks into the flame, looking away after one glance.

"Home? You been home?" Billy Dick asked incredulously.

"Plumb back home," Tug said. "We taken trains when we could fin' one, 'cause Cap'n was a wounded officer. An' we walked some, and onct I stole a mule for him to ride on."

"You damned brigand!" Morgan said.

"An' I come back, an' along the way I fin' this here."

From beneath his jacket he pulled a small slab of cured bacon.

"Dear Jesus," Martin Hasford said, touching the meat. They all swore and touched it.

"Some pore civilian hongry tonight," Zack said, and they all laughed.

Morgan took the bacon and began slicing it, and they pulled ramrods from their rifles to spit the meat over the fire. Still not looking up, Cass fed more sticks into the flame, and it flared up brightly in the small enclosure.

"Yankees comin' into Arkansas, folks all in a muddle," Tug said.

"Damnation!" Hasford said.

"An' more picket lines an' provost guards than you ever seen, an' a pore li'l nigger jus' movin' along."

"Tell me about home," Cass said suddenly, his eyes still downcast.

They moved back then, and Tug crossed the space between them and squatted before Cass.

"All Cap'n Gordy's niggers done run off," Tug said, "an' no matter much. Las' year's cotton still in the warehouse, an' no plantin' this year, I suspects."

"My wife wrote me that."

"An' yore Missy Cass still sellin' that rice, an' her niggers still on de place, but hongry times comin' at Cap'n Gordy's."

"So you left."

"Cap'n Gordy give me da paper."

"Oh? A freedman now?" For the first time Cass lifted his head and their eyes met.

"Tha's what I be. A freedman."

They squatted together, looking at each other, their gazes unwavering, one bold and just a little short of insolent, the other cold and detached, with only some deep fire showing. The boy's hands hung between his knees, brown and cinnamon-flecked like his cheeks, and beside him the white man, his own hanging hands dark, too, as dark as Tug's.

"So why didn't you run off to the Yankees' country?"

"I ain' got no folks yonder. I allowed I'd come back here."

"There's men trying to stay out of this old army."

"I tol' Missy Cass I'd come cook fer you. An' I allowed I wants to look after your horse."

"I haven't got a horse."

"Well"—still looking at the white man, the same smile on his cinnamon-flecked face—"maybe you'll get one."

Then both looked abruptly away, and Tug rose to join the others again, with the laughing and jostling and backslapping once more. They sliced all the bacon, Morgan using the bowie that had come to be called the "vaccination knife," moving to the fire with the fat meat dangling on the ends of ramrods, and Cass moving back into the shadows of a far corner.

The next morning they saw observation balloons above the eastern slopes along the river, the first they had seen.

"What good's them thangs for?" Noah asked. "You can't get a cannon up there."

"They're watching us," Cass said. "Maybe they're getting ready to make another move."

"Good!" Zack said, squirting a stream of tobacco juice into the gray snowbank alongside the hutment. "I'm ready to get shed a' this boar's nest."

"Soon enough," the Black Welshman said. "Soon enough, now."

# ELEVEN

IT WAS good to be out of winter quarters, but they weren't out of winter yet. The day they marched through Richmond there were flurries of white, but somehow it didn't seem so cold as the snow along the Rappahannock.

There was the knowledge of a new spring coming, when all the fields and meadows and rolling woodlots would be greening. Already they had heard larks and seen the darting little black-masked Carolina chickadees.

Part of the feeling was the reception they received in the city, marching through the capital's streets, red banner going before them with the holes of the Antietam showing in the fabric. Young women came out to cheer them. There were others, too, not so young, and a good many civilian men well dressed. But seeing mostly the young women, they strutted in their ragged uniforms, their faces shining like their weapons.

Noah was exuberant. Spring had always affected him so, and although it was a little early this year, the feeling was stronger than ever before in his memory, this excitement at being alive. Zack told him it was his sap rising, and it was true. Getting shed of those dismal little huts and away from the frozen mud and constant drill on snow-packed fields, wondering what the Yankees were doing across the river with their observation balloons, and going hungry most of the time, it was good to be away from Bobby Lee's army. It couldn't help but make the sap rise, Noah allowed.

But there was no joy in Martin Hasford. He had received a letter from Benton County informing him that his daughter, Calpurnia, had married a Yankee officer. Martin's face was dark and scowling as they marched through Richmond's streets, and even the sights of such a splendid place could not change it.

"A battle right in my dooryard," he grumbled. "And me off in this damned Virginny. And Cal married with a Yankee, and an officer besides."

"You knew about that Pea Ridge fight a long time ago," Zack said. "You read about it in one a' them Yankee newspapers we was always seein'."

"I didn't know about that Yankee officer, though."

"To the victor belong the spoils," Morgan said.

Martin's face contorted in fury, and for a moment it appeared he would break ranks and sail into the Welshman. "Mind your own affairs, you son of a bitch," he snarled.

"No offense, Parson. I hear the Yankees in the West are sometimes nearly civilized, not like the ruffians we've got here. Take no offense from a poor soldier, hear?"

Hasford's face beneath his full growth of beard had reddened, and his head was bowed.

"A flare of temper, Liverpool. No call for using such a tone. And I take back the name I called."

"Worse I've been labeled, and not a drop of blood shed for any title yet bestowed."

"This war's too far gone," Noah said, grinning. "I'm beginnin' to understand what you talk about, Welsh."

"All the mystery goes out of life in the end, little brother."

They went into camp on the southeast edge of the city, a place where countless troops had billeted before. There were wall tents and company streets and even a distribution of pots for cooking.

And there was plenty to cook, a larder fat and unbelievable. There were hogs and cattle and plenty of forage for the animals, so much that they had enough left over to load out north to Lee's men, still hungry behind Fredericksburg.

"A dismal pity," Bev Cass fumed, "when the army has to look out for its own because the damned Jews and mountebanks in the government are incapable of it."

No one doubted his wisdom, nor would they have disputed him now anyway. Cass was the newly elected company sergeant, a man of power, a member of the noncommissioned-officer caste. But he had always acted like a sergeant anyway, staying aloof from them and watching them coldly. He continued to mess with them, which they took as some small form of comradeship.

But it was still Morgan's squad.

"Welshman, watch how you tread," Cass said. "You've done enough to be shot seven times over, and if I catch you breaking regulations again, I'll have you before Ole Jury Duty, and you can wager strong on that."

"Aw," Morgan said. "The hardships of war, is it?"

But later, Tug whispered to Morgan, "Never you fret on Mister Beverly. He ain' gonna put no court-martial on one a' his own."

"I have no aim to test him, you gingerbread bandit!"

They had hardly settled into the Richmond encampment when Cass appeared with a fistful of yellowed slips of paper, each bearing the signature of the brigade commander.

"Here are the furloughs," he said. "Into Richmond for twenty-four hours, and twenty-four hours only, mind. And leave part of the town still standing."

"Gawd, I thought they'd forgot what furloughs was," Zack said.

"General Hood said let 'em all go." Cass passed out the slips of paper, fragile but worth more than money.

"A benevolent gentleman," Morgan said.

"No, a smart one. If you didn't have passes, you'd go anyway, and half the division would be caught by the provost guard and brought up for charges."

They stripped naked in the chill air to pick the lice from their clothes, squatting along the company street, using two rocks like hammer and anvil to smash the little critters. Among them were one dull needle and a ball of coarse thread, and these were passed from one to the other for last-minute mending.

Pap's razor came out, and with it Zack trimmed Morgan's beard and he Zack's mustache. All of them shaved those portions of their faces they desired to be bare, using the bottom of a scoured mess tin for a mirror. They made ribald jokes about Billy Dick Hysel scraping at his downy cheeks.

"Like takin' the blade to a baby's arse," Zack said.

"You oughta let the cat lick it," Noah suggested, and all howled.

"Well, I'm after me a shirt," Billy Dick said, laughing too, not caring a whit if they made fun of him. "Ain't had the feel of a shirt on my back sinct we was with Ole Jackson in the valley."

"Me for a hat," the Black Welshman said, wiggling two fingers through holes in his little river cap. "And then for the ladies!"

"We need to find that Texas barber man," Noah said. "Them Texas outfits ought to be aroun' hyar somewheres."

"You look lovely, little brother," Morgan said.

"Well, I'm not going in at all," Martin Hasford said sullenly.

"The hell you ain't," Zack said. "A little taste a' town'll make you forget Benton County fer a while."

"You may as well give in," Noah said. "Iffen you don't, he'll tie you an' carry you in."

Across the camps came the thrilling notes of a bugle. They tensed, stopped their preparations, and stood listening, each thinking that in this last instant they would be called back into ranks and marched away toward Yankee guns.

"What the hell call is that?" Billy Dick said. "I don't hear no long roll with it."

"By God, I think that's paymaster call," Morgan said incredulously.

And paymaster call it was. Like children lining up for cake and lemonade, they jostled one another toward a large wall tent at the far end of the compound, where a number of grim-looking armed guards—all with clean and unfrayed cadet-gray uniforms—stood sentinel. Inside the tent was the paymaster himself, wearing tiny eyeglasses and glaring at the piles of yellowbacks on the folding field table before him.

"Line up, Gawd dammit," a sergeant bellowed, and Ole Jury Duty appeared with his roster, that same wrinkled paper they had all marked at March Landing so long ago, now with long wavering pencil lines drawn through many of the names and the notations afterward: killed at West Mountain; killed at Aquia Creek; killed at Sharpsburg; killed at Sharpsburg; killed at Sharpsburg.

They were paid in treasury notes, few of which bore the same signature. The confederacy was issuing paper money so fast that no single person could sign all of it, so the task was jobbed out to ladies of Richmond who had handsome penmanship and wanted to do their part. It was almost worthless stuff, but at least there was a lot of it.

It was nearing nightfall when they were ready. Before they started off, Tug plucked at Morgan's sleeve, grinning with all his cinnamon face, drawing the Welshman behind a tent.

"I'll wager you some a' dat pay, Mister Welshman."

"You black scoundrel, that's town money. Sacred it is. Besides, what might you have to place a wager?"

From the folds of his massive overcoat Tug drew a gold coin and held it up, glistening in the late sunlight.

"Well, I'm damned! That's my double eagle!"

"Yas suh, ah still got it. An' I'll make a throw a' de dice fer it again all de leaf money you got."

"All the leaf money? Why, hell's on fire, boy, I got nearly thirty dollars in my pocket, and that's only a twenty."

"Yas suh, but dis hyar is all in one piece, an' it ain't no paper."

"Damn! You ought to be the secretary of treasury in this Confederacy."

Morgan looked over his shoulder and saw the others waiting impatiently in the company street, Noah waving to him.

"All right. But no dice-throwing. Never will I throw a die with you again. But a flip of that coin. I'll call, and winner take all."

"Le's see dat leaf money, then."

Swearing, Morgan produced the wad of bills.

"Flip the damned coin, African."

The coin arched up as Tug flicked it from his fingers and Morgan called it heads in the air. It landed heads, and the Welshman snatched it quickly from the ground as though afraid it might sink into the mud. Tug was still grinning.

"All right, then," Morgan said. "But you come along with us. A slab of good beef I'll buy you, and a dram of whisky."

"Naw, naw, I ain' goin' in no Richmond town. Somebody stuff me in a tow sack 'an sell me south to the cottonfields."

"Then take a few of these leaf dollars, so you won't be cleaned complete."

"Naw, naw, I ain't never cleaned complete," Tug said, grinning and insolent. "I still got some lef'. I had me a little time wif dat river cap'n a long time ago, when we still had Big Red an' Cap'n Gordy. You see?"

He held up a second double eagle. Morgan stood gaping, then suddenly laughed and slapped the boy so hard across the shoulders that it staggered him, but the grin—perhaps a smirk—was still there.

"You chocolate heathen!"

As they trooped along the company street, Bev Cass stood and watched them go, his eyes hard and his mouth a grim little slash in his Vandyke beard. Tug moved up beside him, watching, too.

"I got a batch of po'k chops an' white flour," he said. "I can make up some meat an' gravy."

Their eyes met, and as always the man was not sure what lay behind the boy's eyes, the boy knowing still what his mother had told him long ago, before the war, before anyone had marched away from the cotton and the rice. Tug had held that knowledge like an old knife-wound scar, a grudge with no purpose and perhaps not even any malice. It was tempered now with delight at being close to this white man who was his father, and all the while knowing Cass could only guess at what he, Tug, knew. Insolent and taunting, perhaps a little arrogant.

"Yes, I'd eat that," Cass said, looking for only a moment more into the boy's eyes. "We can eat it together."

THE streets of the capital city were swarming with people that spring. Fine animals were there as well, the best-looking livestock that any of them had seen for a long time, pulling the hacks and surreys and street coaches, and some ridden by gentlemen groomed as finely as the horses, or by ladies sitting sidesaddle under their little ribbon-tied hats and in billowing skirts with countless petticoats beneath.

Moving among the throngs of civilians were the soldiers, a few in neat uniforms but most as tattered and unpressed as were the men of Morgan's squad, many of whom were happy to call themselves "Lee's Miserables."

They passed the tree-lined streets where the residents of Richmond made their homes, the houses set back behind picket fences whitewashed and unmarked by bullets and intact because no soldiers had searched for firewood here. The wide porches and neatly curtained windows where the lamps were already shining through the dusk were framed among the white oaks and basswood and holly.

Then the commercial district, where there were shop displays showing merchandise as yet not pinched out by the blockade, but with prices gone mad.

Mostly, Morgan's squad was interested in the food. Bacon had gone for twelve and a half cents a pound before the war, but was selling now for more than a dollar. More than that in the black market, they were told, because Yankee control of the avenues of trade was enough to have created an underground economy. There one had to pay up to seventy cents a pound for salt, and even that the reconstituted kind, brown and dirty looking, taken from brine vats and old smokehouse floors. Coffee was two dollars and fifty cents a pound on the open market, and hard to find there.

But Billy Dick Hysel did find himself a shirt for only three dollars in a small haberdashery where they all crowded in and looked so wicked the storekeeper was afraid to ask Billy Dick for more. It was rough fabric and a dirty gray, purporting to be white. Leaving, they heard the man complaining to his wife about the war bringing all sorts of barbarians into the city.

They waited in line at the shop of a Daguerrian artist on Broad Street, and each then sat for his portrait, Zack and Noah together, trying to arrange their jackets so the patches in the elbows wouldn't show.

The tintype reproductions of their faces showed them all

hairy and grim looking, each holding an old musket long since worthless but provided by the photographer for his subjects to make them appear more fierce and warlike. The thin iron sheets, black-enameled, were slipped into a paper envelope with a cut-out window to reveal the images, and with a flap that could be sealed and the whole business mailed to Benton County or Pine Bluff or the valley of the Buffalo.

A bath, then, in the rear of a barbershop and surgeon's office, where claims were posted on the wall that social diseases could be cured here. And on along the route, a short sip of whisky in the more than occasional saloon.

Near the hill where the Capitol stood, they saw their first prostitute, painted and smiling. Noah gaped as Zack pulled him along with the Black Welshman behind, laughing. There, too, they saw men of all shape and fashion, some well accoutered and perhaps lawmakers of this Confederacy, others in slouch hats or bowlers, with shifting eyes and the smell of pickpocket about them, so Morgan allowed.

"By Gawd," Zack said, so far least affected of them all from the whisky sipping, "we passed enough able-bodied men to make up four good regiments."

"Yeah," Noah said. "An' I never knowed there was this many niggers in the world."

"You ain't never worked a south Arkansas cotton patch," Billy Dick snickered.

It was near the river that Morgan got a new hat. They were watching a passenger train coming into the Richmond and Petersburg rail station from the South, and at the opportune moment the Welshman leaped up and knocked the hat from a gentleman leaning from the window of a coach, who was trying to see the upcoming platform. The hat was quickly retrieved from the cinders, and they all ran, even Martin Hasford, laughing now.

Under a gaslight behind the paper mill, Morgan cast aside the little river cap. The hat was almost new, a narrow-brimmed affair that was too small. It sat on top of the Welshman's head like a thimble astride a ripe plum.

"Likely need a shoestring to tie this thing on," he said.

"It makes a helluva good target," Zack said, gnawing off a cud of tobacco.

It made Noah uneasy. Not the stealing part, but the fact that now the Welshman would no longer look the same, no longer have that little billed cap they had seen him wearing since Little Rock. A bad omen. But he forgot it when Morgan led them into a small café for their dinner—hog liver and onions, because that was the cheapest thing on the bill of fare. Morgan bought a small bottle of brandy, which Billy Dick gagged at drinking.

"Good brandy," Morgan said, swirling the brown liquid in his glass. "Mostly it's so expensive, a man doesn't buy it until he's too drunk to appreciate the value of his money, and then it's too late to enjoy the taste. But not tonight, what, lads?"

The restaurateur was heard to make remarks to customers at another table concerning President Davis's propensity for shrouding the government's activities in such mystery that the good citizens never knew what was happening. The result was circulation of wild rumors that kept things in a constant state of agitation. All of which infuriated the Black Welshman.

Afterward, Morgan disappeared into the kitchen and made his gamble with the proprietor, cutting cards for dollars until he had won more than enough to pay for the meal and the brandy, too, and pocketed his winnings to the protests of the café man, showing him the bowie knife and explaining that he was a nephew of General Winder, the Richmond provost marshal who was known to send people to prison if caught taking advantage of common soldiers. They left the place in good cheer.

Leading them through the dark streets, Morgan seemed to move instinctively. They came to a large row house that sat flush to the sidewalk, in front of it a tall black man well turned out in the livery of a racetrack bugler, complete with red jacket and high hat and cape. There was a hanging lamp on either side of double doors, and the lower windows were heavily draped inside so that no light escaped. The windows along the upper story had elegant louvered shutters, all drawn tight.

As they approached, the doorman watched them warily, his head back. But when Morgan stopped before him and bowed, the man touched his hat with his fingertips.

"Yas suh."

"What place is this, my good man?"

"Dis hyar Miz Rozella's Afternoon Tea Sippin' Society an' Billiard Hall."

"Is there dancing herein?"

"Aw, naw suh, ain't never no dancin' in Miz Rozella's. Miz Rozella's a high-quality place."

Morgan smiled and turned to the others, the new thimble hat perched precariously on the back of his head.

"And now, lads, for the rest of it," he said.

SOLDIERS in Richmond searched for the things soldiers have always sought in wartime cities: strong drink, food, gambling, and women. The search was never difficult, because all of it was there in abundance.

They came with money and left broke, and some of them remembered very little of it afterward. Some drank themselves into oblivion early and lay on the sidewalks or in the gutters, the outraged citizens stepping over or around them, cursing the prostrate forms of men who were veterans of the railroad cut at Second Manassas or the thickets of White Oak Swamp or the stone wall at Fredericksburg.

But in whatever condition they were, the shopkeepers were ready to take their money, meager though it was; the gamblers took it, too, in rigged games, as did the profiteers in back streets for broken shoes or beefsteaks turned black with age or jackets made of shoddy that would not last out the month, even in good weather. And the saloonkeepers also ready to take it, for their cups of scalding liquor. And the whores, large fee or small.

Some effort was made by the established police and by the newer military police to stop prostitution in the city, but their efforts were mostly futile.

So many whores! Some of the ladies worked the streets,

taking rooms in boardinghouses where they were becoming the only tenants because of rising rents. Others worked the saloons near the railroad stations and the warehouses. These were often seen hustling staggering soldiers into dark alleys, the business conducted there upright against a wall.

Some worked with pimps, who not only procured but might appear suddenly during the act of love with a leather stocking filled with buckshot, sapping down the passionate hero to empty his pockets and even take his shoes and trousers if they were salable.

And then there were the established houses, like Miz Rozella's Afternoon Tea Sippin' Society and Billiard Hall. Here were found the most desirable and most expensive women, the most professional of all the Richmond whores. some imported from France or Russia or even China. And here the pressure of purity from among the good citizens was considerably less than on the streets, because here there was more money involved, and where there was money, there were also policemen ready to share some of it.

Miz Rozella was a myth. Rumor had it the place was actually owned by one of Richmond's more successful profiteers, growing rich on the war. But there was always a hostess at the door claiming to be Miz Rozella, dressed richly, with high ruffles on neck and sleeves of a silk or taffeta gown that might be from Europe—surely as dear as gold, having come through the blockade—and a large ivory brooch at her neck with the profile of some Greek goddess, likely Aphrodite.

All the ladies in Miz Rozella's were well dressed and modest. At least when they were downstairs. There they showed bare skin as stingily as did the good matrons of Richmond, and when they went abroad, the ladies of the Tea Room never rouged their cheeks or touched their lips with color. They were the uppermost echelon of whoredom.

There was actually a billiard room in the downstairs, also a bar and a sitting room and a dining room. In the last a man could purchase beefsteak and potatoes for only eight dollars a plate, attended by large black men in short white jackets. If one had the money, these attendants could produce the finest wines and richest brandies. Bar whisky was poured from a water pitcher.

The decor was heavy and plush—deep red and gold-flecked draperies, polished walnut and shining brass cuspidors and footrails along the bar. Oil paintings hung on the walls, mostly showing goat-men chasing fat and naked maidens beside limpid pools. In the dining room, a string trio played genteel music.

In back was the gaming room, with card table and wheel, run by one of Richmond's many gamblers. And in back, too, was the stairwell leading to the rooms above, so that a man might escort his lady of the evening to her bed without being observed by others taking their leisure on the lower floor.

It was all around the most astonishing establishment Zack and Noah had ever seen.

And Martin Hasford thought, Here shows the incongruity of the Confederacy. Amid the golden splendor moved the hard faces and the bony hands still grimed with dirt from trenching and crusted with black powder. At the wheel stood the bedraggled private who laid claim to wide estates, and in the sitting room the captain who owned nothing, sipping Madeira, counting his ancestry for a century before the Revolution, knobby arms showing through the ragged sleeves of his jacket.

There were men who had fought in battles from Big Bethel through the winter campaigns of 1863. They wore their rumpled uniforms as a badge of honor. And then there were the well dressed, who had heard the guns only when McClellan had threatened Richmond along the two great rivers, James and York, and had come close enough for his artillery to shake the windows of the town.

Men from the tidewater and the mountains, from the cotton South and the Delta. But no flags or rank or weapons here, and the night's acting Miz Rozella, like the captain of a ship at sea, seeing to it that all were treated with complete impartiality. So long as they had the requisite money.

Noah was dizzy with it all. The whisky helped. Light

sparkled from the crystal chandeliers; the carpets underfoot were deep and soft, the faces of the women dusted with rouge, pink-mouthed and laughing.

There was a barrel of oysters packed in ice, and a black lad to open them, one pop of the blade and the shells dropped into a washtub, the milky meats into cups of melted butter. Platters of shad fried in cornmeal and crisp as November oak leaves. Cinnamon buns and taffy, and even oranges from Africa.

Noah watched the money passing back and forth, the yellow treasury notes, Federal greenbacks, and coins. All the money in the wide, wide world. And all the women, too—smiling, inviting.

Zack was at the playing table, his long fingers dirty under the nails holding the cards delicately, as though feeling the texture of a quail's breast meat. Billy Dick sat pop-eyed in a corner, a giggling woman hovering above him like an old hen, stuffing jelly and crackers into his gaping mouth. Hasford was still in the anteroom, seated in an overstuffed chair, looking out of place and humiliated, but drinking the glasses of Bahaman rum as fast as Noah could bring them from the bar.

"I never knowed a war was like this," Noah said breathlessly.

Laughing, he looked over all of it, felt the tender eyes and the soft voices and the alabaster fingers on his sleeve, plucking, and thought, I never knowed they done all this stuff in houses like this. I only thought they . . . But stopped there, took another drink from the barman, and laughed with Morgan, who stood nearby, throwing money down, a woman on each arm.

DAWN was beaming its gray light in the bedroom window, and Noah moved over to pull back the curtain. He looked down into an alley where there were barrels of trash and a cat, gray like the sky, hunting rats among the refuse. It was raining, and he felt a chill in his feet, but only because he had just come from the covers of the large brass bed. The woman was dressing.

"You like to stay longer, it's another five dollars," she said, bending to lace high shoes.

I don't even know who she is, Noah thought. I don't even know her name.

His mouth was raw and had the texture of old felt. All that whisky last night, bought by the Welshman or by Zack, who hadn't left that table all night, so far as Noah knew. Surprisingly, it had been Zack, not Morgan, playing bluff. And Noah recalled his amazement at Zack winning, too crafty or lucky or maybe hard looking for anyone to try cheating.

"You're gonna have to go now," she said, and all the gentleness of the evening was gone, and all the laughter, too. She was a gray shape now, lifting her arms to allow the dress to fall over her chemise.

"I'm goin'." He started searching for his trousers in the half-light. He didn't see her leave, but only heard the soft click of the door when it closed.

He sat on the bed, watching the rain against the windowpane where he had pulled back the curtain, and wondered what in hell he was doing here. He thought about the farm back in those Ozark hills, but somehow at this moment thinking of his own people made him ashamed. Instead, he thought of the others, of the squad and the company and the regiment. Only that seemed real to him now.

A grin touched his lips as he recalled Morgan at the bar downstairs, women around him as he spun tales of Indians and bandits and places he had never seen, all in such good humor that his laugh infected them all, shouting in his thick Welsh accent and drinking from a leaded glass, the overflow glistening through his beard.

Noah found Martin Hasford sleeping in that same anteroom chair and woke him. Without speaking they moved to the door and outside, standing between the two lamps that still burned, watching the gray rain.

They could hear a locomotive in the yards nearby, and shuffling boxcars, and the heavy thump of machines at the Tredegar iron works. While they waited for the others, wagons began to pass. The city was waking and going about its early routine, the people bent against the rain and the horses steaming.

Martin spoke first, almost reluctantly. "I had no business in such a place."

"All you done was sleep in a chair. Your wife couldn't fin' nothin' hard 'bout that."

"My wife doesn't even know such places exist. I had no business here."

"It's just another damned saloon," Noah said, but he thought, I like a nice old smokehouse better'n anythin' I had hyar. And the face of Luanne Lacy came to mind, an image now vivid and painful.

While they sheltered in the doorway a few other men left Miz Rozella's, passing them with heads down, not speaking, collars turned up against the rain. Then Zack came, looking drawn from lack of sleep and wadding a roll of yellow treasury notes into a ball, then shoving it into a pocket.

"You been at it all night?" Noah asked.

Zack nodded. He spat a soggy cud onto the sidewalk and wiped his mouth on his sleeve.

"That gamin' fever the Welshman's got is catchin', I see."

"When the cards run, it is," Zack said. "I won almost a hundret dollars all tol'."

"Whata you aim doin' with it?" Noah asked, and thought, That's more money than Pap ever made in a year . . . all done in a single night in a whorehouse!

"I'm gonna buy us some trousers an' shoes," Zack said. "An' whatever's left I'll give to the Welshman, part pay for what he spent on us las' night."

"I'd as lief have a new hat."

"Trousers an' shoes is what you'll get."

They stood a long time, each nursing his own aches. When Morgan appeared he had Billy Dick Hysel by the scruff of the neck.

"Back to the pits," he said. "Come on, lad, wake up now and move. This rain will refresh your soul."

"Mine needs some," Hasford said softly.

They moved onto the sidewalk, bent against the rain, walking toward the center of the city. They could feel the water on the cobblestones soaking through their shoes.

"Damn!" Billy Dick snorted, awake now and walking steadily, his hands thrust deep into his trousers pockets. "Her name was Silvia, an' I couldn't do nothin'."

"Other times there'll be, old soldier," Morgan said.

"I never done nothin' like that before. I didn't know how."

"A good woman does the showing."

"She jus' laughed at me. An' I couldn't do nothin'."

They walked silently then, the Welshman with an arm across Billy Dick's narrow shoulders. Soon they were like the day, damp and cold and dismal, heads down and faces grim, hard-eyed and thinking of all that had gone before. And Martin Hasford alone thinking too of what lay ahead: Rain-soaked soldiers they are, damned and marching straight to perdition. But wicked as they may be, I'll stay with these men right to the end of it.

# TWELVE

THEY weren't long for Richmond and the sinful life. Soon they were marching south with the rest of Longstreet's Corps, through Chesterfield and Prince George and Surrey and Isle of Wight counties, names that meant nothing to most of them, although such had come from the heritage Zack and Noah Fawley could claim.

"Bloody English," the Black Welshman muttered, but not so loud that Noah could hear him.

At Suffolk they had their first round of trench warfare, and none of them liked the taste.

The Yankees were all along the Nansemond River in their gunboats and in the fortified line around the city. Hood's division moved into positions where entrenchments were only partly completed, and shovels were issued. While they dug, Union gunboats along the river lobbed shells at them.

The missiles were large and slow-moving, mostly river mortars, and could be seen coming. While the rest of the company shoveled, Billy Dick Hysel was posted on the parapet to watch and give warning.

"Hyar comes another one a' them black bastards," he would shout, and all would go to ground with their faces in the dirt like moles, Billy Dick himself scrambling down to join them at the last moment, panting with excitement and self-importance.

This was a country different from any they had seen. On the upper elbow of the Dismal Swamp, it was like breathing water rather than air. The heat was stultifying and the cold bone-chilling.

Zack, more than the others, noted the character of this land, the wildlife and the timber. There were scarlet tanagers and cuckoos, small terns and blue herons, and thousands of birds that he knew well and had seen before. The trees included the black gum called tupelo and the sweet-bay magnolia, the sourwood and willow oak.

"Like to hunt this country," he said, throwing dirt from the deep trench.

"It's Yankees we hunt, lad, and not far from here," Morgan said. His new thimble hat was tied to his head by a shoestring, as he had predicted might be required.

Just beyond good rifle range were the Union works. There was artillery there—rifled pieces, outranging anything Longstreet had. Ole Jury Duty fumed about those guns until they began popping at the Southern lines, which seemed to give him relief.

"It's the uncertainty that raises hell with digestion," he said.

So then they had to put up with the guns and the mortars both, shaping their ditches and revetting them with woven willow branches and heavy timbers, ducking when the shells exploded, or diving onto their faces when Billy Dick gave his shrill warning.

The Yanks always stopped firing at dusk, letting the war rest out the night and the men sleep uninterrupted . . . at least until John Bell Hood started thinking about night operations.

There was a salient in the line that thrust out toward the Federal trenches, its nose barely five hundred yards from the nearest hostile gun position. The blues had cut a firing port into the parapet opposite so that the artillery piece could be run out and fired like a naval gun, then rolled back out of sight. But Ole Jury Duty, poking his head dangerously high, found an exact spot from where some of the Federal gunners could be seen deep in the emplacement when they recharged the piece.

"Nut-cutters!" he exploded. "We'll damn sure see about this now."

Two days later he was in the trench with a strange-looking weapon. He called Zack out of the work detail.

"Now, boy, you start earning all that pay the government has been kind enough to give you."

Zack stared at the rifle slack-jawed, rubbing his mud-caked hands on his trousers. As Ole Jury Duty held it out to him, he took it gingerly.

"What the hell is it?"

"It's a Sharps," Ole Jury Duty said. "I got it from Hood's headquarters."

"I seen a Sharps before. I never seen one like this. She's a heavy son of a bitch."

"That's the barrel," Scaggs said. He pointed to the long tube that ran the length of the piece from the small of the stock to the muzzle. "This is the telescope sight."

"Well, I'm damned."

"Get up there and take a look through 'er."

Holding the rifle as though it might be a newborn baby, Zack moved up onto a fire step and peeped over the top of the parapet. He pulled the rifle up, rested it on the turned earth, and squinted through the sight.

"Well, I'm damned," he breathed.

"See anything?"

"It's like bein' right in amongst 'em."

"Could you get off a shot?"

"If I waited long enough, one would likely hold still."

To Zack it was a marvel. He had seen set triggers before, but never such a telescopic sight. There were a detachable false muzzle and a plunger bullet starter that fit on the barrel, allowing the tight bullet to be seated in the bore. After loading, these came off for the firing. Zack tinkered with it for a few minutes, and finally Ole Jury Duty handed him a tin box with cartridges, caps, and .45-caliber, conical lead bullets.

"You're our new sharpshooter."

"It's better 'n shovelin'," Zack said.

It only lasted three days. Zack took his position at the nose of the salient each afternoon when the Federal fire was most intense. His shooting played havoc among the gunners at that one emplacement. He never said anything to anybody about how many of his shots went home, and Scaggs didn't bother to ask him. The decrease in the volume of Yankee fire was evidence enough for His Honor.

Zack concentrated on the mechanical part of the job. It

took a while to get the range, and after that he never thought about what was happening when his bullets arrived at the Union position. It was simply that there were targets over there, each taking his own chance just as Zack was taking his, every day of this war, every hour.

Then the sharpshooter from Hood's headquarters came down to reclaim his weapon and take a few shots himself. He was a strutter and let it be known that he belonged to a company of marksmen—although there were only eight in all that Hood had scattered around, using them where they were needed.

"I captured this beauty during the Seven Days' Fight," he said, patting the rifle affectionately. "Part of the old Fourth Texas, I was. Ain't she a honey?"

He then rose to take his first shot with his fancy rifle, and a Yankee bullet struck him just above the eyes. He slipped back into the trench like a dried cornhusk.

Ole Jury Duty and Zack stood in the trench, looking down at the young man. He lay on his back, the unfired rifle still in his hands, on his face an expression of utter surprise.

"Damn! Looks like the Yanks run in a few sharpshooters of their own."

"You want me to do it some more?" Zack asked.

"Hell, no. Let Ole Hood send his special shooters, if he's all that excited about it. Help me drag this poor boy to one of the grub trenches, and I'll get him carried back to Hood." All the transverses that led to the front were called grub trenches, because that was the route food came up each night.

"Maybe we can keep the rifle," Zack said, taking the dead man's feet.

"Not likely," Scaggs grunted, lifting the boy's shoulders. "Dammit, how'd I come to get the messy end?"

That night in his roll, Zack thought a lot about Hood's sharpshooter getting his head blown mostly off. He had never bothered much with such thinking before, after those hot fights along the Antietam, where there had been bedlam and everybody shooting everybody else. But now he did, because this was a different thing somehow—a single shot, a single head over the parapet, one dead man. An' except for Ole Hood wantin' his own man down hyar, it woulda been me!

Zack had never been a religious man, but now he had to admit to himself that some force might have been involved, sending that boy to stick his head up at the very moment a Yankee sharpshooter was waiting.

Maybe Pap's been right all along, he thought. Maybe a man's time comes when it's supposed to, no matter what he does.

It was small comfort, this philosophy of most infantrymen . . . though how else could they face those close-quarters firefights, so devastating and vicious?

But, Gawd dammit, a man oughta have some say in what happens to him. There oughta be some selection that makes a difference in the end.

He thought about Noah then, working with a trenching detail somewhere toward the rear. He hadn't seen his brother in four days. Pap said look out for Noah. Mama said it, too.

Nobody looks out fer nobody, 'cept his own self. Even when a man wants to, he caint do it.

Dimly, then, he perceived that as smart as Pap was, he knew nothing about war. Only some faint knowledge of it, maybe. But he couldn't *know*.

Well, I'll look out fer him as best I can. Only he's gettin' so damned big an' tough, maybe it's him oughta be lookin' out fer me.

And dimly perceived, too, was the point that his own control of himself in battle came from the will, not from any lack of fear. For Noah . . . hell, he acts like there ain't nothin' can hurt him. I think he enjoys it!

It started to rain, but the chill was still bearable, and rolled in his blanket Zack slept and dreamed of the women in Miz Rozella's Tea Room and Billiard Hall—stroking his arm as he sat at the poker table, and he agreeing to himself that he would soon stop playing and carry that fat one upstairs. But then it was dawn and too late. And he never got around to it in his dreams, either.

---

IT WAS during that time of watching the Yankees in their trenches around Suffolk that Zack took two days' absence without leave. Noah fretted, wondering aloud if a Yankee raiding party had come and dragged Zack off in the night, while actually worried that Zack had deserted for the long trek back to Arkansas.

The squad took elaborate measures to hide the fact from Ole Jury Duty. Martin Hasford answered to Zack's name at muster, and if he hadn't known better, Noah would have sworn it was Zack's voice.

Even Cass went along, never pausing in his calling of names from the roster, his loyalty to messmates stronger than the authority of his new sergeant's stripes.

"No fear, little brother," the Black Welshman said, sensitive to every Fawley emotion by now. "He'll be back, that Zack!"

And he was, just before bedding time on the second day of his disobedience, with the night gone cool and somewhere in a nearby trench the whispering call of a chuck-will's-widow.

Zack was drunk. He came staggering into the light of their fire, gripping a large brown bottle from which he offered no drink to the others. He just squatted and blinked, holding the bottle between his knees.

"Now it's him back again," Morgan laughed.

"Where the hell you been?" Noah asked.

"Them Texas boys. They ain't liars worth a hoot," Zack said, his voice loud and strident. "They took to braggin' 'bout how fas' thangs grows in Texas. I tole 'em 'bout the punkins. You 'member the punkins, Noy, Uncle Questor used to tell 'bout?"

He paused to take a swig from the bottle, his head tilted back, Adam's apple bobbing. Noah stared in amazement.

"Yes, sir, I tole 'em," Zack sputtered. His hat was pulled down crookedly to one side, giving his head a lopsided appearance in the firelight. "In Newton County, thangs grows so fas' it ain't no use plantin' punkins. They jus' get wore out with the vines draggin' 'em acrost the groun'!"

Zack dropped the bottle and scrambled for it, kicking one foot into the fire, scattering live embers. Everyone laughed except Noah. He squatted immobile, staring bug-eyed, astonishment sagging his mouth.

"They got to jawin' 'bout how big thangs was in Texas," Zack continued, back in control of the bottle. "I tole 'bout that cattle drive the Fawleys made over to Carrol County one time. Pap and Uncle Questor. They come onto the White River, and she was in flood and no fords they could use." Another sip of whisky. "Well, Uncle Questor foun' this hyar holler tree an' they cut 'er down an' felled 'er acrost the river, an' they herded them cattle right through it to the other side. Only they lost a few into the limbs."

"I've heard that one before," Martin Hasford said, chuckling.

Noah's face had flushed with anger. He rose and moved around the fire to stand behind Zack, arms stiff at his sides. All the laughter stopped as the others watched Noah's contorted face, staring down at his brother.

"It's time you was abed," he said.

Zack lifted his face, the light dancing across the long angles of his jaw and glinting in his cornsilk mustache. He looked up owl-eyed and wiped his mouth with the back of one hand.

"It's Gawd's truth," he said. "Cows lost in the limbs."

For a moment Noah stood with fists clenched, the muscles along his cheeks knotted with fury. Then he wheeled and stomped off into the darkness.

"Aw, hell," Zack muttered, dropped the bottle again, retrieved it, then rose unsteadily and moved back along the stacks of rifles to find his bedding. The others were silent now, avoiding one another's eyes. Even the Black Welshman had nothing to say.

ROLLED awkwardly into his shelter half, Zack lay staring up at the stars and thought of the Trippet twins. Big girls, never married, helping their daddy run his sorghum mill in one of the valleys along the Buffalo. Middie and Maudie. Strong as bay mules, by Gawd!

He had known them for years, growing up in the hills. They were about fifteen years older than he. Zack had encountered Middie one night while running trotlines in one of the big pools of the river. She was there doing the same.

They sat together on a large outcrop of rock above the stream, and she offered him a chew of tobacco. After a while she began her explorations, and eventually there on the rock Zack found himself in the damnedest position, birth naked, and having sensations he had never known before.

He would turn sixteen that year, and for the next decade he ran trotlines in summer with similar results. On one such occasion he was in the middle of it when he realized that it wasn't Middie but Maudie. He couldn't tell them apart even in broad daylight, and he wondered then how long they had been switching on him. It didn't matter. It all felt the same.

Gawd damn, he thought. Them gals is almost forty, I reckon. I wonder who's runnin' trotlines with 'em now?

He felt a movement in the darkness and heard Noah muttering to himself, rolling into his own bedding. Zack grinned and, lying there, raised the bottle to his lips and drank again. He thought of Uncle Questor and his tall tales spliced between quotations from Scripture, and about the Trippet twins, and about the blue catfish that came from the Buffalo River.

"What's got into you?" Noah's voice came sharply, furiously.

"Let a man kick over the traces now an' again, will ya, Noy?"

"You shame the Fawleys, goin' off absent an' gettin' drunk an' tellin' them crazy stories. You musta swilled a whole vat, drunk as you are."

"Fawleys has done worse than get drunk an' tell tall stories. Now, iffen you want a drank a' this whisky, come get 'er. If not, hush 'bout it. You're jus' pea green 'cause you ain't havin' no fun."

"You make a man sick, actin' like that."

Zack thought about it for a moment, listening to the chuck-will's-widow and sipping the whisky noisily.

"A sober man is a pious man," he said, echoing Martin Hasford, and laughed abruptly, happy with such wisdom. "I reckon you thank I shoulda jus' crawled off in the swamp an' slept 'er off, so's not to shame the Fawleys." He laughed once more. "But I never. So now I reckon you'll hafta write 'nother one a' them letters a' yours an' tell ever'body 'bout what a soaked-up son of a bitch I be. Well, have at 'er. I don't give a damn!"

Noah rose on one elbow and started to make a hot rejoinder, then changed his mind and flopped down with a disgusted grunt, pulling his shelter half across his head, mumbling angrily.

Zack waited a long time before he sat up and reached out to touch the dark form beside him. Noah lay stiffly still under his hand, and Zack patted gently, as he would a hound puppy, and lay back and took the last of the Texas whisky.

Ole Jury Duty knew about the unauthorized absence, of course. The next morning he had Zack chained to a tree and put on bread and water for two days. Zack sensed in his still whisky-clouded brain that Noah took some kind of indecent satisfaction from it, especially from the placard Ole Jury Duty hung around Zack's neck that proclaimed him a "shirker and sot."

As he began to sober up, Zack leaned against his tree and laughed about it all, but not so that anyone could see. Just laughing deep inside. With some bitterness in it.

THERE was more than a little ripple of excitement the day General Hood came down to their trench to look at the Yankee gun positions. He was a tall man, light-eyed and with a long nose that stood out strongly above his flowing mustache and the beard where the fine hair was going white in streaks.

With him were a number of staff officers, the brigade

commander, and the regimental commander. Martin Hasford allowed that if the Yankees could place a shell just right, they'd kill half the commissioned ranks in the division at one whack.

None of them knew what the talk was about until later, when the whole regiment was formed up and Hood asked for volunteers for a night attack against those Union guns. Being asked to volunteer for anything was new to them. Maybe because of that, or maybe because it offered a chance to fight the boredom of trench life and strike a lick at the Yanks, the whole regiment stepped forward.

The operation was left to the brigade commander, who passed it along to the regimental commander, who picked a hundred men and Captain Scaggs to lead them. Noah and Morgan were among those chosen, and Beverly Cass.

The excitement mounted then, becoming almost unbearable as the day waned and the shadows began to darken the trenches. Even those not going were jumpy, watching the others prepare. The raiders shucked off canteens and cartridge pouches and other accouterments that might make noise. Ole Jury Duty decreed they would do it with unloaded rifles to avoid shooting friendly soldiers. It would be the bayonet, and that only.

One of the staff men came down to the line carrying a ten-pound sledgehammer and a handful of iron spikes. Ole Jury Duty, peering over the parapet toward the hostile positions, glanced down and saw the stuff. He flashed his crooked little smirking grin.

"Morgan, take that hammer and those nails," he said. "You're the man for that job, and leave your rifle behind."

The only two remaining white shirts in the regiment were confiscated from protesting soldiers, then ripped into bands so that a man could pin a piece to his back and have a flag that would show in the dark and mark him as a rebel.

Noah sat in the darkening trench, shivering. He had been to the parapet with all the others to take a look at the ground they would cross. Now he sat crouched, Zack beside him, neither of them speaking.

This time it'll be me alone, he kept thinking, without Zack there. But anyways, there's the Welshman and Cass. That Bev Cass, he's a hard-shell little bastard. But I'd rather it was Zack.

Or maybe not. We never done this night stuff. Maybe it's pretty dangerous. Maybe it's better one of us jus' stays back hyar in this ditch.

It wasn't fear exactly. It was some uneasiness of the unknown, an apprehension he couldn't define. And because he didn't trust himself to try, he was silent, as was Zack.

Maybe he's feelin' it, too, Noah thought. Whatever it is. Maybe he's wishin' it was him goin' an' me stayin' in the ditch.

Soon the raiders were making their last preparations. They rubbed dirt on their faces. Some took off their shoes because it was quieter walking that way.

Noah thought about his anger of the last week, when Zack had disgraced everyone. Well, it all didn't look so bad now. Like most of Noah's furies, it had passed quickly and was now mostly forgotten.

He reached over and tapped Zack's knee with his doubled fist.

"This ain't gonna take long," he said.

"I reckon not," Zack said, but he didn't sound convinced.

"We'll give the Yanks time to get off to sleep," Ole Jury Duty muttered, stalking up and down the trench, stoop-shouldered, his tall hat showing against the coming stars.

The hours went slowly. They heard an early whippoorwill somewhere toward the Yankee lines. Beyond that was the faint cough of steam engines as the gunboats in the Nansemond shifted their positions.

Finally, it was time.

"Fix bayonets," Cass said, and there was the soft grinding of metal on metal.

"Let's go, boys. Keep closed up," Ole Jury Duty called along the line, and Noah scrambled up the slope of the trench and over the parapet, Zack pushing his butt from beneath.

It was a simple, straightforward attack. They moved four abreast in a close column, across the dark ground. Noah stumbled often over the pocked earth, bumping the man in front of him. He could feel the men on either side of him and see ahead the pale strips of white-shirt flannel. Behind, he could hear Morgan's heavy breathing.

"Keep closed up, dammit," Cass whispered from alongside the column.

The war was sleeping, which was something they had counted on. They heard not a single picket's rifle, nor any movement behind the Union lines. Even the gunboats were still now.

It took a long time, so long that Noah began to fear they were going in a circle, with Ole Jury Duty up ahead, lost in the dark and heading toward North Carolina. It took so long, Noah expected to see dawn lighting the eastern sky, behind enemy gun emplacements.

But then he saw the rising black shape of the Federal parapets. They stumbled closer, and then the gun positions were there.

We ain't even got charges in these guns, Noah thought, almost frantically. There was some of that chest-thumping thrill again, but nothing like the charge into the smoke at Sharpsburg. It was like wading into a barrel of black sorghum molasses, and maybe with wasps swimming there.

"Move!" he could hear Ole Jury Duty snap, already in the Union trench. "Don't go beyond the guns, either way. Don't get in their traverse ditches. Move, Gawd dammit!"

Beverly Cass was running to the left along the trenchline, bent forward, the others following.

The troops were moving up the parapet, dropping into the first line of works, the two files on the left going in one direction, the two files on the right in the other. They began to stumble over sleeping men, wrapped in blankets at wide places in the trench.

In the dim starlight, Noah followed the white flannel patch before him. There seemed an inordinate amount of noise, enough to wake the whole Union army. He was panting, and sweat soaked his jacket collar.

Two Union sentries, likely asleep, were surprised at their posts, disarmed, and taken prisoner, their eyes shining pale in the night.

"Round 'em up, boys, round 'em up," Ole Jury Duty kept hissing. "Over here, boys, get 'em all over here. Take them pieces back with you."

Then Noah and four others were into a small dugout where there was a fire and a group of blues were sleeping along the walls, seven of them. They leaped at the bedrolls, jabbing with the points of their bayonets. Noah kept one eye closed, to save his night vision.

Sleep-slackened faces appeared, the eyes going wide at sight of the naked steel. Someone swore and another started praying.

"Time for that later, Yank," one of the raiders snarled. "Get your arse outa that blanket and keep them hands in sight."

The startled, half-sleeping Federals groped for shoes, but were pushed to their feet and out the opening into the trench.

Jesus, Noah thought, ever' one of 'em got on socks!

All along the trenchline where the gun positions stood, they were moving quickly, barking curt orders to the stumbling Yankee prisoners. Ole Jury Duty was scrambling from one end of his line to the other, cursing softly, shoving men aside, and at one flank Bev Cass stood squarely in the trench, preventing them from going too far into the darkness.

There was the hard, stinging sound of hammer on iron. Coming from the dugout, prisoners before him, Noah saw the Welshman. Morgan was astride one of the cannons, feeling for the primer hole with the point of a spike. Finding it, he tapped the spike with the hammer, then slammed down the maul with all the force of his powerful arms, driving the spike into the firing port.

"There, you black son of a bitch," he whispered.

Then, leaping down, legs spraddled like a bird's, he ran along the trench to the next gun, leaped up and groped for the port, and drove in the iron.

Before it was finished, there was a single report, a rifle fired from somewhere farther along the trenchline, and then a shouted Yankee challenge. But by then they were coming out of the position, the guns spiked and useless now, pushing their prisoners before them toward friendly ground. The blues moved like cattle, most of them in their sock feet, cursing, prodded along and covered on the flanks by men with white flannel hanging down their backs.

Noah had never seen anything so welcome as the outline of the regiment's revetments. His heart was pumping, and his hands were so wet he could hardly hold the rifle. But he began to laugh then, and dropped into the trench to find Zack and the others waiting.

Bev Cass was already there, counting off the men as they dropped into cover, to be sure none had been left behind.

After the last of them had leaped into the ditches, the prisoners having been hustled away to the rear, Ole Jury Duty went back up the parapet and bellowed with cupped hands.

"Hey, Yank! We appreciate your hospitality!"

A single rifle shot snapped overhead, and as Ole Jury Duty scrambled down, a cheer went up along the line.

Zack was hanging on to Noah's arm as though afraid he might slip away into the darkness and be lost. Noah was shaking like a frightened cur, but still laughing.

"Gawd, it was easy," he panted. "I never allowed it would be so easy. Gimme a chaw. My mouth's like dust."

"You're soaked through. You best get in your blanket 'fore you catch the vapors. I got a little hunk a' cornbread an' sowbelly."

"Gawd! It was so easy!"

IT WAS, indeed, a fine success. No casualties—except for the shirts—six guns spiked, and more than a hundred prisoners taken. But the regiment remembered the aftermath more than the raid. Not to include Ole Jury Duty, they thought what happened next was a high point of the war.

No one was sure how it came about. They knew that Scaggs had gone back to division headquarters the day after the night attack to receive the congratulations and compliments of General Hood. The whole business upset Ole Jury Duty because he wanted the time to scribble notes in his log of the company's operations, a task he had spent much time on, writing in a battered, clothbound ledger book that he called The Record.

Somewhere along the route—on his way back to the regiment, it was rumored—a Mississippi captain named Buford intervened. One story held that words were passed about the effectiveness of Arkansas troops, whereupon Ole Jury Duty let fly some of his best purple oaths, coupled with the certain observation that Mississippi troops had been seen running the wrong direction during a fight.

This in turn brought a slap across Ole Jury Duty's face with leather gauntlets, and with it a challenge to personal combat, him to choose the weapons. Scaggs chose Enfield rifles at forty paces, and stomped back to the regimental position in a foul frame of mind, muttering about down-South cotton planters.

Everyone knew that dueling was against the laws of the Confederacy and the regulations of the army. But they also knew that Ole Hood was not likely to interfere, being himself a man who never stood back from a good fight. They whispered about it, pretending it was a secret, although there were few men in the division who were not aware of it by nightfall of the day the challenge was thrown down.

The prospect of danger never entered their minds. After facing a whole brigade of charging Yankees on various fields, they were disdainful of any harm a single rifle could do.

On the day before the appointed time, Scaggs appeared in the company trench area—grown much quieter now since the Yankees had thus far failed to replace the spiked artillery pieces—and called Zack aside.

"I've got a contest of honor in the morning," Ole Jury Duty said, his face working under his stubble of beard. "I don't expect you'd know anything about such things."

"No, I don't," Zack said. "Except you an' some other officer has decided to take shots at one another."

"Fawley, you know firearms as well as anyone in this army. So I want you to go along with me and Bev Cass, who's acting as my second because I don't want any other commissioned ranks involved in this. I want you to come along and see those guns are loaded right. And I want you to pick two of the best rifles in the company because I've got to choose my weapons, and by God, I want Arkansas rifles."

"You want one that shoots a little wide?"

"Hell, no," Ole Jury Duty sputtered. "This here is a contest of honor. Besides, he'll get first pick, and he might leave me with the bad one."

So it was that Zackery Fawley prepared to see his first duel.

It was predawn dark when the three of them left the company area. Most of the men were awake. A few passed remarks of encouragement as the silent trio walked near them.

"Shoot his arse off, Cap'n."

"Aim fer the bastard's belt buckle."

"Don't give 'em no first shot, Cap'n."

A little farther along, the sky growing lighter now, they passed a Mississippi regiment, and the comments were not so encouraging.

"Hey, mister, ain't we seen you in the circus?"

"Oh, you, Arkansas, come out from under that tall hat. We know you're in there. We can see your arse a-wigglin'."

Ole Jury Duty swore mightily, and Zack wondered if a man in such temper could hit anything with either of the rifles he carried.

They passed along a road fenced by railings and finally into a marshy glade where the willow oaks were thick, their leaves dripping. They found the Mississippians waiting, a grim little group of four, the offended Captain Buford wearing a cape. His coat collar was pulled up to hide any white, even though like all the others he had not owned a white shirt in a long time.

While Cass went out to palaver with the other second

about rules, Zack heard someone coming along the path they had followed. The surgeon nephew of Sidney Dinsmore appeared, carrying a small black bag.

"What the hell are you doing here?" Ole Jury Duty snorted.

"I thought you might need my assistance."

"I don't suppose you're sober."

"As sober as ever."

"That's what I was afraid of. I hope them Mississippi people have brought a doctor with them."

Zack squatted well back from the others, holding the two Enfields he had brought from the company—his own and Martin Hasford's. Both shot true.

There was a little wrangling about Bev Cass acting as a second and him not an officer, but it was finally decided that this duel had nothing to do with rank, only with state pride. Soon Cass was back to take the weapons, and Zack followed over to the other group and watched closely as the referee started to load.

"Them's Yankee cat-ridges," Zack said. "They're a mite big fer them guns."

"Not when the barrels are clean," the officer said, his eyes darting as he surveyed Zack's rumpled and patched trousers and jacket, looking much the way his own did.

"They're clean as your tooth," Zack said, looking the other square in the eye.

"Same advantage to either side," Cass said.

"No," Zack said, "them guns oughta have ammunition made fer 'em, an' not some Yankee stuff."

Zack produced two paper cartridges, and they were closely inspected.

"You can use your caps if you want, but we ain't gonna shoot without you tamp them Enfield loads into the guns."

It was done, and Zack moved back to the line of willow oaks and squatted once more, working off a cud from his plug of tobacco. He could hear the Mississippi officer acting as referee explaining the rules.

"Gentlemen, you will stand back to back, weapons at the trail. On my command you will pace twenty steps, my counting. At the count of twenty, you will raise your weapons to present, turn, and fire at will. Is that agreeable, Cap'n Buford?"

Buford, still wrapped in his cape, nodded.

"And with you, sir?"

"That's just fine," Ole Jury Duty said.

The two combatants took their positions in the dawn light, holding the rifle butts on the ground. The Mississippi group moved to one side, out of the line of fire, Cass and Dinsmore's nephew opposite them. The referee stepped backward a few steps and started the procedure.

"Gentlemen, are you ready?"

"Ready."

"Ready."

"Gentlemen, march! One . . . two . . . three . . ."

Zack could see Ole Jury Duty's face working, his eyes squinting under the brim of the stovepipe hat. He could hear the two men's tread, crunching into the moist, mossy soil with each count. He stopped chewing, the cud held immobile in his cheek.

At the count of twenty, both men turned, bringing up their rifles. Immediately, Captain Buford fired, flame and smoke spouting and the willow oaks trembling. Ole Jury Duty stood blinking, the hat gone from his head with a quick snap, his hair standing in disarray.

"You may fire, sir," the referee called.

"That's my intention!"

"No conversation by contestants," the referee shouted, and Ole Jury Duty ground his teeth and took aim.

The second shot made a sharp crashing note among the trees, like the first. Ole Jury Duty's frail frame jerked back with the shock of the recoil, and the smoke boiled around his face. At the far end of the field, Captain Buford seemed to quiver a moment, like the willow oak leaves. His rifle fell to the ground and slowly he lifted a hand to the side of his head. Zack could see a gout of blood there. Ole Jury Duty had nicked the Mississippian's earlobe! By Gawd!

Both surgeons ran onto the field to assist Captain Buford to a nearby fallen log, and as he sat down he pushed them aside. Blood was running down his neck.

What the hell happens now, Zack wondered, watching as Cass and the Mississippi second conferred in the center of the glade. Ole Jury Duty walked across to Zack and stood with the smoking Enfield butt down, watching, too.

When Cass returned, he said the Mississippi gentleman considered his honor intact now that blood was drawn. Cass had retrieved the tall hat, and now handed it to Scaggs.

"By God!" Ole Jury Duty said, glaring at the .557-caliber holes in the crown.

Sidney Dinsmore's nephew came to them and opened his satchel and produced a black bottle. His Honor took the bottle and drew the cork, passing the rifle to Zack. He took a long jolt and handed the bottle to the others.

While they sipped the whisky again, one of the Mississippi officers came across to them with the second rifle, and Zack took that one, too.

"Captain Buford's compliments, sir," the Mississippian said. "And he asks that you join him in a libation."

"Good," Ole Jury Duty said. "I'll bring some of my own, too."

"These gentlemen are welcome as well," the man said, waving a hand in the general direction of the other three.

"We'll decline," Cass said coldly. "Not being of the officer caste!"

The Mississippian's face reddened, and he turned and stalked away, but Ole Jury Duty and Dinsmore were close behind. There was handshaking and bowing when they reached Captain Buford's log. The two former contestants sat side by side.

"I wonder what Ole Jury was aimin' at," Zack said.

"For the eyes, I suspect."

"Not a bad shot at that."

"Damned foolishness," Cass muttered.

It took a while for the whisky to be consumed. Conversation became rather loud and animated. When it was done, there was more handshaking and bowing.

On the way back to the regiment, Dinsmore's nephew fell twice, scattering bottles and medical instruments from his bag. Ole Jury Duty had begun to expound the virtues of Mississippi troops. Once they had to stop and rest, Scaggs puffing and blowing, spittle in his beard. His eyes were red-rimmed, and he smelled almost as bad as Dinsmore's nephew.

"Look at that, by God," Ole Jury Duty said, taking off his stovepipe hat and pointing at the two holes made by the bullet's passage. "It looks to me like Cap'n Buford was trying to bark me."

"Where was it you taken aim, Cap'n?" Zack asked.

For a long moment Scaggs stared at him, licking his lips with a pointed pink tongue. He slammed the hat back on his head.

"Fawley, I'll only say this. If it'd been you out there doin' the shootin', that Mississippi son of a bitch would be dog meat now!"

# THIRTEEN

THE NIGHT attack and the duel and their ducking mortar shells from the gunboats were about all the action they saw behind Suffolk. The weather was oppressive and the ground sticky. They were never shed of sweat in the day and of shivering at night. And the mud clinging on their feet and trousers was heavy as a wet wash of bedclothes, impossible to avoid, impossible to shake off.

It was a time for short tempers.

Billy Dick Hysel took a head cold, and his constant sniffling and snufflng began to grate on Noah's nerves like a drip from a leaky roof. Billy Dick whined about getting a sick furlough so he could go home to Pine Bluff and eat his mama's chicken and dumplings every day. His harping on that made them all edgy.

Only Morgan seemed to retain his sense of humor, regaling them each night with tales of Sicily and its dark-eyed women.

"Came from that same area did the original Welsh," he said. "Dark and hot-blooded."

"I had supposed from my reading that some of the original Romans were blond and blue-eyed," Martin Hasford said.

Morgan drew back in mock horror.

"Romans, is it? Who's speaking of Romans? Sicily is what I tell of, and dark and hot-blooded they are."

Then came the evening when Billy Dick came in from picket along one of the forward trenches, sniffling and watery-eyed and not watching his next step, and kicked mud in their hominy. They were in one of their revetted ditches with a small cooking fire, and along the trench in either direction were the other fires of the company, strung like glowing beads along the string of the entrenchment.

"Gawd damn you," Noah snarled, and was up from his squat and swinging both fists. Billy Dick dropped his rifle and staggered back against the wall of willow matting, cowering with his arms up, the blood already streaming from his nose.

"Whatsa matter with you?" he wailed. "I ain't done nothin'!"

Noah leaped at him, lips peeled back and fists ready, but Zack was up, too, and caught the arms cocked like pistol hammers.

"Back off hyar," he snapped, and at the sound of his words Noah drew away, but still snorting, his fists balled. Billy Dick lay against the side of the trench, his arms up before his bleeding face.

"Crazy little son of a bitch," Noah panted.

"Cool off," Zack said, his face close to Noah's and his hands flat against Noah's chest. "Jus' cool off now."

The others had not moved, shocked at the unexpected viciousness of the attack. Except for Cass, who knew a little about sudden rages himself. But each of them was aware that it was words alone that had saved the boy from a good mauling—not main strength at all, but the gravelly words from Zack's mouth, some family tone. Only Billy Dick was oblivious to it, thinking just of his own jeopardy.

Zack then turned to the boy, still holding his arms before his face protectively, and pulled them down. Blood was running freely from his nose, across his twisted mouth, and dripping from his fuzz-covered chin. He was crying.

"Hush your blubberin' now," Zack said. "You ain't hurt. Anybody got a piece a' rag?"

"Use mud," Cass said, knowing what Zack had in mind.

From the wall of the trench Zack pinched a wad of mud and kneaded it in his palm, squeezing out all the moisture. When he had a roll the size and shape of a small pecan, he pushed it into Billy Dick's mouth, tight under the upper lip against the gum.

"Ain't even broke," Zack said, feeling the bridge of Billy Dick's nose.

"Yes, it is! It's bleedin' bad an' it's broke. He done broke it!"

"No, he never. Wipe your face."

Billy Dick lifted the ragged tail of his jacket and swiped the blood from his chin. It colored the cloth like walnut stain.

"Why, a hero now," the Welshman said, and his laugh broke the tension. "They'll think you been wounded by the Yanks."

"Ole Hood likely will make a speech about it," Hasford said, smiling sourly but joining in the spirit. Even Billy Dick laughed and continued to wipe his nose and his eyes with the tail of the jacket. But Noah stood well away from them along the trench, glaring, his fists still clenched.

Zack gripped one of the boy's skinny shoulders and shook him, his long teeth showing in a wide grin. Hasford and Tug had begun to clean the dirt from the frying pan, careful to keep the white puffed kernels from spilling out.

"Hominy's jus' hominy. You caint hurt it none," Tug said, shaking his head and grinning as well.

"Looks like a squirrel with his jaws fulla nuts," Zack said.

Billy Dick touched the bulge in his upper lip. There was still a trickle of blood from his nose, but he had stopped crying.

"Making ready for winter, our wee drummer squirrel," the Welshman said. "With mud acorns."

Now it was all fun, and Billy Dick squatted with them and showed the bloodstains on his jacket proudly and said he'd get mentioned in dispatches. Noah was still well back from the group, standing in the trench with his jaw set. Zack moved to him and spoke softly so the others would not hear.

"Don't ever do nothin' like that again," he said. Noah started to speak, but Zack cut him off, reaching out to touch Noah's chest with the tips of his fingers. "You listen an' do like I say. Don't you ever do nothin' like that again. I may not be able to whup you, but by Gawd I won't be as easy as that dumb kid. You remember that, Noy, 'cause you do it again, you got me, not him!"

Noah looked into his brother's eyes for only an instant and

saw nothing there but a calm resolve. He wheeled and stalked away along the trench, his back stiff with indignation. They didn't see him again until the following morning, and by then the anger was gone, although Billy Dick wasn't too confident. As Noah squatted near the breakfast fire, the boy watched him with wide eyes, ready to bolt if required. But when Noah finally spoke, even Billy Dick relaxed.

"I see from the blood on your jacket that the Yankees has wounded you."

They were all glad of one thing: Billy Dick after that tried to be a little less obnoxious, not whining about home and sniffling and wiping his nose on his sleeve. At least for a few days.

A LARGE box arrived for Bev Cass while they were still in the ditches. All the way from Arkansas.

"Maybe it's a ham," Noah said, remembering Harper's Ferry.

When Tug pried off the lid with a bayonet, a small stack of books was revealed, packed with newspapers along each side. Cass read the newspapers first. They were three months old. He scowled through most of the reading as though it were all bad news. When he was finished he threw the papers aside, allowing Tug to use them as fire starter. After stalking up and down the trench for an hour, his face working, Cass told them part of what he had read, enraged and half reluctantly, yet telling them anyway, as though to hold such vile information within himself, bottled up, might rupture his spleen.

"The Yankees have started organizing what they call Arkansas Volunteers of African Descent. In the occupied counties."

"Bet a token some a' Cap'n Gordy's niggers is wearin' Yankee suits right now," Tug said, grinning. But if he was trying to gouge Cass, it was unsuccessful. Cass ignored him.

"And we lost another fight at home. At Prairie Grove. That's close to your place, Parson."

"Yes. Near Fayetteville."

"Well, we lost it. Now the bluecoats are thick as gnats all over the state. They took Arkansas Post the first of the year."

They received that news silently, grimly. They could each remember passing Arkansas Post on the way to Virginia, remember the people who had come to the river's edge there to wave flags as they passed.

"I guess them Yanks is in Pine Bluff, too," Billy Dick said.

Cass glared at him but made no reply.

He hoarded his books like coffee, reading some each evening after drill or duty in the forward lines. But each day the Black Welshman dropped his hints, subtle as case shot, until finally Cass opened his little cache of literature for the rest of them, Tug acting as librarian to keep track of who had what.

"You can't even read, you black heathen," Morgan said.

"No," Tug said, grinning, "but I can see the color of 'em."

Actually, Hasford was the only one to show much interest in campsite reading. He went through *The Count of Monte Cristo* in a week. *Ivanhoe* took longer.

Noah struggled through a contraband copy of *Uncle Tom's Cabin* and decided if they were all like that he would go no further. It aroused only enough interest for him to inquire of Cass if the things written down were true. He had always supposed that the written word was truth simply by the nature of its existence, as with Mama's Bible.

Cass stared at him a long time, his hard little mouth a thin scar in the black beard.

"I never whipped a nigger," he said. "Nor sold a family south."

"Sold a family south?" Noah asked.

"No Cass sold a child away from a mother, nor a wife away from a husband," he said. "I can't speak for any of the others. I can't speak for my cousin Gordy. But I can speak for myself and my father. And that's the rub. They multiply like mice and not enough work for all of them and every one that issues from a woman is obviously whelp of some member of your tribe. You can't keep them all busy, and you can't drown them like unwanted kittens. I speak for the Cass family. I can't speak for the others."

"Well, I was wonderin'," Noah started, and then changed his mind. There was a vicious resentment in Cass's voice that seemed to turn the conversation off. Besides, if he got into this question of carnal knowledge with the slave women, he might hear things he didn't like. So he said no more.

But when he was alone at the outpost, or sometimes before he slept at night, he thought about that book. It disturbed him in a way he couldn't explain. So he thought, Well, if books is like that, the best thang is to jus' stay clear of 'em.

PART of Longstreet's people had already started pulling out of the Suffolk area when they heard about the battle of Chancellorsville. And a few days later, the news went through the army with a shock that Ole Jackson was dead from complications that set in after his wounding by friendly troops on the night of the fight.

In the regiment, where no love had ever been lost between themselves and the Blue Light Presbyterian, there was a sense of doom. No one in either army could have been unaware by then that Jackson was a tactical master of the battlefield, and they heard that Bobby Lee had said he had lost his good right arm. And if Bobby Lee said such a thing, it was something a man could inscribe in his ledger.

It was a dismal time. They had missed a good fight, thrashing around in these southside mud holes, and on top of that they had lost one of their own—and not to Yankee fire, either.

Their spirits rose somewhat when they were issued horses and told they were mounted infantry.

"Dragoons, by God," the Welshman said. "They'll let us fight this war in style yet."

"Don't count too heavy on keeping these horses," Bev Cass said darkly.

Most of them had ridden horses and had little trouble with the brutes. But Billy Dick had not only never been on a horse, he was afraid of them. He fell off seven times the first day.

What was perhaps worse, the horse seemed to sense its advantage and with every opportunity bit Billy Dick's butt. This continued until Martin Hasford started saddling the animal for the boy, and the first time the horse tried to bite him, Hasford cracked the old sorrel square between the eyes with the butt of his rifle.

Cass was right about not keeping the horses. They rode north out of the Suffolk area, skirting Petersburg and Richmond on the west side on the way to rejoin Lee's army. When they arrived, the horses were taken away from them. With not enough horses for the artillery and cavalry, their own chances of staying mounted had been slim from the start.

"Back to shank's mare," Zack said. "I never liked them horses anyways. Too big a target."

"Not if Ole Jury Duty's shootin' at 'em," Noah said, and they all had their laugh.

And Cass thought, It's good they can laugh now. I've got the feeling we won't find much to laugh about from here on.

He was right about that, too.

# FOURTEEN

SOME called it the Shoe Campaign. A few actually found a new pair on this second invasion of the Yankee land. It started as a long walk, a picnic, with nothing to worry them but state militia shooting from long range before fading away. But then the old Army of the Potomac showed up, and the picnic was over.

For each of them who came back to Virginia afterward, there were memories both bitter and sweet. The late-June days were sometimes hot on the march, but there was often cider and they could always raid the beehives and cherry orchards of the good Dutch and German farmers.

The army purchased sauerkraut in some quantity, too, and although that was a new experience for many, Martin Hasford ate it with relish, reminded of the crocks of fermenting cabbage his own mother had brewed when he was a boy, and later his wife, Ora, dipping the shredded kraut from the crock and warming it with a little bacon drippings and sugar mixed in.

The farms they passed were magnificent, even more solid than those they had seen in Maryland. The barns were built like fortresses against the cold of winter, the rolling meadowlands were lush, and cattle and horses grazed over them—at least until the commissary officers appeared.

Towns were neat and well planned with wide streets and the houses all painted, the stores set in rows with sidewalks in front. Here, too, the commissary department came to buy grain and vegetables, paying in promissory notes or Confederate treasury drafts. The army was subsisting on the land as it went, with only a minimum of the long, cumbersome trains tagging along behind. It was a practice long used in Europe and brought to perfection by Napoleon, Morgan said.

When the Welshman mentioned the French emperor,

Martin Hasford thought of the faded miniature painting hanging in his home in Benton County. "Picture Grandpapa" they called him, Martin's grandfather who had gone off to fight the French before the family had come to America—and had been lost on the battlefield at Waterloo.

"Aw, a heritage of soldiering, then," the Welshman said.

"No such thing," Martin replied. "A wild hair turned into his brain and another into mine, too, for coming all this way to fight Yankees, and now they're through all of Arkansas like the pox."

As always when he thought of home, he was reminded that his daughter was married to one of those Yankees now. But at least the thought had ceased to sour his stomach, as it had at first and for some time. He reflected on his wife, Ora, and it was painful to him that she was not so much on his mind now as before, when the war was young.

The turnpikes were hard-surfaced, tough on tender feet, unlike the mud and dust of Virginia roads. But they marched in good spirits, singing sometimes, the people coming out from their farms to line the fences, or from the town houses to wave Yankee flags. When one of these was a pretty young woman, defiantly holding the stars and stripes, they would cheer and doff their hats as they passed.

There were strict orders against pillaging. General Lee himself had said that looting and destruction or theft of private property would not be tolerated, an order they took not to include bee gums and orchards. Anyway, rations were good now. Yankee grub, they called it, and the taste was made even better by knowing that it had been grown in enemy country but would never pass Federal lips.

Much of their meat came on the hoof, the cattle being driven to their camps and left standing for them to butcher. One cow was all they needed to ration the regiment for a day. There were only four hundred men left, and in the company less than forty.

Each of them having had experience in the slaughter of livestock, the work went quickly at the end of each day's march. With the blood splattered on their trousers they laughed and argued about which mess units would get the choice cuts of loin and neck. But it didn't matter much, there was enough for all.

There were turkeys, too, and by now it bothered them little that they had not enough time to cook a turkey thoroughly before having to move on. Half raw was good enough, and that was the way they ate it.

From one bird Ole Jury Duty confiscated a long tailfeather and had it set on his hat, Tug doing the job with needle and thread taken from Bev Cass's roll, which seemed to hold all manner of things necessary. Scaggs's purposeful stalking, his grim face and stooped shoulders, became incongruous after that, with the feather bobbing jauntily from the crown of the stovepipe hat. As though he were a cavalryman with a cape and yellow neckpiece. And somewhere he had found four brass buttons and set them in twos along the cuffs of his jacket.

"Next he'll be after one a' them officer's coats with the chicken guts on the sleeves," Zack said.

Nights were warm, and the only fires needed were those meant for cooking and evening conversation. They visited back and forth with the Texas men, having become all one family. Burton came over again to cut Noah's hair and stayed to tell tall stories about Comanches and Kiowas and Tonkawas.

It was on one of those pleasant nights, the company sleeping on shelter halves instead of under them, that Zack dreamed of Miz Rozella's Afternoon Tea Sippin' Society and Billiard Hall. Or at least some place like it.

He saw the oranges and the oysters, only in the dream they were handed to him by familiar cinnamon-flecked hands, Tug's insolent grinning face beaming behind the offered delicacies.

He saw Ole Jury Duty and Bev Cass and General Hood, all pushing chemise-clad women toward him, and with one of these there was finally a bed and the gray dawn and the hot, naked form beside him under the clean sheets, and afterward Zack looking up and there was Mama poking with a broomstick into a cast-iron pot steaming over a hickory fire. Washing bedclothes and looking at him with a sad smile.

He woke in a cold sweat, drenched to the skin and thinking frantically, None a' them was there. None a' them seen me there.

And then as he came more fully awake there was the sudden, almost sickening desire to bolt this army and go back to Richmond. Just for a little while.

But as the others rose to cook their Yankee beefsteak spitted on ramrods and bayonets, he regained his composure, brought back to reality by the familiar sullen grumbling of soldiers rising to a new day.

"We're sure'n hell gettin' a long way from home," he said.

They knew what he meant. They had all been in this Army of Northern Virginia for so long now that each of them almost considered the Old Dominion native soil. Maybe it was, too, their being here in the first place to defend it. Maybe, they thought, that's what makes a home—the place a man defends.

Billy Dick Hysel caught himself humming "The Black-Eyed Suzie" and stopped, embarrassed. They all thought about Sidney Dinsmore and Ole Dad Johnson, buried in Virginia earth. Maybe that helped make it home, too.

They wondered where the Federals were, the real Yankee army. Surely not still sitting on its arse back along the Rappahannock, with Bobby Lee loose in Pennsylvania. And they wondered about their own troops. There were three corps in Lee's army now. Ole Bald Head Ewell had Jackson's Second, and the Third was under Little Powell Hill. Of course, they still had Ole Pete and Hood heading up the division.

Sometimes when they were marching they saw other columns, far away, moving parallel, flags to mark each regiment, the artillery horses kicking up fine plumes of dust. They didn't see much friendly cavalry.

But if they didn't know where everything was, they were confident Bobby Lee did. Knowing nothing of dispositions or destination, they marched on. Almost casually, enjoying the view of the wide countryside, the maturing wheat and the bearing orchards and the clusters of farm buildings, stone and whitewash in the sun, raspberries ripening and larks nesting in the rye and barley.

Then July came, and it was hurry-up. They knew something was happening. They knew something was ahead. They moved to Cashtown on the first day of the month, stacked arms, and waited.

Toward the east they could hear it—the low grumble of artillery, and then the sudden rattle of infantry columns closing to combat. They didn't say much. They didn't look at one another either. They sat on the ground near their stacks, silently, listening to the tune of battle starting up, watching the far roads filled with artillery moving forward.

Nearby was a road sign, pointing. Morgan read it aloud for the benefit of those incapable of reading it themselves:

"Gettysburg."

THE FIRST day was waiting. Then, in the early light of the second, they moved to the low ridge and behind the seminary buildings, to a position overlooking the long valley where a broad road ran north into the town sitting tight against the nose of a dominating ridge. Directly east of them, across the valley and the road, they saw the high knobs of two hills, the southern anchoring structure of that same ridge.

Those far mounds of rock and earth, that was where they were going. Officers came among them and pointed out routes of advance, advising of supporting columns on either side—there, across the road and through the wheat and up the high ground to the flank of the Union position. When they first saw the round tops, there were no signs of Union troops there.

Through field glasses could be seen the gray headstones of a cemetery along the saddle of the ridge. Smoke was there, and the crash of a firefight on the hill over the town. In the lulls of firing, they could hear the infantry drums beating the Federals up and into position among the gravestones. And some thought they could hear the drums from directly beyond the round tops, coming toward the position they intended to take.

Waiting, watching. The whole corps coming up, bayonets already fixed. Crouching along their own ridge. Artillery coming into position among the oaks and elms, unlimbering and running brutal snouts out toward the blue line. Time slipped away, and there was intense thirst and nervousness and gnats nipping at damp necks; and their own drums, too, rattling the long roll behind them as each brigade slipped into place.

Still they crouched as the morning ebbed, smoke rising densely now from the hill above the town, and the clamor of a fight there, three miles away.

Their own artillery began a thunderous cannonade, making everyone cringe. The sound crashed on their eardrums and the smoke choked them. Only a few minutes of it and the Federal guns answered, throwing dirt into their faces, clipping branches from the trees, showering them with bark and acorns.

Some of the crouching units began to take casualties, and the order went along the line to lie down. The Yankee guns roared on, each minute growing in strength until finally all the explosions seemed to melt into one shattering blast.

Still they waited, some of them under fire, the sun going toward the west, the shadows lengthening across the long valley and the Emmitsburg road. Hood was behind them on a lathered horse, red-faced and furious, cursing as he sent off couriers and took their messages when they returned, riding off himself, then back with his troops, more enraged than before.

Scaggs, too, bellowing curses, the turkey feather in his hat seeming to stiffen with each oath.

"Why in the name of God don't we move?"

The hours went down, the friendly artillery slackening due to lack of ammunition, and the Union guns still racketing against them. The infantry strained forward, almost hysterical to march, to go against those Yankee guns.

On the knob of ground directly opposite them—Little Round Top, they called it—there were blossoms of smoke where there had been none before. And they knew that if Federal guns were there, infantry would be close beside them, in force. And the drums telling them that more were moving up.

"It ain't no flank now," Zack muttered. "It's right square into 'em."

Finally the order came. The flags went up and they leaped out from the trees, shouting, aligning their ranks, marching toward the road eagerly, glad to be moving. The uneven ground dipped under their feet until they reached the road, then tilted upward toward the Round Top.

Blue pickets and perhaps a regiment awaited them on line, maybe more in the field ahead. There was a quick exchange of shots and a charge, the blues going back without haste, confident.

Into the wheat, thrashing through growth knee-high, feeling the hot burst of Federal shell around them, they ran to the sharply sloping ground where the trees and boulders stood. The rocks were gray and forbidding, large as houses, even barns, and crowned with the smoke of Yankee sharpshooters.

Noah abruptly went to ground in the thick growth of wheat. He hadn't stumbled, nor was he hit. He simply went to ground because his legs would no longer support him, and the line swept on beyond where he lay.

Beside him was his rifle, and he tried to take it in his hand. His fingers were trembling so badly he had no sensation of touch, no strength to grip the wood and metal. His eyes were smarting even though there were only wisps of powder smoke here, and that quickly blown away. His tongue was thick and tasted of sour brass, and his belly was quaking, legs quivering.

He had seen panic—formation panic when entire units bolted—and he had been a part of such things above Harper's Ferry with the cows, and again running back up the slope toward the Hagerstown Pike at Sharpsburg. But this was not mass fear—contagious, catching like measles one soldier to the next. This was his alone!

The stalks of golden wheat before his eyes were invisible. He had no impression of anything, neither the noise ahead nor the bugles blowing on the heights nor the drums. He stared sightless, heaving, trying to vomit, but then nothing coming up, and the wild, mindless fear shaking him until his hat fell from his head and lay in the wheat.

He was insensitive to the regimental line going by, on into

the blazing tangles at the rising base of Little Round Top. They were driving upward, forcing their way until the ground dropped suddenly into a small streambed, and beyond that the top of the hill blossoming with smoke and flame. They were close enough to the Union guns to see the black muzzles depressed to meet them, sending down canister and case shot. Infantry was there, too, ranks of them firing from behind rocky entrenchments.

Then they saw to their left that no other single grayback soldier was advancing, and the call went up, "Where the hell's McLaws now?" remembering Sharpsburg.

The other brigades made their move, but each came singly, each then butchered by the Yankee fire. One after another, and then another and yet another, fighting through the fields beside the turnpike, the peach orchard where the metal was tearing limbs from trees.

"Hunker down, boys," Ole Jury Duty screeched. "The God damned corps has come in piecemeal, and it's every regiment for itself!"

Where's Noah, where's Noah? Zack kept thinking frantically, looking down the slope they had crossed and along the line, stumbling beside a young man head-shot and lying face up in the rocks. But now too intense with the fight to continue looking, tasting the bitter grit of black powder between his teeth.

"Sons a' bitches!" he gasped, over and over, ramming home the loads, sweating out his water, the salt stains forming crescents under his arms.

Devil's Den they would call it. They could push no farther. They fired until rifles were sweating hot oil, dropping Federal gunners at the top and seeing other blueclads take the place of the fallen. Bullets from the Union position struck rocks and ricocheted off with vicious whines, throwing fragments of stone as deadly as the metal.

They shot the top off Ole Jury Duty's stovepipe hat and the turkey feather along with it, and then shot away the greater portion of his left hand.

"I sentence you to hell!" he roared at the blue lines, the blood streaming and Martin Hasford trying to get a torn-sleeve tourniquet in place on the upper arm.

They killed Tug as he stood beside Cass, frantically reloading a rifle, shot through the throat. No one moved back, and the short, slashing combat continued as the sun lowered.

Hand to hand in some places, too, where the grays forced back salients in the blue lines. Morgan was swinging his clubbed rifle as he had above the Antietam, and then his fists as he had on that snow-lit field the night he retrieved Noah's hat.

In places they were so close their muzzle blasts set fire to blue Union tunics.

Ole Jury Duty gone to the rear now, Martin Hasford thrust his rifle to shoulder like a pitchfork, his deep voice raised with irrepressible swearing.

Zack took a bullet through the thigh, but no bone or artery was touched. He ripped off the shirt of a dying Federal and bandaged it himself.

It took some time for Cass to realize Tug had fallen. When he saw the boy's crumpled form, he lifted the body and carried it back down the hill, the oversized coat still worn even in this heat, dyed red now as it draped the body, the cinnamon face turned the color of old ashes. Cass carried the boy across the wheatfield, across the road, and beyond to the trees where the silent Confederate artillery stood, and beyond that, too, behind the Seminary Ridge somewhere, to bury the boy with his own hands.

When Bev Cass returned, evening was drawing on. He sought out Morgan in the bedlam and held out a glinting coin.

"I think this belongs to you," he said.

He climbed then to the top of a tall boulder, took casual aim at the Federal positions, and commenced firing again and then again, most of the company sheltered behind the rocks and now loading for him.

It was almost dark when Cass fell for the first time, a spout of red along his right flank. He rose, climbed back on top of the boulder, took up the next rifle, and continued firing, methodically, slowly, making his shots go home. There was no expression on his dark face, only the grim slit of his mouth in the beard, as always.

Again he was hit but scrambled up. Firing. The men below shouting to him now, telling him to come down. Ole Jury Duty gone to the rear and Bev Cass now the company commander. But he stayed, and fell once more, the blood across his front so universal that no single wound could be seen.

One last time he fired, and was down again, slipping along the face of the rock. He was taken by many hands and placed gently on the ground. And died there.

Billy Dick Hysel clutched the drum to his chest, nose running, tears on his face, his own rifle hot only because Cass had been firing it. The boy stared down at the dying eyes, sniffing, wiping his nose on his sleeve.

"O Gawd, help us," he bawled, and slid into a squat with his back against a boulder, his face down on the head of the drum, his frail shoulders shaking. It was only then that he realized his trousers were wet, and he had no notion of when it had happened.

Then it was night. And they lay panting among the rocks, quivering in every muscle as they had once before, along the Hagerstown Pike, spent and shocked and wounded, among their dead and dying, among the shattered remnants of the regiment. And the Federal position still intact.

NOAH was sitting in the wheat when Zack found him. It was pure chance in the darkness, Zack coming down from the Round Top with only a forlorn hope of locating his brother and afraid of what he'd find if he did. Noah had his hat off, sitting cross-legged with his rifle in his lap as Zack came running to him through the wheat beaten down by the passage of the regiment that afternoon.

"Noy? That you?" Zack moved in close, bent forward, his hat almost touching Noah's face, his hands tentatively on his brother's shoulders, searching down the sides for the feel of blood.

"I ain't wounded," Noah said quietly but impatiently, pushing aside Zack's hands.

"Where you been?" Zack squatted in the wheat, trying to see the features of Noah's face, but it was only a pale blur in the night.

"Hyar," Noah said. "Jus' sittin' in this ole wheatfield."

Zack knew then, didn't have to be told. He looked off toward the dim slash of the Emmitsburg Road. All along the ridge behind him was the occasional pop of a rifle, and somewhere beyond that he could hear artillery moving. Along Seminary Ridge were pinpoints of cooking fires, and up the valley the wavering glow of a barn burning.

"What's that on your laig?" Noah asked.

"A little wrappin'."

"You wounded?"

"It ain't much. Be a little stiff in the mornin', I expect, an' that's 'bout all it amounts to."

Somewhere back along the high ground they heard a single voice, shouting for the First Texas. Then it was still.

"You want a chaw?" Zack asked.

He offered his plug to Noah, and Noah took it, gnawing off a cheekful. Zack worked off a chew himself, and they listened to one another grinding their teeth on the hard tobacco.

"You hongry?"

"No."

After another long silence, Noah said, "I reckon Ole Jury Duty's likely after me now."

"No, he ain't. Thangs was busy up there today. I don't thank he's thought about it much. They had to carry him off. Bad shot in the han'."

"I heerd some of 'em comin' back through the wheat. I jus' lay here."

"Cass is dead," Zack said. "An' that colored boy a' his."

"Aw, hell," Noah groaned, and spat the wad of tobacco out into the wheat. "I never liked the taste a' that stuff no way."

Once more a silence, except for the whispering sounds of the battlefield, punctuated now and again with rifle shots, individually, with no purpose, no sound of malice.

"Well, I reckon maybe I oughta be takin' you home now," Zack said.

Noah snorted and groped on the ground for his hat. He pulled it down savagely onto his head and rose, supporting himself with his rifle.

"Not yet," he said. "I reckon you better lead me back up there fer the rest of it."

Still squatting, Zack could hear the harsh sound of bitterness, maybe of shame.

"We could make 'er. If you wanta go. I reckon you've served out your time."

"If you wanta go home, go," Noah said. "But I ain't goin' with you. Is the parson and the Welsh still up yonder?"

"Yeah, both kickin'. You thank you're all right now?"

"Well, I ain't gonna set hyar in this wheat an' fin' out."

"Whatcha reckon happened?"

"I don' know," Noah said with amazement and sudden animation, shaking himself, lifting his rifle. "It jus' come over me like a fever. Maybe it was all that waitin', seein' all that groun' we had to go acrost. Hell, I don't know. I jus' spooked, I guess."

"Well, you never run off anyway."

Noah laughed harshly. "Zack, my laigs wouldn't carry me nowhere. Iffen the Yankees had come, they coulda picked me up right off the groun'!"

He stamped his feet as though testing his strength. "Nothin' wrong now," he said.

"I'll take you home iffen you want me to."

"No." Noah stared along the dark valley. It was some time before he spoke. "When I go home it ain't gonna be after somethin' like this. It's gonna be after I've showed somethin' better'n I done today."

"You showed that already. But I reckon it's always the last bite that a man tastes."

"Yeah, an' I ain't figurin' to have such a taste as this all the rest of my days. I'd kinda like to go home an' have Pap be proud a' me."

"He would be. You've did enough fer that."

Noah said nothing. They heard a small group of horsemen move down from Seminary Ridge to the Pike, converse shortly, then rein back toward the treeline where the fires showed.

"I wanta go back," Noah said, finally giving up on saying anything more about it.

"If you thank you can do 'er."

"I can sure as hell try," Noah said, and Zack could hear the old Fawley stubbornness in the quiet tone. He recalled again that cougar on the limestone ledge and everyone running, and the lonely fear that had been his until Uncle Questor found him. And even with the fear, still saying, "Le's go back yonder and get that painter!"

Noah moved off toward the high ground for a few paces, then turned and stood in the beaten-down wheat, his rifle hanging loosely from one hand.

"I'm beholden you come back fer me."

Now it was Zack who laughed mirthlessly.

"You never figured I'd leave you out hyar in the dark by yourself, didja?"

"I pondered on it. After what I done."

"Hell! I can't figure why I never thought a' doin' it my own self!"

He sighed then and rose and moved to lead the way back to Devil's Den.

ON THE third day they waited still, though occupied with sniping at the Yankees and the Yankees at them. To the rear was Seminary Ridge, from whence they had come the afternoon before. They were the right-flank anchor of the Rebel line, and from their high ground near Little Round Top they could survey the sweep of the valley directly before the Union center. They saw there the Southern charge of July 3.

Pickett's division of Ole Pete's corps led, and behind them came the entire Third Corps of Little Powell Hill—against the Union line north of Devil's Den, against the saddle where the headstones stood.

They watched the first of it, their own sharpshooting forgotten for the moment. The Yankees opposite them paused, too. The gray lines were well dressed as the far troops moved, the red flags going before them. After the advance had moved about a half-mile they could see it no longer because of the curve of the ground.

"They'll have the Yanks on the run by messtime!"

"Them blues ain't likely to stand up again that!"

"Ole Pickett'll have 'em sniffin' his perfumed hair before this day is out!"

And Ole Jury Duty back with the dawn, his hand a mass of bandages already blood-soaked, screaming at them, "Tend your own God damned front!"

The earth trembled with the sound of the battle in the center. As the smoke drifted down across the regiment's position they could hear the faint cries, a deep moaning shout, desperate and prolonged. Then they began to see Pickett's men and all the others, going back across the long valley. There were no lines now, only stumbling, straggling men. And fewer flags, and those bowed down.

Shortly their own orders came to retire, too, and Ole Jury Duty raged, clanging his Mexican War saber against the rocks.

"God dammit, we came this far to no purpose, them whore fornicators, them putrid shit boats!"

Nobody knew whom he was cursing, but on it went as they stumbled back down the rocky knoll, across the field and the turnpike and into the trees along Seminary Ridge. There they threw themselves on the ground, and sent watering parties with all the canteens for the nearest stream. Slowly, as the last of them arrived, they were turned back again to face the Federal lines, and waited once more, this time for the blues to make their advance.

They waited through the night and the next day, and no one came.

"It's Independence Day," Martin Hasford said. His own dismembered rifle had been replaced by the one held in Bev Cass's hand the first time Cass had mounted the boulder to do his shooting.

"Maybe the Yanks will give us a salute for the glorious Fourth," the Black Welshman said.

But they waited for that in vain, too. There were no sounds of celebration from across the valley, only the rumble of artillery and trains moving.

They began their long march back to Virginia in the rain, dragging their wounded with them. Zack was using a second rifle as a walking stick, but his own was still primed and ready.

Morgan, trudging through the mud, slipped the double eagle from his pocket and let the rain wash it in the palm of his hand, the coin that had been held secret in the black boy's pocket, its brother spent by Morgan and the others in that Richmond whorehouse. And before that, it too held secret in Tug's pocket since leaving the Mississippi River.

Cursing, the Black Welshman shoved the coin back into his trouser pocket. "That little African bandit," he said. "I never wanted it back like this."

Hasford said, " 'Sufficient unto the day is the evil thereof.' "

"Damn your sufficiency, Parson!"

Over the hills and mountains then to the Potomac fords, now high from the rain. They waited until the pontoons were floated and crossed onto Virginia soil again, no harm from the Federals behind. And on the friendly shore their spirits began to revive. They looked over their shoulders as though half wishing the blue army would come to them—the earth of Virginia seeming to seep courage up through their shoes, to strengthen them once more.

"By Gawd," Noah said, moving beside Zack, "next time we'll clean their plow!"

"Somebody done bad back there," Zack said grimly. "That charge again the rocks was like ever' brigade fightin' its own private war."

"Hit on it you have, brother," the Black Welshman said. "Part of the army fought the first day, part the second, and yet another part the third. And Bobby Lee saying it's all his fault."

"I don't believe that," Noah said harshly. "It ain't his fault. An' you wait. Next time we'll scald their arse."

"Not iffen we try doin' 'er alone," Zack said. "You caint whup that bunch without all the help you got at han'. Maybe not even then."

"Like hell, I say," Noah snapped.

They stumbled on, Ole Jury Duty strangely silent now, head bowed, his ravaged hat poking its shattered crown toward the skyline like the burst muzzle of a cannon, the bandage on his hand wet with a mix of rain and blood.

Noah muttered again, "We'll scald 'em next time. Wait an' see."

There was in him then a bitter, savage desire to erase somehow the memory of his failure in that charge, to blot out the fear that had overcome any ability to move.

The shame sat like a rock in his belly, worse than it had been after that whorehouse in Richmond, worse than when watching Zack drunk and making a fool of himself. Because this had to do with cowardice, he was sure, that same crime for which men had been shot in this army. The crime for which he had always had only contempt because it had to do with being a man—with being a Fawley.

He would burn the memory from his soul. And no more compassion for fear's victims than before. Maybe less, so as to harden himself against it ever happening to him again.

But as the rain dripped from his contorted face, Noah knew he would never be able to forget the wheatfield along the Emmitsburg Road.

AFTER crossing the long pontoon bridge over the Potomac, the company moved south with the rest of the army. All except Billy Dick Hysel. He moved west. At least that was the direction he assumed.

It was night and there were occasional spits of rain. He held the drum in his arms to keep it from banging against his legs, the sticks thrust into the waistband of his trousers.

At first he saw a few farmhouse windows, orange rectangles in the darkness, but as he hurriedly stumbled along the road these became few, and finally he saw none at all. He looked at the stars, when they were visible, and tried to determine the time, tried to remember how Zack Fawley told him to do it. But he couldn't keep it clear in his mind.

I think Ole Zack just felt time in his guts, he thought, an' all that lookin' at stars like they was a clock was a big josh!

He was wet, partly with the rain but more from sweat. His feet slapped the firm gravel mud of the road like poker cards being dealt on a damp table. He had started this campaign with a good pair of shoes, though two sizes too big, and they were still passable.

I wonder how long it'll take to get to Arkansas, he thought. I wonder how I'll get across that big son of a bitch river.

He was cold and knew it wasn't right being cold in July. He thought about the others—Noah and the parson and the Welshman and Zack—likely around a fire at this moment, roasting corn or maybe cooking some good Yankee meat. His stomach turned at the thought, twisted in hunger.

Gotta stop recallin' them boys, he thought. I'm makin' my own way now, outa all this hell's fire an' shootin'. Gotta jes' keep walkin' along this ole road. Gotta stay clear a' provost guards. Gotta get on to Arkansas.

He found the corncrib well before dawn and lay on a mat of cobs, too tired to feel the roughness. He could hear mice in the husks, and somewhere nearby a great horned owl hooted. He shivered.

Hope that ole owl don't come in hyar after none a' them mice, he thought. I don't like them owls with them big ole eyes an' that little sharp beak an' them claws.

His last thoughts before he slept were on that big son of a bitch river.

# FIFTEEN

WHEN Martin Hasford read aloud the copy of the *Richmond Examiner*, Noah was furious.

"Defeat, hell!" he snorted. "We left a pride a' them blues in the dirt!"

"Dead do not a victory make, little brother," Morgan said, "unless the living run."

"There seems to be less and less of running as they go along," Martin said.

"I seem to recall no runnin' amongst them at any time," said Zack, his bandaged leg straight out before him as he sat applying an oily rag to his rifle.

"A tragedy it is," the Welshman said. "In every fight we've had a part of, there has been no running amongst them. From here on, me for the battles where the blues take to their rear."

"By Gawd, they'll never see our backsides!" Noah said.

"A fire-eater, that little brother," Morgan laughed. "But please recall the cows above Harper's Ferry and the hayfield beside the Antietam."

Noah flushed and started to say something, but Zack cut in quietly. "A time to go for'ard, a time to go back. That's what war is, it appears."

"If we'd stayed behind that fence at Sharpsburg where we belonged . . ." Noah let it trail off.

They were resting beside the road as a column of artillery passed. Some of the horses were shining and fat—the ones taken in the north—but mostly they were bags of bone, and some of the limbers and caissons looked as though they might fall apart at any moment.

They were reading newspapers brought along the line by a headquarters courier. A few Yankee publications, too, delivered to the army by some of Longstreet's spies, so they had heard. Morgan was frowning over an issue of the *New York World*.

"My, my, trouble in New York town, with riots and hanging Negroes to the lampposts and troops firing on the citizens."

"Good," Noah said. "It's what we need in all the Yankee towns."

"What's it about?" Martin Hasford asked.

"Draft riots they call them. People out of patience with the war and opposed to Mr. Lincoln's conscription. Gone out on a bender."

"Good," Noah said.

"This anarchy, not a pleasant sight," said the Welshman. "Even amongst the people of an enemy."

"By Gawd, I'll bet this war is finished soon enough, with all them Yankee civilians raisin' Cain. I tol' you we laid so many in the dirt . . ."

"What a fire-eater, this little brother of yours, Zack!"

"He's a caution when he gets thinkin'."

But there was little time for wool-gathering here, no matter the reason. New recruits were coming into the company—conscripts, most of them substitutes for men actually called. Morgan's squad knew that most of them would slip away at the first opportunity.

"A shifty-eyed crew," Martin Hasford said bitterly. "Leeches on a corrupt way of doing things. I wonder how many times they've enlisted or substituted just for the money, then skipped their muster roll to join someplace else."

"Frightful cynic you've become, Parson."

"The damned bastards," Hasford said, and none of them raised an eyebrow now.

Even worse were the ones who didn't come at all and had no need to buy a substitute, exempt from conscription because they owned twenty or more slaves. It was a law resented in this company with harsh bitterness.

"Those with the most to lose eat the least of Yankee lead," Morgan said.

And Martin Hasford added, "Amen. The bastards!"

"Well," Zack said, "Ole Billy Dick's out of it. One way or the other."

"Oh, I suspect he's halfway across Tennessee by now," Morgan said. "And likely in a Yank prison pen, what with the blues in most of Tennessee."

"And in most of Arkansas, too, if he makes it that far," Martin Hasford said.

There was talk of recruiting blacks, to be set free for their service.

"I ain't marchin' with no nigger," Noah said sullenly.

Zack looked at him calmly, chewing.

"You already have with one. An' et his cookin' an' played his three-card monte an' seen him carried off the field by Bev Cass."

Noah started to retort that he had seen no such thing, having been in that wheatfield, but then realized the admission. And realized, too, that Zack had said it for the benefit of the others.

"That was different," he said instead. "He wasn't no sojur."

"Neither are you. Jus' a rock-hill farmer with a rifle."

"Well," Noah said, furious at both Zack and himself for getting into this, and all over some darky, "well, hell, ain't we all sojurs?"

"I ain't gonna get in no fuss today," Zack said easily. "You wanta fuss, pick out one a' these other fellas."

They knew there was a movement coming. The rumors were floating through the army like butterflies on spring breezes, hard to catch but brilliant and tantalizing. Longstreet and most of his corps were going off to some other theater, they had heard. Maybe to the west. Maybe all the way to Arkansas, Hasford hoped.

"Small chance," the Welshman said. "Ole Pete off to Tennessee, I'd wager."

"If that's it, I don't like it," Hasford said. "Ole Pete's all right, but we didn't seem to work so well when we were at Suffolk away from Bobby Lee."

"Yes, Parson, I speak it for us all," Morgan said. "When the large cards go down, it's me for the Gray Virginian. And all of us!"

"Ever' day this war goes on, you two talk more like generals," Zack said, spitting an amber stream at his feet.

Now there was the hurried activity of the division taking on provisions and new men—drilling, issuing new weapons, teaching the new arrivals what they knew, what they had learned from hard experience. They watched the recruits with stoic detachment, feeling no real involvement.

Their own mess group remained the same. Ole Jury Duty would stalk by with new men trailing him like a gaggle of geese, and the eyes of Morgan's squad would meet his with obvious resistance. Scaggs would pass on, leaving them intact as they had been from March Landing. Intact yet shrunk.

"Easier cooking for only four," Hasford said.

"And most of them cut and run at the first hint of artillery," Morgan said. "Bounders all."

Noah glanced at Zack, but the elder Fawley was staring at the ground.

"Yeah," Noah said, "bounders all."

Once, Scaggs returned after assigning new men and stood before them, chewing his teeth furiously.

"You hill-stompers seem to have outlasted some of our Delta boys," he said. "Don't take it as expectation of special privilege!"

"Oh, no, Cap'n," Morgan said, grinning. "I have been meaning to suggest that you need a new hat. The better to impress these new men. And besides, that one lets in the rain, I'd expect."

Ole Jury Duty stared pop-eyed for a moment, his jaw working, then wheeled indignantly and marched away, his Mexican War saber clanging. He was holding his bandaged hand well out to one side, as though he were carrying a dripping ham.

While they had their laugh, Noah looked at the Welshman and marveled at the shrinkage of solid flesh. Morgan's arms were slender now, and his jacket hung on shoulders that showed bone. Above the great beard his cheeks were as hollow as every soldier's in this camp. I hope he don't run acrost that Irishman again, Noah thought. He ain't much stouter lookin' than me now.

Since Pennsylvania, Noah had lain awake many times thinking about carnage. He could recall the first time he had watched Pap butcher hogs. It had been a horrifying thing, but fascinating as well. And before he was fairly old enough to talk, the gore and laying open of pork had become commonplace, unaffecting. But pork's not men, he thought, even if the blood's the same color. You can get used to pork, but not so easy to men. Yet as time goes along a man has to rassle with those sights for less an' less time afterward.

He watched the new men each day. They acted hard, but Noah could see the apprehension in their eyes. They'll get their chance to rassle with it like all the rest of us has done, he thought. They'll see soon enough they ain't nobody hard enough to forget them sights on a battlefield. An' some will cut an' run. They be most generally a scabby lot a' red-eyed thieves.

He pondered the obvious. After Gettysburg, just as the rations seemed to grow worse, so did the recruits. It seems to me, he thought, that we're runnin' outa both!

But he was ready for it again. Maybe just to prove to himself and Zack that his lapse along the Emmitsburg Road was only that, a lapse. If we could jus' get shed a' this Gawd damned drill! Anything's better'n this Gawd damned drill!

BILLY Dick Hysel thought he had walked long enough to be in Texas, but since he had still not come to that big son of a bitch river, he suspected a miscalculation. Actually, he had ended close to the Shenandoah Valley, what with taking the line of least resistance on mountain roads and being so scared he often lost all sense of direction, traveling at night as he did.

It was almost a relief when the hard-faced old farmer with white chin whiskers gouged him out of a hayloft with a pitchfork.

"What're you doin' in my barn, boy?"

Billy Dick sat up with hay and hair equally mixed, and rubbed his eyes.

"I was jus' sleepin' a spell."

"You steal that drum?"

"No, sir. My paw got me that in Pine Bluff, Arkansas."

"That's a far piece from here."

"Yes, sir. I been the drummer boy for my regiment."

The farmer poked at the blue trousers with the tines of the fork.

"Them britches you're wearin' makes you a Yankee, I guess. You're a little out of your bailiwick, ain't you?"

"No, sir. No Yankee. Confed'rate. These hyar was Yankee plunder an' issued by Gen'l Lee's commissary department."

The old man scratched his chin whiskers, the fork down now. He stared at Billy Dick's face with watery blue eyes.

"You're a deserter, ain't you?"

Billy Dick swallowed hard and yanked on his hat, then pulled the drum tight against his belly. "I been in the army two years and reckoned it was time somebody else done it."

"Uh-huh. Well, come on in the house. The old lady likely got some breakfast ready."

The man pronounced *house* as though it were spelled like *moose*, and Billy Dick figured he was still in Virginia. But he didn't care. He didn't care if the provost guards caught him and shot him out of hand so long as he could get a bellyful of food first.

"We're tidewater folks," the man said as they walked from the barn toward the small whitewashed house, set around with flower beds. "Come up here a few years before the war."

"My paw's a preacher an' a storekeeper," Billy Dick said.

"Well, let's get some breakfast."

It didn't amount to much—boiled poke greens and fried hominy. There was some cornbread, too. Billy Dick ate furiously, his gaze darting around the little kitchen as he stuffed his mouth.

The old lady reminded him at once of his mother, skittering about the room like a waterbug in her half apron, a bun of hair at the nape of her neck, gray as the old man's whiskers. She exclaimed over the drum and the pretty red sides and the bullet hole there that was from the Maryland campaign.

"My land, you was hungry, wasn't you?" she said. "We used to have eggs each mornin'."

"And biscuits," the old man said. "Not much white flour hereabouts now. Not much grain left. No chickens."

"The army comes and buys everything."

"No army bought the chickens. They was stole, right straight out of the coop."

"All of it goes to our soldier boys," she said, ladling another heaping mess of greens onto Billy Dick's plate. "So long as we have enough not to starve, it's all right, goin' to the soldier boys."

"The chickens was stole," the old man said.

"It don't leave much, this war," she said. "But you're welcome to what they is."

"I never took much to chicken thieves or deserters," the man said, but without anger, his watery old eyes unwavering on Billy Dick's face.

"First year wasn't so bad," she said. "But times grow hard now."

"It was likely Yankees stole the chickens," the man said. "When they was in the valley under that Banks or some other general."

"We've seen lots of Yankees on horses."

"Good horses, too."

"Sometimes we see our boys. But we're kinda out of the way here."

"Never could abide deserters."

The old lady finally sat with them at the table, eating daintily, like Billy Dick's mother always had—a little piece at a time, chewing at the front of her mouth.

"My ma fixes poke greens lots of times," Billy Dick said. "With a chunk 'a sowbelly."

"My land, I don't use much fat anymore, so little of it."

"They bought the hogs, too. And all the fat they can get," the old man said. "They take that fat to Richmond and make gunpowder. You know how that works?"

"No, sir," Billy Dick said. "I don't know much about makin' gunpowder."

"They say they use fat for that. I never heard of any such thing. But that's what they say."

Billy Dick was feeling guilty, especially after the second helping of hominy. There had not been over two cupfuls at the start. Here he was, running back to Arkansas, with these nice old folks and the Yankees about to come down on them if he wasn't there to help stop it.

"Both my sons was with Jackson," the old man said.

"No need to fret about that now," she said. "But it's true. Both sons, one still there, but Jackson dead, Lord rest him."

"And rest Hershel."

"Yes. Our youngest gone to his reward, killed in glory at Manassas."

The guilt grew even heavier as the old woman brought out a tintype photograph of two boys, looking grim and very young. While Billy Dick held it, the woman pointed to one of the images.

"Hershel was about your age when he was taken."

He had no inkling what it was—maybe the photograph, or maybe exhaustion from night walking alone in a strange country, or maybe simple lonesomeness for the old squad—but when the old man brought out a Winchester newspaper, the guilt was like solid shot in his belly.

"You see this, son?" the old man asked, pointing to a story. "President Davis has issued a proclamation of amnesty for any of you boys who want to come back."

"Am'sty?"

"That's right. It means anybody who has left the army and wants to come back won't get in trouble."

"Won't get in trouble?"

"That's right. Says right here. But you have to go in

yourself. If you don't, and they catch you, they'll likely shoot you."

"What if a man was goin' back and the provost riders got him?"

"Just show 'em this paper."

"I wouldn't want to take your paper."

"It's all right. I read it already."

And that was the end of it—the night walking and sleeping in barns and looking over his shoulder for the horsemen with black armbands on their sleeves and sabers in their hands.

He didn't know it yet, nor until after they had given him a chunk of cold cornbread to carry with him and he had walked almost a mile.

Then he stood, in broad daylight, looking toward the mountains westward and back to the line of the Shenandoah. He knew that beyond that valley was the Blue Ridge, and then the rest of Virginia. And somewhere there was Lee's army, and Morgan and the Fawleys and all the rest.

So he turned east with the folded newspaper in hand and thought, By Gawd, we vet'rans has got to see it all through.

It felt good with each step. Back to the regiment. There was a bounce to his walk, just like that first march up from Lynchburg two years ago. He swung the drum over his shoulder by its strap and let it bang against his thigh as drummer boys were supposed to do.

That ole army's where I belong, he thought, somehow forgetting the shock of battle and his utter terror, the smoke and noise and torn flesh along the Hagerstown Road and at Devil's Den. This is where all my friends is at. An' Gawd love 'em, Maw and Paw back in Pine Bluff expectin' me to do good. Iffen I was there, wouldn't know how to talk or act, with all my cussin' an' waitin' to play the long roll. This ole army . . .

"YOU ain't said much about home lately."

They were leaning on a rock wall, Zack and Noah, watching a regiment of South Carolina troops pass.

"Am I supposed to?" Noah asked.

"I reckon not. But there was a while you harped about it all the time."

"Not much time to think on it now, I guess."

A mounted officer rode past, and someone among the Arkansas regiment resting beside the road shouted, "Hey, mister, here's your mule!"

The officer ignored it, but it brought a return chorus of jeers and obscenities from his troops.

"This ole rock wall reminds me a' that one Uncle Questor tried to build on the south end a' his barn lot," Zack said pensively.

"Yeah," Noah laughed. "An' it was allus fallin' down 'cause he wouldn't use no mortar in it."

"Yeah, an' Tyne pushed 'er down twicet."

"The hell he did! I never knowed that."

"Yeah, Tyne's got a mean streak in him wider'n White River. A little bit of the devil, Mama says. 'Member the time he had you stick your tongue to that axe blade, dead a' winter?"

"I thought you was gonna kill him."

"I never got on too good with him."

Zack took his plug from his pocket, brushed off the lint, and gnawed off a chew. "Me an' Britt, we allus got on all right. Britt, he's like a houn' dawg pup. He ain't too bright, but he ain't mean. Pap says he misplaced some a' his brains somewheres along the way."

" 'Member that time he pulled a possum out from under the house an' it bit him?"

"Mama poured enough coal oil on it to set fire to the whole Ozark woods."

"Yeah," Noah said, laughing. "I don't know what Mama'd do without her coal oil. An' that damned sulphur an' molasses. 'Member how she'd give us that stuff ever' fall a' the year?"

"Man ever takes sulphur an' molasses, he's boun' not to forget." Zack was grinning, too, both of them recalling calmer times. The tail end of the Carolina column passed, and they watched it going away in the hip-high cloud of dust. "An' that Cadmus, he was almost as mean as Tyne, an' randy as a young goat."

"He was?" Noah asked. "I never knowed that, either."

"Hell, you was too young to know nothin'. You was too busy pokin' into thangs. Like that time you found Pap's shotgun an' shot a hole through the kitchen roof. You musta been about four."

Noah shook his head. "Gawd, he like to of took my rear end off fer that."

"Yeah, ole Cadmus started slippin' down into town at night when he was about sixteen. Randy as a goat."

"I reckon you an' me's the onlest ones a' the whole bunch worth a damn."

Zack looked sideways at his brother and chuckled, shifting the cud that made a grotesque bulge in one long cheek.

"Yeah." He spat a long amber stream into the road. "I reckon so."

They turned their backs to the road then, bellies against the wall and facing the company sprawled about in the old field. They said no more, but they were still remembering home.

THAT was the period of Martin Hasford's final changing, between Gettysburg and the day Billy Dick came back.

Martin had always been a man of strong character, as he saw it—sure of his convictions, his only sins those committed in his mind, and such transgressions quickly conquered. There had never before in his life been a year when such things were different. He had grown within his family, those men and women come from Germany in the generation of his parents, and later the Hasfords like a closed clan separate from all others, marrying cousins and nurturing the hearth where man and wife had mutual grandfathers.

So coming among a group of men not of his thinking—not

of his family—was bound to have its effect. He had expected it, and expected equally to come away whole, as he had been before. That had been the measure of his confidence in the strength of family ties, its hold on his soul.

But it hadn't worked that way. By Gettysburg he knew it. But he didn't know why.

He tried to recall the transition. At those revival meetings behind Fredericksburg he had been pleased to find others like himself who had always disdained oath-making but who in heat of battle found the urge for swearing irresistible.

At first, he had been openly embarrassed and privately shocked by it. Now there was little embarrassment, only a kind of quiet astonishment, and prayers asking forgiveness for breaking the commandment whispered almost mechanically, as though from habit alone.

That night he had spent in the anteroom of Miz Rozella's Afternoon Tea Sippin' Society and Billiard Hall was a victory of will, and only he knew of what magnitude. For on that occasion he had lusted for the same thing Morgan and Noah and the others had lusted for, and was only sustained by strong rum, which unaccountably had increased his resistance rather than weakened it, as with most other men.

And the gambling. It was perhaps the most astounding thing of all. His life had been spent extolling the virtues of thrift and good money management, a scheme of things where gambling held no place. Yet he had played Tug's three-card monte and had lost, as he had lost a number of times at euchre.

At first he had written many letters home, receiving few in return, and had agonized over it. Now he wrote almost none at all, and even the few letters he had from Benton County seemed inadequate to inspire his correspondence. He explained himself in this by the observation that paper had become almost extinct in the army. But he knew that was a dismal excuse.

Not that his homesickness had ever really dissipated, as it had in some of these other men. It had simply become more bearable, like a persistent backache, nonetheless irritating yet at least expected, and therefore presenting no unpleasant surprises.

A man can erect defenses against troubles of the soul, he thought.

His primary defense was a close association with the others around him. As though they had become a substitute for the family he had left behind, their welfare his own.

He came to realize this most fully the day he read the letter to Zackery Fawley.

Noah and Morgan had been gone from the regimental encampment all day, doing detail work with the commissary people. The daily courier arrived from division with the usual drill instructions for the next day and with three travel-worn letters. One of these was addressed to Zackery and Noah Fawley.

Zack held the envelope in his hand, a fragile membrane with bold address on the front, the watery ink faded already. He could make it all out, but with some difficulty.

"News from home, I take it," Martin Hasford said.

"I reckon so," Zack said, chewing thoughtfully. He turned the letter in his hand, inspecting it closely.

"You like me to read it for you?" Martin said quietly.

Zack looked at Hasford for only a moment, and then passed the letter to him.

They were sitting on an old cistern beside the foundations of a farmhouse long ago burned and pillaged by passing troops. The July sun was hot against their backs, the army encamped all around. There was even tentage here, and some of the new men had taken to pairing up to use their shelter halves as intended, making the little dog tents that had crudely lettered signs on them reading "Home Sweet Home" or "Bitch in Heat."

To the west was the sharp outline of the Blue Ridge, and eastward the land rolled away to tidewater. It was a lazy day, with heat waves dancing along the horizons where there were no groves of trees. Zack seemed to have the mood of the moment, unhurried in his desire to hear what the folks at home had written. He chewed his cud like an old contented cow, unconcerned with the flies that were biting fiercely enough to portend rain. At least, Mama always said biting flies meant rain, though sometimes it didn't work out that way.

Martin carefully opened the envelope, not tearing it badly so that it might be used again. He cleared his throat and read aloud:

> Dear Zack and Noah,
>
> I am having the high sheriff do this letter because he writes a good hand. It is yet another winter now . . .

Martin and Zack glanced at one another and laughed, the sweat shining on their faces.

> . . . and there is some snow and ice. It has been a good year but a lot of the men are away in the armies. Union troops are all through Arkansas now, but we seldom see anything of them here. Last summer was a good crop year. Corn came on early and stayed. We were able to butcher four hogs and one yearling steer. Sorghum cane was the best in a long time. Your brother Tyne has went to Missouri to join the army. It had been gnawing at him a long spell so he finally went and took up with the Yankees. We are all well. We had a Christmas wedding and thought of you and Noah and that blackberry wine. Lucinda has a little boy now and another babe due in the spring. Mama wants you to come home as soon as you can. She worries about you staying warm in this kind of weather. And I could use your hands once more to help on the place because with Tyne gone north and Cadmus taking up his own farm, it keeps me and Britt busy. It was Cadmus got married to Luanne Lacy and they taken up housekeeping along a spur of Hog Scald Hollow ridge. You can expect another niece or nephew sometime in the summer, or next fall at the latest. We have been hearing about some of the battles there in Virginny.
>
> Pap

Martin refolded the letter and slipped it back into the envelope. Zack had stopped chewing and was sitting on the rock wall, staring down across the regimental encampment.

"Nice letter," Martin said, handing it across to Zack. Zack took it quickly and stuffed it inside his jacket. He started chewing again, slowly. When he turned to Martin his eyes were cold and unblinking.

"Don't say nothin' to Noy about this hyar letter," he said.

Martin started to speak, then thought better of it and turned his gaze down to his hands locked across his thighs. He nodded and knew it was the girl, this Luanne Lacy.

"I'll show it to Noy in good time," Zack said. "Thanks fer readin' 'er to me."

Zack slipped down from the wall and walked away, and Martin watched him go.

"Damnation," he said aloud, knowing as surely as he sat there that Noah Fawley would never see the letter.

THEY were encamped along the edge of an old woodland, one that had escaped the axes of each passing generation, leaving some of the oaks as large in the trunk as rain barrels.

It was a quiet place, even with the First Corps spread all around it, making the sounds and gentle noises and mutterings an army makes at nighttime, after the animals have been picketed, the last bugle call sounded, and the men rolled into bedding near the fast-dying fires, bundled against the chill.

Zack lay awake, listening to the movement of the limbs in the soft wind. He heard Noah's heavy breathing beside him, felt rather than saw Martin Hasford still crouched beside the fire, reading the last of Bev Cass's books—Martin's eyes traversing the lines, the strain of deciphering the small print in the light that grew less and less.

And he could feel the letter from Buffalo River against his side, under his jacket. It was heavy as a full cartridge pouch, dragging against his thinking.

Maybe tomorrow I'll tell him. An' maybe not.

He pondered the letter with a sad, resigned intensity, had

in fact been thinking of little else since Martin Hasford read it to him. He thought of its origin, in Town along the Buffalo, and of all the intervening space and time from there to this Virginia woodlot.

He wondered why soldiers so looked forward to these letters from home, because as frequently as not they were messages of sorrow and regret: one of the young'uns has died of measles, a wife has run off with a leather profiteer, the crops have failed, the Yankees are occupying home counties.

He'd as soon have a nation of illiterates so there would be no opportunity for transmitting news of such disasters. There were disasters enough here in the army without having to worry about those from far distant, over which a man had no control.

Maybe I can work up the nerve to give it to him tomorrow. The longer I hold it the madder he'll be fer my doin' it. An' no matter when I show it to him, he ain't gonna like it.

He had known from the first about Noah and Luanne Lacy—not the details but that something had passed between them that was to Noah serious and permanent. He could tell from the look in Noah's eyes each time the name was mentioned, could somehow feel the swell of tenderness.

It wasn't like the Trippet twins, all of a sudden and for the moment, but something especially lasting, like maybe the increasing affection between Pap and Mama as they grew old together.

Why, Pap had even taken to hugging Mama right in front of people. Zack could recall being hugged only by Mama, never by Pap, and that only dimly when he had been a sprout and most of the brothers not even born yet.

But he imagined Noah might be a hugger, like Uncle Questor. Uncle Questor was always hugging somebody, even if it was only one of his foxhounds. It always embarrassed Pap when Uncle Questor came for Sunday pork chops, going around to all the boys and Lucinda before she was married and left home, and to Mama, too, hugging them all and quoting Scripture.

As a matter of fact, it always embarrassed Zack, too—

Uncle Questor squeezing and smelling of old leather and wood-smoke. Noah never seemed to mind. Come to think of it, Mama had always embraced Noah more than she did the other boys, more than Lucinda even. And he hadn't minded that either.

So maybe Noah's the same way, a hugger.

Why couldn't he jus' run aroun' awhile, like normal men, Zack thought. Why couldn't he jus' mount one now an' again an' go on about his business? Not get walleyed over one in particular?

Jesus Gawd, I'm gettin' worse than Noy used to be, all this home thinkin'. He used to get that far-off, glassy-eyed look ever' day.

The wind in the trees above him was gusting gently now. He heard Martin Hasford finally go to his bed, by which time the last faint light of the company's fires had faded and no longer outlined the lower trunks in flickering orange color. Still he lay awake, feeling the letter.

A group of cavalrymen passed along the road nearby. He could hear the soft tinkle of bit chains, the squeak of leather, and the padding sound of shod hoofs in the dust. He could smell their droppings, a sweet and pleasant odor. It reminded him of the vine rose Mama had growing up one of the porch posts, fertilized each spring with the leavings of the horse stalls.

Somewhere back in the woods he heard a sentry challenge, and then there was a low exchange of words. But finally there was only the sound of wind in the trees.

Maybe I'll get up the nerve come mornin'. At least lately he don't seem inclined to mention her too much. Not as much as he done when we first came out here. Damnation!

He had always looked forward to sleeping because it meant rising to a new morning. Anticipation of what the dawn would bring him made him rush into sleep, so he could hurry and feel the soft breeze coming up from the valleys as he stood alone on the front porch, none of the family yet awake, the sky only just turning gray in the east. Life in the deep timber began to stir and make its presence known after sleep, after the last calls and movement of the night creatures denning, the foxes and owls and possum.

But it had been a long time now since he had looked forward to dawning. Each night it seemed harder to sleep, because waking to a new day had somehow become hateful.

Damn that weddin' wine an' Noy so full a' new manhood because a' Luanne Lacy, showin' his mettle, stealin' that pig with Ben Shackleford. An' damn Ole Jury Duty an' his judgment, an' damn that long trek to a foreign country, an' damn the marchin' an' the scratchin' fer food an' the bare feet in wintertime. Damn it all!

The beautiful dawns were gone.

ZACK acquired the hat at the regimental medical station. He had decided to find one any way he could. Noah put so much store in his hat, and the one he was wearing had seen better days.

Zack had no money and nothing to trade except Pap's Dragoon revolver, and he had no intention of parting with that. At first he thought he'd have to steal one, which didn't bother him much. But then he thought of the medical station, where bits of clothing of all fashion were left behind by the sick and wounded evacuated to hospitals. He had to make three trips of it, but at last his patience paid off.

The regimental medical facility was located near the headquarters of corps artillery. The gun parks were impressive, though Zack noted as he passed among the cannons each day that many of the pieces were patched together, stocks wrapped with baling wire and some of the wheel spokes looking hand-whittled.

Amongst the guns he found the yellow hospital flag, and beneath it there was a canvas fly, a small wall tent, and a line of smaller sleeping tents. Medical corpsmen lounged about with no business to speak of, but the surgeons were nowhere in sight.

Zack saw the hat on the third day, lying on one of the

folding cots under the fly. It was fairly new, Yankee headgear of fine, thick felt.

The only reason that hat is still hyar, he thought, is because these medical corps boys gets all the wearin' gear they need from them as pass through. An' some goin' no farther. He noted that the corpsmen lying about were a well-dressed lot compared to most of the men in this army.

"Who belongs to this hyar hat?" he asked.

"Artilleryman," one of the loungers said. None of the others showed any interest, just went on with their napping. "Puttin' a new barrel on a Parrott gun an' the thang slipped the chains an' rolled off the trunnion onto his laig. Hadta ship him off to Richmond."

Zack scratched his chin, looking over the surgical equipment neatly arranged on a folding table with a white cloth. The sight of the saws and blades made his skin crawl. There were white coats hanging from the tent poles, with most of the bloodstains washed out.

He moved along the line of sleeping tents, each with its walls rolled up, and saw lying there men he assumed to be doctors. All napping. He found Dinsmore's nephew in the last one, snoring and with a small bottle and tin cup on the ground under his cot. It took a long time to wake him.

"You 'member me, Doc?" Zack asked. "Your Uncle Sidney was in my comp'ny."

"Wha' say? Wha' say?" Dinsmore's nephew sputtered, trying to get his bloodshot eyes open. "I remember. Wha' is it? Whatcha want here? You wounded?"

"No, I ain't hurt. I come to ast a favor a' ya. Man in my mess squad, a good man," Zack said. "But his hat's wore out. I thought you might help me. It was him comforted your Uncle Sidney before he died at Sharpsburg."

"He did?"

"He sure'n hell did. I was wonderin' . . ."

On the walk back to the company, Zack thought, Gawd Almighty! I'm gettin' as bad as that Welshman makin' up lies!

He gave the hat to Noah that night before evening muster,

away from the others in the oak grove where they had been making their bed this past week.

"Damnation!" Noah exclaimed. "That's a good 'un, ain't it?"

He pulled off his old hat and started to replace it with the Union blue one, then paused, looking at Zack's slouch, bent out of shape and brim limp.

"You need it bad as me," Noah said. "That 'un you're wearin' gonna fall apart on you one a' these days."

"No, it ain't. Still another year er two left in 'er. Go on. Try it."

Noah was grinning. The Yankee headgear fit perfectly. "Damnation! That feels good. Where the hell'd you come by it? You slip off an' shoot a bluebelly?"

"No. That there's a present from Ole Sidney Dinsmore, you might say."

"What?"

"Never mind. Come on. Lessee what that Welshman's got in the fryin' pan."

They walked back toward the mess group and found Morgan and Hasford bent over a small fire. Noah strutted, grinning. But the old hat was still clutched tightly in one hand.

"What's the bes' thang to do with the ole one?"

"Hell, burn 'er," Zack said. "She ain't no use to nobody now."

"Kinda hate to part with 'er. But by Gawd, this new one's a jim-dandy!"

"Well, try an' keep anybody from takin' it away from you."

BILLY Dick was a soldier again, forgiven by President Davis for his lapse of patriotism, and forgiven by his messmates as a matter of principle. He was issued a new rifle, a .557 like the others, only this one bought not with Arkansas cotton money but with Confederate treasury drafts and come through the blockade.

The Black Welshman gave the boy a welcoming bear hug. It embarrassed Billy Dick to the point of tears, but he tried to hide it, showing them how brave he was. They all turned to jostling each other, pretending they hadn't seen the damp on Billy Dick's cheeks.

Some of the veterans in other companies took it badly, this mollycoddling of deserters. But Noah's baleful glare under the new Union hat and Morgan's doubled fists kept the discontented at bay. This was family, and nobody else's business.

"You sure taken a serious attachment to that boy, ain't-cha?" Zack asked.

"No, I ain't," Noah said. "He's still a snivelin' little bungler. But what we do in this hyar comp'ny ain't none a' them other boys' put-in!"

"He's back where he belongs," Morgan said to anyone who cared to listen. "Come back himself, and not a moment of combat with the Yankees lost in the bargain."

Billy Dick stayed with them after that all the way to Tennessee.

It was true—Longstreet was off to join Bragg. They boarded boxcars and noticed the dilapidated condition of the rolling stock, and of the tracks, worn and uneven, showing little sign of maintenance, only long wartime wear. They inched along as they left Virginia, going slow to avoid the cars leaving the tracks and setting off in their own direction.

It appeared that John Bell Hood would not be among them on this excursion. He had been wounded in the arm at Gettysburg. Only temporary, it was said, and they hoped so. Hood had always been a favorite, most especially after he had made no effort to discipline Ole Jury Duty for the affair of honor behind Suffolk.

But then, as they passed near Richmond, Ole Hood came out from his hospital bed to wish them well. They went wild, with cheering and hat-throwing and frenzied yowling such as had never been seen before. Of course, such a lack of dignity would never be displayed in front of Bobby Lee. Maybe the uninhibited nature of it helped Hood make up his mind. To hell with the hospital! He would come along and lead his troops! Wounded arm be damned!

So they made a fine trip of it, stripping the sideboards off the cars so they could watch the passing countryside.

In that process the Black Welshman broke the blade on the vaccination knife. It made a loud pop, and everyone in the mess group stood silently a moment.

"Well, a good friend gone to rest," Morgan said, and tossed the two parts of the bowie off along the railside.

Noah shivered and looked at Zack with some terrible light in his eyes.

"It's bad luck to break a knife," he whispered.

"Aw, hell, that's somethin' Uncle Questor put in your head, all that bad-luck business when natural thangs happen. It was jus' a wore-out ole knife is all."

But it took a while for Noah to get fully back into the spirit of their journey. Zack watched him closely, thinking, Maybe it's true, maybe it's the bad luck Martin Hasford read in that letter.

The landscape of the Carolinas along the right-of-way was soon enough taking its effect, and Noah forgot the knife.

Trouble in min' fadin' away as fast as his temper, Zack thought. But, by Gawd, that temper. He's gettin' to where he keeps a pretty good han' on it. Maybe the hat helps.

Some of them rode the roofs. They shouted and sang the old songs, even "Hell's Broke Loose in Georgia." Billy Dick grinned and tapped his drum. They missed Dad Johnson's banjo, but one of the new men from another company had a French harp, and that was almost as good.

Down to Atlanta they rode, and then a wide swing back north toward Chattanooga, a detour required because Yankee cavalry was threatening some of the rail lines that would have made their trip shorter.

They didn't give a damn. They enjoyed the travel, saving leather, riding the cars. When the pretty girls came out to wave them along, they cheered furiously and cavorted like monkeys.

At one such time a new recruit made what Noah perceived

to be an untoward remark, and Noah hit the man with his fist. There was nothing more serious about it than a bloody lip, and that was part of the fun, too.

They ate raw pork and fresh peaches and threw the pits at telegraph poles as they passed. Some of the men had new shoes, good shoes, perhaps even English-made and passed through the blockade. They told jokes about the Yankee president and roared out obscene stanzas to the tune of "The Battle Hymn of the Republic."

But all of that ended short of Ringgold, where they took to shanks' mare again and moved north, toward the sound of guns.

Afterward Zack could never keep it all straight—which fight came first, or which rainstorm. There was Missionary Ridge and Lookout Mountain and Knoxville. Old John Bell Hood was shot off his horse with a wound so bad the surgeons had to amputate his leg.

There was a scrambling night attack, at least one embarrassing withdrawal, and the telegraph wire they ran into before one Federal position, strung shin-high on solid posts, wire that cut their flesh and sent them sprawling as they tried to charge.

Ole Jury Duty was growing weaker by the day, his still-bandaged hand hurting more with each hour, looking ugly. Until finally he was relieved of his command and sent on detached service to whatever area of Arkansas he could find not occupied by Yankees, there to recruit new men.

Ole Jury Duty's oaths on that day were as good as any he had ever used in battle, and, listening, everyone shivered with admiration. But then he was suddenly subdued and a little tearful as he came to Martin Hasford with the old worn ledger book in which he had been inscribing the company history.

"Hasford, you're an intelligent man," Ole Jury Duty said gruffly. "Take this book and write down the things that happen. And someday your grandchildren can read it and be proud of you."

Then he stomped away, the frayed crown of his stovepipe hat flapping in the wintry wind. They watched him with mouths clamped tight shut, seeing their company eroding away before their eyes.

"Who's head man now?" Noah asked.

"Sergeant Napier," Morgan said. "Color-bearer these past months."

"Scissorbill!"

"Well," Zack said, "Napier's got luck. He's been haulin' that flag around a long time an' not a nick on him yet from blue lead."

There was mud and cold and rain and then snow, and the rations became so meager they took to stealing corn from the cavalry horses.

It just wasn't the same in Tennessee. They didn't even look forward to a fight with the same old spirit. After Hood fell, they never knew who might be commanding the division, what with various brigadiers competing for the job. And Ole Pete raising hell with everybody and threatening to court-martial half the officers in the corps.

Their worst fears were being realized. Away from Lee, the old First Corps was not the same. They would recall each miserable moment as a direct result of their being somewhere they weren't supposed to be. Even with their victories, it was a terrible time.

In all that campaign, Zack would remember most vividly the first fight—as surging as Sharpsburg, as vicious as Gettysburg, and their lines going forward under the red banners, the shout raised and bayonets up, attacking in column of companies.

It was there that Zack came across the drum, lying on the field, the head splattered as it had been that first day at March Landing, only now not with rain. Now with red.

A few steps farther on lay the doll-like figure of the boy, already growing cold when Zack reached him and bent down to take up the rifle from clutching fingers. Later, when he wormed the barrel, Zack found six unexploded charges.

Afterward the Black Welshman would say to Martin Hasford, "Did you see it? He held that boy and cried. Sure he is the most deadly man in this company, even in the regiment, I'd wager. But there for a moment, tender as his own mother was he!"

And later still, Zack would say sadly, "Never taken a single shot at them that done him up the flue."

Zack discarded his own rifle, companion since March Landing and now worn down in the barrel so that it looked like a shotgun. He took Billy Dick's Enfield, fired only a few times.

"I don't like it," Noah complained. "Takin' up a piece with bad luck on it."

"It's a good piece," Zack said. "No need to let some scissorbill get his hands on it."

So Zack used the weapon throughout the rest of that dismal winter, all the while Noah grumbling about it, thinking of the boy. William Richard Hysel. Regimental drummer. Chickamauga. Sixteen years old!

# SIXTEEN

THEY came to the Wilderness in springtime. Only a year before, Bobby Lee and Ole Jackson had gone into that tangled wildwood and whipped Joe Hooker and sent him back across the Rapidan. Then they had been in Southside, but now they were back with the Gray Virginian and damned glad to be there, shed of Tennessee and Bragg, the mud and rain and short rations.

They continued to change. They were now gaunt and hard and leathery, with little semblance of uniform among them. Some still wore Union blue trousers, which they called Yankee diapers. Their hats showed every style of the decade, and their jackets were various in all except the patches at the elbows and the frayed collars. Many were without shoes again, a condition they had come to expect with each changing season. At least it was better to be barefoot now than in the fall, facing a winter campaign.

After the scanty grub in the west, they felt themselves to be living like officers. There were even fewer oaths taken against the God damned commissary department. They ate salt pork and boiled turnips, and sometimes fresh fruit, which they credited to Bobby Lee's initiative. And there were poke greens found along the roadsides.

They had come to Gordonsville on the rattly-bank rail system that was falling apart. Though slower than walking, it gave them a rest and helped their spirits. They knew the other two corps were watching the blues across the river, and they knew it would be only a short time before something happened. They were as ready as they ever had been, even though rumor held that the Potomac Yanks now had over 115,000 men.

There had been changes, what with former color sergeant

Napier now running the company, a flatland farmer promoted to lieutenant before they left Tennessee. It didn't take much running. They had come to know what was expected of them and what duties could be safely shirked. And Napier knew the futility of strict discipline among so rowdy a bunch of individualists. He should have known; he was cut from the same pattern.

A few more recruits were in, and some of the shattered units had been reshuffled. Their own company had been consolidated with another after Knoxville, but they could only muster thirty-five rifles as they lay in camp at Gordonsville.

Sprawling in the warm sun, looking at the roll of farm country gone fallow with war, they saw no fences in sight, or telegraph poles. Just a few deserted houses and barns, the wood long since stripped from their sides by armies passing across this ground. The growth was green and lush but untended, fairly to the outskirts of the town. All of it had the look of desolation. No livestock grazed, no bee gums buzzed, no civilian traffic ran along the dusty roads.

Martin Hasford stared at the forsaken land and shook his head sadly. His eyes followed the contours of the old fields where saplings were already sprouting, and he measured the length of the furrows that should have been there. But even he was not immune to the subdued excitement that grew in them at the prospect of action.

There were little clusters of blue-gray violets where the tobacco and corn had once grown. From one of the abandoned farmyards Liverpool Morgan had picked a spray of yellow jonquils and was wearing them in his lapel. They had seen goldfinches feeding near the stunted cedars of dooryards, and there were migrating spring warblers and jays in the low pines that marked the country lanes. There was the smell of new life, and the feel of it, too.

The sap was rising in Noah stronger than ever, he coming into his twentieth year.

"Maybe after the next whack at the blues, we'll get another run at Richmond town," he said. "I hear the big chicken guts has started passin' out the furloughs."

---

They were lying along what had once been a fieldside fenceline, nothing to mark it now but the brush and straggling weeds. Zack and Noah and Morgan and Martin Hasford, on their backs in the high grass, hands locked behind their heads, watched the high white clouds in the blue Virginia sky.

"Ain't likely to be much furloughin'," Zack said, "with the Yanks nearby."

"More of the elephant soon, lads," said Morgan, his thimble hat cocked down over one eye. "And no ladies for the poor soldier until the fall."

"So long as the grub keeps comin' in," Noah said. "I never much liked turnips until I got in this ole army."

"We never grow any in Benton County," Hasford said. "Plenty of yams, though. Like a bait of yams about now."

Zack shifted on the grass and grunted, holding a hand to the leg wounded at Devil's Den.

"That thang still bother you?" Noah asked.

"I thought it was the cold weather an' the wet," Zack said. "But warm weather hurts it, too."

"You should have turned in to the hospital," Martin said.

Noah snorted. "Yeah, an' likely to be a one-legged man now. Zack, 'member that one-legged man lived on the farm west a' the Lacy place?"

Zack grunted again, and thought about the letter he had been carrying all winter.

"This ole man whittled hisself a peg leg," Noah said. "I never seen anything like it. Durin' butcherin' time, that ole man jump aroun' in the pen with his hammer, knockin' them hogs on the head."

Maybe after the next fight, Zack thought, when he's still squirmin' like a hot stud. But not now.

It would not be the same at home, and the letter made him almost constantly aware of that. Place all changed, people shuffled around, new faces. Lucinda would be with two young'uns now, Luanne with at least one. Him and Noah would be uncles three times over. He couldn't look at Noah and think of him as an uncle.

Maybe some old faces gone. He wondered if Uncle Questor was still alive. Hell, that ole bastard'll live on past us all!

Nothing the same now. He figured when he'd left the hills he was a man come to his full growth. But maybe there had been more growing since, like with Noah. He'd sure as hell seen some things he had never imagined before!

That Noy. Never talks about Mama's roast pig no more. Maybe I oughta jus' grab the scruff a' his neck an' drag him on home. Next shoot he's liable to do the same thang he done in that wheatfield at Gettysburg, an' that'd kill his soul. Well, maybe not, either. He done all right in Tennessee. He never got spooked a single time's I know of. But they say them thangs come on unexpected.

But what the hell, it'd take me an' Hasford an' the Welsh throwed in to drag him off from this ole army. Only this ole army maybe ain't gonna las' much longer.

At least he felt better than he had during that winter with Bragg. It wasn't as good as it once had been. Maybe it was the spring sap rising in him as it always did in Noah.

Gawd Almighty! An' me comin' on thirty!

Even so, I'd favor runnin' a few trotlines with one a' them Trippets. Nex' furlough I ain't wastin' no time with poker.

He could almost smell the Buffalo in the night, hear the bullfrogs under the limestone bluffs that dropped straight down to the water, feel the full flesh of Middie or Maudie Trippet, whichever, giggling in the darkness and chewing plug tobacco.

"Fresh sausage," Martin Hasford was saying, looking at the sky where he could see bread biscuits in the clouds, puffed and steaming from his wife's oven, ready to be split and covered with honey.

Hasford thought of Benton County now with longing for the comforts of it, forgetting the hardship. The cooking and good beds and work to be done with his hands seemed far distant. But there was no longer that heart-squeezing loneliness he had known only in association with this war, and through this war had learned to control.

Noah watched all the movements around him now with an increasing inquisitiveness. He could tell from a plume of dust whether it was cavalry or infantry moving along a road out of sight. In the darkness he could determine from the sound alone whether a battery of Napoleons was passing or a column of heavier guns. He could identify outfits from the various states at greater range than any of them. He could spot an open flank developing as quickly as any of the officers.

"On the general's staff you should be," Morgan said. "Born to your work, you are."

Noah seemed to have gained weight in Tennessee, despite the sorry rations. Or maybe he had only grown another inch or two. Whatever, there was a maturity in his eyes that had not been there before.

The Black Welshman had changed least of all, though in appearance most. His great head now seemed to sit precariously on a body grown too slender for it.

"Aw, for the women," he said, as he had from the start, a twinkle of delight in his eyes under the black brows. "Maybe furloughs in the fall, say Zack?"

Zack looked startled, constantly surprised at this man and how he was capable of looking inside Fawley thinking. A by-Gawd min' reader. Uncle Questor said he knows an ole lady onct who was a min' reader.

These hours of leisure—when they could lie in the sun and watch the birds and the clouds and the coming of green—lasted only a little while. General Lee came out to their camp at the end of April to review Ole Pete's First Corps and welcome them back into his army.

After the troops passed in review they broke ranks, and many of them gathered around the big gray horse. Noah was close enough to touch the bridle. Lee tipped his hat to them and smiled, and his dark eyes were alight as he looked into their faces and told them he was glad to have his war horses back where they belonged.

"That ole man!"

"By Gawd, that Bobby Lee!"

"I'd foller Gen'l Lee to the gates a' hell!"

Martin Hasford was so inspired that he wrote a letter home

for the first time in months. He had a hell of a time finding paper and ink.

When he wrote, the exuberance at seeing Lee was heavy in his prose, but at the last he noted: "It seems an age ago when all these men first came flocking to the army in a fit of patriotism. It seems a time gone by. Now, many regret they came at all."

He reread that passage five times and thought to scratch it out, but in the end left it intact.

It wasn't long then. The news came through the army grapevine that the blues were moving, moving to cross the Rapidan. Morgan called it the Rubicon, and of them all only Hasford knew what he meant.

"By Gawd," Noah said, and his eyes had the same glint of light that Zack could recall seeing in Maurice Gordy's eyes when this war was only a year old, "the old Army of the Potomac!"

Morgan spat into his hands and rubbed them together, Martin Hasford read his Judges, Zack carefully looked to his rifle.

After Tennessee, where they all felt themselves to be strangers from the first, this was something they could understand. The Army of the Potomac! It would be like going out to meet an old and respected friend!

"Yes, lads," said the Black Welshman, "were it not for my modesty, there is but a single army in history I could name better than the Army of the Potomac."

THEY marched straight into this one, making the last leg in darkness. All day they had been moving up the Orange Plank Road, and ahead they could hear someone catching seven kinds of hell. The artillery was not so intense as on other fields, but the volume of rifle fire told them there was a furious fight.

They rested in the fields beside the road as darkness fell and the sounds of battle died with the day. Then they were up at two o'clock, on the road again after a mouthful of cold, raw bacon. The air was crisp, and they moved quickly toward the dawn and with first light heard it again, closer now and more vicious—the crash of infantry weapons like hailstones against a metal roof.

Here we go again, Martin Hasford thought, and with the new men too ignorant of what's coming to be more than a tad frightened, the rest of us knowing but hardened to it in some way I have yet to comprehend.

At first it seemed there was a heavy mist hiding the rising sun, but then they saw it was smoke, and below that the jagged outline of the Wilderness. Already on either side they could could see the stunted pines and the low oak trees, growing thicker as the column advanced. Then a quickening of the heart as the word was passed.

"Trouble ahead, boys! The Yanks has broke the line of the Third Corps."

"Double-quick time now, boys!"

Trotting, Noah suddenly recalled how they had dropped their rolls along the Hagerstown Pike. Now the rolls were so small that nobody bothered. Each went in with everything he owned on his back and small hindrance.

Soon they were close enough to hear the individual rifle shots and yelling. But this wasn't their own shout. It was deep and measured, and they knew it was Union infantry. They began to pass ammunition trains deployed off the road in the timber, the underbrush now standing to a horse's belly. They passed staff officers on horses, together in hurried conversation. There was a column of reserve artillery and a clearing with the yellow flag above it, the surgeons working in the open field with the wounded lying in the tall grass.

"Deploy to your left flank," came the order shouted by Colonel Manning and repeated along the line, the company and the regiment peeling off the road, coming into battle formation. No skirmishers out. They knew where the enemy was—dead ahead—and the rifles came down from shoulders, bayoneted, as they thrashed through the undergrowth.

A pause then as other units moved abreast. The Fourth Texas was there, and Noah saw Burton, his mouth open, waving his hat. Then came the command to advance.

First there was a line of artillery pieces, a battery with guns smoking, almost hidden in the woods, the tall grass before them blazing from the muzzle blasts. The gunners saw them coming and cheered.

They passed the guns and saw the first retreating grayjackets. These men were not running but falling back slowly—firing, a few hurried paces to the rear, then firing again. They were ashen-faced and trembling, and their faces looked scorched.

"Jus' give us a little spell of time, boys," one of them shouted.

"We ain't out of this yet!" another gasped. "Jus' hold 'em off a mite."

They parted to allow these men to pass through their own ranks, taunting them with vicious catcalls.

"You sure ain't part of Bobby Lee's army, takin' to the rear!"

"The Yanks ain't thataways, boys. You're a-goin' the wrong direction!"

Noah remembered the gibes they had themselves taken after the affair of the charging milk cows above Harper's Ferry. Now the glove was on the other hand but it was not cows coming at these men.

Suddenly along one flank there was a wild commotion, and the line slowed to a walk, then stopped. Noah saw the gray horse there and recognized the rider. Trying to lead the charge! Soldiers were yelling, milling around the gray, pointing to the rear. One sergeant had the bridle in his hand. A group of staff men appeared, their own mounts rearing and walleyed. They swarmed around General Lee and soon had him moving back to safety.

"That ole man!" Noah gasped, but nothing more as the shout went up and the line surged forward.

The last of the stragglers came through their formation, and then they were onto the advancing Federals, a solid mass of them, shouting through the trees, crashing in the underbrush that was already burning in some places. Shoulder and fire into the contorted faces, into the blue chests, bite cartridge, going forward still, shouting, ram, hammer back, cap, shoulder, trigger, fire. Blood the color of sorghum molasses in the smoke-shrouded timber!

The blue lines were breaking before them, and their own entangled in the trees and undergrowth. On either side of him Noah felt his own people, though unaware who they were, sensing only the targets before him and the crash of fire, the galling taste of black powder on his tongue. A great bearded face was suddenly there, and the Enfield misfired as Martin Hasford lunged in with the bayonet, a hard thrust and a choking sound above all the others, the face no longer there, hammer back, recap, fire.

Deeper into the trees then—pressing, charging, the smoke from burning timber stinging his eyes. The roar of Napoleon guns sounded nearby. Canister and grape and rifle bullets sheared off the limbs of trees and the brush, carpeting the woodland floor with a bramble of instant abatis, almost as impregnable as those their own engineers sometimes constructed of sharpened stakes to create barriers to an advancing line. All of it catching fire. Already there was the stink of burning flesh, like bacon dropped in hot embers, and the screams of fallen men caught by the flames and trampled by the rush of others.

The smoke cast a gray dome of fog over the woods, an oily smudge that gave everything the color of faded slate. Hands and faces were like flour paste in the flashing gloom, wounds opening like black mouths, teeth gleaming pearl.

They stumbled over their own fallen and felt the squirming wounded underfoot. In a frenzy they smashed at one another, recoiled, and smashed again, fresh lines of troops coming up from both sides. Brittle brush flared up suddenly among them in a burst of light and heat—searing, catching trousers afire. The whip of missiles was felt through the thickets.

The intensity and frightfulness of it were such that they grasped only fragments of it to recall later—the bark of oak flying into faces as bullets struck; a single blooming jack-in-the-pulpit standing pinkly serene amid the carnage; a soldier rising and walking before them unarmed, the ripped back of his jacket showing where the ball had passed through, then pitching headlong into a flaming briar patch; the Federal soldier down and slamming a rifle butt against his own head to quiet the agony of a groin wound; the dead lying in the thickets, all stripped of their shoes and some with pockets turned out.

"The biggest Gawd damned elephant of them all!" Noah was screaming, not willing the words, not even understanding their meaning. Incomprehensible, incredible, the quick jerking motions of attack and load and fire and fall back, and then attack again. He was a stunned automaton.

He came to the first Federal trench, a line of fallen logs, not so good as Lee's men were now expert at constructing in only a few moments, but a barrier nonetheless. Leaping with the gray shadows on either side, Noah was up and over it, stabbing into the ranks beyond, hearing Martin Hasford now screaming obscenities in the best tradition of Ole Jury Duty. The line was writhing along its course, dense with yammering men in one place, thin of troops in another—screaming, firing, jabbing with their pointed steel.

Only a little farther then, and forced back once more. Noah felt the sting of a Minié ball across his neck and another along the old Sharpsburg wound. His left side was running red; even in that furious moment Noah recalled that the shot he had taken along the Hagerstown Pike had been unnoticed at the time. But these two he felt as they left their marks on his skin.

"Just don't hit no bone, just don't hit no bone," he gasped.

Some of their number went beyond the others and were shot down. The lightly wounded were dragged away as prisoners. Colonel Manning was captured, and others, too. But each time the line seemed on the point of disintegration, it flowed together again, bending forward.

"Into it, Texicans," someone was bellowing. The line went forward hard, over the first entrenchments, and beyond it stubbornly, the blues falling back just as stubbornly. They were into an area now where the dead were mostly blue-clad, and they knew they were beyond the starting point of the battle yesterday.

But only a few more yards, and then no more—the next line of parapets higher, stronger, and the old tree stumps scattered everywhere giving shelter to the Federal marksmen.

Finally, both sides were down, blowing like winded horses, lying among the heaps of dead, firing into one another from less than twenty yards' range. Neither side seemed able to sustain an assault. Between shots, the grays frantically dug mess plates from rolls and scooped up the loamy soil and threw it before them, blanketing with Wilderness earth the bodies of the men down.

Looking to either side, Noah could recognize only Martin Hasford. In the movement forward men had come loose from units, units had become lost and entangled in the wild growth. The cohesion of many companies was gone, and each man was fighting with whomever he found beside him.

There was another braying cheer from the deep woods ahead, and the blue line was coming on. From their prone positions the grays swept it with fire and shattered it, and then were themselves up and rushing again. But only a few steps, then back to their hasty entrenchments and out with pans and plates, and with hands, too, throwing up more protective soil.

Ammunition was being expended at a fearful rate, but there was no lack of it. It was lying all around them in the pouches of the fallen. Noah refilled his own belt three times from the dead, never seeing or caring if it came from comrade or enemy.

"Where's Zack?" he shouted through the swirling mists of woodsmoke, and Martin Hasford stared at him with blank expression, his face a black crust of powder above the beard. The beard had been singed down to a stubble, and along one side the jaw was still smoking.

"Where's Morgan?" But Martin made no reply, glassy-eyed and ramming in a load mechanically, lying on his back behind the parapet made of loose dirt and flesh.

Then pioneer troops appeared from corps headquarters,

not to stay but to drop real entrenching tools. Martin Hasford took up an axe as though glad to be shed of the smoking, blistering rifle, and expertly began to fell timber to buttress the fortification. Noah then with a shovel, throwing soil over the logs. They stayed under fire, building a defensive line.

The day had come on hot, and in their covering of woodsmoke it was suffocating. The sweat drenched their jackets, and water became a problem. The salt stung their eyes and their hurts. Martin had a slashing scalp wound and was bareheaded now, his hair and beard soggy with blood.

But his eyes had finally lost that doll-like glaze. Touching his wound, he grinned.

"Blood put out the fire in my whiskers."

To their right and far into the woods, a great intense firefight was beginning. Even as their own fight continued, the word was passed down—Mahone, with a makeshift division of three brigades, was making a flank attack and would soon sweep along the line before them.

"Watch your front! Watch your front for our boys!"

But they learned later that in the confused flanking movement Longstreet had fallen, just as Ole Jack had fallen in this same timber the year before, almost to the day. Longstreet, like Jackson, a victim of friendly fire! At least, it was not a mortal wound.

ZACK lay in the deep thicket, his face against a white oak log, watching the line of ants moving in a frenzied column away from the flames eating the husk-dry fallen leaves at the other end. They scrambled along the rough ridged bark, and a few came close to the rifle lying across the log and executed a quick detour away from the hot metal.

The sound of combat was all around him, but he could see nothing of troops, his own having pulled suddenly back into the growth of post oak and red cedar to the rear. Beyond the log was a brushy glade and a line of shadbush, some leafed out and others still showing their white sprays of spring blossoms.

Behind the screen of shadbush he could hear the Yankees, officers shouting orders and men swearing. Everywhere he could see the fires, eating the fallen leaves of last autumn and bursting the stunted pines and cedars into flame. The odor and snap of burning resin was thick through the smoke around him.

He had been here only a short time, as time was measured in this whirlwind—lost in a tiny eddy of the battle. He had been shot through the lower spine and was unable to move anything below the waist.

It taken 'em a long time about it, he thought. But when they got me, they got me a good 'un!

He was aware from searching fingers that his trousers were wet with urine, a different feel than the sticky blood along his backside.

They'll think I was afeared an' wet myself. What's the difference, Zack Fawley? They ain't gonna know who you are anyway, onct this fire gets finished with it.

Then he thought of the letter, crumpled still beneath his underwear and soaked through with sweat many times over.

My name's on 'er, but likely faded out. Maybe they can read it. No, when the fire gets hyar the letter'll be gone, too.

He wasn't sorry he had held the letter back, never shown it to his brother. He knew now that no matter the good intentions he imagined, he had never intended showing it. It was a rebellion somehow, a rebellion against this insult of being dispatched to look out for Noah. Him, Zack, with all that responsibility, and then supposed to be the one to explain that the beautiful Luanne Lacy was now bedded each night with Noah's brother Cadmus.

He wasn't sorry. Noah would have to find out in his own sweet time.

There was no pain. Just a dull numbness at the hips and no feeling at all in the legs. But his stomach had begun to cramp, and with a violent retch he threw up against the log. Nothing but bile, a chunk of raw meat, and a black cud of tobacco.

Musta swallered that when the Yanks got me.

Twisting against the log, he managed to pull his plug from

a trousers pocket. The tobacco was soaked with blood, and after staring at it a moment he tossed it aside.

By Gawd, it's hot. No breath of air in this timber. Noy may be dead, the Welsh, too. Ain't seen neither one of 'em since the boys made Bobby Lee go to the rear.

He thought almost casually about his situation. He still didn't believe a man's time came according to some predestined rule. Usually when it came, it was a man's own fault.

Iffen I'd stayed where I belonged an' not been so fast after that one Yank an' got myself out in front, then the ball never woulda found me. That's always been my trouble in this war. I ain't one to shoot in their general direction. I gotta pick me a particular target. An' this time it got me in trouble. Like a boy after his first deer—don't think, jus' ramble. No matter what Pap says.

Luck. Chance. A bad draw a' the cards, as the Welsh would say, and devil take the hindmost.

It was past now, done, and nothing he could do about it. It was over like this war, although he knew the character of the army well enough to realize that the fighting was a long way from finished. And Noah right at the front end of it, yelling about whipping the blues.

He pulled his mind away from it and looked at the smoldering trees, the hat brim low over his eyes, the eyes behind the rear sight of the rifle, the rifle resting on the log, muzzle toward the shadbush. There were black gum trees there, too, some of last year's leaves still clinging to the limbs like tiny cake knives blushing crimson. And trees he didn't recognize, and brush, and much of it burning.

He knew the hidden blue line before him would soon come on again. He could hear them working up to it. And he had no notion of being hauled away to some Federal prison pen to die there without the use of his legs.

I'd as lief take 'er standin' an' not on the ground like a squealin', gut-shot hog.

He almost smiled, because his thinking was beginning to sound like Noah's defiant talk. But he wasn't defiant, only certain of what would happen, and the part of it he could make happen. He was resigned to it as he had been resigned to most of what had happened to him throughout his life. Because he couldn't change a lot of it.

Maybe that's what Pap means. And what Mama means when she says, "To ever' man his season." Some season!

That Noah! A good man. Only a boy starting into this thing, but a man grown in it. And Zack wasn't sure whether such growing was good or bad.

Why'd he hafta steal that Gawd damned pig? We might still be home in the hills. But ain't no use thinkin' 'bout that, neither. Caint do nothin' 'bout it. Damn, this war's made me go addled in the head, all this thinkin' an' none of it any good.

He checked the cap on the nipple of the Enfield, hammer back and waiting. With a low grunt he pulled Pap's old Dragoon revolver from his waistband and looked at the cylinder. Five chambers primed. He cocked it and fumbled in his pouch and came out with another percussion cap. His fingers were gummy with blood. He pressed the cap into place on the sixth chamber and lay the pistol on the ground behind the log, close at hand and still cocked.

The line of ants before his face was thinning out, only a few left, scurrying along the fallen log.

Stragglers, by Gawd, but double quick an' some amongst 'em playin' the long roll, I expect.

He thought of Billy Dick Hysel, long rotted in his shallow grave in Tennessee. He patted the stock of the Enfield and spoke aloud.

"Well, boy, your Ole Bess has laid a pride of 'em in the dirt. Paid 'em back with interest."

Why do so many of us boys call our guns by ladies' names—Betsy an' Mabel an' Ole Nell? Why not men's names? Why any name at all? Jus' "gun"!

He twisted into a firing position behind the rifle and felt a stab of pain along the groin. One of his legs jerked convulsively. He didn't feel the leg move but was aware of it all the same. Like being aware of a deer hidden nearby—and, sensing him, suddenly going stiff with apprehension.

Beyond the shadbush he heard them beginning their low,

cadenced yell. He heard the crash of underbrush and sighted along the rifle. Sparks from the burning trees fell with little hisses onto the brim of his hat.

The first figure to break cover was a Federal captain, and Zack pressed the trigger, hardly feeling at all the kick of the rifle, and reached for the revolver.

DURING the night the Wilderness burned. It burned through the next day as well, the hardwoods resisting the flames and the pines flaring up. They waited in their trenches, Noah scrambling along the lines asking for his brother.

"Likely scattered into one of these other outfits," Napier reassured him. "He'll turn up, that Zack!"

By midafternoon the Welshman was back, his left trouser leg torn off and a bloody bandage around the thigh. When Noah saw him he almost broke down, and seeing that, Morgan made light of it all.

"Just malingering I was," he shouted, gripping Noah's shoulders for a moment in his huge hands. "That Dinsmore's nephew's a good surgeon, even when he's drunk."

He produced a small clay flask, enough for each of them to have a good drink, and Hasford, too. Smacking his lips, Morgan looked around at the log and earth and body revetments.

"By God, lads, it looks like a real fort," he said. "Where's Zack?"

"We haven't seen him since yesterday," Hasford said.

Morgan pounded Noah's shoulder and laughed.

"Hell's on fire, he'll be back, that Zack!"

Noah was so nearly exhausted that the few sips of whisky almost made him drunk. Carrying parties had brought water, and a good thing. The whisky made him even thirstier than before, and after taking all of his own water and most of Hasford's besides, Noah slept against the revetment. But only for a little while.

They waited, watching the woods ahead, but the Yankees did not come again. Finally, Martin Hasford went to his Bible as he always did after a fight, making atonement for his language and knowing all along that the same language would come again when the blues did.

Then with the stub of a pencil he prepared to write a few entries in the log Ole Jury Duty had bequeathed him. As he pulled the ragged ledger book from his waistband he stared in disbelief. Embedded in it was a .58-caliber bullet.

"By damn!" Morgan said. "If Ole Jury Duty was still here and tending that book, you'd be gut-shot now, Parson."

"I didn't even feel it," Hasford said.

" 'Only fools rush to their own folly.' "

Hasford lifted his face, the stubble of burned beard gleaming in the smoke-filtered sunlight. He stared at the Welshman for a long time.

"You know the Book of Solomon?"

"I know a good deal from your Book, Parson," the Black Welshman said, and grinned. "I know a good deal from it."

"You never showed it."

"Each in his own fashion."

They waited still, the day sweltering and the woods around them burning. Toward the end of that day they sent skirmishers forward, and a shout went up that the blues were gone.

"By Gawd, they taken out fer the Rapidan fords, jus' like Hooker!"

A long, high-pitched cheer started on the right flank and moved along the line like a wave, sounding through the Wilderness from one division to the next, from one corps to the next. And when the last was stilled in the far distance of the left flank, it started once again on the right and rolled along the front again.

"We whupped 'em, we whupped 'em!" Noah shouted, waving his hat, his thought of Zack gone in the exuberance of the moment.

But the cheers had hardly died when they knew the same truth Bobby Lee had suspected all along. The Army of the Potomac was not recrossing the Rapidan. It was moving headlong to Lee's right flank, moving to impose itself between the Army of Northern Virginia and Richmond. Moving toward a small crossroads at a place called Spotsylvania, where a county courthouse stood.

They looked at one another with grim, glowing eyes from the darkened faces. They had been in this game long enough to know the obvious military fact.

"Lads," the Black Welshman said, "if I come to any sense of what's happening here, we need to get to this Spotsylvania first!"

# SEVENTEEN

THEY started the run for Spotsylvania just before midnight, along a road cut through the woods that same afternoon by artillery-men, pioneers, stragglers, reserves, and walking-wounded infantrymen, and anybody else Lee could lay hands on. It was a terrible road, only a rough lane really, with stumps in some places a foot high and both sides littered deep with the timber felled to form the pathway.

Men moving in the darkness from battle positions were lost from their units and simply joined the line of march where they found it, falling in among the troops of other companies. From the very first Noah lost sight of the Welshman, and in the glowing night he felt a sudden dread of being left alone. Now and again he reached out to touch the back of Martin Hasford going on before him, to reassure himself that someone familiar was still there.

Stumbling and staggering along the stumpy route, he looked back into the faces of the men behind, barely discernible as faces in the pulsating red light. Looking for Zack but not expecting to see him. Yet still looking while they ate away the miles—slowly, agonizingly.

I oughta fade outa this march an' go back for him, Noah thought. He come back for me alongside the Emmitsburg Road.

But he didn't. They pushed along through the smoking night, trapped in the column like bullets in a red rifle barrel, unable to break free. Besides, Noah knew that back there where the fighting had been the troops were no longer, and he had a dreadful fear of being caught on a battlefield after the armies were gone and him alone with the moans of wounded and the lanterns of the medical corpsmen searching in the darkness for the dead.

The burning forest was on their left, sending its red glow against the clouds of smoke overhead like hell's own door opening and reflecting inner light on the grotesque roof of some primordial cavern.

The flare of the fire, some of it near enough for them to hear the crackling wood, cast dancing shadows across the uneven and spongy road. They fell, tripping over stumps, and were up again cursing, moving on as quickly as the surface would allow. They came to ammunition wagons and artillery limbers, the gunners sweating and trying to negotiate the teams through the stumps. They moved to either side of these obstacles, thrashing through the fresh-cut logs and brush that hemmed the passage.

Eyes smarted as the thick smoke dipped to earth around them, and sometimes they could smell the roasting flesh. But this was soon past, and they were moving on beyond the lines of yesterday's fight and into a new part of the jungle, it burning as well.

There were the grunts of laboring men, feet gouged by the snags. There were the squeal of a horse with a broken leg, the shot fired, and then the oaths of the artillerymen as they cut the horse from the harness and dragged the deadweight clear, some of the infantry stopping to help.

There were the officers moving among them on horseback, urging them along as though this were the paved surface of the Hagerstown Pike. One among these was Anderson, who had taken Ole Pete's place and was a man much admired by the Third Corps, having once been a division commander among them.

There was a chaplain, a civilian attached to the division headquarters, standing at the roadside panting and hatless, calling out the encouragements found in Psalms, touching some of them as they passed, blessing them. Some of the men lifted their hats to him, but few said anything, moving silently on toward that small crossroads.

Ammunition pouches replenished just before their movement became heavy now and chafed their sides. The night wearing on toward dawn, some of them threw aside blanket rolls and mess gear.

They felt more than saw the movement around them, the movement of the long line through the burning Wilderness, the bandages on heads and arms and thighs like pale beacons in the red glow of the fire, the gleam of brassy light dull along the barrels of their shouldered rifles. For a time the fire seemed to move as fast as they did, but finally the men at the head of the column took deep gulps of fresh air, the smoke behind them now.

The column moved with fits and starts, and sometimes they ran hard against the man in front, jabbing one another with the hammers and butts of rifles. They swore softly and bent to retrieve hats lost in the collision, and were bumped into by men behind. Or the serpentine army would lengthen and they would have to hurry to stay up, tripping and stumbling and swearing again.

They rested for ten minutes in each hour, collapsing in the road because there was no place along the sides to find a place not scattered with the windrows of fallen timber and brush, and many not wanting to move into the woods for fear of becoming lost. They lay heaving among the stumps, gulping their water, wiping sweat from hatbands, adjusting slipping and moist bandages on their wounds.

Noah noticed a deadly silence about this column, unlike any he had known before. No singing, no shouting insults, no banter among them. They were coldly serious and grim-faced and nearing exhaustion, jaws set and eyes bright, hands gripping weapons. No drum beat the long roll, no bugle marked the passage of the hours.

At last there was the sign of light in the east beyond the head of the column. They marched as though coming from a black pool toward the bright surface. Visibility improved, and instead of the vibrating glow of red to mark their path, the coming sun showed gray shapes around them.

They moved more quickly, stretching out the length of the column. Toward the front their footfall came once more in the measured cadence it always had on real roads. Their thin shanks coiled and flexed, and the feet reached expectantly, the new day bringing strength from some reservoir that always seemed to be there.

Here the roadside was less cluttered with the debris of the road's making, and as the pale dawn came they were ordered to the sides for breakfast. Meat issued the night before with the ammunition was eaten raw because they knew it would be only minutes before they'd be called back into line. And very little energy to kindle fires anyway. No man that Noah saw was without his ration now, in an army of men who usually consumed every bite as soon as it was passed out to them, so great was their intensity.

Another brigade passed along the road as they ate. Even now there was not the usual exchange of insults between them—as with the artillery, the Napoleons they had passed in the night, the gunners up and riding the limbers.

And then the old familiar sound. Gunfire ahead. Growing in volume. Frantic couriers dashed along the road, conferring with officers. Word was passed. Some of Beauty Stuart's horsemen were up there at the crossroads, trying to hold off the Federals.

Why, hell, the cavalry couldn't hold off advancing infantry, not for long, and even before the orders were barked out they were wolfing down the last bite of meat and scrambling back into the road.

When they broke into the scattered clearing around Spotsylvania they found a line of fenceposts the cavalrymen had racked there as hasty fortification. They ran now, shouting, the silence of the red night gone. And beyond the fenceposts, issuing from the forest, came the line of blue infantry. Not sixty yards away! And behind that, others, unseen as yet, but with their drums beating forward the rest of an entire corps of the Army of the Potomac, attacking in column of brigades.

Noah threw himself down behind a pile of posts and leveled his rifle. And thought, That son of a bitch over there may try Bobby Lee's flank, but we'll allus be there to meet him!

It was the kind of thing they said or thought or tried to will—a barricade against the sudden fear, a foundation for resistance to whatever came. Noah knew that now, knew the bravado it typified. And knew after the wheatfield at Gettysburg how fragile courage could be. So he thought it again, aloud, bellowing it at the top of his voice as the crashing fire began.

At this moment there was among them a shared hatred of this new enemy. New because he didn't fight like the others had, a day or two or three at most, and then pull back and give everyone a chance to lick wounds and fill bellies and rest aching feet. This one kept on coming, bull-headed, not knowing he was whipped, throwing in the fresh brigades of blueclads with their despised low bellowing.

And, besides, there wasn't a man in the army who did not know that the new man over there—Grant—had prohibited Federal sutlers from crossing the river with his army. So, even if the grays broke a line here and there, stole a march, captured a wagon park, there would be no chance for that delicate booty. It was not only unheard of but unfair. That son of a bitch!

A CRUEL month was May 1864. Noah, like the rest of them, felt the hatred ebb, and in its place came bewilderment, and then admiration for this pugnacious Union host. And with it the growing determination that if Grant wanted to fight it out on this line all summer, they'd do what they could to accommodate him.

"Great stubbornness you'll always find in a civil war," the Black Welshman had said once. "And bitterness, too, and hatred and, yes, admiration for the soldier on the other side sometimes. Cruel it is like no other, lads."

It became a horrible dream world of shock and violence, did May 1864. And well into June, too. No respite from the hardest campaign any of them had ever known—and at a time when rations were scant and manpower diminishing. If they weren't in a death struggle at one point, they were marching to one just down the road. And each march now was a race against the ever-expanding flanking movement of an enemy obviously intent on cutting them off from their capital, or else driving them into immobility in the trenches on the outskirts of Richmond.

After the Wilderness came Spotsylvania, more vicious than Antietam, more prolonged than Gettysburg. Noah watched the army coil into position on a long, wide half-circle, there in the southern edge of the jungle where the attacks came as regularly as each new dawn, each new midday, each new evening. They had their names for some of the positions: Salient, Mule Shoe, Bloody Angle.

No moment of daylight rest. When the enemy was not actually coming on the attack, they were felling timbers, erecting impenetrable barricades that charging Yankee regiments would penetrate anyway. Counterattack and drive them out, then throw the dead from the ditches, up onto the face of the parapets.

Dig and chop and burrow rifle ports, snipe and take their hurried meals, wait for the next assault, chop and dig.

And sometimes the blues so close on the other side of the entrenchments, they stabbed at them with bayonets through chinks in the logs!

Once, in the evening, the Federals moved into their position so quickly they were caught cooking and were set upon before they could run to their stacks of rifles—slashing at the invaders with chunks of firewood, with rocks, with frying pans, until a friendly reserve regiment countercharged and drove out the blues.

Sun and then rain, and wet powder bringing on the misfires. And always the dead heaping up before their position, Union advances harvested man by man with volley fire and canister from enfilading artillery.

At night they crept across the killing ground and collected rifles and ammunition, gave water to the wounded, and returned—until each man had at hand a dozen loaded rifles standing in the trench beside him for the next exercise in rapid fire.

The Federal bands serenaded them sometimes. They could hear the music from only a short distance behind the opposing lines: "Nearer My God to Thee." The mournful notes came through the black of night from where the blues had constructed their own trenches, and some of the hard-faced veterans, Martin Hasford among them, sang the words quietly, tears mixing with rain on their faces.

They began to rotate from front to reserve. The first time the regiment was replaced in line by an Alabama unit, and they moved back beyond the Brock Road, where Noah collapsed in a stand of bullet-marked pin oaks and slept for twenty-four hours without rising, even to eat.

But usually these reserve times were quickly interrupted. They would hear the angry crash of fire from across the road, usually just as they had meat half cooked. They would grab up rifles and run back to support hard-pressed friends or drive out blue incursions with a furious charge.

Always now the heavy dispute of their own artillery with the Union guns. The longer they were here, the more trees were felled to create positions for the batteries. Finally, it seemed there was as much bombardment as there had been along the ridges at Gettysburg.

Rain came again, followed by blistering heat. They had begun to smell the rotting flesh, the space between the lines so fiercely contested that no burial parties dared work there, even in darkest night. They had the smell of it with the powder smoke thick around them, the smell of it when they worked to rear their fortifications higher still, and the smell of it when they slept or ate. They were never rid of it. It clung to them like mold, a stench no one could become accustomed to, nor ever forget.

It had been a long time since they had seen vegetables, and in some units there was scurvy. In the First Corps they recalled fondly those few boiled turnips at Gordonsville. Now they dug the roots of sassafras and wild grape, stewing the stringy substitute or gnawing it raw. The day's ration from the commissary department was usually a quarter-pound of hard pork and two rock-textured biscuits.

In their dumb shock they tried to comprehend the news that Jeb Stuart had been mortally wounded at a place called Yellow Tavern.

Well, they said to one another, if you consider cavalrymen soldiers, he was the best of the lot. It was a compliment only these infantrymen could fully appreciate.

It rained the day the Federals made their last assault, then slipped away, flanking to Lee's right again. They made their own move, feeling they had been on the Spotsylvania line forever and glad to be away from it, starting another race on the roads toward Richmond—this time to the North Anna River, where they expected the blues to try a crossing.

And through it all there was no sign of Liverpool Morgan.

THEY rested beside the muddy road where the artillery horses were struggling to heave the guns farther south. Always farther south now.

Here the land was not so ravaged by war. They saw tended farms, and the people in little hamlets came out along their route to wave them on. Sometimes there was a pitcher of buttermilk for the troops lucky enough to be first along the roadside fences.

Martin Hasford squatted beside a hedge of crabapple that second day away from Spotsylvania, watching the bony cavalcade of horses straining in the mire. He shook his head sadly.

"They ought to do all this with men alone," he said, "just to save the horses."

Beside him, Noah laughed, a harsh, mirthless sound. He was sitting in the mud, his legs up and his arms resting on his knees.

Leaning against the wall behind them were their rifles. They had come away from Spotsylvania with a number of Yankee pieces, but the weight had soon become too much for them and the others. The roadside was littered with discarded rifles. Now ordnance-department wagons were coming on behind, and each of the Yankee weapons was being carefully retrieved for future use.

"I've give up now, Parson," Noah said, and he lowered his face to his arms.

Martin Hasford looked at him, blinking, a little startled. By now he had come to accept the name he was called, accepted it so completely that he no longer even worried at its meaning.

"Give up?"

"Yeah. He ain't comin' back to us. Zack ain't."

"Why, of course he is."

"No." Noah's voice was muffled, his head still down. "Three weeks now since we come outa that fire in the woods. He ain't comin'. He'd a' found us by now iffen he was."

"Why, he's likely turned in to a hospital. He's likely clear back in Richmond with good grub and the women to look after him."

"No. He ain't comin'!"

Noah lifted his face and stared across the road where the long column of artillery and wagons had passed, and now regiments of infantry moved, their flags cased and rifles across shoulders, some with bayonets still fixed and crusted as though with rust. Their faces were leaden, gray as the cloudy skies.

Suddenly, Martin Hasford moved close to Noah and put his arms around the younger man's shoulders. Noah almost cried then, but he clamped his jaw and the tears did not come. Only a shudder. Martin moved back, embarrassed, his own eyes shining. "He was like my brother, too," he said.

"Yeah," Noah said bitterly. "All of us is brothers, ain't we? The ones that last, they all get to be brothers, don't they?"

Martin Hasford tried to think of some appropriate verse from his Book, but none came to mind.

There are blessings in all things, he thought. Thank God for this hard campaign because with it there is little chance for this boy to think on Zack, only time to think of survival, of ravenous wolfing of meager rations, exhausted sleeping in the mud, nothing more.

Boy, I call him, Martin thought. Because he's of an age with my own son, but by age and experience a boy no longer. Three years of this and on it goes. He tried again to recall some verse that might be comforting, but once more could not.

"I reckon that's the size of it," Martin Hasford said.

"Yeah. All brothers. Even the horses!"

There was only a moment of anguish in Noah's voice. Recalling those years in the hills when Zack's strength had grown until he surpassed even Pap for dependability, he had come to believe that Zack was invulnerable, indestructible. The rock of the family! Calm and clearheaded, those pale eyes showing the toughness of the best of his breed.

But now he knew Zack was gone. He didn't know how he knew, but he knew. Somehow, some way, if Zack was alive he would have found a means of communicating it. So he was gone.

They'll kill us all, Noah thought.

He had seen so many fall, and at first there had been shock and disbelief, watching flesh turned to pulpy mush, seeing skin go bloated black, eyes turned to lifeless jelly. It dismayed him now. Dinsmore and Johnson and Tug and Cass and Hysel. Now Zack. Dismayed him because Zack, who had always been a being extraordinary, had become simply another of the fallen. No more, no less. Even a point of pride, maybe, and that thought made him recoil with horror. But it was true. A point of pride that his own brother could be listed with all the rest.

All of them one family, he thought. Family was the strongest symbol in his mind, and this old army had become that now, more family than anything else he had ever known. He knew it better than his own dooryard in the hills above the Buffalo. He knew the men in it better than he knew his own Pap. He knew its texture and its pride, its roughness and its character, more surely than he had ever known his own brothers. More surely even than Zack, except that Zack had been a part of this old army, too, and he had come to know Zack only after they had made it to Virginia—before that only vaguely, only the shadowy, taut form moving through the timber after game.

"They say Gen'l Lee passed on ahead last night," Martin said.

"Yeah, that's what they say."

I wonder why so many a' these boys call him Marse Robert, Noah thought. Slave talk! Hell, he ain't no Marse Robert. He's Bobby Lee!

And he wondered if all those dead on the ground of Pennsylvania and Maryland and in the Wilderness were family in the General's thinking. He wondered if Bobby Lee felt the way he was feeling now, seeing yet another man fall.

But there was no more time for pondering. Napier was moving them out into the road again. Noah heaved himself up, the mud sucking at his trousers, his rotten shoes slipping in the wet soil.

"You all right?" Napier asked, looking closely into Noah's face. "You look a mite drawed out."

"Jus' show us some Yanks," Noah said, shouldering his Enfield. "We'll whup their arse!"

But the old hell's fire was gone from his voice.

THEY won this race, too. By the time the Army of the Potomac arrived along the North Anna and the Totopotomay, they were waiting. So this time the blues made only a few tentative approaches and then backed away to slip toward the flank once more.

The days were going fast, coming close to June. The heat was becoming unbearable. After the North Anna they watched the landscape change again. Marshy country now, much of it, and the little streams meandering toward the rivers haphazardly as though lost in their direction. They were coming into the area where Lee had fought his first battles—Mechanicsville and the Chickahominy.

On the road near Hanover Junction they found Ryan, Pugilist. He was standing like a tree beside an artillery caisson, his great rugged face shining with sweat, his orange beard dripping.

"Hey you, Arkansas!" he bellowed, snaggled teeth showing as he grinned. "Still got your hat, I see."

"I'll be damned," Noah said, and he moved off the road

and extended his hand. "I still got a hat. You eat any more snowballs lately?"

Ryan threw back his head and laughed. "By God, I'd trade this damned cannon for a mouthful of that Fredericksburg white now, I would."

Martin Hasford came over, too, and he and the Irishman shook hands. Martin winced a little at the grip.

"Been wonderin' if I might see you lads, I have," Ryan said. "Seen one of your boys lately."

Noah stared, his heart suddenly thumping, unable to speak.

"Who? Who'd you see?" Martin asked.

"That big bully of a Welsh you set on me that night in the snow. Him as gave me the knuckles and minus these." He pointed with a grimy finger at the gap in his line of front teeth.

Napier had come up, and he pressed close to the pugilist, face intent.

"Where'd you see him?"

"Why, hell, he was with us on that little walk to the Mule Shoe," Ryan said. "He got in with our column in the dark somehow and first pop out of the box we're in the line and the Yanks are comin'. Took him off prisoner, they did."

"Like hell!" Noah said savagely. "They wasn't no Yank alive could carry off the Welsh!"

"Oh, it took a few. That wild man! Usin' his rifle like a club, was he. They shot him down. Only enough to bleed him a little, and him bellowin' like a swamp alligator. They dragged him off, did the Yanks. Him and a few others of our boys."

"Like hell," Noah said weakly.

"Where was he hit?" Napier asked.

"Just a nip at the collarbone. But they laid a rifle butt acrost his head, an' that put him low, like old rags, but still makin' his voice heard above the racket."

Noah stood limp, stunned, unhearing as the others talked. Who's left to steal the chickens now? he thought wildly. Who's left to flip the double eagle? Who's left to swim rivers?

Ryan was slapping Noah's shoulder, still grinning.

"No worry, boy. He's in one of them blue prison pens now. Eatin' off the fat of the Yankee land."

"More likely hog slops," Napier said.

"Well now, boy, it couldn't be no worse than what we're gettin' in this army, could it?"

Napier propelled them back to the road then, and as they hurried to catch the company, Noah looked back. The big Irish prizefighter was still watching them, grinning through the gaps in his teeth.

Noah could see in his mind that snowy, moonlit field behind Fredericksburg, and he could hear the sounds of Morgan's quick hands against Ryan's hard jaw.

They'll kill us all, he thought.

ACROSS the path of the advancing Federal army they entrenched again, quickly and effectively. They would beat the Yanks here, too, with time to spare. A line without reserves, five miles long. But brutally strong.

Lying in the trench, Noah could see the sweep of the cleared ground to the front where the blues would have to move if they persisted in taking this route to Richmond.

"They'll break off here, too," he said to Martin Hasford. "They'd be fools to try us on this line."

Artillery was up, a lot of it. There were rumors that some batteries had come out from the Richmond defenses, even some of the twenty-four-pounders captured in this same area from McClellan when he made his run at the capital in 1862.

It rained again that first night, but they kept their ammunition well covered. Their spirits were high because there was the prospect of fighting from a strong position. Besides, pots of steaming boiled beans had appeared at evening, giving them their first good meal in weeks. Out from Richmond the beans had come, and cooked with salt pork. There was bread, too, and most of it edible.

The rain itself was good after the boiling hot day, a day of frenzied digging and felling of trees. They had even had time to implant sharp stake abatis to their front.

In the darkness and the rain, Noah and Hasford lay close together. Before they slept, Noah said it again: "They'd be fools to try us here."

But the Yankees did try, with dawning skies clearing and the sun coming on strong. They came with brigades on line, looking fresh, and their regimental musters filled out as though there had not been almost a month of killing.

They came with the drums and with the low cheer. They came with thunderous barking of artillery, marching with their striped banners up.

The first attack was butchered, well short of the defensive line. The second attack came only a few paces closer, and the third did no better. Still they came, shouting through the smoke. They were cut down like the corn in Sharpsburg's field.

"Gawd Almighty," Noah shouted. "Iffen the ammunition holds out, we'll clean up the whole blue army."

It held out. Doggedly the blues came and were dropped in rows. Noah could see the white slips of paper pinned to blue jackets, with names inscribed so identification might be made when they fell.

At other points along the line the Federals might have enjoyed more success, but not here. The bodies heaped up in the murky cloud of fumes. The wounded of the first, second, and third attacks were screaming, trampled underfoot by the fourth.

Behind their barricades, Noah and Martin worked with calm quickness—loading and firing, faces caked with black once more. Hasford swore only occasionally and then softly, almost to himself. There was little excitement in this, no thrill of danger. Behind the earth and log parapets it was the casual work of execution.

It began in early morning and by noon was finished. The clearings before the grayback lines were literally covered with a carpet of blue—squirming and writhing bodies, and the calls for water coming through the heated day, sending the chills along Noah's back.

He was crying. He had no notion why. He rubbed his wet

cheeks with fingers blistered on the hot barrel of his rifle, and his hand came away from his face covered with the black-powder mud.

"Send some more, Gawd damn you," he sobbed. "Send some more a' them poor dumb bastards!"

But they sent no more. Once again the blues pulled back and moved away, their march this time taking them far south of Richmond. And after that it would be the Petersburg trenches and the end.

Noah, Hasford, and Napier didn't know it at the moment, nor Ryan, Pugilist, nor the Mississippi captain with Ole Jury Duty's nick in his ear, nor Burton, the Fourth Texas Indian fighter and barber.

Seeing those hordes of blue uniforms and looking along their own tattered and unshod columns, seeing the condition of worn-out horses and worn-out guns, they struggled to keep the same spirit they had shown in 1862. But somehow, even without knowing what lay ahead, hope was dying, just as so many of those fine Union regiments had died under their guns that morning at Cold Harbor.

# EIGHTEEN

IT WAS not the last fight he saw, nor certainly was it the worst, but for Noah, New Market Heights was a thing that hung heavy in his craw like an unchewed chunk of raw pork. It was there that they first came face to face with black troops.

After Cold Harbor they had no chance to see Richmond again, but marched south to pass it on the east, finally taking trench positions near the James River. They expected the blues to hit them there quickly, striking toward the capital, but the Army of the Potomac crossed the river downstream and laid siege to Petersburg, farther south.

Like all veterans, they knew a great deal more about what was happening now than they had in the first years of the war—that mad thrashing around the valley with Old Jack, the march to Harper's Ferry, the fury at Antietam, each day looking no farther than the next file ahead and perhaps not caring.

Now they had a grasp of the larger scheme of things. They knew they had been maneuvered into fixed positions, and it was a situation nobody liked, from the newest recruit right up the line to Bobby Lee himself.

Their awareness was perhaps less attributable to their experience than to the fact that General Gregg, who commanded the brigade now, believed in passing information along to his troops. Whatever the reason, they knew that getting penned in front of Richmond and Petersburg was bad. They talked about breaking out into the open again, where Bobby Lee could move, could find flanks. But the wiser men among them knew the chance of such a thing was slim.

Their intelligence sources soon informed them that on Northside, where they were, the Army of the James opposed them.

"Who the hell is the Army of the James?" Noah asked

from his post along the parapet, from where he could watch the engineers building abatis and stake obstacles along the marshy, wooded creek below the position.

"It says in the newspapers that it's commanded by Ben Butler. They call him the Beast," Martin Hasford said. He was sitting on a fire step, jotting entries in Ole Jury Duty's log.

"Why do they call him that?"

"Maybe because he's got a lot of U.S.C.T. outfits under him."

"What the hell's that?"

"United States Colored Troops."

Noah stared incredulously. He hopped down and sat on the fire step beside Hasford, bending toward him.

"*Infantry* niggers?"

"That's what they say."

"Not jus' ditch-diggers an' road-scrapers? You mean they're liable to throw nigger infantry at us?"

"That's what they say."

Noah sat stunned. If he had heard it from anyone but Martin Hasford, he wouldn't have believed it.

Like many others in this First Corps, he had developed an instant dislike for the Army of the James without ever having fired a shot at it. They were supposed to be fighting the Army of the Potomac. That was the strangely beloved enemy, the one they hated but at the same time had come to know so well. The Army of the James! And to make matters worse, the prospect of black soldiers coming at them.

This hyar is like some foreign country, Noah thought once again.

He wished Liverpool Morgan were with them. The Welshman could set it straight. Noah had to sift through his thinking alone now, with only the parson to help him, and Hasford was more and more spending his time and thought on that damned book of Ole Jury Duty's.

For three years now he had known that this war was being fought for a lot of reasons, depending on who was telling of it. But no doubt about it, one of the reasons was slavery.

Like most of his hill-country associates, he preferred to

believe that he was not going through all this simply to keep the colored man on somebody else's plantation. He was doing it for freedom, sure enough, but the freedom of locals to determine their own destiny. White locals!

Until he had come to this war, the only black faces he had ever seen were those two men who worked the Town sawmill beside the Buffalo. He had never passed a word with either of them, nor been close enough to them to do so even if inclined.

They had been strange and rather outlandish creatures, and all he knew of them was what Zack or Pap or Uncle Questor had mentioned after going into the valley for lumber on one occasion or another. What Noah got from it all was that neither Zack nor Pap nor Uncle Questor could themselves understand a word of what the black men said.

He had seen plenty of them since joining this army. He had always remained intentionally aloof because he could claim no experience from such associations. Besides, he was a little afraid of them.

There had been Tug, of course. The strange attachment between him and Bev Cass. The familiarity between the boy and the Welshman. Through all of that, Noah had looked on Tug as something akin to a house pet, taken from some unknown wilderness and trained to speak and cook and tend horses.

He had even touched Tug once. On that winter day behind Fredericksburg when the black boy had returned from taking Cap'n Gordy home, Noah had actually slapped the boy's shoulders. A number of times. It had surprised him then that Tug felt just like any other man—flesh and bone and blood. But he never touched the boy again after that, even though they had spent countless nights around the same cookfire.

Now there was the prospect of having to shoot at these people, and they at him, and it disturbed him deeply in a way he could not comprehend.

"Them'll be free niggers from New York an' other such places," Napier said.

"Not all," Martin Hasford said, not looking up from his

ledger. "The newspapers say some are slaves, run away or liberated, and enlisted by the Yankees."

"God have mercy on any of 'em I get hands on," Napier said, and Noah could hear in his voice a viciousness he'd never heard before.

It was this hatred that confused Noah even more than all the rest of it. He could feel the searing heat of it, the rage, in the voices of the men around him—men from the cotton lands, from the big riverbottoms, and from the Texas regiments.

There had always been times for despising the enemy—no doubting that—but tempered between by periods when the fury subsided and they could speak of the blues with admiration for their courage and competence. And early on, those times when they crossed the lines and traded tobacco for coffee . . . the swims Zack and the Welshman had made across the Rappahannock.

He realized with a start that in those earlier times it had been he, Noah, who had been so bitter and unwavering in his hatred. But now the anger of the others over this U.S.C.T. business was beyond his understanding. He wondered whether he had slid back or had simply stayed the same and now the others had passed him.

Maybe most perplexing of all, Noah wondered: Surely the Yanks know how this ole Confed'rate army is gonna feel about usin' colored again 'em. Why would they enlist 'em when they already got more'n enough white men for their army?

And with that he began to perceive dimly how bitter and unrelenting this war had become, in fact had been all along, though hidden beneath the exuberance of the early months, that dulling spell of frenzied flag-waving and speechmaking and proud bullheadedness that seemed to make it all so simple and straightforward.

"Parson, I'll never understand the Yankees," he said.

"And some of our own? The flatlanders?"

"Hell, I don't understand them either!"

Hasford smiled at him then, and it was some comfort to know that perhaps Martin was aware of his inability to fit all the pieces of this war into their proper place.

I reckon, Noah thought, that a sojur is supposed to jus' do what he's told an' not worry 'bout all this other stuff. It makes a man's head hurt.

THE ARMY was catching hell south of the river. But Northside was calm, and because of that was thinly held, many of the positions only partially manned. They could hear artillery in the direction of Petersburg almost every day, and sometimes rifle fire and smoke like thunderclouds rose from the banks of the James.

There was always time for joking, and they heard the new one going around, the result of a government directive that asked ladies to save the contents of their chamberpots for use in the manufacture of niter. Two years earlier, Noah would have been astonished and embarrassed to hear such things said about females and their basic bodily functions. But now he laughed along with the rest.

Even Martin Hasford had a chuckle, though he tried to avoid thinking about his wife and daughter at such times.

Northside was good duty, considering. Rations were coming out from Richmond on a somewhat regular basis. Sometimes sections of troops were entertained at local villages and farmsteads. There was even dancing. Civilians seemed immune to the thought of any Yanks taking Richmond. After all, McClellan had failed.

But that had been in 1862, and this was 1864, and it was not McClellan over there either.

"We got one chance," Napier said. "Slaughter enough of them blues so in the elections this fall the Yankee voters will be sick and tired of it an' put Ole Lincoln outa office."

"We ain't doin' much slaughter standin' around in these ditches," Noah said. "Maybe the boys south of the river is."

"Count your blessings," Martin Hasford said. "The best time for being a soldier is when you don't have to kill somebody."

It was so quiet that even Noah's apprehension about fighting black troops began to fade.

"Prob'ly jus' one a' them rumors the Yankee spies started," he said.

"I doubt it," said the parson.

There was an afternoon of agony and delight at a local farm on the Darbytown Road when Noah was instructed in the shoddish by two giggling girls, daughters of the farm owner who was holding a fish fry for some of the men in the Texas Brigade. . . . Agony because his shoe soles flapped hopelessly against the hard-packed ground of the yard, like pistol shots above the noise of the fiddlers on the porch, and he couldn't forget the patches on his trousers and the traces of trench mud at his elbows, impossible to remove even with scrubbing and brushing. . . . Delight at the soft touch of a woman's hands and the sight of her smiling face. And not just one, but two of them. They seemed so young!

Finally he was able to see beyond his own embarrassment and realize that all the civilians looked pretty threadbare, too, so he threw himself into the dance, feeling the slender waists with his callused hands and smelling their soapy fragrance. And once he thought, Hell's afire, I'm pert' near as good a dancer as Zack. But quickly put that from his mind so as not to spoil the moment.

He took a few too many sips of elderberry wine, and before the afternoon was through he was moderately but excusably drunk. It reminded him in the red waning light of another such day on the slopes above the Buffalo when Lucinda was married and he and Ben Shackleford had stolen the pig. And then he thought for the first time in a long while of that abandoned smokehouse and Luanne Lacy.

Twice Noah stole kisses, one from each of his two dancing partners. The soft lips' gentle caress against his own made him more giddy than the wine had power to do.

Burton entertained them all with his Comanche scalp dance, which his comrades had seen many times before and which they noted was a little different with each rendition.

If it was a good day for Noah, it was no less so for Martin Hasford. He sampled the wine and, sitting at one end of the porch away from the fiddlers and with their host beside him, discussed the best ways of fermenting wild fruit. They spoke of the Scriptures, too, and the farmer said the Lord came to things in a curious way sometimes, but it was His will just the same. Martin agreed out of courtesy rather than conviction. He could not accept all that had passed in recent months as the Lord's doing.

The realization was a little frightening to him. But it was impossible to avoid. And impossible to avoid as well the fact that even though he was continuing to read his Bible each day, he was doing it more for passing time than for inspiration. It had been months since he had attended a religious service. He consoled himself in this by noting that throughout the army there seemed less religious fervor for such things as there had been, say, that winter behind Fredericksburg.

They ate the fish taken from the James River and with it corn dodgers and sweet potatoes baked brown on open coals and bathed in butter. With the music and the dancing feet stilled, they could hear the faint notes of church bells in Richmond calling worshipers to Sunday-evening services. Across the fields came the calls of larks. The war seemed very far away.

Going home to the trenches in the dusk, Noah walking beside him and humming one of the shoddish tunes, Hasford thought, No, He has not ordained the transactions in this thing. He has allowed the war to run its course along a man-made path. And if I am mistaken, then I hope He will forgive me for being too small-minded to see it otherwise.

But, he thought, it is sometimes comforting to think that He does each thing with His own hand. That way a man can console himself in saying that he has had nothing to do with these disasters himself. As with a hailstorm.

IT WAS in that week of the shoddish dancing that they saw the black infantry. A small fight, as such things are reckoned, but reminiscent of Cold Harbor with the brigade entrenched along Darbytown Road on the slopes of New Market Heights, in strong positions and with sweeping fields of fire before them.

They came at dawn, and the brigade waited for the mists to rise and for the leading companies of the attacking formations to hang up on the abatis along the streamline. Then came the volley fire. It was devastating.

The second wave came shortly afterward, with good longer-range visibility now for the artillery. The blues floundered through the marshy ground and struggled through the obstacles in a killing fire.

Mostly they were so far away when they fell that Noah could make out no expressions on their dark faces. Yet it was a strange and terrible sensation firing into those ranks, watching them fall and writhe on the low ground, hearing their cries.

On one of their later assaults, a few broke into the thinly held Confederate trenches. Only a small number were allowed to surrender. Noah watched with amazement, then numbing dispassion, as Napier shot one who had thrown down his rifle and stood in the trench petrified, hands held empty over his head. In the Texas trenches they killed a number of others that way.

After they had met the attack, General Gregg ordered them back to another line, to strengthen it until reinforcements could come out from Richmond. Behind them as they hurried into new positions they could hear the last of their rear guard firing, then breaking off into silence, and finally they heard the cheers of the black soldiers as they occupied the trenches.

Many of the men around Noah were grumbling and swearing, furious to have been denied a last-ditch bloody fight with the niggers, but he could think only of the new, neat uniforms, the shining brass buttons, the gleaming weapons. And the black faces hung in the abatis.

"You all right?" Martin Hasford asked, touching his arm.

"I reckon. My breakfast ain't settin' too well on my stomach is all."

They fought again and marched and fought yet again, in the rain or in the sun of Indian summer. It had been a hot and dry year, and when they moved, a cloud of dust accompanied them, except in the marshlands where the ground was fine as gunpowder. At least the marches were short, by old standards, moving them from one trench to another, positions for the most part prepared when the Yankees had threatened Richmond in 1862.

Between fights and movement they stood in their ditches exchanging shots with snipers.

Then at last it was November, and still Richmond had not fallen, the Beast and his U.S.C.T. all turned back and be damned.

But the word soon passed along the trenches: The Yankees have up and reelected that damned Lincoln!

And with that, some of them groaned and lost all hope. Even Noah.

# NINETEEN

FEW OF the Confederates imprisoned at Fort Delaware had the slightest notion of its location, but like most soldiers in the Southern armies they knew its reputation. Perhaps Elmira was as infamous, but if so it was only because of the cold weather in upstate New York.

In fact, Fort Delaware wasn't much worse or better than the other Northern pens wherein, by the end of 1864, the death toll of imprisoned rebels had reached about twenty thousand.

It stood on an island twelve miles downstream from Wilmington. At that point the river was tidewater, so that the solution which passed its shores was saline at high tide. Shaped somewhat like a shoe sole, the island was a scab of rock in midstream, level and featureless, covered with a thick layer of gummy gray mud. A mile to the north was the flat shore of New Jersey, and equidistant to the south was Delaware City. In the best of times it had been unbearable, and after the Union established a prison there, it got worse.

At one end was the billet area of the Federal garrison, mostly men who had been conscripted but were not fit for field duty. The rest of the island was surrounded by walls of rough lumber or wire fences, all about twelve feet high and with watchtowers located along the perimeter. On the outboard side of the fence was a walkway, elevated a few feet above the surface of the river, and inside the walkway and the fence was the compound yard and prisoner barracks.

The yard was divided by another fence into an area for officers and a larger one for enlisted ranks. In Privates' Pen were common criminals from the blue army, court-martialed for various offenses and doing their term here. From time to time one of these was found strangled, the body dumped in one of the drinking-water cisterns located about the island.

The compound yard was mostly below river level, the water held out by the guard walkways acting as dikes. Constant work by the prisoners was required to keep these levees in repair. Water seeped up continually through the bedrock to moisten the soil in the yard, and any increased depression brought a seepage of turbid muck as thick as pea soup and smelling like vomit.

The barracks were little better than ragged tents. After General Grant put an end to prisoner exchanges because they were proving more advantageous to the South than to the North, more and more prisoners arrived and none left. Bunks were racked one above the other, in some barracks three high. Only the healthier men could use the top bunk in a three-tier affair because of the arduous climb required.

From time to time the cisterns would go dry, due to lack of rain. Then a boat would come out from Delaware City, and water would be pumped directly from the river into the cisterns. This was the worst time for drinking water on the island. It was murky and filled with dead leaves and fish heads and wiggly things. No one ever recorded the Fort Delaware cisterns being cleaned out.

In summer the mosquitoes came in swarms, along with the flies. In fall there was no sight of turning foliage from the far gray shores. In winter the inmates suffered terribly from head congestion and what they termed the galloping consumption. In spring there was no greening.

Not many prisoners escaped from Fort Delaware. But in the early months of 1864 there was a successful break, even though the Federals refused to believe it.

LIVERPOOL Morgan pushed back the one tattered blanket they allowed in this place and sat with his feet hanging over the edge of the rickety wooden bunk. For a moment before he wrapped on the burlap strips that had been passing for shoes these many weeks, he stared at his bare feet. All the toenails were rotting off.

His shoulder hurt, too, as always. When they had brought him here in the summer his collarbone had been broken. The Yankee prison pen doctor had made a few probing inspections and finally let it heal without further application of medical expertise.

It had left an ugly scar and bone splinters under the skin, and what the Welshman knew would be a lifetime sore shoulder. At least his left was still intact. He had proven that once when he caught a fellow prisoner trying to steal his trousers off the washline. One hooking blow was enough to crack the fellow's jaw.

Morgan had little sympathy for the man, a thief and a Yankee besides—one of many felons from the blue army who shared this compound with the prisoners of war.

"Rise from them butts and get your grub," a blueclad soldier shouted from the doorway where no door was hinged, burned long since in the single tub stove that was supposed to heat the barracks. "This crew's got cart detail today, so eat hearty, you Reb bastards!"

"Cart detail, is it?" Morgan said. "And a good day for fresh air and lively work for the poor soldier."

"Go to hell," somebody muttered.

Morgan laughed, wrapping his feet. At least now the surface of the compound yard was mostly frozen, so toenails would not become spongy from the slimy mud. Of course, one might instead lose the entire foot with frostbite.

Breakfast was the usual fare. Each man had a tin cup—his only utensil—and this was filled with rice soup, four grains to the quart of water, so they said. Then two hard crackers. It was all they'd have until the end of the day, when there would be four more crackers and a two-ounce chunk of meat unidentifiable as to origin and in such a rancid state that it was impossible to tell whether or not it had been cooked. Sometimes there were weevils in the crackers, and sometimes there were white worms in the meat, dead or still squirming, depending on how long it had been consigned to the cookpot.

Morgan always ate the meat no matter its wildlife, gagging

it down with gulps of prison cistern water that tasted like fish scales.

On this morning, as on all others, he stood in the grub line at the end of Privates' Pen and wondered where the regiment might be. There was a concentrated effort by the guards to keep any news of the war from them, and since summer he had been only vaguely aware that Lee's army was in the maze of trenches around Petersburg and Richmond.

Out of there they are by now, surely, he thought, doing what they do best: maneuvering in open country, marching to the good defensive ground or to the Yankee's flank, using their feet and their firepower in the rolling meadows and wooded country of the Old Dominion. Well, that's how it once was, anyway. Not likely now.

"Move it along, Reb." The Union soldier was dipping out the soup, as sour-faced as most of the guards, not liking it any more than the prisoners.

"When's the next bread ration?"

"Two days."

"Glory be!"

Twice each week they were treated to half a loaf of bread each, when a civilian baker was ferried over from Delaware City and spent the day cooking. It was the high point of their existence. Crusts of bread were hoarded, swapped, bartered, gambled for, and fought over. Half a loaf of bread could be traded for a week's ration of the bad meat, or for five chips of tobacco, or for a single nice fat river rat.

The rats had started coming into the compound with cooling weather, creating a nightly hunt with clubs. Morgan had become one of the best of these hunters and a good rat cook besides. The meat was light-colored when properly roasted over the open flames of the tub stove. With salt, it was fairly good. The Federals gave them all the salt they wanted. Some put it in their water to kill the taste.

Morgan sat with his barracks mates in a long row not far from the open-pit latrine that ran the length of one side of Privates' Pen. They were accustomed to the smell—could have done nothing about it anyway—yet, even so, they hated latrine detail. It was worse than the carts. New sanitary ditches were never dug because of the limited space in the yard; the old one was simply cleaned out with shovels, the accumulated deposits carried off in buckets and dumped in the river. Working the latrine was called Perfume Factory detail.

Some of the cisterns were near the latrine, and during the summer a number of men had died of typhoid fever. Many had been taken off by smallpox, too. But Morgan had escaped both. He thanked Bev Cass for that homemade vaccination and his mother and da for giving him the constitution of a railroad spike.

They were a shaggy, lousy, bedraggled-looking crew. Most of them still had on what was left of garments they had been wearing when captured. Now and again cast-off Yankee uniforms were issued, actually dumped in a pile just inside the Privates' Pen gate. It created a scramble that was sometimes bloody.

On this morning the Black Welshman wore a pair of Union trousers too large for him and a blue cavalry cape too small. No hat, and only the burlap wrappings for shoes. He was luckier than most. He always asserted himself when they threw the Federal uniforms into the pen and usually came away with a new change of clothes.

"Little Yankee fornicators!"

The man was sitting next to Morgan, finished with his meal and now picking lice from his beard.

"True it is," Morgan said. "They say the blues import this special breed of prison-pen critters. A bite much sweeter than a good honest field-army louse."

"Go to hell!"

Morgan could see the carts at the Privates' Pen gate. They were massive two-wheelers, with ropes attached for pulling. Twenty men to the cart, but still not enough when the carts were loaded.

Someone had decided they needed a chapel in this prison, so each day the men quarried gray slab rock from the surface of the compound and hauled it to the chapel site in Officers' Side. That was beyond the Privates' Pen fence and looked no different except that there the chapel walls were rising. Officers lived in the same drafty barracks, wore the same discarded blue uniforms, ate the same rice soup and roasted rats. Sometimes they even worked the carts or the Perfume Factory.

The quarrying operation had left the compound yard pitted with holes. Each depression was filled with water, filled in fact as soon as the stone was lifted out of the ground, and each of these had become a sink, stinking and slimy.

A Union sergeant with a detail of three men moved along the line of prisoners, giving each man a thimbleful of vinegar. Morgan took his with relish, enjoying the sting in his throat, his eyes watering.

The vinegar was to prevent scurvy. Earlier in the year, before the vinegar rations began, they had lost a few men to that, too.

And they had lost one man in late summer who apparently went mad and made a dash for the high wooden fence that surrounded the prison compound. He was trying to claw his way out when a Union guard shot him. It created such a wicked feeling in the yard that for three days the guards were afraid to come inside. Food was passed through the partly open gate with a platoon of Yanks standing ready with cocked rifles.

And some died from despair. They simply curled up in their bunks and were gone.

It became a day like all the others, unmarked by anything that might distinguish it. Most of them had stopped trying to keep the date in mind, even though this was information most of the guards were willing to give without expectation of bribe. But what difference did it make? Each day was the same.

Back and forth the carts, Morgan with the rope halter hooked across his left shoulder, pulling from the quarry pits across Privates' Pen, through the gate into Officers' Side. Rocks loaded at one place, thrown off at the other, scarecrow workers, scarecrow masons, scarecrow draft animals.

At least the men attached to the carts were spared lifting

the scaly stones. They squatted in the traces and watched as others placed the rocks into the carts and still others unloaded at the chapel site.

There was a sutler's break at noon. For thirty minutes the work stopped and the men rested or went to the sutler's shed that stood astride the fence between Privates' Pen and Officers' Side. Went, that is, if they had chits and wanted to spend them.

Money came into the compound by letters from relatives, but usually this was Confederate and not honored. A few men had work from time to time in the garrison buildings doing repairs and clean-up, and were paid two bits a day for their labors. One way or another there was always a bit of commerce in the compound.

Morgan glanced over at the shed. It wasn't much, as sutlers went. The little civilian entrepreneur stocked candles and tobacco chips and sometimes canned fish. Some of the men wrote letters at night, so there was a brisk business in the candles among these, though sometimes the candles were stolen and eaten by barracks mates. Tobacco was the universal currency inside the compound, sold in small cubes about the size of two Minié balls and almost as hard. It was traded back and forth, finally chewed, then dried and smoked. The value of a chewed chip was almost as great as one fresh from the sutler's barrel.

Morgan had stopped smoking. He had lost his clay pipe at the Bloody Angle, and besides, smoking another man's chewing, or even his own, had no appeal.

Miraculously he had arrived at Fort Delaware with his double eagle, the one from Cass's hand at Gettysburg—no factor of honesty among his captors, he figured, but one of oversight. Like the money of all prisoners, it was confiscated, and in its place he was issued chits for the sutler.

Twenty dollars' worth of chits was enough to fill two socks, except that no one had socks. The Welshman kept his treasure secreted about his person and slept with it, too. After the affair of the trousers and the broken jaw, the other prisoners showed little inclination to steal from him.

For a while he had been a rich man among beggars, but only a few chits were left now.

"What day is this?" Morgan asked.

"Saturday. I think it's Saturday."

The Welshman rose from the line of prisoners reclining in the gray day, and walked over to the sutler's shed.

"My good man," he said, "would you be kind enough to tell me the date?"

"December twenty-fourth."

"Aw," the Welshman said, and smiled. "I'll buy one of your candles."

"You, a candle?" The little man's eyebrows went up. "I've better things than candles to eat."

"Not much you haven't. Just a candle, if you please."

And that night when all the prison was sleeping, Liverpool Morgan slipped from his bunk, went into the compound yard before the barracks, placed the candle on the frosty ground, and lit it. The wind was down, and the small orange flame flickered gently as he stood back from it and lifted his head.

The Black Welshman sang four old songs from his father's land and in his father's tongue—Christmas carols. In the stillness his voice reached to both ends of the prison. After a brief flurry of excitement and rifle cocking, the guards in the watchtowers let him sing.

"It's just that crazy Reb," one said to the officer of the day, arrived to determine the origin of these notes, "the one who talks like he was a butler to Queen Victoria."

"That son of a bitch can sing, can't he?" another guard said.

The officer of the day turned away in the darkness.

Morgan finished his serenade with most of the officers and men in the prison pen listening, lying in their bunks and staring into the blackness. His finale was not a carol but the old Welsh lullaby he had first heard from his mother, and he sang it in English:

"*. . . O'er thy spirit gently stealing, visions*
*of delight revealing,*

*Breathes a pure and holy feeling, all through the night."*

Then he blew out the candle, ate what was left of it, and went back into the dark barracks.

HE COULD hear the wind under the eaves, coming up now in the hour before dawn. From the garrison he heard the faint note of a single bell stroke, marking the time. And around the compound each of the guard towers called their report.

"Post number one, and all's well."

In the darkness he lay, half sleeping, half awake, his mind drifting without direction.

Red satin in Richmond and black hands popping open the oyster shells. The scent of pine trees in the Ouachitas. The gray-green olive groves along the slopes of Sicily.

Crowded wharves along the rivers framing the City of Brotherly Love, a handful of men shipping off to Garibaldi, bright young eyes, laughing mouths, and wounds that would not stop bleeding.

Dice thrown against a wooden breadbox and regimental formations coming up on the flank like blue waves along a Mediterranean shore. A boy, shouting gloriously and colors in his hand, head suddenly gone in the instant passage of a solid shot.

Pink silk, shining billiard balls, and the faint moan of violins. Muted grumble of artillery fire beyond far hills where the gray infantry columns hurry forward like flowing seams across the patchwork quilt of Virginia farmland.

The water of the Rappahannock cold to the bone. Mouthful of braised mutton.

God of hosts, hear us pray here in the snow with the spires of Fredericksburg above the dim distant mist; lead us through the wheat there beyond Emmitsburg Road; spare us the fire and agony in Spotsylvania's Wilderness.

Jesus, and the kisses! Richmond paid for kisses solicited and sought, bargained and bought, taken and taught. Once more, twice more, and once again yet out of the grime and taste of powder and of murky water. Jesus!

Ah, Cass! Owner of niggers. On that rock above the fight, above it all except for searching missiles, a personal thing unto yourself alone. Li'l Cousin to the captain. Bitter, sour-faced uncle to them all.

A hand reaching, rings there on the fingers, golden bands. The sweet, hot-smelling moisture of passion, the fingers clutching softly. Whores in soldier suits, taking in the profit down the nights in a muddy hutment.

Is this Da speaking to his lonely son? Is this brine and sweet salt air coming off southern France? Is this me? Is this meat pie on a cannon barrel?

Violet blue and jonquil yellow, redbud purple, apple blossoms on the road to Lynchburg. Bud of pin oak transformed, shape intact, to Minié ball, hollow base, set off to drive into the meat and bone of enemies, friends, who knows, God damn!

Push me one more time, bastards! Try me, blue! And go up the flue. Try me wet mouth, sweet glowing breasts, sweat-soaked thighs and brow and loins. One son I would have, one son only, beautiful and strong from any woman. So long as her voice has the gentle Welsh tone to it and her eyes the gentle Welsh shining. But always a devil lurking there, too, and fire and thunder.

Marching. Knee joint out of time but "The Black-Eyed Suzie" going down the line. Waving hats to any mounted general standing by to watch them pass. The muck and mud of roads in foul weather, the bursting time of green in Shenandoah Valley and captured Yankee eyes gone wide with fear, all of them, braced against the stone of Harper's Ferry walls.

Spare me more salt pork and only let me chew the bark of trees. Spare me not the movement of the cards from king to queen and ace and straight! Look there, across Chickamauga's field, and see the enemy standing like a rock, blue-boned and colors up. Look there at Sharpsburg's Dunkard church thrust up white and scarred, the limbs of guns and men and horses all around like shrubbery. See the low horizon of Suffolk town hemmed with ditches meant alone for moles and badgers and mud-caked soldiers.

Ah, Parson. Dear Benton County Hasford. Did you hear the voice of God and make His words known in battle with a blasphemous mouth?

Foamy kisses and the valleys of bushy exploration, and God help the one who catches clap. But almost worth the price at that—at the moment anyway, yes, Parson? You'd not know, not you, with your higher cause for killing.

Girlish cheeks ablush in Little Rock and Dalton and Palermo, hot Italian lips and shattered canteens in the white rocks, punctured. Stump of a leg, hollow face above, and maggots in the unhealing wound.

Ah, Scaggs. Your Honor pleads guilty to foul mouth and tender heart. Earlobe shooter, hero home among a captured people, crying in the night.

Snow of Tennessee in winter, freshets in the mountains with the spring. Oak staves thrown into the glowing furnace, paddlewheels dipping, the flat, wide, brown river twisting around the Crescent City. Rice and red beans!

Cavalry. Charging. Caught in the crossfire of Minié ball and case shot, horses down and screaming, blue riders trying frantically to free themselves from slashing hooves sky-pointed.

Ah, Noah. Little brother. Hot and cold like flaming coke gone from red to ash-gray embers, innocence and arrogance, coupled like the wedding of a kiss and a balled fist!

Splinter bone like a needle in the pillow of a red-flowing face. Bare feet blue in the cold rain. Drive in the skirmishers! Richmond taffeta, Ringgold ginger snaps, and the Old Army of the Potomac coming on.

Ah, Zack. Wolf-eyed. Cold as midnight sweat. No fun for you, this, but mechanical like ricking firewood against the cabin wall. Killer.

Aim for the officers, boys—and the brave ones and then their colors, too. Let them fall, the others, from the casual wasps of lead, flame-born, and flesh their burial ground!

Pecan pie in autumn. Sweetbreads and the musty odor of sage in dressing. Fluff-tailed squirrels and spiders large as dinner plates in the fallen needles of the cedar. Kisses!

Morgan was on the top bunk, and from below someone was reaching up, shaking him.

"What?"

"You was lettin' out a yell like you was chargin' the Yanks again, Welsh."

"Oh, that was it? Just a dream. But dream no more!"

IT WAS a rainy afternoon. The wind from the east brought the smell of the sea and pushed the dark clouds low along the surface of the river. Sometimes one could not make out the Delaware shore.

A detail of prisoners was on Perfume Factory duty. Once they had emptied all the latrine buckets into the river on the downstream side, they were allowed to move back along the island's shore and bathe. They went into the water clothing and all, doing two jobs at once.

It was only later when the guards were counting the men back into the compound yard that they realized two prisoners were missing. They shrugged it off and reported the pair victims of drowning.

But there had been no drowning. Both men made the New Jersey shore. One of them was Liverpool Morgan.

It was April 9, 1865, the day Bobby Lee surrendered his army at Appomattox.

# TWENTY

RICHMOND! But it was not the same city they had seen before marching north into Pennsylvania.

After they had come out and stacked their arms with the Federal army looking on, then passed in gray regiments before the salute of raised rifles, there had been some intense yearning to go back once more and look at the place that represented what they had fought for, to see the capital of what they were already calling the Old South, this city on the James they had defended these several years.

Noah and Martin Hasford and Burton had walked along the roads with other paroled soldiers, veterans of Lee's army marked all alike by their ragged clothes and gaunt faces. On the same roads, formations of blue cavalry and infantry marched, and long lines of former slaves moved in search of the new life and food. Anyone who wanted to go to Richmond had to walk because none of the railroads were working except for a single line the Yankees had rebuilt from the North.

The farms they had passed seemed deserted, like those they had seen along the Rapidan in 1864. The people were staying closed in, locked away, hiding.

Once inside the city, they were sorry they had come. Blueclads an' niggers, Noah thought, and where in hell do they all come from?

They wandered aimlessly through the streets, gawking at the spectacle of a place burned and looted. Along the waterfront stood the skeletons of buildings, stark, black, an hollow, charred brick walls reflecting in the waters of the Jam and the Kanawha canal.

There were ruins where the flour mills had stood, and ironworks and railyards. Libby Prison was intact, squar ugly like the thing it was, a tobacco warehouse that had seen no tobacco in four years. And the curious coming down from the North on that single line of track the Union army maintained—gaping, pointing, taking their hurried excursion among the defeated and then back to the cars to be in Washington again before nightfall.

There were no dogs or cats on the streets, an evil sign. And there were whisperings of danger after dark with thugs in the alleys. A curfew had been imposed, what with no lights in the streets after the gasworks had been blown to hell. The townspeople were like sleepwalkers, still in shock—not so much from the Yankee occupation as from the memory of their own kind pillaging the town after the gray army left and before the blues arrived.

Noah headed then to Miz Rozella's Afternoon Tea Sippin' Society and Billiard Hall, Martin Hasford making no complaint, perhaps because he expected what they would find.

The building had not been burned, but the doors and fancy louvered shutters had been torn off, and all the pane glass was shattered. Even the two lamps that had hung on either side of the entryway were gone, taken for the brass.

They moved cautiously inside and found the floors bare of carpets, all the draperies and furniture and paintings gone. The billiard table was still there, too heavy to cart off in a hurry, but the green felt cover had been cut and shredded as with a cat's claws.

In one corner of the barroom was a small pile of char and half-burned chair legs where someone had kindled a fire. Beside this was one of the big mattresses from upstairs, cover stripped, stained with tobacco juice or blood, one end torn off and the cotton batting spilled out across the floor.

"Les get outa hyar," Noah said softly, shivering. "It's like the rest a' this town. Gone to ghosts."

Capitol Hill was pocked with digging, dotted with tentage and the litter of paper and boxes and rags. The stately old building at the crest stood desolate and grim. Within sight of it were some of the soup lines. The food came each day on the army railroad and was doled out by Federal commissary officers—to freedmen and former Confederate soldiers mostly, the latter with parole slips in their hands. But the citizens of Richmond were there, too, looking ashamed. For many it was soup line and Yankee charity or starve.

"I've seen enough of this," Burton said. "Only before I go, I'd like to place these tared ole eyes on the house where Marse Robert's stayin'."

It took a long time to find someone who knew the location of Lee's temporary town quarters. Finally they had the information from a Yankee provost-guard sergeant, who also gave them each a lemon. They moved along Franklin Street and found the place, not difficult with the crowd milling in the street before it.

They stood well away along the sidewalk, looking at the people. There were Union soldiers with rifles before the small entryway, and from time to time someone would pass between them and go inside. The tourists twittered among themselves like sparrows and stared at the brick façade, sometimes tiptoeing to see inside the windows. It was a tall, narrow house, austere as any town house could be, with the look about it of Colonial Virginia. The windows were high, too, paned with glass that showed delicate waves of light when the sun shone across them.

"By Gawd, boys, I'm goin' in to see him," Burton said, his jaw set in the flowing white beard that covered his face to the eyes.

"Hell, you caint jus' walk up an' see Bobby Lee in his own house," Noah said. But the thought made his heart thump as though he were hearing the sound of infantry drums coming near.

"If them Yankee soldiers at the door don't stop me, I can," Burton said stubbornly. "Why, hell, boys, me an' the general, we're jus' common ole civilians now. You comin'?"

"Not me," Martin Hasford said. "I think we oughta ju take in one of these Yankee grub lines and then light for home."

Noah wanted to go, but as the Texan looked at him knew he wouldn't. It was one thing to be marching wi column of men and come onto Bobby Lee beside the road, or to be making a charge and see the gray figure close enough to cheer him. It was something entirely different to walk right through his front door as though you were an equal.

"Me neither. We'll wait right hyar an' watch them blues gouge your arse with bayonets."

Burton grinned. "I heerd you wasn't afeared of Yank bayonets."

"Not if I got one, too."

"Well, by Gawd, boys, the worst part about decidin' somethin' is the decidin' an' not the doin'. So here I go."

They watched the old man make his way along the street, through the curiosity seekers, straight toward one of the Union soldiers. There was a brief confrontation, and they could see Burton's head bobbing with emphasis as he spoke. Then he moved around the sentinel, passed through the iron gate, mounted the seven stone steps to the small landing framed by two white columns, and tapped on the door. After a moment the door opened and Burton disappeared inside, pulling off his hat as he stepped across the threshold.

"I'll be damned," Noah said.

"Never saw a Texas man yet that didn't have pure gall," Martin said, shaking his head.

They stood for a long time in the cool April breeze that ran along the street, hearing the rustle of last year's dry leaves in the ivy that clung to the walls of the brick houses. Once they saw in one of the third-story windows of Lee's house the shadow figure of a woman, looking down for a few seconds and then moving back.

Can't be Bobby Lee's missus, Noah thought. We heerd she was an invalid now, in her age.

Their hats were stained, the brims torn and limp. Their jackets were gone at the seams and marked with mud, washed out to a pale butternut color. Only Noah had a shirt, and Martin Hasford's underwear was showing at neck and wrist. Their trousers were patched, and hung about their ankles like windblown Spanish moss. Hasford's shoes were held together by old leather thongs, and Noah was barefoot.

Feeling the gaze of the passing tourists, Noah knew the blood was rising in his cheeks. He glared back at them.

The ladies were in trim little bonnets and flowing skirts, holding tight to the elbows of their escorts. The gentlemen wore striped pants as unwrinkled as stovepipes, well-brushed bowler hats, studded shirts. Some had canes, and some tapped the sidewalk with umbrellas. To Noah, they all smelled like bay rum.

"Ain't they ever seen sojurs before?" he muttered, but then felt foolish saying it. Without weapons, they were only derelict civilians.

But, by Gawd, we are too sojurs, he thought.

He drew himself up and looked at the passing faces boldly, his tatters flapping in the breeze, and thought, Shit! The parson stands there hangdog like he was ashamed 'bout somethin'.

"Like scarecrows," he heard someone say.

"Mule turd," he said aloud, then thought, Gawd, I best forget all this army kinda talk 'fore I get back to the Buffalo. But to hell with these people. We fit with Bobby Lee!

"Here he comes," Martin said softly.

Burton came down the short steps and through the gate and into the street, pulling his hat on and walking toward them with his head down. When he came near he raised his face, and they could see the shine of moisture in his old eyes.

Burton stopped, shifting his feet, not looking into their faces. His jaw muscles were working under the foliage of white hair.

"Well, what happened?" Martin asked.

Burton waited a long time to speak, swallowing. Once, he brushed his hands across his face. He blinked and cleared his throat.

"They was some officers in the parlor," he finally said. "They allowed Marse Robert was too busy to see any visitors today. So I says I served with him since the Seven Days and thought I'd say goodbye before I walk back to Texas."

He stopped and swallowed again, not looking at them. Then he went on in a rush of words.

"But one of 'em—I think he was a Lee—he says wait, an' he went up the stairs an' pretty soon he come back down an' right behind him was the general."

"By Gawd!"

"Marse Robert come over an' he put out his han' an' I taken it. An' then I left."

Noah and Martin leaned forward expectantly, waiting, watching Burton's face. There were tears now, running down into the white beard.

"Well, what did he say?"

Burton was swallowing hard now. "He never said nothin'. I never neither. I couldn't."

He choked and lowered his head, and his hands covered his face again but only for a moment. Then he was looking at them for the first time, sniffling violently and blinking and wiping his beard.

"But I taken his han', by Gawd, boys, I did. Lordy, he looks old."

"By Gawd!"

Noah and Martin looked along the street to the narrow little house, and Noah thought of that old man in there. Then he, too, swallowed, and his throat was hard.

"Boys," Burton said, "I'm away from here. I've seen enough of the elephant to last three lifetimes. I'm gonna go down by way of Georgia, see some relatives I got there. I expect you boys'll be goin' another direction."

"I expect so," Martin said.

Burton held out his hand, they took it in turn, Noah thinking, By Gawd, the han' that shook Bobby Lee's!

"I enjoyed cuttin' you boys' hair. Ever come to Texas, look me up. Fort Worth or thereabouts, I reckon. We'll scalp us a few Comanch' an' drink some Mexican whisky."

"It's been good shootin' at Yankees with you," Noah said.

Burton paused for a moment, then grinned. "Yeah, some of it was all right."

They watched him hurry up the street, moving quickly and surely through the people. Noah sighed.

"Well," Martin said. "Let's find us some of this charity grub. And light out for home."

THE countryside was greening. There was the smell of spring, of new life budding, and welcome rain, warm and sweet-scented on the fields and in the timber, making the roads soft but not sticky. Martin Hasford had thrown away his battered shoes because they were more hindrance than help.

When they paused for the night on a Powhatan County road, they had three Irish potatoes shared between them and drank the cold water taken into canteens at the last clear stream crossing. The canteens were all that was left of their army equipment.

The two men sat near the road, chewing the raw potatoes, watching former slaves walking toward Richmond. They came in dark clots—men, women, and children—carrying little baggage, some of them singing. The old were usually lagging far behind, struggling to keep pace.

After one group passed, there would be a long interval and then another would appear. Some of the men turned bright eyes toward the two Confederate soldiers, and sometimes they smiled.

"Gwine cross Jordan," one young man shouted, and those following muttered their A-mens.

"Where they all come from?" Noah asked.

"Out of Egypt," Martin said, chewing. "And no Moses to lead them on."

It was growing dark, and the sun had left a pale orange light in the western sky. They could hear mourning doves somewhere across the fields among rows of small cedars. Noah called them rain crows.

"Good weather comin'."

"Red clouds at night, sailor's delight," Martin said.

"What're you gonna do now, Parson?"

"Go home and work my farm like before."

Always now "before" meant the years preceding the war.

"Time to make all my jularky dreams come to pass, I reckon," Noah said.

"You're a young man and supposed to dream of jularkies."

Noah laughed. "Jus' an ole man now. Times wasted an' me twenty-one, an' no wife ner young'uns yet."

"Plenty of time for that," Martin said. "Plenty of time."

"Gonna end like my brothers, an ole bachelor." And he laughed again as though it were hard to believe. Then he spoke quietly, seriously, gazing off across the twilight fields.

"It's kinda spooky, goin' home now after all this time an' all the thangs we done. Seein' all of it that we have."

"Yes," Martin Hasford said. "A little spooky."

I wonder if Zack ever showed him that letter, Martin thought. That girl, what was her name? Luanne something. I wonder if Zack ever told him. Maybe I ought to.

But he decided against it. Family business was something he didn't like nosing into. Some things you just don't nose into, he thought, even with friends in the army for years. At least not me.

"What're you gonna do with that book you been keepin'?" Noah asked.

"Thought I'd go by March Landing and look up Scaggs. Give it to him. He's the one started it."

"Ole Jury Duty. That's the son of a bitch got me in this army."

"Yes, I know."

"I got somethin' for him, too," Noah said.

He unbuttoned his jacket and opened his shirt, on which there were no buttons. From around his waist he pulled a long bundle that looked almost black in the twilight. Slowly, gently, he unfolded it and spread it on the ground. Martin Hasford bent over it, then gasped.

"Dear God," he said, "it's the colors!"

In the dim afterglow of sunlight the crossed bars of the banner showed, the thirteen stars the color of apple blossoms. The edges of the flag were frayed, and there were many holes and rips in the cloth where Yankee metal had passed through. For a long time they sat staring at it.

"I wondered what happened to it," Martin said. "That day we marched out to surrender, all we had was the naked staff."

"I figured we was givin' 'em our guns, so maybe somebody oughta keep the colors."

Like we hadn't surrendered all of ourselves, Martin thought. He touched the flag with his fingertips and it felt gritty, impregnated with the dust and grime of battlefields from southside Virginia to Gettysburg, from the Rappahannock to the Tennessee.

"Dear God," he said.

"You bundle 'er up with that book. Take 'er to Ole Jury Duty. He'd like that."

"Yes. He'd like that."

Martin Hasford slipped the ragged old ledger book from beneath his jacket—the old ledger book with the place names, the roads and mountains and streams and towns, the old ledger book that showed for all these years of service that the company had recruited one hundred and forty-five men.

And showed, too, in the last entry, that eleven had been left to stack their arms at Appomattox.

He wrapped the ledger in the flag and pushed the whole business back inside his underwear.

What strange symbols men take unto themselves, he thought. I hope He doesn't consider this another golden calf.

"How far you figure to Arkansas?" Noah asked.

"About a thousand miles."

"Hell! We can do that in less'n two months."

"Yes. Home in two months!"

It was a long time before Noah slept. He lay beside Martin Hasford, watching the stars turn in the sky above them.

Back in the hills he had often lain awake deep into the night, listening to the sounds of the others sleeping, listening to the creak of windblown limbs on the trees beyond the walls, and sometimes the call of a hunting owl or a whippoorwill or even a wolf on some far ridge, marking the passage of the moon with his howling. It had always been the time for his thinking, buried in a goosefeather tick.

But in the army he had acquired the talent for sleeping quickly in any place, at any time, taking his rest where he could get it. That talent seemed to have deserted him now. He lay wide-eyed, his mind busy with things he could not comprehend.

He was rebelling at thinking back to things past, though aware of an intense, almost painful relief that the fighting was finished, the flaming, murky battlefields left behind.

Yet there was a vague dread, too, an uncertainty. It was as though he waited expectantly for the savage fury, even while knowing that all of it was over now—like holding his breath for the next flash of lightning in a thunderstorm after the last of the clouds were gone.

A passion now for home. But that was unsettling, too. All the images seemed somehow blurred, the memories dim, the people strangers moving in a strange land. Each time he tried to recall a vivid impression of the morning mists above the Buffalo, Pap with an axe in his hand and heading toward the timber, all his mind could bring forth was the spires of Sharpsburg lifting like flat bayonets above the haze of dawn along the Antietam.

IT WAS predawn when they started again. As with so many marches they had made, they moved out without breakfast and in the darkness. Except now there were only the two of them.

They walked without speaking, taking long strides, arms swinging, but rather awkwardly now because there was not the rifle held over the shoulder, a weight so long with them they had become conditioned to it, felt almost unbalanced from the lack of it.

At first there were open fields and the road running pale in the darkness before them. Then they were in a dense woodland, and it was darker here. They moved almost by instinct, seeing little ahead of them, feeling tentatively but surely with their bare feet for the surface of the road.

They felt the pressure of being alone, perhaps some of that

early apprehension they had felt the evening they moved on Harper's Ferry, unsure of what lay ahead. Perhaps, too, that was why they turned and ran when the challenge came sharp and loud from the darkness.

Martin Hasford could never recall how far he had run when the shot came. It couldn't have been but a few steps, the rifle flashing behind them almost instantly with the call to halt. He was aware of the ringing report and then the heavy chuck of sound, a sound he had heard many times. Then a heavier thud and a grunt, and he knew Noah was down. The second bullet whispered past his head without his even having heard the shot, and he threw himself belly-down in the road.

"Don't shoot!" he shouted. "Paroled soldiers. Paroled from Lee's army. Don't shoot! Don't shoot!"

He lay panting, waiting, the cold moisture of the road seeping up into his flesh. He shivered. No shots came now, and then he heard them—heavy boots thumping nearer—and then he saw the dark forms of legs around him like tree trunks. They pulled him to his feet, and in the growing light he could see the outline of forage caps and cavalry capes and repeating carbines. Martin counted about a dozen of them.

"Get up here," someone ordered. Martin could see the chevrons on the man's sleeves. "Go over him. You move, Reb, you're a dead man!"

They searched him roughly, their cold hands inside his jacket and his trousers.

"What's this!"

"A Bible."

"No, this here."

"Just a logbook," Martin Hasford said, his voice shaking.

"Make a light."

A match flared and then a lantern was lit. One of the soldiers held it up, the orange glow in Martin's face.

"What's this wrapped around it?"

"Just a cloth."

"Cloth, hell! It's a God damned Reb banner! Where you think you're a-goin' with this Reb banner? Lemme see your parole paper."

Martin showed him. The soldier held the light to his face again.

"You're shakin' like a peach-seed dog, ole man," the soldier said. Martin could see that they were all young, even the sergeant.

The sergeant moved back along the road. Trying to control the tremors in his muscles, Martin watched him go in the growing dawn, moving toward an officer with a saber. The sergeant talked with him. Beside them in the road was a dark lump.

"Bring him here," the officer called.

They shoved Martin along with the muzzles of their carbines. In the lantern light Martin could see Noah lying face down, his arms folded under him.

"Sweet Savior," he gasped, and ran the last few steps and bent to the still form. Gently he turned Noah onto his back, and saw the dark stain glistening on the chest where the ball had passed through from behind. Noah's eyes were open. "Sweet Savior!"

"Take off your cape and make a pillow," the officer said.

"Hell, Cap'n, he's dead."

"Do what you're told!"

One of the soldiers slipped off his cape and folded it, and Martin pushed it under Noah's head. The others stood silently in a tight circle, looking down, the lantern shining on their faces and the dawn etching the outlines of their caps as though with ice.

"My God, my God," Martin said. His trembling was gone now, but his voice began to shake with rage. He looked up at the captain, his face twisted. "Why'd you do this? We ain't even armed."

"Why'd you run, Reb?" the sergeant asked.

"You haven't got any business out on the roads," the captain said.

"How do you expect us to get home? Paroled and going home, and you did a thing like this."

"Travelin' in the dark right now is dangerous, don't you dumb Reb bastards know that?" the sergeant asked.

"Dangerous? The war's over, for God's sake."

The captain and the sergeant looked at one another.

"You haven't heard the news?" the captain said.

"Heard what news?"

"The president was shot last night. We're ordered to investigate any stragglers on the roads."

"The president? President Davis?"

"Davis!" the sergeant spat. "We'll damn sure hang his arse when we find him."

"All right," the captain said. "No, not Davis. President Lincoln. In Washington City."

"What?"

"President Lincoln. In Washington City."

Martin moaned and lowered his head. "For God's sake, don't you know how far we are from Washington City?"

"It ain't all that far," the sergeant said.

"Orders. Anybody looks suspicious, we're told to investigate," the officer said. "My sergeant tells me you looked in a big hurry, and in the dark."

"Sweet Savior, look what you've done to this boy!"

"Boy, hell!" one of the soldiers muttered. "That's the kinda boy been layin' our men in the ground, Cap'n."

"All right. Let it alone."

The sergeant turned to the captain and held out the ledger book and the tattered flag and the Bible. "He had these on him."

The captain took the ledger book and glanced at a few pages in the light of the lantern. He did not touch the Bible or the flag, leaving the sergeant standing with them in his outstretched hand. After a moment he handed the ledger to the sergeant.

"Give it back to him. And the Bible, too."

"What about this rag?"

"Give it back to him."

"Jesus, Cap'n, this here is—"

"Give it back," the captain cut in harshly. "Give it all back to him. And his parole paper, too."

"What about this boy?" Martin's voice was choking in his throat.

"We'll take care of it. We shot him, so we'll bury him."

Martin Hasford felt a movement under his hand and bent to Noah's face. The eyes were clear now. In the light of coming sun, the outline of the face was growing sharp.

"Parson?" Noah whispered.

"I'm right here, Noah," Martin said. He could see blood framing Noah's mouth.

"Tell Zack. We got 'em in flank."

Martin felt the form beneath his hands shudder.

"Listen, Noah. Listen. 'The Lord is my light and my salvation. Whom shall I fear? The Lord is the strength of my life. Of whom shall I be afraid? When the wicked, even mine enemies and my foes, come upon me . . .' Noah?"

"He don't hear you, Reb," the sergeant said.

"Let him finish."

"No, Cap'n," Martin whispered. "I'm through now, Noah."

It was over then, all of it, and Martin rose and took the Bible and the flag and the ledger book. His lips were clamped tight shut. These bastards won't see me cry, he thought.

"You'd best take his effects," the captain said. "Sergeant, empty the man's pockets."

Martin watched with dread as the Yankee cavalryman bent to search through Noah's clothes.

"Wait," he said. "Bury it all with him," thinking Noah's Pap would want it this way.

The sergeant paused and the captain nodded. Likely a big mistake, Martin thought. That watch will surely end in one of their pockets.

"His name was Noah Fawley," he said. "You'll mark his grave?"

"Take it down," the captain said, and the sergeant produced a small note pad from his hip pocket and penciled in the name. It was light enough now to see without the lantern, and the soldier holding it lifted the globe and blew out the flame.

"Third Arkansas Infantry," Martin said. "He was a hill boy but a good soldier. He never knew what this war was about. I never did either, I guess."

"Well, by God, I can tell you what it was about," the sergeant said.

"All right," the captain said. "Never mind that. You want to stay while we put him in the ground?"

"No!" Martin said vehemently. "No, I don't. But I'd like your word that you'll mark his grave."

"I can give you that. You can share grub with us before you go."

"No, I don't want your grub."

"All right. Be on your way then," the captain said. "I'm sorry this happened."

"Be sorry for yourself, you son of a bitch!"

The soldiers muttered and bent forward, their carbines up, but the captain waved his hand.

"All right. Let it go. On your way, old man. And be a little more careful until you're well shed of Virginia."

"Virginia!" Martin gasped, and now he couldn't stop the tears. They ran down through his beard and into his mouth. "I wish to God I'd never heard the name."

He moved out of their surrounding circle and walked quickly along the road toward the west. The hard knot in his throat finally was gone, but he could still feel the wetness on his cheeks.

The trunks of trees alongside the road were showing clearly now in the early daylight. The buds were out on the lacy limbs, and above them the sky was turning from pale gray to deep blue. Through the woods he could hear the hard hammerblows of downy woodpeckers, and beyond, in the cedars that bordered the fields, the mourning doves calling.

Dear God, I know it well. The planting time, the turn of earth, the beginning of life once more, the smell and feel and taste of coming green. The smell of sap and blood and expectations never known before, though repeated every year. Again new, each season again fresh, each drop of rain and tear salty on the lips. Always the new coming.

He lengthened his stride toward the west, toward Tennessee, then the Mississippi. Toward home. Less than a thousand miles away, and his legs feeling the strength of spring.

## In Appreciation

To Bell Irvin Wiley for his *Johnny Reb* and *Billy Yank*, and to Henry Steele Commager for his *The Blue and the Gray*. Here are the letters and diaries written by the men of both armies.

And to Douglas Southall Freeman for his *R. E. Lee* and *Lee's Lieutenants*. Here is the substance of the Virginia army.

And to the men of the Third Arkansas Infantry and the record they made for themselves in a strange land.

And to all of those who have preserved that record.

And to Jeanie Donovan, librarian, whose assistance was invaluable.